W9-CQT-370

By the Authors

JODI PICOULT

JENNIFER FINNEY BOYLAN

MAD HONEY

MAD HONEY

A Novel

JODI PICOULT AND
JENNIFER FINNEY BOYLAN

BALLANTINE BOOKS
NEW YORK

Mad Honey is a work of fiction. Names, characters, places, and incidents are the products of the authors' imagination or are used fictitiously. Any resemblance to actual events, locales, or persons, living or dead, is entirely coincidental.

Copyright © 2022 by Jodi Picoult and Jennifer Finney Boylan

Published in the United States by Ballantine Books, an imprint of Random House, a division of Penguin Random House LLC, New York.

BALLANTINE is a registered trademark and the colophon is a trademark of Penguin Random House LLC.

LIBRARY OF CONGRESS CATALOGING-IN-PUBLICATION DATA
Names: Picoult, Jodi, author. | Boylan, Jennifer Finney, author.
Title: Mad honey: a novel / Jodi Picoult & Jennifer Finney Boylan.
Description: First edition. | New York: Ballantine Books, [2022]
Identifiers: LCCN 2021055844 (print) | LCCN 2021055845 (ebook) |
ISBN 9781984818386 (hardcover) | ISBN 9781984818393 (ebook)
Subjects: LCGFT: Novels.
Classification: LCC PS3566.I372 M33 2022 (print) | LCC PS3566.I372
(ebook) | DDC 813/.54—dc23/eng/20220127
LC record available at https://lccn.loc.gov/2021055844
LC ebook record available at https://lccn.loc.gov/2021055845

International ISBN 978-0-593-50096-5

PRINTED IN THE UNITED STATES OF AMERICA ON ACID-FREE PAPER

randomhousebooks.com

4 6 8 9 7 5

Book design by Elizabeth Rendfleisch
Art by Adobe Stock/Татьяна Гончарук

This one's for my *other* co-author, my brother-from-another-mother, Tim McDonald, who made me fall in love with writing all over again. I'll work with you over any buggy collaboration program anytime, anywhere, and will lock you in the Writers' Cage only when strictly necessary.

—JP

Susan Finney, my sister-in-law, is a lover of books, stories, red wine, dogs—and me. Openhearted and generous, she has guided Boylans—and Finneys—on many journeys, even when we did not know the way. She's a sister, a mother, and a grandmother, but above all: an angel.

I dedicate this book to you.

—JFB

Life can only be understood backwards,
but it must be lived forwards.

Søren Kierkegaard

MAD HONEY

OLIVIA ⬡ 1

The day of

From the moment I knew I was having a baby, I wanted it to be a girl. I wandered the aisles of department stores, touching doll-size dresses and tiny sequined shoes. I pictured us with matching nail polish—me, who'd never had a manicure in my life. I imagined the day her fairy hair was long enough to capture in pigtails, her nose pressed to the glass of a school bus window; I saw her first crush, prom dress, heartbreak. Each vision was a bead on a rosary of future memories; I prayed daily.

As it turned out, I was not a zealot . . . only a martyr.

When I gave birth, and the doctor announced the baby's sex, I did not believe it at first. I had done such a stellar job of convincing myself of what I *wanted* that I completely forgot what I *needed*. But when I held Asher, slippery as a minnow, I was relieved.

Better to have a boy, who would never be someone's victim.

MOST PEOPLE IN Adams, New Hampshire, know me by name, and those who don't, know to steer clear of my home. It's often that way for beekeepers—like firefighters, we willingly put ourselves into situations that are the stuff of others' nightmares. Honeybees are far less vindictive than their yellow jacket cousins, but people can't often tell the difference, so anything that stings and buzzes comes to be seen as a potential hazard. A few hundred yards past the antique

Cape, my colonies form a semicircular rainbow of hives, and most of the spring and summer the bees zip between them and the acres of blossoms they pollinate, humming a warning.

I grew up on a small farm that had been in my father's family for generations: an apple orchard that, in the fall, sold cider and donuts made by my mother and, in the summer, had pick-your-own strawberry fields. We were land-rich and cash-poor. My father was an apiarist by hobby, as was his father before him, and so on, all the way back to the first McAfee who was an original settler of Adams. It is just far enough away from the White Mountain National Forest to have affordable real estate. The town has one traffic light, one bar, one diner, a post office, a town green that used to be a communal sheep grazing area, and Slade Brook—a creek whose name was misprinted in a 1789 geological survey map, but which stuck. *Slate* Brook, as it should have been written, was named for the eponymous rock mined from its banks, which was shipped far and wide to become tombstones. *Slade* was the surname of the local undertaker and village drunk, who had a tendency to wander off when he was on a bender, and who ironically killed *himself* by drowning in six inches of water in the creek.

When I first brought Braden to meet my parents, I told him that story. He had been driving at the time; his grin flashed like lightning. *But who,* he'd asked, *buried the undertaker?*

Back then, we had been living outside of DC, where Braden was a resident in cardiac surgery at Johns Hopkins and I worked at the National Zoo, trying to cobble together enough money for a graduate program in zoology. We'd only been together three months, but I had already moved in with him. We were visiting my parents that weekend because I knew, viscerally, that Braden Fields was *the one*.

On that first trip back home, I had been so sure of what my future would hold. I was wrong on all counts. I never expected to be an apiarist like my father; I never thought I'd wind up sleeping in my childhood bedroom once again as an adult; I never imagined I'd settle down on a farm my older brother, Jordan, and I once could not wait to leave. I married Braden; he got a fellowship at Mass General;

we moved to Boston; I was a doctor's wife. Then, almost a year to the day of my wedding anniversary, my father didn't come home one evening after checking his hives. My mother found him, dead of a heart attack in the tall grass, bees haloing his head.

My mother sold the piece of land that held our apple orchard to a couple from Brooklyn. She kept the strawberry fields but was thoroughly at a loss when it came to my father's hives. Since my brother was busy with a high-powered legal career and my mother was allergic to bees, the apiary fell to me. For five years, I drove from Boston to Adams every week to take care of the colonies. After Asher was born, I'd bring him with me, leaving him in the company of my mother while I checked the hives. I fell in love with beekeeping, the slow-motion flow of pulling a frame out of a hive, the Where's Waldo? search for the queen. I expanded from five colonies to fifteen. I experimented with bee genetics with colonies from Russia, from Slovenia, from Italy. I signed pollination contracts with the Brooklynites and three other local fruit orchards, setting up new hives on their premises. I harvested, processed, and sold honey and beeswax products at farmers' markets from the Canadian border to the suburbs of Massachusetts. I became, almost by accident, the first commercially successful beekeeper in the history of apiarist McAfees. By the time Asher and I moved permanently to Adams, I knew I might never get rich doing this, but I could make a living.

My father taught me that beekeeping is both a burden and a privilege. You don't bother the bees unless they need your help, and you help them when they need it. It's a feudal relationship: protection in return for a percentage of the fruits of their labors.

He taught me that if a body is easily crushed, it develops a weapon to prevent that from happening.

He taught me that sudden movements get you stung.

I took these lessons a bit too much to heart.

On the day of my father's funeral, and years later, on the day of my mother's, I told the bees. It's an old tradition to inform them of a death in the family; if a beekeeper dies, and the bees aren't asked to stay on with their new master, they'll leave. In New Hampshire, the custom is to sing, and the news has to rhyme. So I draped each colony with black crepe, knocked softly, crooned the truth. My beekeeping net became a funeral veil. The hive might well have been a coffin.

BY THE TIME I come downstairs that morning, Asher is in the kitchen. We have a deal, whoever gets up first makes the coffee. My mug still has a wisp of steam rising. He is shoveling cereal into his mouth, absorbed in his phone.

"Morning," I say, and he grunts in response.

For a moment, I let myself stare at him. It's hard to believe that the soft-centered little boy who would cry when his hands got sticky with propolis from the hives can now lift a super full of forty pounds of honey as if it weighs no more than his hockey stick. Asher is over six feet tall, but even as he was growing, he was never ungainly. He moves with the kind of grace you find in wildcats, the ones that can steal away a kitten or a chick before you even realize they've gone. Asher has my blond hair and the same ghost-green eyes, for which I have always been grateful. He carries his father's last name, but if I also had to see Braden every time I looked at my son, it would be that much harder.

I catalog the breadth of his shoulders, the damp curls at the nape of his neck; the way the tendons in his forearms shift and play as he scrolls through his texts. It's shocking, sometimes, to be confronted with *this* when a second ago he sat on my shoulders, trying to pull down a star and unravel a thread of the night.

"No practice this morning?" I ask, taking a sip of my coffee. Asher has been playing hockey as long as we've lived here; he skates as effortlessly as he walks. He was made captain as a junior and reelected this year, as a senior. I never can remember whether they have rink time before school or after, as it changes daily.

His lips tug with a slight smile, and he types a response into his phone, but doesn't answer.

"Hello?" I say. I slip a piece of bread into the ancient toaster, which is jerry-rigged with duct tape that occasionally catches on fire. Breakfast for me is always toast and honey, never in short supply.

"I guess you have practice later," I try, and then provide the answer that Asher doesn't. "Why yes, Mom, thanks for taking such an active interest in my life."

I fold my arms across my boxy cable-knit sweater. "Am I too old to wear this tube top?" I ask lightly.

Silence.

"I'm sorry I won't be here for dinner, but I'm running away with a cult."

I narrow my eyes. "I posted that naked photo of you as a toddler on Instagram for Throwback Thursday."

Asher grunts noncommittally. My toast pops up; I spread it with honey and slide into the chair directly across from Asher. "I'd really prefer that you not use my Mastercard to pay for your Pornhub subscription."

His eyes snap to mine so fast I think I can hear his neck crack. "*What?*"

"Oh, hey," I say smoothly. "Nice to have your attention."

Asher shakes his head, but he puts down his phone. "I didn't use your Mastercard," he says.

"I know."

"I used your Amex."

I burst out laughing.

"Also: never *ever* wear a tube top," he says. "Jesus."

"So you *were* listening."

"How could I *not?*" Asher winces. "Just for the record, nobody else's mother talks about porn over breakfast."

"Aren't you the lucky one, then."

"Well," he says, shrugging. "Yeah." He lifts his coffee mug, clinks it to mine, and sips.

I don't know what other parents' relationships are like with their children, but the one between me and Asher was forged in fire and, maybe for that reason, is invincible. Even though he'd rather be caught dead than have me throw my arms around him after a winning game, when it's just the two of us, we are our own universe, a moon and a planet tied together in orbit. Asher may not have grown up in a household with two parents, but the one he has would fight to the death for him.

"Speaking of porn," I reply, "how's Lily?"

He chokes on his coffee. "If you love me, you will never say that sentence again."

Asher's girlfriend is tiny, dark, with a smile so wide it completely changes the landscape of her face. If Asher is strength, then she is whimsy—a sprite who keeps him from taking himself too seriously; a question mark at the end of his predictable, popular life. Asher's had no shortage of romantic entanglements with girls he's known since kindergarten. Lily is a newcomer to town.

This fall, they have been inseparable. Usually, at dinner, it's *Lily did this* or *Lily said that*.

"I haven't seen her around this week," I say.

Asher's phone buzzes. His thumbs fly, responding.

"Oh, to be young and in love," I muse. "And unable to go thirty seconds without communicating."

"I'm texting Dirk. He broke a lace and wants to know if I have extra."

One of the guys on his hockey team. I have no actual proof, but I've always felt like Dirk is the kid who oozes charm whenever he's in front of me and then, when I'm gone, says something vile, like *Your mom is hot, bro.*

"Will Lily be at your game on Saturday?" I ask. "She should come over afterward for dinner."

Asher nods and jams his phone in his pocket. "I have to go."

"You haven't even finished your cereal—"

"I'm going to be late."

He takes a long last swallow of coffee, slides his backpack over his shoulder, and grabs his car keys from the bowl on the kitchen counter. He drives a 1988 Jeep he bought with the salary he made as a counselor at hockey camp.

"Take a coat!" I call, as he is walking out the door. "It's—"

His breath fogs in the air; he slides behind the steering wheel and turns the ignition.

"Snowing," I finish.

DECEMBER IS WHEN beekeepers catch their breath. The fall is a flurry of activity, starting with the honey harvest, then managing mite loads, and getting the bees ready to survive a New Hampshire winter. This involves mixing up a heavy sugar syrup that gets poured into a hive top feeder, then wrapping the entire hive for insulation before the first cold snap. The bees conserve their energy in the winter, and so should the apiarist.

I've never been very good with downtime.

There's snow on the ground, and that's enough to send me up to the attic to find the box of Christmas decorations. They're the same ones my mother used when I was little—ceramic snowmen for the kitchen table; electric candles to set in each window at night, a string of lights for the mantel. There's a second box, too, with our stockings and the ornaments for the tree, but it's tradition that Asher and I hang those together. Maybe this weekend we will cut down our tree. We could do it after his game on Saturday, with Lily.

I'm not ready to lose him.

The thought stops me in my tracks. Even if we do not invite Lily to come choose a tree with us—to decorate it as he tells her the story behind the stick reindeer ornament he made in preschool or the impossibly tiny baby shoes, both his and mine, that we always hang on the uppermost branches—soon another will join our party of two. It is what I want most for Asher—the relationship I don't have. I know that love isn't a zero-sum game, but I'm selfish enough to hope he's all mine for a little while longer.

I lug the first box down the attic stairs, hearing Asher's voice in my head: *Why didn't you wait? I could have carried it down for you.* Glancing through the open door of his bedroom, I roll my eyes at his unmade bed. It drives me crazy that he does not tuck in his sheets; it drives him just as crazy to do it, when he knows he's just going to crawl back in in a few hours. With a sigh, I put the box down and walk into Asher's room. I yank the sheets up, straightening his covers. As I do, a book falls to the floor.

It's a blank journal, in which Asher has sketched in colored pencil. There's a bee, hovering above an apple blossom, so close that you can see the working mandible and the pollen caught on her legs. There's my old truck, a 1960 powder-blue Ford that belonged to my father.

Asher has always had this softer side, I love him all the more for it. It was clear when he was little that he had artistic talent, and once I even enrolled him in a painting class, but his hockey friends found out. When he messed up doing a passing drill, one of them said he should maybe stop holding his stick like Bob Ross held a brush, and he dropped art. Now, when he draws, it's in private. He never shows me his work. But we've also gotten college brochures in the mail from RISD and SCAD, and *I* wasn't the one to request them.

I flip the next few pages. There is one drawing that is clearly me, although he's captured me from behind, as I stand at the sink. I look tired, worn. *Is that what he thinks of me?* I wonder.

A chipmunk, eyes bright with challenge. A stone wall. A girl— Lily?—with her arm thrown over her eyes, lying on a bed of leaves, naked from the waist up.

Immediately, I drop the book like it's burning. I press my palms against my cheeks.

It's not like I didn't think he was intimate with his girlfriend; but then again, it's not like we talked about it, either. At one point, when he started high school, I proactively started buying condoms and leaving them very matter-of-factly with the usual pharmacy haul of deodorant and razor blades and shampoo. Asher loves Lily—even if he hasn't told me this directly, I see it in the way he lights up when she sits down beside him, how he checks her seatbelt when she gets into his car.

After a minute, I mess up Asher's sheets and comforter again. I tuck the journal under a fold of the linens, pick up the pair of socks, and close the door of the bedroom behind me.

I hoist the Christmas box into my arms again, thinking two things: that memories are so heavy; and that my son is entitled to his secrets.

BEEKEEPING IS THE world's second-oldest profession. The first apiarists were the ancient Egyptians. Bees were royal symbols, the tears of Re, the sun god.

In Greek mythology, Aristaeus, the god of beekeeping, was taught by nymphs to tend bees. He fell in love with Orpheus's wife, Eurydice. When she was dodging his advances, she stepped on a snake and died. Orpheus went to hell itself to bring her back, and Eurydice's nymph sisters punished Aristaeus by killing all his bees.

The Bible promises a land of milk and honey. The Koran says paradise has rivers of honey for those who guard against evil. Krishna, the Hindu deity, is often shown with a blue bee on his forehead. The bee itself is considered a symbol of Christ: the sting of justice and the mercy of honey, side by side.

The first voodoo dolls were molded from beeswax; an *oungan* might tell you to smear honey on a person to keep ghosts at bay; a *manbo* would make little cakes of honey, amaranth, and whiskey, which, eaten before the new moon, could show you your future.

I sometimes wonder which of my prehistoric ancestors first stuck his arm into a hole in a tree. Did he come out with a handful of honey, or a fistful of stings? Is the promise of one worth the risk of the other?

WHEN THE INSIDE of the house is draped with its holiday jewelry, I pull on my winter boots and a parka and hike through the acreage of the property to gather evergreen boughs. This requires me to skate the edges of the fields with the few apple trees that still belong to my family. Against the frosty ground, they look insidious and witchy, their gnarled arms reaching, the wind whispering in the voice of dead leaves, *Closer, closer.* Asher used to climb them; once, he got so high that I had to call the fire department to pull him down, as if he were a cat. I swing my handsaw as I slip into the woods behind the orchard, twigs crunching underneath my footsteps. There are only so many trees whose feathered limbs I can reach; most are higher than I can reach on my tiptoes, but there's satisfaction in gathering what I can. The pile of pine and spruce and fir grows, and it takes me three trips to bring it all back across the orchard fields to the porch of the farmhouse.

By the time I've got my raw materials—the branches and a spool of florist wire—my cheeks are flushed and bright and the tips of my ears are numb. I lay out the evergreens on the porch floor, trimming them with clippers, doubling and tripling the boughs so that they are thick. In the Christmas box I carried down earlier is a long rope of lights that I'll weave through my garland when this step is finished; then I can affix the greenery around the frame of the front door.

I am not sure what it is that makes me think something is watching me.

All the hair stands up on the back of my neck, and I turn slowly toward the barren strawberry fields.

In the snow, they look like a swath of white cotton. This late in the year, the back of the field is wreathed in shadow. In the summertime, we get raccoons and deer going after the strawberries; from time to time there's a coyote. When it's nearly winter, though, the predators have mostly squirreled themselves away in their dens—

I take off at a dead run for my beehives.

Before I even reach the electric fence that surrounds them, the smell of bananas is pungent—the surest sign of bees that are pissed off. Four hives are sturdy and quiet, hunkered tight within their insulation. But the box all the way to the right has been ripped to splinters. I name all my queen bees after female divas: Adele, Beyoncé, Lady Gaga, Whitney, and Mariah. Taylor, Britney, Miley, Aretha, and Ariana are in the apple orchard; on other contracts I have Sia, Dionne, Cher, and Katy. The hive that has been attacked is Celine's.

One side of the electric fence has been barreled through, trampled. Struts of wood from the hive are scattered all over the snowy ground; hunks of Styrofoam have been clawed to shreds. I stumble over a piece of broken honeycomb with a bear print in it.

I narrow my eyes at the dark line where the field turns into forest, but the bear is already gone. The bees would have killed themselves, literally, to get rid of their attacker—stinging until it lumbered away.

It's not the first time I have had a bear attack a hive, but it's the latest it has ever happened in the beekeeping season.

I walk toward the brush near the edge of the field, trying to find any remaining bees that might not have frozen. A small knot seethes and drips, dark as molasses, on the bare crotch of a sugar maple. I cannot see Celine, but if the bees have absconded there is a chance she is with them.

Sometimes, in the spring, bees swarm. You might find them like this, in the bivouac stage—the temporary site before they fly off to whatever they've decided should be their new home.

When bees swarm in the spring, it's because they've run out of space in the hive.

When bees swarm in the spring, they're full of honey and happy and calm.

When bees swarm in the spring, you can often recapture them, and set them up in a new box, where they have enough room for their brood cells and pollen and honey.

This is not a swarm. These bees are angry and these bees are desperate.

"Stay," I beg, and then I run back to the farmhouse as fast as I can.

It takes me three trips, each a half mile across the fields, skidding on the dusting of snow. I have to haul out a new wooden base and an empty hive from a colony that failed last year, into which I will try to divert the bees; I have to grab my bee kit from the basement, where I've stored it for the winter—my smoker and hive tool, some wire and a bee brush, my hat and veil and gloves. I am sweating by the time I am finished, my hands shaking and sausage-fingered from the cold. Clumsily, I grab the few frames that can be salvaged from the bear's attack and set them into the brood box. I sew some of the newly broken comb onto the frames with wire, hoping that the bees will be attracted back to the familiar. When the new box is set up, I walk toward the sugar maple.

The light is so low now, because dusk comes early. I see the motion of the bees more than their actual writhing outline. If Asher were here, I could have him hold the brood box directly below the branch while I scoop the bees into it, but I'm alone.

It takes several tries for me to light a curl of birch bark to ignite my smoker; there's just enough wind to make it difficult. Finally, a red ember sparks, and I drop it into the little metal pot, onto a handful of wood shavings. Smoke pipes out of the narrow neck as I pump the bellows a few times. I give a few puffs near the bees; it dulls their senses and takes the aggressive edge off.

I pull on my hat and veil and lift the same handsaw I used on the evergreen boughs. The branch is about six inches too high for me to reach. Cursing, I lug the broken wooden base of the old frame underneath the tree and try to gingerly balance on what's left of it. The odds are about equal that I will either manage to saw down the branch or break my ankle. I nearly sob with relief when the branch is free, and carry it slowly and gently to the new hive. I give it a sharp jerk, watching the bees rain down into the box. I do this again, praying that the queen is one of them.

If it were warmer, I'd know for sure. A few bees would gather on the landing board with their butts facing out, fanning their wings and nasonoving—spreading pheromones for strays to find their way home. That's a sign that the hive is queenright. But it's too cold, and so I pull out each frame, scanning the frenzy of bees. Celine, thank God, is a marked queen—I spy the green painted dot on her long narrow back and pluck her by the wings into a queen catcher, a little plastic contraption that looks like one of those butterfly clips for hair. The queen catcher will keep her safe for a couple of days while they all get used to the new home. But it also guarantees that the colony won't abscond. Sometimes, bees just up and leave with their queen if they don't like their circumstances. If the queen is locked up, they will not leave without her.

I let a puff of smoke roll over the top of the box, again hoping to calm the bees. I try to set the queen catcher between frames of comb, but my fingers are stiff with the cold and keep slipping. When my hand strikes the edge of the wooden box, one of the worker bees sinks her stinger into me.

"Mother*fucker.*" I gasp, dancing backward from the hive. A cluster of bees follows me, attracted by the scent of the attack. I cradle my palm, tears springing to my eyes.

I tear off my hat and veil, bury my face in my hands. I can take all the best precautions for this queen; I can feed the bees sugar syrup and insulate their new brood box; I can pray as hard as I want—but this colony does not have a chance of surviving the winter. They simply will not have enough time to build up the stores of honey that the bear has robbed.

And yet. I cannot just give up on them.

So I gently set the telescoping cover on the box and lift my bee kit with my good hand. In the other, I hold a snowball against the sting as a remedy. I trudge back to the farmhouse. Tomorrow, I'll give them the kindness of extra food in a hive-top feeder and I'll wrap the new box, but it's hospice care. There are some trajectories you cannot change, no matter what you do.

Back home, I am so absorbed in icing my throbbing palm that I don't notice it's long past dinnertime, and Asher isn't home.

THE FIRST TIME it happened, it was over a password.

I had only just signed up for Facebook, mostly so that I could see pictures of my brother, Jordan, and his wife, Selena. Braden and I were living in a brownstone on Mass Ave while he did his Mass General fellowship in cardiac surgery. Most of our furniture had come from yard sales in the suburbs that we would drive to on weekends. One of our best finds came from an old lady who was moving to an assisted living community. She was selling an antique rolltop desk with claw-feet (I said it was a gryphon; Braden said eagle). It was clearly an antique, but someone had stripped it of its original finish, so it wasn't worth much, and more to the point, we could afford it. It wasn't until we got it home that we realized it had a secret compartment—a narrow little sliver between the wooden drawers that was intended to look decorative, but pulled loose to reveal a spot where documents and papers could be hidden. I was delighted, naturally, hoping for the combination to an old safe full of gold bullion or a torrid love letter, but the only thing we found inside was a paper clip. I had pretty much forgotten about its existence when I had to choose a password for Facebook, and find a place to store it for when I inevitably forgot what I'd picked. What better place than in the secret compartment?

We had initially bought the antique desk so that Braden could study at it, but when we realized that his laptop was too deep for the space, it became decorative, tucked in an empty space at the bottom of the stairs. We kept our car keys there, and my purse, and an occasional plant I hadn't yet murdered. Which is why I was so surprised to find Braden sitting in front of it one evening, fiddling with the hidden compartment.

"What are you doing?" I asked.

He reached inside and triumphantly pulled out the piece of paper. "Seeing what secrets you keep from me," he said.

It was so ridiculous I laughed. "I'm an open book," I told him, but I took the paper out of his hand.

His eyebrows raised. "What's on there?"

"My Facebook password."

"So what?"

"So," I said, "it's mine."

Braden frowned. "If you had nothing to hide, you'd show it to me."

"What do you think I'm doing on Facebook?" I said, incredulous.

"You tell me," Braden replied.

I rolled my eyes. But before I could say anything, his hand shot out for the paper.

PEPPER70. That's what it said. The name of my first dog and my birth year. Blatantly uninspired; something he could have figured out on his own. But the principle of the whole stupid argument kicked in, and I yanked the page away before he could snatch it.

That's when it changed—the tone, the atmosphere. The air went still between us, and his pupils dilated. He reached out, striking like a snake, and grabbed my wrist.

On instinct, I pulled back and darted up the stairs. Thunder, him running behind me. My name twisted on his lips. It was silly; it was stupid; it was a game. But it didn't feel like one, not the way my heart was hammering.

As soon as I made it to our bedroom I slammed the door shut. Leaning my forehead against it, I tried to catch my breath.

Braden shouldered it open so hard that the frame splintered.

I didn't realize what had happened until my vision went white and I felt a hammer between my eyes. I touched my nose and my fingers came away red with blood.

"Oh my God," Braden murmured. "Oh my God, Liv. Jesus." He disappeared for a moment and then he was holding a hand towel to my face, guiding me to sit on the bed, stroking my hair.

"I think it's broken," I choked out.

"Let me look," he demanded. He gently peeled away the bloody cloth and with a surgeon's tender hands touched the ridge of my brow, the bone beneath my eyes. "I don't think so," he said, his voice frayed.

Braden cleaned me up as if I were made of glass and then he brought me an ice pack. By then, the stabbing pain was gone. I ached, and my nose was stuffy. "My fingers are too cold," I said, dropping the ice, and he picked it up and gently held it against me. I realized his hands were trembling and that he couldn't look me in the eye.

Seeing him so shaken hurt even more than my injury.

So I covered his hand with mine, trying to comfort. "I shouldn't have been standing so close to the door," I murmured.

Finally, Braden looked at me, and nodded slowly. "No. You shouldn't have."

. . .

I HAVE SENT a half dozen texts to Asher, who hasn't written back. Each one is a little angrier. For someone who seemingly has no trouble interrupting his life to text his girlfriend and Dirk, he has selective communication skills when he wants to. Most likely he was invited to eat dinner somewhere and didn't bother to tell me.

I decide that as punishment, I will make him clean up the evergreens still strewn across the porch, since my bee-stung hand hurts too much for me to finish stringing the garland.

On the kitchen table is a small bundle of newspaper, which I carefully unwrap. It was placed in the decoration box by mistake, but it belongs in the one with our Christmas ornaments. It's my favorite—a hand-blown glass bulb in swirls of blue and white, with a drippy curl of frozen glass at the top through which a wire has been threaded for hanging. Asher made it for me when he was six, after we left Braden behind in Boston, and I got a divorce. I had a booth at a county fair that fall, selling honey and beeswax products, and an artisanal glassblower befriended Asher and invited him to watch her in her workshop. Unbeknownst to me, she helped him make an ornament for me as a gift. I loved it, but what made it truly magical was that it was a time capsule. Frozen in that delicate globe was Asher's childhood breath. No matter how old he was or how big he grew, I would always have that.

Just then my cellphone rings.

Asher. If he's not texting, he knows he's in trouble.

"You better have a good excuse," I begin, but he cuts me off.

"Mom, I need you," Asher says. "I'm at the police station."

Words scramble up the ladder of my throat. "What? Are you all right?"

"I . . . I'm . . . no."

I look down at the ornament in my hand, this piece of the past.

"Mom," Asher says, his voice breaking. "I think Lily's dead."

LILY ◆ 1

DECEMBER 7, 2018

The day of

From the moment my parents knew they were having a baby, my father wanted me to be a boy. Instead, he got a daughter: boyish in some ways, I guess, but not in the ways that would have mattered to him. Every day he took time to remind me of all the ways I'd disappointed him, not because of anything I'd done, but simply because of who I was.

Sometimes I think what he liked best about seeing me in my fencing gear was the fact that he couldn't see my face behind my mask.

I could have told him, *You can't always get what you want.* Everyone recognizes that as a song by the Rolling Stones, but did you know that Keith Richards takes off his low E string to play guitar? Once, a long time ago, when this song came on the car radio, I mentioned this to my dad.

He switched off the volume. We drove along in silence for a while, and finally he said, *You don't know everything.*

I wanted to yell at him, but instead I said nothing: a pretty good strategy for dealing with Dad. Of *course* I don't know everything. But I want to.

Last summer, when my mother and I left Point Reyes for New Hampshire, Mom said, *This is our second chance,* and I thought about how she said *our,* like it was her chance, too.

We were driving along the northern edge of the bay, through the wildlife refuge, the so-called scenic route. Mom does have a thing for back roads. It was the beginning of our long trip east, a trip that would take ten days, including the stopovers for college tours and auditions. I wondered whether I'd ever come back.

"Are you okay, Lily?" Mom asked.

I started to tell her that I was fine, because that's what she needed to hear, but instead my throat closed up. I turned away, as if I were suddenly fascinated by the highway signs. NEXT EXIT VALLEJO. "I'm a mess, is all," I said.

Mom reached over and took me by the hand. "You're not a mess," she said. "You're a hero."

I glanced down at the scars on my wrist. I wondered what the kids in my new school were going to think if they saw them. I figured I could wear a scrunchie, or friendship bracelets for a while. To cover them up. I wondered if this was going to be the new beginning my mother thought it would be, or the same old bullshit.

"I'm not a hero," I told my mother. "I'm just somebody who finally figured out how to stop being sad."

ASHER KEEPS SAYING, *I have the best Christmas gift for you, ever! It's so good it's coming early.* Maya thinks he's going to give me his grandmother's ring. "She used to take us for these crazy expeditions," Maya says. "One time she drove us to Santa's Village—in July— which was *sick,* because they make actual snow in the middle of the summer. And Asher pitched a fit because he wanted to go down the road to Six Gun City and pretend to be a cowboy so we stayed over- night, like, on the spur of the moment, at a shitty motel where Asher and I had to share a bed." Then she glanced at me, as if she realized what she had actually said. "I mean, we were like six years old, so you don't have to be jealous or anything."

I'm not jealous, not like she thinks. But Maya has known Asher since they were in kindergarten together. That's a piece of his life I won't ever have, and sometimes, I am so hungry for the parts of him that I don't know yet I feel like I've been starving for decades and he's a feast. I try to remind myself that even if Maya played house with him once, I'm the one he sketched this fall, hair up, top off, wearing the autumn sunshine like a cape.

Asher's going to be here any minute. I take one more look in the mirror. It's December in New England, so it's not exactly bikini weather. But my hair has grown out long and curly—I haven't cut it since we came east. I'm wearing lapis earrings that make my eyes look more like jewels and less like a brackish pond, and the shirt Maya and I found at the hippie store last week. It does not have long sleeves, just three-quarter, but I don't care about Asher seeing the scars. He already knows the whole story.

He says it doesn't matter, but it matters to me.

I head down the stairs. Mom's sitting by the fireplace with a glass of wine. She's still wearing her National Forest Service uniform— the khaki shirt, the green pants. The shirt has her badge over her left breast and her name tag over the right shirt pocket: AVA CAMPA- NELLO. On one sleeve is the green patch with the gold pine tree and the letters that spell out U.S. and the words FOREST SERVICE up top and DEPARTMENT OF AGRICULTURE on the bottom.

Her silver Stetson felt hat is upside down on the floor next to Boris. I call him a black Lab, but he's mostly gray.

FIVE THINGS ABOUT MY MOTHER
THAT MAKE HER A BADASS

5. She can track anything: wildcats, black bear, porcupines, coral snakes, opossums. Also: humans. After I brought Asher over to the house for the first time, I found her in the yard the next day looking at his boot print in the mud. I said, *What?* She said, *Your boyfriend is left-foot dom- inant, so likely left-handed.*

4. She taught me how to remember the signs of the zodiac in order, with the sentence *The ramble twins crab liverish; scaly scorpions are good wa- terfish.* (Ram, Bull, Twins, Crab, Lion, Virgin, et cetera.)

3. She knows exactly what knot you need in every situation, and how to tie it: clove hitch, bowline, sheet bend, square knot. "And then there's

the Gordian knot," she says. "Which you can only untie with a sword."
Does Mom have a curved ornamental sword that she got in Japan, and
which she has hung on the wall above the fireplace? Yes, she does. She
says it is called a *katana*.

2. By the time Mom had graduated from Syracuse with her forestry degree, she had already been skydiving, rock climbing, bungee jumping,
and shark-cage diving. Also, I think she had seen the Grateful Dead
fifteen times, although she doesn't like to talk about that. She is still
angry at Jerry Garcia, she says, for "dying like a beached whale."

1. Her best friend is me; her second-best friend is herself. I call her
Ranger Mom. On the surface you'd think she's this calm, sweet-
tempered person. Which she is, unless you try to mess with her
daughter. At which point she would pull the brim of her ranger hat
down low, and say, *Mister? You have just made a serious mistake.*

MOM LOOKS OVER at me and smiles wearily. She's been looking
more and more tired this fall, in part because she traded her park
ranger job in Point Reyes for the desk job here in New Hampshire
with the Forest Service. At least I *think* that's why she looks tired—
but there might be other reasons, too, ones that have to do with me.

"You look nice," says Mom.

"Yeah well, *you* look kind of wrung out. Are you okay?"

She takes a sip of wine and smiles. "I'm fine. Don't worry." Her
long braid hangs down over her left shoulder. I think, *Boris isn't the
only one who's turning gray.*

"Too late. I *do* worry. If you're not working, you're asleep. Or talking to the dog."

She smiles again. "He's an excellent listener."

"Mom, Boris is deaf."

Mom looks down at Boris. "My secrets are safe with him."

"You have secrets?" I ask, and I'm only half kidding.

She waves me off. "Asher's taking you out? On a Sunday night?"

"He's giving me an early Christmas gift. He says it's too good to
wait."

Mom nods. "What are you giving *him*?" She gives me a hard look, as if maybe I'm supposed to read into this question.

"Christmas isn't even for twenty-three days," I tell her. "How do I know?"

She takes another sip of Chablis. "I am assuming this *big gift* of his will be in full public view? And the recipient will be fully clothed?"

"And I'm assuming that we will both pretend you didn't say that," I answer. "Christmas gifts are so stupid anyway. They're a complete misreading of the tradition."

There's a pause before she says, "We're talking about what tradition now?"

"The gifts of the Magi. Even if the three wise men *did* exist, they didn't visit Jesus the night he was born. It was weeks after—possibly years."

Mom raises one eyebrow. "You're reading the Bible now?"

"I read everything," I tell her.

Mom picks her ranger hat up off the floor and puts it on the raised hearthstone. "All I know," she says, "is it's nice to give people gifts. While you are both not naked."

"Oh my God. Stop. Just stop."

Mom laughs. "You be sure to tell Asher exactly that when he gives you his special gift."

A text dings on my phone; Asher's here. "And on that note," I say. Boris doesn't raise his head.

I put on my heavy down jacket and my mittens and I glance at myself in the hall mirror. "Lily," says Mom. "You really do look nice."

I smile at her, and I rush out the door into the cold New Hampshire night.

Asher's ancient Jeep is idling out in the driveway. There's a little snow coming down, drifting lazily in the cones of his headlights. I open the door and there he is, with a smile that splits his face into fractions, and green eyes that make me think of June, when everything is in bloom. He leans in to kiss me and it is electric as fuck; my heart jumps like an engine being restarted.

After a minute, or maybe a lifetime, he pulls back. "You ready?" he asks. He puts the stick into reverse.

We head down the road. The radio is playing softly, some oldies station. I put my hand down on top of Asher's as he's shifting the gears on the Jeep. He steals a glance at me.

"Well?" I ask him.

"Well what?"

"Are you going to give me a hint?"

He pretends to mull over this. "Hm, I'm thinking no."

"Are we going to be gone for a while? Because I didn't pack a toothbrush."

"I'll try to have you back by morning," says Asher.

A cash register chimes in the song on the radio, and now I recognize the tune. "Money," by Pink Floyd. It's one my father used to sing.

"God, I hate this song," I mutter.

He glances at me. "You want me to change the station?"

I shake my head. "It's in seven-four. It's a weird time signature."

Asher doesn't say anything right away. "So the time signature is what upset you?"

I don't want to go into it. "You know what else is in seven-four? 'All You Need Is Love.' The Beatles. And Blondie's 'Heart of Glass.' Soundgarden's 'Spoonman.'"

Asher smiles. "I can't believe the stuff you remember," he says.

We both fall silent for a little bit. We don't say it out loud, but we're both thinking: *It would be nice if there were some things you could forget.*

We drive toward Adams. To the right is thick pine forest. There's a trail in those woods along the Slade Brook that leads from Presidents' Square almost to our house. The first week after we moved here I walked along that path and found what I'm pretty sure was bear scat.

"I've never seen a bear," I tell him.

"You'd be fine," says Asher. "You'd tell him all about the time signatures of pop songs. Next thing you know, he'd roll right over. You could scratch his belly."

"My mom told me if you're hiking someplace where they have grizzly bears, you're supposed to carry a little bell with you."

Asher looks at me uncertainly. "Were there bears in Point Reyes?"

"Well, not grizzlies. Bears had been extinct in Marin County for a hundred years. Then a black bear showed up a couple of years ago. He was eating garbage behind a pizza place."

Asher laughs.

"What?" I ask.

"I'm just thinking about what kind of pizza bears like."

"Maybe Hawaiian?"

"No one likes Hawaiian. Not even bears."

"Shut *up*," I argue. "It's awesome."

"Lily, if you like Hawaiian pizza I'm afraid that might be the dealbreaker in our relationship." But he's smiling, and I think, *Fuck, I can't believe he is mine.*

We pass the opera house and there's a sign out front that says, WHITE MOUNTAIN SYMPHONY ORCHESTRA. ALL MOZART CONCERT. Is Asher taking me to the Mozart concert? Is this the big surprise? But he just keeps driving.

In Presidents' Square, snow falls on the statue of Franklin Pierce. "Poor dude," I say. "He looks cold."

"He's used to it."

"His son died in a train wreck, a couple months before he became president," I say quietly. "The kid was only ten years old. Pierce never got over it." We're crossing over the train tracks, passing by the old mill. "You see that with people all the time, something bad happens and it wrecks them. They turn into ghosts." I can feel Asher looking at me. I try to pull the sleeve of my coat down over my right wrist.

"You're not a ghost," says Asher.

Which is ironic, because I am positive Asher is the only person who truly sees me.

We pull into the parking lot of the A-1 Diner. "You ready?" he says, and turns off the engine.

"This is my surprise?" I ask, looking into the diner. There's a man drinking coffee at a booth, and a bored waitress reading a newspaper behind the counter. I'm trying not to feel disappointed.

Asher, on the other hand, is radiating excitement.

"Come on," he says.

We walk up the stairs into the A-1. Asher holds open the door. I step in and immediately smell French fries and coffee. The waitress looks up from the paper.

So does the man in the booth.

I haven't seen him in two years. I've never seen him with a beard before. It's almost completely gray. "Dad?" I say.

"Hey, Champ," he says, standing up.

"Merry Christmas, Lily," says Asher.

This is not happening. This is not my life anymore. But there is Asher, and there is my dad, like potassium and water. Any second now, there will be an explosion.

Everything starts to spin around me, and I look in panic, first at Dad, and then at Asher. *What the fuck?* I want to ask him. Of all the things you could have given me, you brought me to see the one person I hate most in the entire world.

FIVE MINUTES LATER, I'm on a park bench across from Town Hall, snow settling in my hair. The single traffic light in town blinks yellow.

I pull out my phone and stare at it for a full minute. What I want is to talk to somebody who *knows* me. Which is who, if it's not Asher?

My mother, but I can't tell her *this.*

I could call Maya, I guess, but I know she'll just take Asher's side. It's what she always does.

So I sit, shipwrecked on the park bench with the snow coming down on the glowing glass of my phone until it goes dark.

The last time I saw my father was at a fencing match—two years ago, I guess. I was down on the piste with my sword pointed toward the foilist from Hartshorn Academy. Thirty seconds into the match I flèched my competition with an ear-piercing yell. And the kid from Hartshorn *screamed* and ran back to his bench. Everyone in the field house laughed, applauded. The ref gave me the point.

Then, from the bleachers, I heard that voice. It had been four years. But I knew who it was without even looking. And that he was drunk. I remembered what it was like to have him in my life, what it was like to spend so much time so incredibly scared. On any given day, you never knew which dad was going to show up. Sometimes there was the nice one, the one who called me "Champ."

Then there was the other one.

That's my kid! he shouted. *That's—*

I dropped my foil and ran.

The snow is gathering in my hair and my teeth are chattering from the cold, but I feel like I'm being incinerated from the inside. From inside Town Hall, I hear people applauding.

"Lily." I glance up to see Asher. He looks like he's been shot with a bow and arrow. My first thought is *Good.*

"I don't really want to talk to you," I tell him, and I get up and start walking away.

"Lily, wait," he says, and he grabs my arm.

"Let go of me."

"Please. Let me explain." His pretty face is pale and scared now. "*Please?*"

He's gripping me *hard*. I can tell without even checking that I'm going to wind up with a bruise. It wouldn't be the first time.

"I was trying to do something nice for you."

"You thought it would be nice to stage a reunion for me with the person who ruined my life? Why would you think I'd *ever* want that?"

"Because I know what it's like. Not having a father."

"Lucky you!"

Anger flickers in Asher's eyes, but is quickly banked. "It *wasn't* lucky, Lily. Not for me. It was like having a giant black hole in the middle of everything."

"I would rather have had a giant black hole in the middle of everything than to have that *asshole*," I tell him.

"You don't mean that."

"How do *you* know what I mean? You weren't there!"

I start to move away, but he grabs me by the arm again. "You're right, I wasn't," he says. "I was *here*. Without my own father. And I thought maybe if I couldn't fix that for me, I could fix it for you."

I look him hard in the eye. "You," I say slowly, "can get your fucking hand off my arm."

I twist out of his grasp and start walking through the snow. It's five miles to the house, but I will walk a hundred if it means I can stop having this conversation.

"Don't you think he deserves a second chance?" Asher calls.

"No," I snap.

"Lily," Asher says. "You gave *me* one."

Again, I stop in my tracks. The snow is coming down harder now. "Maybe that was my first mistake," I say, and head toward the trail that leads through the dark woods to my house.

FIVE DAYS LATER, I wake up sick. Correction: *still* sick. It's my third day home from school. I can hardly remember Monday and Tuesday because I spent both days trying to avoid Asher and everyone else at Adams High. Whatever I've come down with started the night I walked through the woods, and keeps getting worse.

Although to be honest it is hard for me to separate how crappy I feel from being sick from how crappy I feel about Asher.

I don't even know how in the living *fuck* he found my father. Social media? A private detective? Obsessing over it makes me crazy. What if Dad is still around here? What's to keep him from coming over and knocking on our door? It'd be easy enough for him to find us. It's a small town.

The bruise I got from where Asher grabbed me is greenish blue. Yesterday, when I told Mom I wanted to stay home, she looked at it and said, *Lily. Talk to me.*

But what could I tell her? I didn't have the words.

Lily, she said. *If that boy is hurting you, you have to tell me.*

I opened my mouth, but instead I just started crying. So Mom put her arms around me and held me and we just sat like that for a long time. *He did hurt me, Mom,* I whispered. *But not like you think.*

I'D ALMOST FORGOTTEN that today's the day I find out about the early decision from Oberlin. To be honest, all I want to do is sleep. At lunchtime, Mom comes in to check on me again. She's not wearing her Forest Service uniform, which means she's taken the day off to take care of me. She carries a mug of tea, which she puts down on my nightstand before placing a hand on my forehead. "You're hot," she says.

I take the tea and sip it. It is Irish breakfast, my favorite, although I wish that we had some of Olivia's honey.

If I'm breaking up with Asher, that means I'm breaking up with his mom, too, I guess? Which is sad, because I really liked her. Once Olivia called me a *pixie*, although clearly she didn't know the mythology. In England pixies were thought to be children who'd died before being baptized.

She sits down on the edge of the bed. "You look terrible."

"You're supposed to love me unconditionally," I say, but my voice is basically a croak.

My mother's long braid swings down over her right shoulder. "Maybe we should take you to a doctor."

"I'm fine," I say. "I just want to sleep."

"Lily." She clenches and unclenches her jaw. "I didn't move us all the way across the country for you to be afraid of some"—she's searching for the word—"boy."

I roll over and close my eyes. "I'm not afraid of him. I'm afraid of me."

"What are you afraid of?" she says.

How can I tell her? Mom, who's done everything in the universe for me, who's moved us twice, who got herself a job in New Hampshire just so we could start over again? "I'm just afraid—" I say. "It's not enough to make me happy."

She thinks this over. "Some people," she says gently, "have to fight for that harder than others."

I think she is talking about me, but after a second I realize Mom is describing herself. She hasn't really dated anyone since we left Seattle seven years ago. She doesn't have friends she goes out for coffee or wine with. I feel bad for her sitting behind a desk at the forest headquarters in Campton, while all the teams that answer to her get to go out into the wild. I think Mom's the kind of person who gets lonelier in an office with other people than when she's on the Appalachian Trail by herself.

She stands, pausing at the bedroom door. "Don't forget your tea," Mom says, as her cellphone rings. She starts walking down the hall.

It feels like ages since we moved cross-country. Was it really just August when we shouted every time we crossed a state line? Nevada, the Sagebrush State. Utah, the Beehive State. Nebraska, Iowa, Illinois: Cornhusker, Hawkeye, the Land of Lincoln. The cornfields of Indiana, how they went on and on for days. The campus of Oberlin. Niagara Falls.

We crossed the Connecticut River late that same day. New Hampshire, the Granite State. *Granite,* I had thought, *is unbreakable.* I felt myself grow lighter as I read the sign: WELCOME TO NEW HAMPSHIRE: LIVE FREE OR DIE!

Like it's that easy.

MIDAFTERNOON. ANOTHER KNOCK. Mom, with a thermometer and more tea: Lapsang souchong this time—the first black tea in history.

I pull the thermometer out of my mouth. "Mom," I say. "I need to tell you something."

There's a dramatic pause and then Boris waddles into the room. He walks over to my bed, spins around three times, then collapses on the floor with a groan.

"It's Dad. He's *here*. In Adams." I get this far and then I can't tell her any more.

"I know. I talked to him this morning."

"I don't want him here!" I burst out.

"Don't worry. He flew back to Seattle yesterday."

I heave a sigh of relief. Only now do I realize how much I've been dreading him suddenly showing up at the house. Maybe that's what's been making me sick—the fear of Dad swooping in to wreck everything again.

Mom inserts the thermometer into my mouth again. "He told me Asher was the one who contacted him, and invited him out here. I don't know what that boy was thinking."

"That was the big Christmas gift. A *reunion*." I speak around the thermometer.

"Lily, can you just not talk for one minute?" She looks pointedly at my lips, which I clamp around the thermometer.

She is quiet for a long beat. Finally she says, "We don't know anyone as well as we think we do. Especially the people we love."

Finally the thermometer beeps. "So am I supposed to forgive him?" I ask, as she squints to read my temperature.

Mom says, "A hundred point eight. I'm calling the doctor." She stands up.

My phone pings and I know who it is even without looking. This will be the latest in the series of texts I've been getting from Asher begging me to talk to him.

"Should I text him back?" I ask Mom. I haven't responded to him once. I've barely written to Maya.

"Why don't you wait till you feel better," Mom says, "before you make any decisions."

DR. MADDEN SAYS I need rest and ibuprofen. If I'm still sick tomorrow, or if my temperature spikes, I should come in. Mom heads to CVS to get Advil while I sit with a banging headache and a phone still blowing up from Asher. *Aren't you going to answer me? At all?*

I don't write back.

Then: *Hello?* I don't write back.

Then: *Lily, promise me you won't hurt yourself again. Just promise me that.*

I don't write back.

Then: *Lily, please.*

I get a text from Maya: *Do u want me to get your homework or anything from yr locker?*

I reply: *Im all set with HW thx just need sleep.*

The next one from Maya reads: *I need 2 talk Asher is flipping OUT what happened*

I don't write back.

I give up and check the Oberlin site. They still haven't updated my admission status.

I'm also applying to Berklee, and the Curtis Institute, and the Manhattan School of Music, and the Peabody. If I don't get into Oberlin I'll survive, I know that. But there was something about that campus. I could imagine myself there, the green quads, the buildings with their red-tile roofs. For the first time, I could really see my future.

I go downstairs, planning to kill time by practicing. Our home is very New England: all raw wood and exposed timbers and fireplaces. The only thing missing is a moose head on the wall.

I like it—but sometimes I miss the bay.

I sit down by the fireplace and get my cello out of the case. Drawing my bow across the strings, I close my eyes, and imagine waves crescendoing toward the shore.

Then I play the Bach Cello Suite No. 1 and go where that music takes me. The first time I played cello, it felt like holding the body of a woman in my arms. Even as a little kid, I thought, *Who is she?* And the obvious answer: the person I'd eventually grow up to be.

My fingers know this piece so well they move without my even thinking about it consciously. There are times when it's like the cello is playing me, when I'm the instrument and the music is pouring through my blood.

I remember the mist rising up from the water when we stood by Niagara Falls. The guide talked about people going over the falls in barrels. One kid who fell into the river north of the falls was washed downstream. He didn't even know he was about to go over Niagara Falls until he was already past the edge and hurtling downward.

According to our guide, he lived.

IT'S NOT A long piece, the Bach No. 1, maybe four minutes tops, but when I finally lift my bow I feel like I've been gone a long time. My head doesn't hurt quite as much, and I'm hungry. I decide to make myself lunch when I hear the sound of someone whistling outside.

I throw open the front door, and a blast of cold air rushes in. In the front yard is Dirk, who is the co-captain of the hockey team.

For many reasons, I am not a huge fan of Dirk.

But Asher is, and technically, without Dirk, I would not be dating Asher, so I give him the benefit of the doubt. "Dirk," I say. "What are you doing here?"

He stops whistling, as if he didn't expect to see me coming out of my own house. "I heard you were sick," he says. He looks at me like he's surprised I didn't call him to tell him all the details.

"It's probably just a virus," I say.

"I don't mean to bother you," he says. "I'm just— I'm kind of messed up."

A gust of wind blows his baseball hat off. The weather vane on top of the garage spins again, squeaking. Dirk scoops his hat up from the ground, flicks the snow off, and looks at it in his hand as if he's trying to figure out if it's too cold to put back on his head.

I do not want to babysit Dirk. I do not want to be his confidante. I have enough problems of my own.

"Messed up how?" I ask.

He's holding his hat by the brim with his thumbs and index fingers, suspending it like he's a puppeteer and his Red Sox hat is his marionette.

"Well, you know I got a likely letter from UC Boulder, right?" He casts a shy little glance up at me. "But I have to keep my grades up."

The UC Boulder's hockey team needs a goalie bad enough that it promised Dirk during junior year he could have a free ride, unless he failed out as a senior. Which, judging from the look on his face, he's about to do.

"I was hoping you could read the paper I wrote for Chopper?"

Everyone except for me lives in fear of Chopper, our English teacher. Dirk reaches into his jacket and pulls out a bunch of papers.

"Dirk," I say. "I'm sick."

"Maybe when you're feeling better?"

I sigh, take the paper from him, and read the title: "The Not So Great Gatsby."

Dirk twists the visor of his Red Sox cap. "Your mom home?"

I think about this question for a second. Then I say, "Did you need something else, Dirk?"

He smiles, and it transforms him. I suddenly understand why girls at school might hook up with him and brag about it, instead of feeling ashamed for falling under his spell. "I know something's not right between you and Ash," he says.

Everything in me freezes. "What did he tell you?"

He shrugs, then takes a step toward me. "Listen, I know it's none of my business, but like—if you need a friend, Lily? I can be a friend."

I *do* need a friend, somebody I can talk to about this whole mess. Somebody who's not Asher, and somebody who's not my mother, and somebody who isn't Maya. But I'm damn sure the person I need is not Dirk.

He takes a step closer. His words are clouds, a whole weather system between us. "I could be *more* than a friend," he adds.

"You should go home," I say.

"Okay." He puts his cap back on his head, like he's decided something.

"I'll email you," I say. "After I've read your paper."

"And I'll come back," says Dirk. "Whenever you're ready." Another flash of that grin, like he's giving me a secret for safekeeping. He heads back to his car, a beat-up old Dodge, whistling.

Back upstairs, I lie down on my bed with Dirk's paper. The first sentence is *Jay Gatsby in the Great Gatsby by F. Scot Fitzgereld is said to be Great, but is it really?*

Oh, Dirk.

I open my laptop and log on to the Oberlin site. STATUS UPDATED.

Dear Lily:

The admissions committee of the Conservatory of Music has completed its early action deliberations and has deferred a decision on your application until the spring. We received more than 5,000 early applications, and we had many more qualified candidates than we could admit.

Your decision will be reconsidered in February and March with the entire applicant pool. Please be sure the Mid-Year School report is sent to us as soon as

I shut my laptop, hard. *Fuck.*

I pick up my phone and open up my favorites and my thumb is just about to press down on Asher's name before I remember that we're not talking. What do you do when you really need to talk to someone about your boyfriend, and your boyfriend is the person you want to talk to him about? I remember his parting words to me, telling me I should give my dad a second chance. *You gave me one.*

My father used to call second chances *mulligans.* He thought of me as his chance to get his own life right the second time around. That was a stupid thing for him to think, and an even stupider thing to say. Nobody is a do-over of anybody else, and if you get to do anything at all on earth it's live your own life, not be some sort of ghost version of somebody else's.

I look at my watch. It's almost four. There must have been a crazy-ass line at the pharmacy. The salesclerk there is about 120 years old and no one has the heart to tell her to retire. My headache is back and Mom is taking forever to get the Advil. I wish that she was here. Because all at once I realize the person I need to talk to is Mom, and what I need to tell her is everything.

I walk downstairs again to the kitchen, thinking I will make coffee. The caffeine will help the pounding in my head. But I get distracted by the big butcher block with knives sitting right there on the countertop. How very, very sharp a knife is.

The doorbell rings. For a second I just stand there, listening to the quiet. Then, there's a knock that echoes the throb in my head. Whoever has come to visit is not going away.

OLIVIA ◆ 2

Three hours after

The police department is an unremarkable square building hunkered on the edge of town, the kind of place you do not notice unless you need it, which in Adams means filing a complaint because your neighbor cut down a tree over your property line, or reporting a pothole that bottomed out your car, or taking the Boy Scouts on a tour of the facility. I remember once asking my father what the officers did all day, since crime was basically nonexistent up here. "Only the crimes you can *see*," he said cryptically, and it wasn't until years later, when I was married, that I understood what he had meant.

I pull into the tiny visitor parking lot so fast that my truck straddles the two spots. I realize that I have literally run out of my house without taking a purse, my license, anything. Inside, there is a wall of Plexiglas with an officer and a dispatch operator sitting behind it. To my left is a locked door. Behind it, somewhere, is my son.

"I don't have any ID but I'm Asher Fields's mother; he doesn't have the same last name as me because I'm divorced, and he called to say he's being questioned—"

"Whoa." The officer holds up a hand and speaks through a tinny speaker. "Take a breath."

I do. "My son is here," I begin, and the locked door to my left opens.

"I've got her, Mac," a voice says.

Lieutenant Newcomb is the sole detective in the small Adams

PD, but long before that he was Mike and he took me to my junior prom. I knew, when I came back here, that he had never left; our paths had crossed a few times—at a sidewalk market where I was selling honey and he was on security detail; at town Christmas tree lightings; once when I spun out on black ice and my truck hit a guardrail. There's gray in his black hair now, and lines at the corners of his eyes, but superimposed over this man is a flicker of a boy in a pale blue tuxedo, chasing a runaway hubcap on the shoulder of the road while I waited and twisted a corsage on my wrist.

"Asher—"

"—is fine," Mike interrupts. He holds the door to the interior of the station open, so that I can walk through. "But he's pretty worked up."

"He said that Lily was . . ." I can't even shape my mouth around the word.

"She was taken to the hospital. I haven't heard anything else, yet. I'm hoping Asher might help us figure out what happened."

"Was he there?"

"He was found holding her body."

Body.

Mike stops walking, and I do, too. "He asked me to call you, and I didn't think it could hurt."

Asher isn't a minor, so they didn't have to wait for me before taking his statement. I realize Mike is doing me a favor—maybe because we have a history, maybe because Asher is so upset. On the phone with me, Asher's voice had been a saw, serrated with shock. "Thank you," I say.

He leads me to a room with a closed door and turns to me. "You should prepare yourself," Mike says. "It's not his blood."

With that, he opens the door.

Asher is huddled in a plastic chair, his tall body curved like a question mark, one knee restlessly bobbing. When he looks up, I see his shirt, streaked red. His eyes are swollen and raw. "Mom?" he says, in a voice so small that I swell forward, folding him into my arms, cocooning him with my body, as if I could turn back time.

. . .

ASHER IS FIDGETING, frustrated. Every time there is a noise in the hall, his head swivels hopefully to the doorway, as if he expects someone to walk in with the information that everything is fine, that Lily is all right. A foot away, on the table, is the recording device that Mike has set down. An untouched glass of water sits in front of each of us. "What were you doing at Lily's house?" the detective asks.

"She's my girlfriend," Asher replies.

"For how long?"

"About three months. I went over there to talk to her."

Mike nods. "Didn't you see her at school?"

"She was out sick. She hadn't been answering my texts. I was . . . I was really worried." He lets out a long breath. "Look, I want to help you. But . . . do you know if she . . . if she's . . ." I see the moment he decides to err on the side of optimism. "Is she still at the hospital?"

"I don't know," Mike says. "As soon as I get word . . ." He clears his throat. "So, you went to her house to check on her?"

"Yeah."

"How did you get in?"

"The door was open," Asher says.

"When you came into the house, where was Lily?"

He swallows. "Lily was . . ." Asher looks down, and his hair falls into his eyes. I watch his throat work for a moment, caught around the rest of his words. "Lily was at the bottom of the stairs and she wasn't moving."

I think, quickly, of Lily—who somehow always had seemed in motion, even when she wasn't; hands moving to punctuate her sentences and her smile flickering in the spaces between words. I think of how she would hold Asher's hand, and her thumb would rub over his knuckles, as if she needed to convince herself that he was solid.

"There was blood under her head," Asher says. "I tried to get her to wake up?" His voice scales upward, a question, like he can still scarcely believe it himself.

"How?" the detective asks.

"I shook her, I think?"

"Why didn't you call 911?"

Asher looks as if he has been slapped.

"Mike," I murmur. "He's just a *kid*."

He looks at me, not in warning, but not in sympathy, either. "Olivia, you're going to have to let him answer these questions."

Asher's eyes meet mine. "Oh my God," he says, "why *didn't* I call them? If I had . . . if I had would she be okay now? *Is this my fault?*"

"Asher." I gently put my hand on his shoulder, but he shrugs it off.

"What happened to her?" he demands of Mike.

"We're trying to figure that out," the detective says, grim. "Was anyone else there?"

"Just her dog."

He nods. "Let me get this straight. When you got to the house, you found Lily at the bottom of the stairs. But when the officers got there, Lily was on the couch. Who moved her?"

"I guess I did, but I don't really remember doing it," Asher admits. He shakes his head. "The next thing I knew, Lily's mom was standing in front of me asking what happened. She called 911 and then she kneeled down in front of Lily and I . . . I backed off. And then you guys showed up."

Mike flicks the button on his pen twice. He stares at Asher, then nods. "Okay, Asher. Thanks for answering my questions. I really appreciate it."

He stands up, but Asher remains in his chair, gripping its arms. "Wait," he says. "How did she fall?"

"I don't know," the detective says. "We're still trying to determine what actually happened." Suddenly there is a buzzing, and he pulls his phone from his pocket and holds it to his ear. "Lieutenant Newcomb." I watch his face, but it remains smooth, implacable. "Thanks. I understand."

As he hangs up, Asher rises on a current of hope.

Mike shakes his head, meeting Asher's eyes. "I'm sorry," he says.

Asher folds in on himself, crumpling onto the floor. He draws up his knees, buries his face in his hands as he sobs.

He is making a noise that is inhuman. With muscles I did not know I have I help him to his feet. As we are walking out of the conference room, Mike puts his hand on my arm. "Keep a close eye on him," he murmurs. "We don't need another tragedy on our hands."

THE NEWS THAT the American colonies had won the Revolutionary War took two whole weeks to reach Adams, New Hampshire. For that reason, when I was growing up, the town celebrated Independence Day two Saturdays after the Fourth of July. There was a little parade, a petting zoo on the green, and a fire engine and police car for little kids to climb in. When Asher was four, Braden happened to have Adams Day weekend off, so we made the trek from Boston to visit my mother. We sat on the curb and let Asher catch candy that was thrown from the parade floats that limped past—antique cars bearing politicians seeking reelection, a local barbershop quartet, the Girl Scouts. While Braden stood in line to get us cotton candy, Asher spotted the police car and darted toward it.

I chased after him. The blues were flashing, which is why it took me a minute to realize that I knew the officer who was lifting kids in and out of the car in a regulated flow. "Oh my God, Mike," I said, before I could stop myself. "You're still here?"

He grinned. "Hey, Olivia. Old habits die hard."

Braden walked up, holding the cone of spun sugar. His arm snaked around my waist. "Who's this?" he asked, smiling.

"Braden, Mike," I introduced. "We went to school together a thousand years ago."

As they shook hands and made small talk, Asher climbed into the open rear door of the police car, curling his chubby little fingers through the wire mesh of the cage that served as a divider. Mike reached for him. "If you're going to ride in a police car, buddy," he said, "you definitely want to be up front." He swung Asher into the driver's seat.

Later that night, when we were getting ready to go to bed, Braden stood beside me at the bathroom sink. He watched me rub moisturizer onto my cheeks, my neck.

"Did you date him?" he asked.

I laughed. "Mike? I mean, for a hot second. But we were kids."

Braden's eyes met mine in the mirror. "Did you fuck him?"

I closed the jar of moisturizer. "I'm not going to dignify that with an answer," I said.

Suddenly his hands were at my throat. My gaze flew to the mirror, to his fingers pressing against my windpipe. "I could make you," Braden replied.

As stars started to narrow my vision, Braden abruptly released me. Coughing, I pushed past him. Instead of going to my old bedroom, where we had left our overnight bags, I went to my mother's sewing room, curling onto my side on a narrow couch, trying to make myself as small as possible.

Hours—or maybe minutes—later, I woke to the shape of Braden kneeling beside the couch. It was so dark that he was only a shift in the seam of the night. He held out his hand to touch me, and I flinched. "I just can't stand the thought of you with anyone else," he whispered.

"I'm yours," I told him, as he fitted his body against mine.

For days after that, Braden would leave me love notes—on the bathroom mirror, in my wallet, in the stack of Asher's folded clothes. He brought me flowers. He kissed me, just because. Until it got back to the point where, when he touched me, my body instinctively softened, instead of going tense.

WHEN WE GET HOME, I am surprised to see the pine boughs and wire and Christmas lights on the porch where I left them. It feels as though I've been gone for months, not hours. Asher, shell-shocked and silent on the ride, gets out of the car before it even rolls to a complete stop. His movements are jerky, shuddering, those of a wooden puppet instead of a boy. I hurry after him, but he is already halfway up the stairs when I get inside the house. "Ash," I call out. "Let me get you something to eat."

"Not hungry," he mutters, and a moment later, I hear the door to his room slam.

I hang up my coat and go into the kitchen. Even though Asher has turned down dinner, I heat up some soup and bring it to him. When I knock on his bedroom door, he doesn't answer. I hesitate, cognizant of his privacy, but then remember what Mike said. I balance the tray of food on my hip and briskly turn the knob, as if I've been invited in. Asher lies still on his bed, staring at the ceiling, his eyes so red it looks as if all the blood vessels have burst. He isn't crying. He's barely breathing.

"I know you said you aren't hungry," I say softly. "But just in case."

There's a canyon between us.

"If you want to talk—"

The slightest shiver, a *no*.

"Maybe if you eat something, you'll feel better . . . ?"

Silence.

I retreat to the door again, realizing that there isn't any food I could cook that would fill the hole inside him. That I brought him a tray to make *me* feel better, not him.

AN HOUR LATER, I knock on Asher's door again. He is in the same position, his eyes still open. The soup is untouched.

This time I don't bother with words; the ones we need don't exist in the English language. Even the syllable *grief* feels like a cliff, and we've fallen.

I FIND AVA CAMPANELLO'S phone number in the PTO directory of the high school, a PDF I filed in a saved folder on my computer without ever looking at it. I have talked to her only twice: once after an orchestra concert where Lily was featured performing a stunning cello piece, and once when she came to pick Lily up from our house to go to a dentist's appointment. Both were polite, friendly conversations—people who do not know each other and yet are linked by circumstance. It made me think of how, when you pull a frame from a hive, bees create a chain across the space: me, then Asher, then Lily, then Ava.

I am not surprised when she doesn't answer. She must have . . . people. Friends or relatives . . . someone who is with her at this moment. And yet, I vaguely remember Asher saying something about the father being out of the picture, and I know Lily was an only child.

I *hope* she has people.

"Ava," I say, to the blank space of voicemail, "this is Olivia McAfee. Asher's mom. I just . . . I wanted . . ." I close my eyes. "My God. I am so sorry."

I hang up as a tsunami of sadness sinks me into a kitchen chair. You read about tragedies in the paper, where a student athlete falls dead in the middle of a basketball game or a National Honor student is killed by a drunk driver or a school shooting claims the life of a preteen. In the news you see their faces, braces and cowlicks and freckles.

You tell yourself this wouldn't happen in your hometown.

You tell yourself this isn't anyone you know.

Until it does, and it is.

IN THE MIDDLE of the night I hear it—a note like an oboe, vibrating in the heart of the house. I bolt upright in bed, thinking of the bear that decimated my hive, and then the rest of the day fills in the empty spaces in my conscious mind. Reality hits like a fist.

The floor is cold on my bare feet as I follow the thread of sound. I know I am headed to Asher's room, and I throw the door open to find my son curled on his side, sobbing uncontrollably. "Ash," I cry, gripping his shoulder. "Baby, I'm here."

It doesn't stop, this waterfall of pain. It comes pouring out of him from a source that refills as quickly as it is emptied. I touch his arm, his face, his hair, trying to soothe. With a little jolt I realize that Asher is sound asleep.

Imagine a sorrow so deep that it batters the hatches of sleep; imagine drowning before you even realize you've gone under.

I don't know what to do. So I curl around him the way I used to when he was little and had a nightmare. Except now, he is bigger than I am, and I'm more like a barnacle than a protective cloak. I whisper in his ear, lines that used to slow his pulse, calm his heart.

> The owl and the pussy-cat went to sea
> In a beautiful pea-green boat,
> They took some honey, and plenty of money,
> Wrapped up in a five-pound note.

I repeat this, letting it pull at him like a current, until I fall asleep.

THE NEXT MORNING—SATURDAY—I am awakened by the buzzing of Asher's phone. I gingerly sit up, making sure not to disturb him, and look at it. On the lock screen are notifications from Dirk. I remember suddenly that there is a game at 4:00 P.M. today, one that Asher will obviously not be playing in. Then I realize that Dirk likely isn't texting about the game. By now, I am sure, news of Lily's death has spread.

I power down the phone so that Asher won't be disturbed, and leave it on his nightstand. I rush through a shower and braid my hair, then mix up 2:1 sugar syrup. I put on boots and a parka, grab a top hive feeder and the crate that holds my bee kit, and hike across the frosted field to my hives. I don't want to disturb the colony that was attacked yesterday, but I don't have a choice. I have to free the queen, feed them sugar solution, and insulate the box—even though I know this is still a losing battle.

When I reach it, I light my smoker first and remove the cover. I'm surprised to see a couple of drones—male bees, with their big heads and giant eyes and helicopter noise. By this time of year, drones are mostly gone. Their only purpose is to mate with the queen in the spring, and they die in the process. While waiting for their big orgy, they do practice flights, the bee equivalent of flexing. But they don't collect pollen or nectar, even though they are allowed to eat it anytime they want. They don't make beeswax. They don't clean. They're allowed to enter other hives, like goodwill ambassadors. But because they are basically a giant energy suck on a hive, in the fall, any drones that are still alive are attacked by the worker bees, literally dismembered and tossed out.

We could learn a lot from bees, frankly.

Girls run the bee world, and worker bees are all female. They feed baby bees, shape new cells out of beeswax, forage for and store nectar and pollen, ripen the honey, cool down the hive when it's too hot. They also are undertakers, working in pairs to drag out the dead. But their most important job, arguably, is taking care of the queen, who can't take care of herself—feeding and cleaning her while she lays fifteen hundred eggs a day.

It's hard to spot a queen bee if she's unmarked. She is the largest—longer, skinnier—but she tends to look more frenetic, and to run away from the light with her ladies-in-waiting. When Asher was younger, we'd play a game where I'd pull out frame after frame until I found the queen for him. *How do you know it's her?* he would ask, and I'd say, *She's wearing that tiny, tiny crown.* In truth, the way you spot a queen is usually by sussing out the proof that she's alive. If you don't see eggs in all stages of development, the queen of a colony is probably dead.

The first time Asher brought Lily to our house, I was with the bees. I saw him crossing the field with her, holding her hand as if he thought she might fly away—a balloon untethered, a dandelion puff. I was debating whether to add another super to Ariana's hive when they stopped, about twenty feet away. In his free hand, Asher carried his beekeeper hat. But tucked beneath his arm was also an old brimmed pith helmet with face netting, one that used to belong to my father and must have been in the attic.

Asher had dated before, but he'd never gone the extra step of introducing me to a girlfriend. Granted, I knew all the kids in town. This one, I had never seen before.

"Mom," Asher said, after he'd helped her don her makeshift bee gear. "This is Lily."

I glanced up, smiling through my own netting. It was September; the winding down of bee season. In a few weeks I'd do the second honey harvest, but for now, there were still plenty of blossoms and forager bees diving into the entrances of the hives with leg baskets full of pollen. "Ah," I said. "The famed Lily."

She glanced at Asher with her eyebrows raised.

"I talk about you," he said, grinning. "Maybe a lot."

"It's nice to meet you, Mrs. Fields," Lily replied.

"It's McAfee," Asher and I corrected simultaneously, and when Lily blushed, embarrassed, I shook my head. "Don't worry. Just call me Olivia." I glanced up at her. "First rule of beekeeping: don't stand in front of the hive."

Lily darted to the right, shrinking from a curious bee that circled her head.

"Are you allergic?" Asher asked.

"No," she answered. "I mean, not that I know of?"

"You'd know," I said. At that, she shied back a tiny bit, closer to Asher.

"These hives are pretty chill," I told her. "They won't bother you if you don't bother them."

Asher slipped an arm around her, his hand in the pocket of her jeans. "I promised Lily some honey," he said.

I twisted the frame in my hand to reveal its back side, glistening. "There it is." I showed Lily. "But it's not quite ready yet. They have to cap it first."

"Bee vomit," Lily said. "Isn't that how they make it?"

"The nectar is regurgitated, sure," I agreed. "But *bee vomit* just doesn't look quite as enticing on the label."

"It's an enzyme they add that breaks the nectar into glucose and fructose," Lily said.

"Yes, invertase," I confirmed, taking another, longer look at Lily.

"Lily is ridiculously smart. She's like Google," Asher said. "But cuter."

I watched her cheeks pinken again, and looked back down at my busy hive. Sometimes, when I opened a deep hive body, I got the sense I was invading the colony's privacy. I felt the same way, at that moment, with Asher and Lily.

In spite of his compliments, though, her eyes were on me as I worked methodically through the super, inspecting the new white wax the bees had added to the comb to build out between the frames, creating the right bee space for them to move comfortably in, and making the cells deeper to hold the honey. It always looked to me like wafer cookies, or white chocolate.

"It's like a dance," Lily said, mesmerized. "Like you're moving through honey."

I smiled. "What else do you know about bees?"

I expected her to know the usual factoids: that 80 percent of crops are pollinated by bees; that one out of every three or four bites we eat is a result of their work. But instead, Lily surprised me.

"In 1780, outside of Philly, there was a Quaker girl—Charity Crabtree—who was taking care of bees when she came across a wounded soldier. He asked her to ride his horse to General Washington, to let him know that the British were about to attack. She did, but she could hear the army behind her, so she threw down the hive she was carrying and the bees swarmed the enemy soldiers. Washington supposedly said that it was bees that saved America."

I blinked at her.

"I told you so." Asher laughed.

"I like this one," I told him.

Gently, I fitted the telescoping cover on top of the super and ratcheted tight the nylon ties. I dug my heel into the soft earth and made a small divot where I could dump the embers from my smoker and stamp them out with my boot. "In 1925," I told Lily, "in a book called *The Mummy*, there's an account of a group of Egyptologists who came across a big sealed jar in a tomb. When they opened it and found honey, they tasted it because they knew honey doesn't spoil, and they thought it would be amazing to taste something from thousands of years ago. But one guy found a hair wrapped around his finger . . . and then they pulled out the body of a toddler from the honey, still dressed and perfectly preserved."

"That is *vile*," Asher said at the same moment Lily said, "That is *awesome*."

"I know a lot of bee lore," I said, laughing. "I trot it out at cocktail parties."

"When was the last time you even *went* to a cocktail party?" Asher asked.

In my previous life, I thought immediately, remembering the get-togethers with Braden's colleagues. Instead, I just laughed.

Lily's eyes sparked. It made me think of those cocktail parties, actually. How sometimes I would see someone else standing alone across a crowded room and catch her gaze and nod and know she, too, was thinking: *These people, who do not really see me, have no idea what they are missing.*

We walked away from the hives. As I fiddled to reanimate the electric fence, Asher turned Lily to face him, and he lifted up the bee veil from her face. In that moment, I saw his future. I could so easily imagine him on his wedding day, repeating the movement with delicate lace, revealing a girl who looked at him the same way Lily looked now.

It was the moment I realized that my son wasn't a boy anymore, but somehow, when I wasn't paying attention, had become a man.

NOW LILY WILL never be a bride, I suddenly think.

She'll never grow up.

My knees give out beneath me and the frost bites my legs as I sit on the frozen ground, shaking. Lily is not coming back. I will not see her holding Asher's hand as she crosses the strawberry field. I will not hear her draw from an endless well of ephemera and factoids over a roasted chicken. I will not watch her bang through the front door or tease Asher out of a funk.

We are so lucky to have our children, even for a little while, but we take them for granted. We make the stupid assumption that as long as we are here, they will be, too, though that's never been part of the contract.

I cannot bring Lily back. But I can keep Asher from following her to a place from which he can't return.

When I stand up again, there are spots of thawed green grass where my palms were a moment earlier, proof that—against all odds—winter doesn't last.

INSIDE THE HOUSE, I stamp my boots, and feel the burn of blood rushing into my feet. From the living room, I hear a British voice.

Asher sits on the couch holding his laptop. He is wearing the same clothes he wore yesterday; his hair is sticking up on one side. His eyes are an unholy red, and he is barely blinking as he stares at the computer. I see the yellow chyron of the History Channel in the corner. A World War I plane streaks across the screen as the narrator says something about the Red Baron.

"What are you watching?" I ask.

Over his shoulder I see a fiery missile punch a hole in the broad body of the plane. You know it's only a matter of time before it's going down.

"That," Asher murmurs. "That's what it feels like."

I take the computer from him and close the clamshell. "Will you come with me?" I ask. "To tell the bees?"

It takes him a long moment to answer, but finally, Asher nods.

"It's cold," I say. "You're going to want a coat." But in the end, his hands are shaking too much to work the zipper, and I wind up kneeling in front of him, fastening the metal teeth, as if he is small again.

For the second time that morning, I make the trek across the fields to the hives. This time I am carrying yards of black crepe from the attic.

Lily wasn't family, technically, but she was one of us. It is the beekeeper's job to let the bees know of the loss, and I'm superstitious enough to think that if I don't, a perfectly healthy hive could deteriorate. With Celine's already bound to fail, why would I take that risk?

Another part of the ritual: it's the job of the beekeeper's firstborn son to shift all the hives to the right.

I lean close to each colony, and sing the first song I can think of.

Neptune of the seas, an answer for me, please
The lily of the valley doesn't know.

"Queen?" Asher asks. His voice sounds like it's hidden at the bottom of a well. He puts his shoulder to Adele's hive, using his strength to budge the wooden frame six inches to the east.

I nod, laying a length of fabric over it. It's a shawl, a shroud. An invitation to mourn with us. It might be my imagination, but I think I hear the buzzing within the hive swell just a little in response to Freddie Mercury's lyrics.

Asher drags Beyoncé's hive a few inches, and then Gaga's. "She loved that song," he says.

FIVE DAYS AFTER Lily's death, there is a memorial at Ricker's Funeral Home, the only one in Adams. Asher is wearing a suit that he's outgrown; the cuffs of the jacket end above the knobs of his wrists and the pants are an inch too short. He sits next to me in the pickup truck, silent as we try to find a parking spot. But he is silent a lot these days, except for at night, when he cries so hard he sometimes cannot catch his breath.

I turn off the ignition and unhook my seatbelt, but Asher doesn't move. "Ash?" I say softly. "You don't have to do this, if it hurts too much."

I am lying as I say the words. I think he *does* have to do this, or he will always regret not saying goodbye.

Asher stares out the windshield, his eyes fixed on nothing. "What do they do with her?" he asks. "Since the ground is frozen."

"Well," I say. "When Grandma died, it was January. We didn't bury her till April, when the ground thawed."

He turns to me, waiting for the rest of his answer.

"I think there's a room at the funeral home where they keep the bodies till winter's over."

Asher's face goes white.

"Or they may have decided on cremation."

"So she might not even be here," he murmurs.

"Yes, but that's not the point. Ash, whatever is . . . left. It's not Lily."

His face goes almost feral. "Don't you think I know that?"

I find myself recoiling from him. Immediately, his face crumples. "I'm sorry. It's just . . ." His voice hitches. "Every morning I wake up and then I realize I'm *in* the nightmare."

"I'm not going to tell you it doesn't hurt." I reach for his hand and squeeze it. "But it's not going to feel like this forever."

When Asher looks at me, he suddenly seems very, very old. "Not because I'll stop missing her. Because I'll get so used to that, it'll become the new normal."

He folds himself out of the car, and this time I'm the one who is left behind. He is right; you don't ever recover from losing someone you love—even the ones you leave behind because you're better off without them.

As soon as we step inside the funeral home, I see the small polished wooden box on a draped table, a framed photo of Lily beside it. Cremation, then. The moment Asher sees it, he stops moving beside me.

There are kids from the high school here, some of whom I know and some I don't. Teachers that look familiar. My arm is linked with Asher's; I feel him tug me forward inexorably toward the table, on which is a spray of—of course—lilies.

I think of Alexander the Great, who died in a faraway battle, and whose body was preserved during the trip home in a coffin full of honey. I imagine Lily, frozen in liquid amber, forever nineteen.

Asher stops walking when we are still several feet away. "You okay?" I whisper, but his face is completely wiped of expression. He is a statue beside me, his eyes vacant and pale.

Suddenly his friend Maya barrels toward him, throwing her arms around his waist and sobbing into his shirt. He doesn't embrace her; doesn't react at all. It's like she is hugging a tree. "Oh my God, Asher," she cries.

A few people turn, watching the encounter. *That's the boyfriend. I heard he found her. Poor kid.*

Maya draws back, tips up her chin. She has long black hair that hits her waist—it's been like that since Asher was six and they were book buddies in kindergarten. They used to play in the tree house my father built for me and Jordan hundreds of years ago, Maya always choosing their adventure: pirates on the high seas, paleontologists finding a new species of dinosaur, astronauts on Mars. There was a time when I was sure they'd wind up romantically involved. But Asher was horrified when I offhandedly mentioned this—that would be, he told me, like kissing his sister. I remember, now, that Maya was the one who introduced him to Lily. That she and Lily were best friends.

I can see the pain glazing Maya's face, and her confusion as Asher doesn't commiserate. "Maya," I say, pulling her into a hug. "I'm so sorry."

She nods, rubbing her wet face against my shoulder. Then she sneaks a glance at Asher, who stands beside the photo of Lily, his back to us. He looks like a sentry, like the queen's guards at Buckingham Palace, who will not show a flicker of emotion, not even if you make silly faces or shout at them. Maya's brow wrinkles. "Is he okay?"

"Everyone grieves differently," I say softly.

"Will you let him know that I'm . . . here?" Maya replies. "I mean, if he wants to talk or anything?"

"You're a good friend," I tell her.

Maya's eyes flicker away toward Asher, and suddenly her mothers are there, embracing her.

We adults acknowledge one another. One of the women—Deepa—shakes her head. "What a tragedy," she says.

Her wife, Sharon, hugs me. "We had to get Maya a prescription so she'd sleep at night," she murmurs. "I can only imagine how hard this has been for Asher."

You can't *imagine,* I think uncharitably. *He loved her.*

I mumble something in response, but my attention is distracted by Asher. He is moving toward the box holding Lily's ashes. He stops six inches away and reaches out one hand as if to touch the wood. Instead, his fingers hover above, shaking violently. He closes them into a fist, with just his pointer extended, and traces the edge of one lily petal.

I step beside him and slide an arm around his waist. I can feel people staring. I try to tug Asher away, but of course he is bigger and stronger than I am.

Suddenly there is a volley of raised voices in the far corner of the room. It breaks Asher's concentration, too, and he turns toward the sound.

Ava Campanello is flushed and red-faced, her eyes nearly swollen shut. She wears a shapeless black dress and is arguing with a man I've never seen before—someone in an ill-fitting suit who holds up his hands in surrender. Two women try to calm Ava down, but she yanks herself free of them and runs out of the room.

The man looks around. With slumped shoulders he starts for the door, veering toward the polished wooden box on the way out. He touches it, then looks up. "Asher," he says and nods in greeting, and then he walks out.

"Who was that?" I whisper, but Asher's face has drained completely of color.

"I'm going to throw up," he mutters, and he races out of the room.

By the time I reach the hallway, where the restrooms are, Asher is already inside one. There are two separate doors with unisex signage on them. Taking a guess, I knock on the closest one. "Ash?" I whisper.

The door opens and I find myself facing Ava Campanello. The collar of her somber dress is damp, as if she has been splashing her face at the sink. Her eyes are too bright.

"Ava," I say. "I am so, so sorry."

I think of how bees that cannot find their queen will choose to be where her eggs are. They will do whatever it takes to come back to her offspring. I think of what it would feel like to be separated from your child for the rest of your life.

"You're *sorry*," Ava repeats. Her voice is a hot knife. "If it weren't for your son, I'd still have a daughter."

Stunned, I blink at her. She shoves past me, her heels clicking down the tiled hall. At its mouth she is absorbed by a flutter of women who glance at me and whisper as they usher her back into the gathering room.

The door to the second bathroom opens, and Asher steps out. Hectic color stripes his cheekbones. "Can we leave?"

"Yes," I say. "Absolutely."

I turn to find Mike Newcomb leaning against the wall, his hands in the pockets of his trousers. His detective badge glints at his waist, like the sun in a rearview mirror that makes it impossible to see the road. "Asher," he says. "Got a minute?"

MIKE TELLS US this is routine; that often, after the fact, there are follow-up questions. We follow behind him in our own car to the police station again. He leads us back into the same conference room we were in days ago, pours us two glasses of water, sets the same small recording device on the table. "Asher, thanks a lot for coming in," he says amiably, but Ava Campanello's accusation tickles the back of my mind. "Now that the crime scene investigators have gone through the house, there are some discrepancies that we hope you can help us clear up."

Two words lodge in my throat. "Crime scene?"

Mike does not even look at me. His eyes remain on Asher's face. "A healthy young girl died. If we didn't look thoroughly at what happened, my ass would be on the line."

My face feels hot. "Asher told you everything he knows."

"Is that true, Asher?" Mike says evenly. "Or would you like to help us?"

"I just want to know what happened to Lily," he replies.

The detective relaxes, and it has a ripple effect. Asher leans back in his chair. Seeing him breathe, I breathe, too.

Whatever Ava said to me must be born of grief. She lashed out because when you hurt someone else, you're less likely to feel your own pain.

"We're trying to put together a timeline," Mike says. "Can you walk me through your day? What happened from the time you woke up, until the time you ended up at Lily's house?"

"I went to school," Asher says, shrugging. "It was . . . school."

"You said last time you were here that Lily was home sick, so you texted her . . . ?"

"Yeah. She was out for two days. I texted her, but she didn't write back."

Mike scribbles something on a pad. "Did she tell you that she was staying home sick?"

Asher flushes. "No. I found out from a friend of ours. Maya."

"Maya . . ."

"Banerjee."

"Why didn't Lily tell you herself?" Mike asks.

"I hadn't talked to her in a few days," Asher replies. "We were in the middle of a fight."

I shift in my chair. Asher and Lily had been fighting? Why hadn't he told me?

"What were you fighting about?" the detective asks.

Asher clears his throat. "Her father," he says, his gaze darting quickly to me and then away. "She hadn't spoken to him in a really long time, and I thought she should . . ."

Because you don't talk to your father, I think.

". . . but Lily didn't want to."

I think about the man at the funeral with the dark eyes and the wrinkled suit who had fought with Ava, who had called Asher by name.

"Was that all you were fighting about?" the detective asks.

"Yes."

He leans forward. "You can tell me, you know, if she was seeing someone else."

"What?" Asher is genuinely stunned. "*No.*"

"So you texted her five times that day, and you really needed to see her—"

"She was *sick*," Asher clarifies. "I was checking on her."

"How'd you get into the house?"

"The door was open. Like, literally."

"You didn't think that was strange?"

"I didn't think about it at all," Asher says. "I knocked and pushed it all the way open and went inside. I called out Lily's name."

"Did Lily answer?"

"No," he says, quietly. "She was lying at the bottom of the stairs."

I open my mouth, because I can see that Asher is about two seconds away from falling apart, and if Mike walks him through Lily's death again, that's exactly what will happen. But to my surprise, Mike glosses right over it.

"Did you go anywhere else in the house?"

"No."

"You didn't go upstairs?"

Asher shakes his head.

"But you've been in her bedroom before."

"I. Uh." His cheeks are flaming.

"You feel uncomfortable talking about this in front of your mom?" Mike asks. "Listen, Asher. This is going to be a lot easier for you if you just tell me the truth."

"I *am* telling you the truth. I wasn't in Lily's bedroom."

"Then I guess you don't know anything about the overturned lamp, the glass on the floor from the broken lightbulb, or the nightstand that was knocked over."

"No," Asher answers firmly, "because I *was not in Lily's bedroom.*"

"That's interesting," the detective says. "Because your fingerprints are."

Asher goes still.

This is a mistake, I think. *This is ridiculous. The only fingerprints in police databases belong to criminals, to kids with records, not kids like Asher.*

I suddenly remember him scrubbing at the pads of his fingers in the kitchen sink last spring, trying to remove the ink. *Hockey camp,* he said, by way of explanation. *All the counselors have to get it done.*

"Stop talking," I say, but my voice is only a wheeze. I grip the arms of the chair and force the words out faster. "*Stop talking, Asher.*" Standing, I look coolly at Mike. "I believe we have the right to an attorney."

He holds up his hands, a conciliation. "I'm just doing my job," he says.

"And I'm just doing mine." I haul my son up by his arm, pull him out of the conference room and through the halls of the police station.

We do not stop until we are in the parking lot. By then, Asher has shaken off his shock. "Mom," he says, "I don't know what he's talking about. I found Lily at the bottom of the stairs. I swear it."

"Not here," I say, gritting out the words, and I unlock the doors of the truck.

When you work with bees, the first thing you do is blow smoke. It's how a beekeeper lulls them into complacency. Or how a teen tries to convince his mother that everything is okay.

Asher gets inside the truck. I lean against its powder-blue haunch and take out my phone. Jordan, my brother, is in Ireland on vacation with his wife and his eleven-year-old son. He is semiretired these days, but he used to be a renowned defense attorney.

It is the middle of the night overseas, and the phone rolls right to voicemail. "Jordan?" I say. "It's Olivia."

I remember the conversation we had twelve years ago, as vividly as a slap—how angry Jordan was, when he found out the truth about my marriage: *My God, Liv, why didn't you tell me? I would have come for you. I would have gotten you away from him.*

"You told me to call you the next time I need help," I say into the phone.

Asher's temple is pressed to the cold glass of the window. His eyes are closed.

I take a deep breath. "I need help."

LILY ⬡ 2

The week before

Afterward, Asher and I start laughing like maniacs, as if we have just robbed a train and are now galloping off with the gold. This goes on for what feels like forever, until at last, out of breath and delirious, we fall silent.

"I think I have splinters in my ass," I say.

"You want me to get some tweezers?"

"I'm good."

This is a lie. I'm *phenomenal*. I am grateful for his arm around my waist, because I need an anchor. I feel like my bones are made of light.

The blankets we brought up here are a tangled mess. I grab an afghan and wrap us up in it.

We lie there on the floor of the tree house looking up at the wooden ceiling. It's quite a fort Asher's grandfather built: a window on each wall, the rafters overhead held together by round pegs. There's a brass telescope in one of the windows, pointing out at the beehives. A rusty lantern hangs down from a chain attached to a thick tree limb. At the far end of the tree house is a hammock slung between two walls, and beneath it a pile of books, definitely worse for wear. The Chronicles of Narnia. The Hunger Games. *Charlotte's Web*. Moldy boxes containing Battleship and Candy Land. Asher's sketchbook. A small wooden box.

In front of another window is a ship's wheel. It is so easy to imagine Asher, age seven, standing there with his hands on the wheel, steering through an imaginary storm.

If it came to it, he'd go down with the ship. And I would go with him.

For a while we just lie there, not talking, the two of us folded perfectly into each other, human origami. Sun pours through the open window of the tree house, and a shaft of light pools on the floor like a spotlight in a theater. I imagine all of the people in the past who've climbed up here before me. Are we the first people to have slept together—*together* together—up here?

"What do you call this place?" I ask him. "The tree house? Does it have a name?"

Asher leans up on one elbow and smiles. "The Stronghold," he says, in a voice kind of like Christopher Lee in those Lord of the Rings movies.

It is impossible not to laugh at this. "That's very—medieval."

He looks around. "When I was a kid, we came up here all the time. I spent days here in the summer, me and Maya. We had a whole world. I was the king, she was the queen." He points to one of the beams on the ceiling, and there are his initials, A.F., and Maya's, M.B. There are other initials, too: O.McA and J. McA. And D.A.

"O. McA is your mom, right? And J. McA is—?"

"My uncle Jordan. My grandfather built this place for them, when they were kids."

"And D.A.?"

"Dirk!" says Asher with a smile.

"Let me guess. He was the court jester?"

Asher laughs. "Not quite. In ninth grade we'd come up here to do bongs. We'd look through the telescope to make sure Mom wasn't coming." He shakes his head a little, caught in the web of a memory. "You should have seen Maya's face when she learned I brought Dirk up here. I thought she was going to punch me. She said, *You're not supposed to get high in the Throne Room!*"

"The Throne Room?"

"Yeah."

I glance around. "I don't see anything to sit on."

Asher pulls me over him, so that my legs fall on either side of his hips. He's hard again, against me. "I'll be your throne," he offers.

I lean down and kiss him. "God save the king," I whisper.

My hair makes a curtain around us. Asher's hands are on my waist and coasting up and my own palms flatten on his chest. Then he lets go of me, and I hear the rip of foil and the shuffle of our hips as he puts on the condom. I think about how you never realize how empty you feel until you are filled. Then I stop thinking at all.

By the end, we have flipped, and Asher is heavy on me, his nose pressed to the curve between my shoulder and my neck. "This is my favorite part of you," he murmurs.

"It's not a super-exciting one."

"Speak for yourself." He nuzzles my skin. "I'm never moving. Forward my mail. I live here now."

I laugh and push at him until he rolls to his side. Then I get up and put on my bra and panties. While Asher searches for his boxers, I move the telescope around, looking out on the world he grew up in. I think about him peering through it as a kid, and about Olivia and her brother, too, doing the same thing when they were little. "*Plus ça change, plus c'est la même chose,*" I murmur.

I can feel Asher's eyes on me. "It's John-Baptiste Karr." I translate: "It means the more things change, the more they stay the same."

I glance over my shoulder, but he's still staring.

"What?" I ask, self-conscious.

"You," Asher answers, and just the way he says this sends a thrill of electricity through me, and I think: *You know, I could just rip my underwear off again and we could go for the hat trick.* Sometimes when Asher looks at me, it's like he's a flower in a field and I'm a strange rain he just wants to drink in.

A second later I feel Asher's arms encircle me from behind and I lean back into him. I don't know how long we stand like that, the two of us. That's the thing I can hardly believe. That we have all this, and there is no end to it.

My eyes fall upon a rafter on the far side of the tree house, where there is another pair of initials. "Who's B.F.?"

Asher lets go of me, goes over to the corner, pulls his pants on.

"Asher?" I say, and he gives me a look. Now he's buttoning up his flannel shirt.

"B.F. is my dad," he says. "Braden Fields."

Whenever Asher talks about his dad, the mood shifts. *I just want to keep the door open,* he says, but I don't really understand why he keeps the door open to someone who's bound to bust it off its hinges sooner or later.

"So that must have been . . . a long time ago," I say. "When he carved that."

"It was," says Asher, quietly, like he's trying to decide whether or not he wants to talk about it. "Before I was born. Mom was pissed that he went and carved his initials, like this place belonged to him. Which it didn't."

"I guess I can see that," I say, carefully. "Maybe your mom wanted, like, one memory that was hers, that she didn't have to share?"

"Well, you're *supposed* to share things when you love people," says Asher, with an edge to his voice that makes me wonder if this is suddenly about him and me.

But then all the heat goes out of him. Asher sits on the floor, deflated. I sink down beside him and put my arms around him. I can *feel* him thinking.

"Sometimes I don't know if he's the asshole for what he did," Asher says, "or if I'm the asshole, because I miss him in spite of all that."

I'm not sure how to respond. I mean, you feel what you feel. I don't know if there's any point to deciding whether it's good or bad.

"I don't know, Asher," I say. "I wouldn't miss him, if it was me."

"You don't miss your dad?" Asher says. "You never wish that he hadn't died, and the two of you could talk?"

Now I feel guilty—because this is the one thing that I haven't told Asher the truth about. It wasn't as if I meant to keep this from him; I honestly had forgotten what excuse about my father I'd made months ago when we first met. But after everything Asher and I have been through, I'm terrified that if he learns there's *more* I hid from him, he'll walk away for good. I ought to come clean, tell him that the reason my father's not part of my life isn't that he's dead. It's that he's a poisonous *fuck,* who would wreck my world if he knew where I was.

"I don't miss him," I say, quietly. "Ever."

From outside, I hear the *whoo* of a mourning dove. It's only four o'clock in the afternoon, but the shadows are already growing long. Autumn days are short here.

"It's not that I forgive my father," Asher says, "for what he did to my mom. But I want to understand him. Because—you know. Whatever I am, is part him."

I don't know what to tell him. I think Asher's father is a first-class bullshit artist.

"I get that. Just . . . be careful. I think he's pretty good at manipulating people."

"You really think he doesn't give a shit about me?"

"If he gave a shit about you," I tell Asher, "maybe he'd see you more than once a month? And not just in a Chili's two and a half hours away?"

"That's *my* idea, to meet way out of town," he says. "I'm trying to protect my mom."

"I know," I tell him. "But why hasn't he invited you to *his* place? Have you ever even *seen* his new wife? Met your half brothers? Shane and Shawn?" *Who sound like cowboys in a Western,* I think.

He frowns. "I'm sorry," I tell Asher, and I am. The whole thing with his father isn't really any of my business.

Wind carves through the open window of the tree house. Here it is, the Sunday after Thanksgiving, and it's unusually warm, considering it's New Hampshire, in November. But I wonder whether this is the last time we'll come up here before spring. For a moment it makes me sad. I'm going to miss this place.

"We should go there," Asher says, an idea dawning.

"Where?"

"Dad's house. This Thursday. We should . . . just show up."

"What's this Thursday?"

Asher raises an eyebrow. "It's *Fieldsgiving,* Lily."

"Fields—*what?*"

"They always do Thanksgiving a week late. Because Dad insists on working in the hospital on the actual holiday."

"Okay," I say, taking this in.

"Don't you see?" Asher says. "This year, we walk in—you and me!—and we look everyone in the eye. Meet Margot, the twins, sit down at the table. They need to know Dad has a past, and that the past is me."

I have to say, it's an interesting idea, although it's also slightly insane. Does the new wife—Margot—does she even know about Asher? Do Shane and Shawn? It would be nice, just once, to see his dad at a loss for words.

"What if he . . . throws you out?" I ask. The last thing I'd want is for Asher to be hurt by his father again.

"I'd like to see him try," Asher says. I can feel it all becoming real to him. "Seriously. We can do this. Make him see us!" He rubs his hands together. "You in, Lily?"

I nod. "Asher contra mundum," I say. But I'm all but certain that whatever's going to happen at his father's house, it is not what Asher is expecting.

"JESUS," SAYS MAYA, waving her hand in front of her face. It's the day after Asher and I were in the tree house, and Maya and I are practicing by the fireplace in our living room. "Did that smell come *out* of him?"

I look down at poor old Boris. "He's getting pretty—pungent."

"Are you sure he's not already dead and decomposing?"

"Show respect for your elders," I say, and pat Boris on the side of his chest. He opens his eyes, but he doesn't raise his head.

Maya brings her oboe to her lips. "Let us try it again," she says, then looks at me over the top of her glasses. "Ready?"

I nod, and Maya starts to play. This piece—the duet for cello and oboe by Eugène Bozza—is in six-eight. Maya gets seven measures all to herself before I come in. I know she likes it, because the oboe almost never gets to play solo. But in this piece, for once, Maya gets to be the star.

Of course, she's the one who gives the first violin the A when the orchestra tunes up. Sure, the first violin gives the note to the rest of us. But the oboe gives it to the violin.

It's basically the only moment when the oboe gets any respect.

I remember Maya's initials carved into the rafter of the tree house, and the story of her getting pissed off when she found out about Dirk and the bongs. I remember Asher and me cocooned in the blanket.

Maya stops. "Earth to Lily," she says.

I've missed my entrance. "Sorry."

"You're thinking about Asher," she says, with a grin.

"That's so wrong?"

Boris releases another dank cloud of swamp gas. Maya raises her oboe to her mouth again. "One more time?" she says. "If you're back from—Ashville?"

"Fine," I say. "Go." She comes in on the five and I listen to her play. Eight measures in, I join her. I love this piece. People don't know Bozza's music, but they should because it is genius. I close my eyes and let it all wash over me.

Two minutes later, we both land on the final D, and hold it. Then I raise my bow and we're done. It does feel, in a way, like excellent sex.

Maya raises an eyebrow. "You were in the tree house again, weren't you?"

There's no point in trying to hide anything from her. I nod. "Yesterday," I say quietly.

Maya smiles. "Your cello sounds different, when you think about him," she says. "You play it the way an astronaut walks on the moon."

"Is that . . . a good thing?"

"Yeah, it's like you've never heard music, and you need to listen to every single note." She glances at me. "You know he's never been in love before." She looks reflective, as if she's remembering the times when *she* was the one in the tree house, ruling over their subjects.

"I'm sorry if I—" I'm not sure how to say this. "If I took him away from you?"

Maya blinks at me. "Lily." She laughs. "We were never a thing."

I want to ask her if that was his choice or hers or what, because it's still not clear to me if Maya is gay, or ace, or what. But when I asked her about this before, she changed the subject. Asher says he's never known her to have a crush on anybody. My guess is, Maya's waiting for someone, and he or she or they haven't yet arrived on the scene.

Boris moans, a ghost in a haunted house. "One more time?" Maya says. "And maybe more legato after measure twenty, you know: the high part?"

I nod. "Got it."

She counts it off. "One, two, three—"

"Maya." She lowers her instrument, frustrated. "Can I ask you something?"

"Are we *still* talking about Asher?"

"No," I say. "I mean, yes." I let the end of my bow touch the floor. "Can I ask you about . . . Asher's dad?"

"Ah," says Maya. "The mysterious Braden. You meet him and think, What a nice man! What a charmer! But he's not a nice man, Lily. He's just figured out how to imitate one."

"Does Asher know all that?"

Maya shrugs. "He knows *I* think that. But he keeps on having those Saturday breakfasts every month in spite of it."

"You know about the Saturday breakfasts?"

Maya nods, like *of course* she knows about the Saturday breakfasts. "I think Asher feels like his father is this broken thing he has to fix."

"He wants—to fix his father?"

"He wants to fix himself."

It hurts me physically, like a stab to the chest, to think that Asher would believe he is lacking in any way. Even if it is how I thought of myself until only weeks ago.

"Let's say that, hypothetically, Asher decided to surprise his father's family, in the middle of a big family dinner. Just show up at his father's house and march in there so the new wife and the kids have to look him in the eye—"

"Wait, what?" says Maya, and for once I have surprised her. "This is real?"

I think about what I've told Asher, and what I haven't. I think about how, if trust is a seed, you give it to someone believing that they will not crush it beneath the heel of their boot. Asher confided in me, and not Maya, for a reason.

"I said hypothetically," I answer.

Maya narrows her eyes on my face. "Well, I hope you hypothetically told him it was a stupid idea."

"I'm not an idiot," I reply, and I lift my bow.

THREE DAYS LATER, I'm hearing the Bozza duet in my head as Asher and I make the drive. Brown leaves by the side of the road swirl around as the Jeep rushes past.

A muscle in Asher's jaw clenches and unclenches. I cover his hand with mine on the stick shift. I want to tell him *You don't have to do this.* But I'm not sure that's true. I think he does.

I didn't play the Bozza for my audition piece at Oberlin last July, but I did play the Saint-Saëns's First Cello Concerto. Badly. There were three people on the committee—a Black woman with gray hair, a young Asian woman with big glasses, and this old white dude with Benjamin Franklin–style half-glasses who scowled at me the whole time like he'd just stepped in dog shit. He had this intense stare, so intense I couldn't stop sneaking these little glances at him, and every time I looked up at him he looked angrier. I started shaking. By the time I got to the *poco animato* I actually dropped my bow. I can still hear the sound of it hitting the floor. It was the sound of my future disappearing in a single second.

I figured that was it, and I might as well wave goodbye to the committee, but the woman with the gray hair picked my bow up for me, put it in my hand, and said, "Ms. Campanello, pretend you're playing for your friends." Which was one of the most generous things anyone has ever said to me.

It didn't stop the Ben Franklin guy from scowling, though. Then the woman with the glasses said, "Start over from the top. You can consider that your mulligan."

There's that word again.

Maybe it's because I figured I didn't have anything left to lose, but the second time *I nailed it.* I played the hell out of that thing. When I finished, the women applauded. Even Angry Ben Franklin nodded. A few minutes later, my cello was back in the hard case and I was wheeling it out to the car, where Mom was waiting with Boris.

"How'd it go?" she asked, and I wondered if I should tell her about the first time or the second. The second, I decided. Because it had erased the first.

Asher turns onto an unmarked dirt road. His father lives in the far suburbs of Boston near absolutely nothing, from the looks of it. "How much further?" I ask.

He glances down at the GPS. "Three miles."

"How are you feeling?"

"Jumpy," he says.

"You know," I say. "There's still time for Plan B. We can go back, see how your mom's doing."

"Oh, she's using the time to scrape propolis off her old frames," Asher says. "She's actually *thrilled* to not have to be cooking all day. Don't worry about Mom."

I look out the window into the dark forest—pine trees and birches and oak. "It's not your mom I'm worried about."

Asher has to slow down because this dirt road has so many potholes and bumps in it. On the GPS map there's a checkered flag now, showing the location of the house. It sits on the bank of a body of water called Cold Pond.

He glances over at me, catches the worried look on my face. "Lily," he says. "This is going to be fine. I promise."

But I can't tell whether he really believes this, or if he's just trying to convince himself.

"You believe your mom, don't you?" I say. I know this sounds harsh, but there's no way to sugarcoat it. "About what he did to her."

"I do," he says, but there's a tone in his voice like *Although.*

"So . . . ?"

"It's what happened to her," he says. "Not what happened to me."

"But it *did* happen to you, too. Didn't it?"

"If he ever did anything to me," he blurts out, "I don't remember it. I barely remember him hurting *her.*"

"That's not an excuse—"

He turns to me. "Do you believe people can change?"

All the breath in my body goes solid. "Yes," I finally say.

"Okay, then," he says, his shoulders relaxing. "I believe that the relationship between him and my mother was toxic. And yeah, it was his fault. But it's been *twelve years.* They've been apart longer than they were married. My mother decided I don't get to have a relationship with him, because she thinks she's protecting me. But that was never between him and me; it was between him and *her.* It's not fair that I have to be on my own."

"You're not on your own," I tell him. "You have your mom. You have me."

"I know," he says, quietly. "But it's different. Not having a father. Even a fucked-up one." He looks at me as if he could will me to understand. "Don't you ever wish your dad was alive?"

"Not if he was an evil *dickhead,*" I say, a little too quickly.

There's a long pause. "What did he die from?" he asks. "Your father?"

"He was in a car wreck," I tell him quietly. "He was drunk."

"Oh, Jesus," says Asher, and he jams on the brakes. We are at a dead stop, on a dirt road, in the middle of a thick forest. He puts the car in park. "I'm so sorry," he says, and he leans forward to put his arms around me. "I'm really sorry, Lily."

But now I feel terrible about lying to Asher, even if it was strangely satisfying to fictionally kill my father off. "Actually." I pull back from the hug. "There's . . . something else about him. I should have told you before."

Asher's eyes darken, until they are the same shade as the boughs that surround us. "Tell me," he says.

But how can I? When I've only just gotten Asher back? "I don't know how," I say, my voice small.

For a while we sit there in silence. "Okay," Asher says, finally. "That's okay, too. Whenever you're ready."

I reach for his hand again, stroke my thumb over the knuckles. "One daddy at a time," I say, and Asher lifts my palm and kisses the center, folding my fingers around it, as if I could hold on to this promise.

He shifts the car into gear, and we move forward again. And then, suddenly, there it is: a huge post-and-beam house with a wraparound porch. There are racks with canoes down by the water, and puzzle pieces of what I guess must be a dock, disassembled for winter.

Through the windows, I see people moving around inside. It makes me think of Olivia lifting the top off a hive, of the bees who bustle around, completely ignoring her.

Asher turns off the engine. "Let's do this," he says, and I see that muscle in his jaw pulsing again.

"You sure?"

He gives me a sad smile. "As ready as I'm gonna be." We climb out and close the doors of the Jeep. Then we start walking.

The picture windows of Braden Fields's house glow golden. There must be a fire in a fireplace I can't quite see, too, because the light shines and flickers. As people move through the light, their shadows play against the walls. There's a long table in one room, and some candlesticks, and a chandelier that hangs down over that. Two little boys are setting the table—they must be Shawn and Shane, the horse thieves. There's an Irish setter wagging his tail. A woman comes in behind them—rosy cheeks, a little plump—Margot. She looks nothing like Olivia, and I am not sure if that is a good thing or a bad thing. I realize I am scanning her for bruises.

She looks happy.

Asher has been watching this scene, too, and as we've drawn closer his steps have come more and more slowly, until now, nearly at the threshold, he's frozen. Until this second, this other family of his father's was just an idea. But now they're real: Margot, two little boys, a dog. As we stand in the shadows, peering in, Braden walks into the room. Margot pivots, and we cannot see her face anymore.

So softly I can barely hear it, Asher breathes, then says, "Turn around."

I do, but he's not talking to me. He's staring at the family in front of him.

"Fuck this." Asher huffs. He strides back to the Jeep, and I have to run to keep up. Before I even get the door closed Asher starts up the car and pulls it into reverse. I twist around to look at the house as we drive off. I can see Braden and Margot and the boys squinting through the picture window into the darkness at the sound of the Jeep peeling away.

Margot and Shawn and Shane look uncertain, as if they've been asked a question they don't know the answer to. But Braden has a different expression entirely. His face is all planes and angles, sharp as a knife, as if he knows exactly who drove up to his door, and just why we came.

ON THE WAY back from Asher's father's house, here are the things we discuss:

1. Whether the Bruins will make the playoffs.
2. Whether a yam is a sweet potato and why anyone would make a pie with either of them.
3. Which president was the first to pardon a turkey (John F. Kennedy).
4. That the land North Adams sits on actually belongs to the Wabanaki.
5. That there should be reparations for indigenous people *and* Black Americans.

6. That Black Friday is the busiest day of the year for plumbers, which doesn't say much about the talents of those who make Thanksgiving dinner.

Here is what we do not discuss:

1. What happened at Asher's father's house.

OUR DINNER THAT night winds up being a bucket of KFC in the tree house. There are drumsticks and breasts and wings and little tubs of mashed potatoes and a carton of brown gravy. We sneak past the house, so Olivia won't hear us. We are getting gifted, I realize, at dodging parents.

"What are you thankful for?" Asher asks me, gnawing a drumstick.

"What am I what?"

"Thankful for. Didn't your family ever go around the table, everybody saying what they're thankful for?"

"Our Thanksgivings were pretty laid back." I lean forward and kiss him, hard. "But I'm totally grateful for this *chicken*."

Asher smiles. "Dirk has a whole theory about girls, comparing them to different kinds of KFC chicken."

"Of course he does."

"He says there are only three kinds of women—Original Recipe, Extra Crispy, and Nashville Hot wings."

I shake my head. "Fucking Dirk."

"I know," says Asher.

I look up from the mashed potatoes. "So? Which one am I?"

Asher thinks it over. "Extra Crispy, I guess."

"What about Maya?"

He wrinkles his nose. "Maya's not chicken."

"*I'm* not chicken!"

"I know, I know . . ." He grins. "Original Recipe, actually. Maya's definitely Original Recipe."

I look up at her initials on a rafter. I think about how she warned me against going to Braden's.

Asher puts his chicken bone atop the small pile we've amassed. It looks like a tiny potter's field, a mass grave. I wonder if Asher, too, is thinking about where things go when they die, because he says, softly, "I'm going to tell him I don't want to meet for breakfast again."

I wait, because I know there's more.

"I just . . ." He shakes his head. "I can't, now. Now that I've seen him . . . there." Asher looks up at me. "Even that one Saturday a month, he doesn't belong to me."

"What do you mean?" I ask.

He shrugs. "It wasn't like I expected. They all looked so . . . happy."

"And that's a bad thing?"

"Yes. I mean, I don't know. It all seemed so *fake*," Asher says. "All I could think was that my mother probably looked happy, too, when she lived with him, even though she wasn't." He takes a deep breath. "I wanted to see her face. Margot's. When he came into the room, I mean. I wanted to know if there was something dead in her eyes, or if she was smiling too hard. If everything was perfect between them . . . or if she had to make it look that way, because of who he is." A shudder runs down the length of him. "I wanted to know if she looks like my mother does, when she talks about him."

All at once it's like Asher has left the room, totally withdrawn somewhere inside himself.

"Fuck," he mutters.

"Ash?" I say, and I move closer to him. "Hey."

But he just sits there bent over, his head buried in his folded arms.

"Fuck," he says again, even more quietly.

I slide an arm around him. Asher's head falls on my shoulder. He's breathing hard, like he's run a mile.

For a while we just sit like that. Then he lifts his head, his eyes wet. "What if I'm like him?" he asks.

"You're not, Asher," I say. "Look at me. You're not."

He shakes his head. "But I could be." His voice is really quiet, but there's an intensity I've never heard before. "There are times I am so fucking angry."

I think of how tender he is with me. Of his slow-motion movements with the bees. How he's always the first to smile, to tease, to interrupt two teammates who are about to come to blows.

But then I also remember that time we had breakfast with his dad, and how cruel Asher was to me in the car afterward, when we were driving home. How I saw something in him that day that scared me.

"Asher," I tell him. "You're the one who gets to decide who you're going to be. You don't have to be like your father."

He tilts his head, looking at me. "You're so . . . fierce." He reaches for my wrist, his hand skating lightly over my scars. "You're the bravest person I know."

"I'm not brave," I tell him.

"You're brave enough to tell the truth," he says.

Now it's my turn to feel ashamed.

"What?" he asks. "Is this the thing about your father?"

"He's not actually dead," I confess. "I barely knew you at all when I told you that."

"You mean I didn't know *you*."

"He's not dead," I continue. "But I wish he was." I pull my hands away from Asher and fold them across my middle. "My mom and I left him when I was eleven. We drove off in the middle of the night. To get away from him."

"Did he—hurt your mom?"

"No," I tell him. "He hurt me."

"See, that's what I'm afraid of," Asher says. "That someday— I could hurt you, too."

"You wouldn't."

"I've *already* hurt you," says Asher, and we both remember that day in the car. *You don't know everything, Lily,* he'd snarled. *There's some shit that's so dark you can't possibly imagine it, ever!*

"That was an accident," I reply. "You didn't mean to."

He looks haunted. "*That*," he murmurs, "is what I remember about my father, when I was little. It's what my mother used to say to him."

I take his hand and squeeze it, *hard*. "You're the most gentle boy I've ever known." I lean forward and kiss him. I fall into him, until the only air I'm breathing is what he's giving me.

"If you wanted"—he says softly—"I could be gentle—some more."

He starts to unbutton my shirt. The whole time he's looking me in the eye, like we are the only two people in the world. Up here in the tree house, it's easy to believe this is true.

I remember how on Sunday it made me sad that I'd never get to be in the tree house again until spring—but here we are, and the warm spell continues.

My shirt flutters onto the floor.

Asher watches it fall, then he looks up at the rafters. "Wait," he says, and then he goes over to the side of the tree house where the hammock is, and opens a wooden box that lies beside a pile of board games. He roots around in the box, and when he comes back to me, he is holding a knife.

For a second my heart stops. My wrists throb.

"Lily," he says, handing me the blade. "Carve your initials."

I clear my throat. "You know . . . they don't call it a Swiss Army knife . . . in Switzerland."

I go over to the rafter where Asher's initials are carved, and chip by chip cut out my own. It takes longer than I thought it would. But he waits, patient, this tortured boy who thinks he has a hurricane brewing under his skin.

When I'm finally finished, Asher traps me in the circle of his arms. The knife drops out of my hand and lands on the floor with a clunk.

"So where *does* the name come from?" he asks.

"It was American"—Asher kisses me—"soldiers who"—he kisses me again—"couldn't pronounce"—and again. This one goes on and on—"*Offiziersmesser*"—and on—"which is the German word for—"

I never do finish that sentence.

When Asher is braced above me, when his hips are flush to mine, I wish I could make him understand that there's nothing inside him I would not welcome inside me. How even if there are broken parts of him and broken parts of me, together we still make a whole.

After, we lie on the blanket, keeping each other warm. We've accidentally scattered the bones from our meal. My bra is hanging off the ship's wheel. "Happy Fieldsgiving, Lily," Asher says, stroking my hair away from my face. He nuzzles that space between my jaw and my shoulder. "Mine," he murmurs.

Being known, I think. This *is what I am thankful for.*

OLIVIA ⬡ 3

Six days after

In my nightmare, I am hiding.

I can taste my own heartbeat, even as I tell myself that staying overnight at my parents' house was the right thing. I'd come to take care of the bees, but heavy rainstorms blew in, and I couldn't risk my toddler's safety by driving home. There were news reports of cars hydroplaning on highways, of fatal accidents. But now that we are back in Massachusetts, Braden thinks this is just a flimsy excuse. He hammers at the door I've locked between us. *You were leaving me,* he says.

I wouldn't, I tell him. *Ever.*

That's funny. Because I'm pretty damn sure you weren't here last night.

He keeps banging, and I sit down on the edge of our bed. Is he right? On some subconscious level is that why I'd stayed the extra night? Because I knew coming home would be like this?

Bang bang bang bang.

Did you see him?

I have no idea who he is talking about. My father has been dead for years.

Did you let him touch you, you slut?

Did he take my son *on a tour of the fucking police station?*

This is about Mike? We haven't seen him for months. I haven't thought about him or talked about him.

Braden, I say evenly, *all I did was check the bees.*

There is another heavy knock, like he's fallen against the door.

You're killing me, Liv. You know that, right? You'd probably love it if I died. You'd be free.

Shivering, I turn the knob. I open my arms to him.

When you're gone, all I can think about is that you're not coming back, Braden says. *If I didn't love you so much, I wouldn't be so crazy.*

We sit on the bed, me holding him, even though my heart is still racing and my mouth is dry. Yet even with Braden on this side of the door, the hammering hasn't stopped.

I ROLL OVER in bed, drenched in sweat, blinking into the darkness. Someone is still pounding downstairs. I glance at my phone: 12:24 A.M.

I pull on a sweatshirt and flannel pants and hurry to the front door. When I open it, Mike is standing there, along with two uniformed officers—one male and one female. It has been only hours since we left the station. Instinctively, I think: *When the police come to your door in the middle of the night, it is never good news.*

"I have a warrant for Asher's arrest," Mike says quietly.

As if he has been summoned, I hear Asher's voice behind me. "Mom?"

He is wearing a T-shirt and sweatpants; his hair is sticking up. He looks like he is tangled in the net of a dream. I put my body between the stairs and the detective.

Mike moves past me. The other two officers are pulled in his wake. I try to make eye contact with the female officer, hoping to see a glimmer of sympathy, but she is already at Asher's side.

"Asher Fields," Mike says, "you are under arrest for the murder of Lily Campanello. You have the right to remain silent. Anything you say can and will be used against you in a court of law. You have the right to an attorney—"

An attorney. Jordan is on his way, on the first flight he could get out of Dublin. He would know what to do, but he isn't here, and won't be until morning.

Mike keeps reciting Asher's rights. "Mom?" Asher says, his voice quivering.

"Mike, this is a mistake—"

"Please turn around and put your hands behind your back," Mike continues, talking over me as if I haven't spoken.

"There has to be a better way. I'll bring him in later. I'll—"

The female officer firmly pivots Asher. The male officer, more roughly, jerks his wrists into handcuffs.

"We also have a warrant to seize and search the contents of your cellphone and computer," Mike says. "Where are they?"

"In my room," Asher says quietly, and the female officer climbs the stairs.

I push forward. "Why do you need them?"

"It's okay, Mom," Asher says. "I have nothing to hide."

"This is a mistake," I repeat.

Finally, Mike turns to me and meets my gaze. "This is routine, Liv. Nothing unusual. We'd be remiss if we didn't secure the electronics."

The female officer clatters down the stairs, holding Asher's phone and laptop and a pair of sneakers. She tosses them onto the floor in front of Asher.

But he is handcuffed.

I kneel down in front of him, slipping one shoe on at a time, tying the laces. The last time I did this, he was five.

"Let's go," Mike says.

With one uniformed officer on either side of my son, they follow Mike out the front door. Asher doesn't have a coat; he is in short sleeves; he will freeze. "Wait," I say, but then realize a jacket is the least of the problems. "Where are you taking him?"

I follow them outside and watch them open the rear door of the police car and duck Asher into the seat. He perches awkwardly, his hands still caught behind his back, his face close to the cage that separates him from the front of the squad car. *You definitely want to be up front,* I think, hearing Mike's voice from a lifetime ago.

I turn to him, standing on the driveway beside his unmarked car. "I'll just grab my keys."

"Go back inside, Liv," Mike says gently. "He's going to the station. You can't come." He hesitates. "Don't make this worse than it already is."

Don't let him see you cry, I think.

I haven't thought that for a long time. I can barely force a reply through my throat. "What do I do?"

Mike's gaze is soft. "Your attorney will know," he answers.

I watch the police car until I cannot see the taillights, like the crimson blink of the creature you once thought lived under the bed or in the closet, the thing that scared you most.

I TRY TO call Jordan, but of course, he's on a plane and not answering. It takes me ten minutes to realize that I am going to ignore Mike, and another ten to get to the police station. Even though it is the middle of the night, there is a desk sergeant behind the Plexiglas, who looks at me with a bored expression.

"My son was brought in here. Asher Fields. He was arrested." The words dissolve on my tongue, bitter as almonds. "I would like to see him."

"Well, you can't."

"I'm his mother."

"And he's legally an adult," the sergeant says. Something in my expression must dig at him, though, because he offers me a crumb of information. "Look. He's getting booked. Fingerprints, photograph, searched, pockets emptied. He'll be in a cell for the night. You can see him first thing in the morning—"

I glance at my watch; six hours till sunrise . . .

"—in superior court," the sergeant finishes.

In a daze I drive back home. I put on a kettle to make coffee, because there's no way I'm going to get any sleep. But while the water is heating, I find myself wandering into Asher's room.

The sheets are mussed and musky with sleep. A bag of pretzels sits on his nightstand, half-empty. The charger of his cellphone curls shyly under the bed. On his desk is a stack of textbooks and the empty space where his laptop usually rests. There's a plastic laundry basket of neatly folded clothes that he has been living out of, instead of bothering to put them away into his dresser.

I sit on the bed and turn on the lamp on the nightstand. Then I pick up the pillow. It smells like Asher.

I have a brief, panicked thought that he might not ever be in this room again.

On the heels of that thought, I wonder if Ava Campanello is sitting in her daughter's bedroom, thinking the same thing. And how much worse it would be to live with the reality of that, instead of simply the possibility.

I quickly place the pillow back against its mate.

I should call Braden, I think. He deserves to know what is happening.

But at the same time, Braden and I do not speak for good reason. I have spent twelve years excising him cleanly from my life and Asher's.

To call Braden is to invite him to take control again, and I don't know if I could survive that.

Maybe I won't need to tell Braden anything. Maybe this will be over and done with in a day, a misunderstanding realized, and we will all get back to our lives.

My gaze catches on the wall directly across from the bed.

There is a framed, signed Bobby Orr photo I got Asher for his birthday when he was fourteen, and a sketch he did once of my old Ford truck. Between them is a hole in the sheetrock.

Asher put it there about a month and a half ago. He'd been in a foul temper, snarling like a bear with a thorn in his paw. I had heard the noise and had run upstairs to find him, red-faced and chagrined, holding his fist. I looked from the smashed wall to my normally stoic son, my mind tamping down the dormant memories of Braden. *Well,* I said, *I hope whatever's pissed you off is worth what you're going to spend on repairing that.* He swore he'd plaster it up and repaint. I assumed it had something to do with hockey—not making the starting line, or disagreeing with a ref's call.

But now, thinking of the timing, I realize that maybe it happened when he and Lily had a fight. When she stopped answering his calls and his texts.

But they had made up.

Hadn't they?

I spend the rest of the night sitting on Asher's bed, waiting for the sun to rise just so I can be sure it will.

IT TAKES A lot of work to make honey. Nectar collected by bees is a runny liquid that has to be processed by worker bees, swallowed, spit up, and swallowed some more. Each time the liquid is exposed to the air, it dries a little bit, until the water content is approximately twenty percent. Meanwhile, bees fan their wings over the comb, an HVAC system to dry it even more.

It takes an equal amount of work to *harvest* honey. The bees aren't happy about it—you're taking away the fruits of their labors, after all—so you have to be smart about the process. For this reason, Asher always helps me during the two honey harvests. This past September, so did Lily.

"How do you know it's ready?" she asked, watching as I blew a stream of smoke over the top of the super, and used my hive tool—a tiny crowbar—to unstick one side of a frame. Beekeeping is gooey, and as if the honey and nectar aren't bad enough, bees also make propolis, which stretches like taffy when it's hot and acts like super-glue when it dries. I repeated this on the other side of the frame and slid the wood out, holding the rectangle of comb between my thumb and forefinger as bees rippled over it. "If it's ripe, the cells are capped with wax. If you see a lot of liquid, it's not time yet."

I don't use gloves when I work—most beekeepers don't, because if you move slowly and gently, the bees generally ignore you. Except, of course, when you're literally stealing their honey, and then they get pissy. This is the only time of the season when I actually wear a com-

plete bee suit. Mine was a set of white coveralls. Asher, too, was fully
suited up in heavy white canvas, with a netted hood zipped into the
neck of the jacket. Lily smiled at him. "You look like you're going to
the moon."

"Is that sexy?" he asked, grinning.

Lily's eyes lit. "Wait," she said. "Please tell me your mother told
you about the birds and the bees by describing actual bees."

I raised a brow. "Please tell me he doesn't need a refresher course."

She laughed. "Birds, bees. It's so . . . coded."

"Science is less messy than emotion," I mused. I met Asher's eye.
"You ready?"

You have to move quickly when you harvest—bees will swarm
the combs you remove. Asher removed the cover from an empty hive
box about twenty feet away, then came back to me. I pulled out the
first frame at the edge of the box—when making honey, bees tend to
work from the outside in, as opposed to how they raise brood, which
is from the center outward. The frame was gorgeous—heavy, ripe
with a uniform capping of comb.

Asher held the frame in a pair of pincers that looked like miniature
antique ice tongs, and we each went to work clearing the frame of bees.
There are ways to do it with chemicals, or even a leaf blower, but I
prefer to take a bee brush and gently push off the workers, who fall
into the box. The bees, who had been calmly buzzing, began to growl—
a different, angrier pitch. They whipped around us in a frenzy, landing
on my veil and sleeves, a cyclone of indignation. While Asher carried
that frame to the waiting hive box, quickly setting it inside and cover-
ing it, I pulled the next frame. We'd do this until all the honey-filled
frames in this super had been removed to the extra box, and hope that
the bees didn't follow us back to the barn, where we did the extraction.

Many McAfees ago, the barn had been used for livestock, but
now it just housed an old tractor. The rest of the cool, dark area was
filled with the tools of my trade. I had two workbenches, one of
which I'd covered with butcher paper; a plugged-in electric hot knife
sat heating on top of it, as well as a honey fork. The second bench was
lower, and Asher set the heavy hive box on it. There was a big plastic

tub with a grate set in the bottom and a valve where material could be drawn off. And of course, there was an extractor, a barrel-shaped machine that removed the honey by centrifugal force.

I took off my hat and veil, and Asher unzipped himself from his suit. "This is where you get to help," I told Lily. I lifted the hot knife and pulled the first comb out of the hive box. "You get to uncap these."

I showed her how, setting the frame on a strut that had been placed across the plastic bin, slipping the edge of the knife into the yellow at the top of the frame. The heat made the capped wax curl away in a lazy peel, revealing the golden honey flowing from the comb. "That's . . . mesmerizing," Lily said. "It's like visual ASMR."

It's harder work than it looks. The frames are heavy, and balancing them takes upper-arm strength. The hot knife is a hazard—I had plenty of burn marks on my hands. And it's sticky, obviously. As the honey gets onto your hands, the knife will shift and slip.

The wax cappings collected in a soggy pile in the bottom of the plastic bin. Asher leaned over and plucked a little bit, popping it into his mouth. He did the same for Lily, slipping it between her lips. "I'm supposed to eat it?"

"Chew it. Like gum," Asher said. "And when the honey's all gone . . ." He spat the refuse into a trash bin. "It's the best part of honey extraction."

When he was little, I used to give him a tiny bowl with the wax cappings. He'd chew on them and watch me as I worked.

I finished uncapping the first side of the frame. Then I handed Lily the knife and turned the frame to the flip side, so that she could try.

She held the knife for a long moment, staring at the burning edge. "Okay," she said under her breath, and she flawlessly mimicked what I'd done.

"She's a keeper," I told Asher.

As she uncapped the frames, Asher and I loaded them into the radial extractor. The combs have to be positioned evenly, or it shimmies like a washing machine with an unbalanced load, walking itself around the barn. The honey will run along the inside of the tank and collect in a reservoir, after going through a straining sieve to remove wax and debris and bee parts. The reservoir has a honey gate, and when it's full, we strain the honey through a second, finer sieve before storing it in five-gallon pails. Some of this I'd sell in bulk for four dollars a pound. The rest I'd bottle myself and sell for eight dollars at farmers' markets.

After the frames were all uncapped, Asher and Lily stayed on bucket duty, waiting for the honey to finish straining through the gate into pails, while I carried the drained supers back to the hives. The bees would eat the remaining honey, finishing the cleaning for me. I had to make several trips, so I kept coming in at different scenes in Asher and Lily's two-person play: trying to outdo each other by coming up with titles of songs about honey—possibly the only list ever to include Barbra Streisand, Cheap Trick, and Tori Amos. Next time I came in, Asher was pressing their initials onto a beeswax heart and giving it to Lily, who was delighted. The third time, I caught Lily holding up her sticky hands, Asher leaning forward to lick her fingers.

I grabbed another empty super and pretended not to watch as Lily kissed the honey back from his lips. "Ash," she whispered, as if he had already been burned.

BECAUSE MY BROTHER, Jordan, is ten years older than I am, I literally cannot remember a time that he wasn't there. When I was a baby, he was my favorite diversion—one I could watch for hours and follow when I learned to crawl. When I was in elementary school, he convinced me that fireflies were broken stars and that if I walked through the strawberry fields at night, I could find them lodged in the plants. When I was a teenager and he came to visit, he used my eyeliner to draw on the bathroom mirror: knock-knock jokes, cartoon worms with monocles, eyes that said *I'm watching you.*

When he walks in the front door at 8:40 A.M., having paid some exorbitant fee to an Uber driver who has likely never taken a fare this far from the Boston airport, I fly into his arms with a sob.

Jordan is six feet tall, with hair that's more gray than brown now, but instead of making him look old it just makes him look seasoned. He is arguably one of the most famous defense attorneys New Hampshire has ever had, given the high profiles of his past cases—which include a teen suicide pact and one of the worst school shootings in the country—but to me, he will always be the guy who swung me onto his shoulders at Adams Day so that I could see the juggler onstage, even if it meant that *he* couldn't. He is one of those people who can eat junk food all day and still have to worry about keeping on weight, and in spite of this I never considered smothering him in his sleep, so clearly his strengths outweigh his flaws.

He holds me for an extra heartbeat, and then pulls back, his hands on my shoulders. "It's going to be all right, Liv," he says.

My brother also knows exactly what to say and when to say it.

When he called me back yesterday after getting my message, Asher was only a suspect. Jordan doesn't even know the worst of it yet. "Asher was arrested last night," I tell him.

He nods, as if this doesn't surprise him. "What's the charge?"

"Murder."

A muscle tics in his jaw. "Jesus."

"The arraignment is this morning at the superior court," I tell him. "I don't even know where that is."

Jordan glances at his watch. "Fuck," he says. "It's in Lancaster."

Lancaster is an hour away.

"Gimme five." He ducks into the bathroom and by the time I gather my wallet and car keys, he is standing in the parlor again, this time in a suit.

"Why did you bring a suit on vacation?" I ask.

"In case I drop dead," Jordan replies, not missing a beat. He gives me directions—*turn here, get on the highway, drive like the cops are chasing you*—because there's an excellent chance that arraignments will already have begun by the time we reach the courthouse. New Hampshire, he tells me, has a Felonies First program. It means all preliminary processing happens in superior court, instead of starting at the lower circuit court level—a building I pass all the time, which is only fifteen minutes away from my home.

As we drive to the superior court, I give him all the meager details I have. "It's a mistake, Jordan," I finish. "Asher's girlfriend was found dead. And he was found *with* her. He swears he didn't do it."

Jordan taps his fingers on his leg. "If they're charging him with murder, they must have *something*." Too late, he hears his words the way I have. "Look," he says. "I don't know the facts yet, but Selena and I will figure this out."

For the first time, I think of Jordan's wife—the mother of his second son, and his longtime investigator. I'm embarrassed that I haven't asked about her yet. "Where *is* Selena?"

"Dropping Sam off at her mother's," Jordan says. "That way she can do a little digging for us. She'll get here tomorrow."

I nod. Jordan always refers to Selena as his secret weapon. "We'll be able to take Asher home, right?"

Just then we pull into the courthouse lot, and I have to jam on the brakes. There are news vans from Concord and Manchester affiliates and a swarm of reporters. "Is it always this busy?" I murmur, and Jordan doesn't respond. He waits for me to realize that they are here for Asher.

For me.

"Don't say a word," Jordan says.

He jumps out of the passenger seat and is opening my door before I can even unbuckle my seatbelt.

I step out into a sea of monsters: Cyclopean cameras, with black, blind eyes staring at me, microphones thrust at me like bayonets.

Did you know Lily Campanello?

Why did your son kill her?

Does Asher have a history of violence?

"No comment," Jordan says. "No comment."

I am shaking so hard that without his arm around me, I would have already collapsed. As Jordan shepherds me into the courthouse, I realize he never answered my question about bringing Asher home.

BECAUSE I'VE BEEN doing ninety on the highway, we manage to slip into the front row of the courtroom just as arraignments are beginning. There's a broad table in front of us on the left that is empty, and a matching table on the right, seated behind which is a woman with an angular black bob. There is also a bailiff, a clerk, a court reporter, and a judge—an old white man whose chin slopes directly into his neck, like that of a turtle. "Do you know the judge?" Jordan asks.

"Isn't it that guy in the black robes?"

He glances at me. "I meant his *name*. If he tends toward harsh sentencing, or if he's a bleeding heart."

"I have no idea," I tell him, wondering why we are wasting time sitting here when my son is somewhere in this building.

"Rhimes," Jordan says, looking at his phone. "That's who's presiding over arraignments today. Selena texted me."

"How does she know?" I ask, stunned.

"She casts runes," Jordan replies drily. "But also, the New Hampshire judicial system website."

"When do we get to see Asher?" I ask.

As if I've conjured him, Asher enters through a side door with a deputy, still handcuffed. He is pale, with dark circles under his eyes. He is still wearing that T-shirt, those sweatpants. His eyes rove around the courtroom, and when he spots me—and his uncle—his shoulders relax.

The deputy leads Asher to the empty table, waits for him to sit down, and removes his handcuffs. "State versus Asher Fields," a clerk announces, passing a file to the judge. "Charge of murder in the first degree."

Beside me, Jordan sucks in a breath. "Fuck," he murmurs.

"Mr. Fields," the judge asks, "do you have counsel, or do you need an attorney appointed for you?"

Jordan rises to his feet. "I'm representing Mr. Fields, Your Honor. Permission to approach the court?" When the judge nods, my brother steps through the gate of the wooden bar. "My name is Jordan McAfee, and I am counsel for the defendant."

"Thank you, Mr. McAfee," Judge Rhimes says. "Have you filed your appearance with the clerk's office yet?"

"No, Your Honor. I just arrived from Ireland. I still have clover in my shoes." The judge doesn't crack a smile. He doesn't even blink. "Right," Jordan continues smoothly. "I will make sure to contact the clerk."

Judge Rhimes grunts, satisfied. "For the record, the State is being represented by Assistant Attorney General Gina Jewett." The woman with the black bob nods at Jordan. "Mr. McAfee, have you had the opportunity to talk to your client about the charges before him?"

"No, Judge. If I can have five minutes, I think we can be ready to move forward."

The judge doesn't even look up from his file. "You have two," he says.

"Understood." Jordan turns to Asher, speaking quickly and quietly. I am close enough, in the front row, to hear every word. "You've been charged with first-degree murder. Do not freak out. We will talk through this outside the courtroom."

"But, Uncle Jordan—"

"Asher," Jordan says, "do you trust me?"

Asher nods. He swallows hard.

"All we're going to do is enter a plea of not guilty. You don't have to say anything else yet. Do you understand?"

"Yeah, I just need you to know that I didn't—"

"I don't want to hear anything, Asher," Jordan interrupts. "Save it for later." He clears his throat and turns back to Judge Rhimes. "Your Honor, we're ready to proceed."

The judge perches a pair of glasses on the end of his thin nose. "Mr. Fields, you've been charged with murder in the first degree. How do you plead?"

Jordan stands, and Asher follows suit. He remains tight-lipped, tugging at the bottom of his T-shirt. Jordan elbows him in the side. "Not guilty," Asher says quietly.

"Let the record reflect that Mr. Fields has entered a plea of not guilty." The judge sounds bored. Tired. As if his entire life has not suddenly come apart at the seams, the way ours have. If you do this long enough, I wonder, do you even notice that the people in front of you are falling to pieces?

Judge Rhimes turns to the assistant attorney general. "Are we going to consider the matter of bail today, Ms. Jewett?"

She rises, a cobra. "Your Honor, as is clear from the record, Mr. Fields has been charged with one of the worst crimes that can be committed, in a town where this, frankly, does not happen. We have evidence that the victim was his girlfriend, that they were in a volatile relationship, and that it spiraled out of control and ended in death for the victim."

Every word she lays in place is a brick, a wall being constructed between me and my son. I stare at the prosecutor. *You know nothing,* I think.

"This is a defendant who is obviously not in control of his anger, and therefore is a risk to the community," Gina Jewett concludes. "The State asks that Mr. Fields be held without bail."

I must make a sound, a terrible sound, because both Jordan and Asher go rigid before me. But you would never know it, from the casual tone of Jordan's reply. "That's ridiculous, Your Honor. Asher has lived here most of his life. He has no criminal record." My brother's voice hitches just the slightest bit, and I realize he is hoping like hell that this is true. "He's a good student, he has ties to the community. He's eighteen and has no substantive income. His mother is a single parent—she's right here, Your Honor." He turns, revealing me in the space between his shoulders and Asher's. I lift my hand in a half wave. "She will make sure that Asher goes nowhere." Jordan glances back to the judge. "The defense asks that bail be set at a minimal amount that—quite honestly, Judge—my client may not even be able to meet."

Judge Rhimes looks up and seems to realize for the first time that his courtroom is packed with reporters hanging on his next words. "Considering Mr. Fields's long ties to the community and lack of a criminal record, but also considering the fact that this is a murder charge . . . the court sets bail at a million dollars cash or surety."

I feel like a butterfly, pinned. A million dollars. That is the stuff of game shows. Of celebrities. Of dreams. Not actual money, in an actual bank account.

What the hell will I do?

"The defendant is remanded into custody unless and until bail can be established," the judge says, and he bangs his gavel. "Next?"

It all happens so quickly. The deputy steps forward and grasps Asher's arm, drawing him away from the defense table. Asher seems to realize at the same time I do that he is not leaving with us. "Uncle Jordan?" he says, his voice shaking. "*Mom?*"

"Let's go," the deputy says as Asher struggles. Jordan tries to speak over this. "I'll see you in jail, Asher," he vows as Asher is dragged out of the courtroom. "I can't come through the same door as you, but I will be there as soon as possible."

But Asher is not paying attention to him. His eyes are locked on mine with a look that I can't place, but that I've seen before. Like he is both haunted by these accusations and hurt by the fact that someone could think so poorly of him.

"I didn't do it!" he explodes. "Mom, I didn't do it. I *loved* her."

It isn't until he is gone that I discover tears are streaming down my cheeks, and that Jordan is by my side. And it isn't until we leave the courtroom that I remember where I've seen that expression on Asher's face before.

On his father.

AS SOON AS Braden actually started making money as an attending, he wanted to spend it. I couldn't fault him—being a resident had not been lucrative—but I also recognized that he had hundreds of thousands of dollars in student loans. He wanted to buy a house in tony Concord, Massachusetts—I convinced him not to by saying that I wasn't sure I liked the school district, and we settled in Natick instead. He surfed the internet for luxury vacations; I said I couldn't leave the bees. So I wasn't surprised when one day, he drove up to our home in a new Audi.

It was deep forest green, with tan leather seats. It had a sunroof. He showed me this, encouraging me to try out the button on my own. He radiated excitement. Surely, I told myself, we could handle this expense if it made Braden so happy. When he was happy, I could be, too.

His delight lasted exactly six days. On the seventh, he left for work as usual. I was washing dishes in the sink, watching the rain strike the window. A moment later Braden was back, fuming. "There's six inches of water on the floor of the Audi."

"What? How?"

"That's what happens when you leave the sunroof open and it pours all night."

"You didn't pull it into the garage?"

Braden stared at me, as if he were shocked that I'd place the blame at his feet. "No," he said tightly. "I did not."

"Will insurance cover the damage?" I asked gently.

He grabbed the sponge from my hand and hurled it at the window behind me. "You idiot," he yelled. "*You* ruined the car."

I was so stunned that I couldn't even form a reply.

"But I—I didn't drive the car," I managed.

"You came home from grocery shopping and left it in the driveway. Or are you too fucking stupid to remember?"

I rubbed my damp hand across my forehead. I had gone grocery shopping, but that was two days ago, wasn't it? And I was positive that I'd pulled the car inside the townhouse garage instead of leaving it in the driveway, because there were pine trees and I didn't want any sap to drip on the hood. But had I just *imagined* I'd done that? Had I gotten sidetracked, and forgotten?

Maybe Braden was right, and this was all my fault.

Reluctantly, I made myself look him in the eye. "I . . . got distracted," I said, swallowing. "It was an accident. I'm sorry."

His eyes were stains of spilled ink. His hands framed my shoulders. For a moment—a blessed, hopeful moment—I thought he would forgive me. "Sorry isn't going to undo this," Braden said, and he threw me against the wall.

. . .

I CAN'T FIND my voice until we clear the double doors of the courtroom. "A million dollars?" I choke out.

Jordan, who is holding on to my arm, squeezes. "We will figure this out," he says calmly.

We turn a corner and are suddenly surrounded by reporters. *A swarm of bees*, I think. *A shiver of sharks. A bask of crocodiles.*

A tenacity of reporters.

Their questions are a tangle of sentences that trip me. Jordan steps forward. "Our thoughts go out to poor Lily and her family," he says gravely. "That said, Asher Fields has done nothing wrong, and we intend to show that his arrest was a misguided attempt to pin blame on an innocent person. It is understandable that when someone as young as Lily passes, the need for answers is overwhelming—but to ruin another teenage life in the process is inexcusable."

He unerringly steers me into the parking lot. This time, he holds out his hand for the keys and gets in the driver's seat. He drives down the divided highway for about four hundred yards before turning and parking in a cul-de-sac. "You okay?" he asks, and I nod. "Good. Then tell me what the fuck this case is about."

"I don't know," I say, feeling my throat coat with tears again. "I don't get it. I was with Asher when the police questioned him. He wasn't a suspect—he was just there to help them figure out what had happened to Lily. He *wanted* to talk to them."

"He was questioned once?"

"Twice," I correct. "After he found Lily . . . he was asked to give a statement. The second time was after her funeral. He was in the wrong place at the wrong time, Jordan," I say. "And now he's being blamed for it."

Jordan considers this for a moment. "Prosecutors don't charge first-degree murder unless there's a reason."

"I don't even know what that means."

"In New Hampshire, you're guilty of first-degree murder if you purposely cause someone else's death. If that act was done deliberately, with premeditation."

"He went over to Lily's house to get her to talk to him, because they had a fight." When Jordan's brows rise, I shake my head. "To *talk*," I repeat. "He wasn't planning to kill her."

"That's not what premeditation is. It could be a half a second. A thought that crossed his mind."

I stiffen. "My son does not think about killing people."

Jordan turns his attention to the wheel again and puts the car in drive. "Good. I'll drop you off, and then go to the jail to talk to him."

"No way. I'm coming with you."

He turns. "Liv. If you want me to be his attorney, you have to let me be his attorney."

"Then you have to let me be his mother, Jordan," I plead. "You saw him. He's scared." Jordan drums his fingers on the steering wheel. "If something happened to Sam," I ask, "would you tell Selena to sit on the sidelines?"

I can tell the moment he softens, because I've seen it before—when he babysat me and I begged him to let me stay up an extra hour; when I called him from college after totaling my car and asked him to lend me money for repairs so I didn't have to tell our parents; when I showed up on his doorstep with a garbage bag full of clothes and a six-year-old hoping to crash for a little while. "If I'm Asher's attorney," Jordan says, "I listen to him. Not you. He's my client and you aren't. When I'm discussing the case with him or making recommendations or weighing strategies, I will listen to *him*." He looks me directly in the eye. "If you start telling me what to do, you're out."

"Understood."

"And if he ever wants to talk to me privately, Liv," Jordan adds, "you have to leave."

I nod. "Deal," I say.

ASHER IS BEING held in West Stewartstown, at the Coös County House of Corrections, but when we arrive, we are told we cannot see him. As a new inmate, he has to be processed, and he has to put our names on a visitation list, which then has to be approved by the administration—all of which will take forty-eight hours. While Jordan argues with the correctional officer, I stand in the waiting area, watching little kids run around their mothers, waiting to visit their fathers. The CO shrugs when Jordan says this is ludicrous. "Maybe so," he agrees, "but it's the rules."

The building is square and white and utilitarian, and the sounds of buzzing and locking doors set my jaw on edge. I try to picture Asher behind those doors, and I fail. Jordan has to drag me back to the car. "Two whole days before we can see him?"

"Liv, we don't have a choice."

"Do you know what could happen to him?"

Jordan looks at me. "Do *you*?"

I type on my phone, scrolling through pictures of metal bunk beds with thin mattresses, of tiered hallways with cells separated by doors. "Inmate found hanging in cell at Coös County Jail," I say, holding up the screen.

"What?" Jordan turns, seriously shocked.

"A year ago."

He rubs his hand over his face. "This is not ideal. But Asher is a smart kid. He will stay out of trouble."

"What if it *finds* him?" I ask. I do not have to add that this has already happened, once.

"Stop letting your imagination run wild." Jordan presses a piece of paper into my hand, one he got from the correctional officer. "If you want Asher out, *do* something."

I read the top line. *Bail Bondsmen—NH.* Then a list of phone numbers.

When we pull up to the farmhouse, I almost expect there to be reporters on the front lawn. But it is quiet; the bitter wind jumps from tree to tree like a rumor. Jordan follows me into the house. His suitcase is sitting where he left it when he entered a few hours ago. "I'll make myself at home," he says, and he carries it upstairs.

I walk into the kitchen, pour myself a glass of water, and then abandon it on the counter.

In the sink is a bowl Asher used last night. There are still grains of Rice Krispies stuck to the sides. He likes it with chocolate milk from a local dairy farm. I trade them honey for it.

I touch my finger to one rice puff.

What will they feed him, in there?

Will he even be able to eat, or will his stomach be too knotted up for that?

Does he know I tried to visit? Will he think Jordan lied, about coming to see him?

Will he think that his own mother has given up on him?

I would trade my freedom for his, in a heartbeat. I would sleep on a metal bunk, starve, waste away, if it meant he could be home in my place. But the next thought crowding that is Jordan's: *Prosecutors don't charge first-degree murder unless there's a reason.*

And the voice of the assistant attorney general herself: *They were in a volatile relationship. It spiraled out of control.*

There are so many euphemisms for hurting someone you love.

Asher is a perfectionist—in his hockey skills, in his schoolwork, in his art.

How does he act if something isn't perfect?

I think about the hole in his bedroom wall.

Almost desperately, I grab my phone and dial the first number on the bail bondsmen list. "Hello," I say, "I, um, have a few questions."

I am sure that the answers I'm getting must be wrong. Jordan walks in after I've hung up from the fourth call. "I took over Asher's room," he says. "I couldn't sleep in Mom and Dad's old bed, that's just gross." He shudders. "Obviously, I'll move when—" His voice breaks off, seeing my face. "What?"

"I can get a million-dollar bail bond," I tell him, "if I pay somewhere between a hundred and a hundred fifty thousand dollars. I won't ever get the money back, no matter what—not if the case is dismissed, not if Asher's innocent, nothing."

Jordan rocks back on his heels, slipping his hands into the pockets of his trousers. "I could have told you that," he says quietly.

My jaw drops. "Why *didn't* you?"

He doesn't answer. Instead, he asks, "What else did they say?"

"That the money needs to be personal collateral, or that I have to have someone cosign on the bond."

Jordan nods. "That's why I didn't tell you."

"I'd pay you back—"

"Liv. That's not the issue," he says gently. "I can't cosign for you, because I'm defending Asher. It's a conflict of interest. If I weren't, I'd bail him out for you in a heartbeat."

All my breath seizes in my chest.

"You want Asher out of jail, I get that," Jordan continues. "You're thinking of the short term. But if you want Asher free permanently, you have to think of the long term. That said, if you want, I will step down. We can get him a public defender and have him home for dinner."

"No," I manage. "No, you have to represent him." Because I trust Jordan. Because Asher isn't just some client. He's his blood.

Jordan looks at me. "There's someone else who—"

"Absolutely not," I interrupt. I know one other person who has enough money to bail Asher out, but to do that, I'd have to tell his father that he is in jail.

I'd have to talk to Braden.

"Don't you think you owe it to him to—"

"No," I say flatly. "I think all my debts have been paid."

Asher has been mine, all mine, for twelve years. Jordan made damn sure during the divorce that my lawyer would get me full custody without visitation. It turns out that getting a restraining order is enough to make someone with a reputation to uphold settle quickly and quietly. Now, Braden lives hours away with his new family. He has had nothing to do with Asher's upbringing, with making him into the young man he has become.

In my mind, I once again picture the hole Asher punched in his wall.

I stare down at the notes I made while I was on the phone calls. I only have $17,483 in savings. If I can't pay a bail bondsman the ludicrous fee in cash, I can use a property bond that is equal to or greater

than the bail amount. "How much do you think this house is worth?"
I ask.

"You can't."

"It's mine." It was left to me, in my mother's will. She had let it
fall apart around her, because she didn't have the money for repairs.
Neither did I, till I sold off more fields, and paid for a new roof and
septic system, replaced the rotting porch, and rewired the house to
code.

What matters is if Asher can come home, not whether he has a
home to come to. I'll figure that part out.

"Jordan," I say, "are you coming with me to the bank or not?"

THE MORNING AFTER Asher's arraignment, I walk down the
long driveway to get the paper. Asher is on the front page, above the
fold, of *The Berlin Sun*. He has been in the newspaper before. They
cover his hockey games. Sometimes, he is pictured in action in the
Sports section, with a special nod to a hat trick.

ADAMS TEEN ARRAIGNED FOR MURDER OF GIRLFRIEND.

It is not even 8:00 A.M.

I crumple up the paper and throw it into the trash.

WHEN SELENA ARRIVES, shortly after ten o'clock, Jordan catches
her around the waist and gives her an embarrassingly long kiss. They
are nearly the same height, and Selena—as usual—looks like she has
stepped out of a magazine instead of taking a red-eye and driving to
the farmhouse. She's dark-skinned and model-thin, wearing a crisp
white shirt and high-waisted pin-striped trousers, with red suede
booties. Her hair is shaved nearly to the scalp; she has giant gold
hoops in her ears. Her lipstick matches her footwear. I could plan
outfits for weeks and still not come off as put together as Selena does
with virtually no effort.

"I missed you," Jordan says.

"As you should," Selena responds. "Or all that Pavlovian behavioral conditioning is going to waste." She turns to me, her smile fading into concern. She wraps me up in a tight, true hug. "How are you holding up?"

"Not great," I manage, my lip already quivering. "I'm sorry," I say, wiping my eyes. "I don't know what's wrong with me."

"I do. Your son was arrested." She glances over my head at Jordan. "Speaking of which, my mother's down to watch Sam for however long we need her. *He's* already renegotiated the amount of screen time he's allowed, and *she* says you owe her big-time because she's missing Casino Night at her church."

"I'm sorry I ruined your vacation," I say.

Selena shrugs. "I hated Ireland anyway. Has to be the whitest damn place I've ever been, and I've lived in *New Hampshire* half my life."

"Because I'm irresistible," Jordan replies.

"Because you pay well," Selena corrects. "Then again, I earn it. I've got information about the AAG. Our friend Gina Jewett is the presumptive heir to the throne of the attorney general of New Hampshire."

Jordan frowns. "She's awfully young to be groomed for that job."

"Thirty-eight. DuPlessis is retiring early because his wife has cancer." Selena faces me. "The AG wants her to cut her teeth on Asher's trial. He thinks it's a winnable case, and it will be prominent in the media and people will hear Jewett's name and remember it when they vote." She turns to Jordan. "That's all I've got, so far. So what's our plan?"

Jordan tangles his fingers with Selena's. "Come upstairs," he says. "I'll fill you in while you unpack."

I realize I am superfluous, and that they are not going to unpack. "I'll go . . . I'm going to check on the bees," I mutter, the first excuse I can think of that will get me out of the old house, where I can hear every little noise.

It's twenty degrees out, and the bees are balled together for warmth in their insulated hives. I'm not going to check on them; I don't *need* to check on them. But all the same I bundle myself up in my coat and hat and gloves and walk the perimeter of the strawberry fields toward my sleeping colonies.

I'm happy that Jordan has such a rock-solid marriage. I can even remember back to when I had the same optimism about the institution. On the day I got married, I had a jar of honey sent to Braden, who was getting ready with his groomsmen.

It was not, as gifts go, a unique idea. Honey has always been a symbol that purity and sensuality can coexist. In ancient Egypt, a groom bound himself to his bride with twelve jars of honey. In an old Hindu wedding ceremony, the bride's forehead, ears, eyelids, mouth, and genitals were streaked with honey. In Hungary, the bride baked a honey cake during a full moon and fed it to her groom to guarantee his love.

Braden sent the jar back to me with a note: *Thanks, but nothing could make this day sweeter.*

P.S. However, save this for the honeymoon. I have plans.

I can say truthfully that my wedding day was the happiest day of my marriage—not because it was so perfect, but because all the others grew progressively worse.

God, I was stupid. I saw what I wanted to see, until it got too hard to justify what was right in front of me. And even then, I blamed myself.

"You're not checking on the bees."

At the sound of Jordan's voice, I whip around. "You're not . . ."

"Having wild, crazy sex in my old childhood twin bed? No. Not yet, anyway." He takes a step closer. "I didn't mean to chase you out of your own house."

"You didn't," I automatically reply. "I just thought you two wanted some privacy."

"We just spent a week together in an Irish bed-and-breakfast. Contrary to popular belief, I don't need to have Selena within arm's reach at all times." He hesitates. "I may *choose* to, but that's a whole different thing."

"I wouldn't know," I mutter.

A shadow passes over Jordan's face, and I know he is thinking about Braden, and how he didn't know the truth about my marriage. Immediately I feel awful for making him second-guess himself. Old habits die hard. "It's okay, Jordan. Really."

"It's not remotely okay," Jordan counters. "I'm your brother. I'm ten years older than you are. I was supposed to take care of you."

"And here you are," I say cheerfully. "Doing just that."

"Do you know how much it hurt me to find out, after the fact?"

"Less than it hurt me *during* it."

He blinks at me. "Why do you do that? Joke about it?"

"Because if I don't," I admit, "I'll cry."

I realize, in that moment, that I have not spent a lot of time with Jordan—on purpose. I've told myself that it's because he was busy, at first, defending Peter Houghton in a school shooting case; then, a couple of years after Sam was born, Selena had a hysterectomy because of endometriosis, and she needed him more than I did. After that, I was raising Asher, dragging him all over the state on weekends to Peewee hockey tournaments. When that pretext was gone, I blamed my hermithood on the bees. But it's not my brother I've been avoiding. It's a conversation I was not ready to have—one where Jordan felt guilty; one where I felt lacking.

He falls into step beside me, and we walk along the edge of the woods. "How come we've never talked about Braden before?" he asks, kicking at the snow.

"Because I don't like to."

He stares at me. "It's been twelve years, Liv."

I stop walking. "What do you want to know?" I am shivering, and I know it's not because of the cold. I feel exposed, flayed open. I am the wound that never healed.

My brother's mouth opens and closes. It is so rare that I see him at a loss for words. "What was it like for you?" he finally asks.

I hesitate. "Like someone stabbed me," I say slowly, "and then blamed me for getting blood on the knife." I suck in a breath. "When that stopped being only metaphorical, I left."

Jordan's eyes darken. "Why didn't you tell me?"

"Because you would have tried to kill him," I say flatly.

"Would that have been so bad?"

"It is if you'd wanted to be a practicing lawyer," I reply.

He looks away, and when he turns back, his eyes are damp. "I should have noticed."

"Braden and I were both really gifted at making sure no one did," I say.

"But it's my job—my *literal* job—to protect people who've been dealt a shitty hand."

"I wasn't your job—"

"No," he interrupts. "You're my little sister." He puts his hands on my shoulders. "I should have been there."

I stare up at him. I remember how, when I was young, he would pick me up at school. Everyone else had mothers who came, or the occasional father, but I was the only one with a brother old enough to drive. He let me sit in the front seat of the truck, even though I shouldn't have, and would always wait till I fastened my seatbelt before he would fasten his own. It was like my safety was directly linked to his.

I slip my arms around him and lay my cheek against his chest. "You're here now," I say. "You can make it up to me."

INSIDE THE JAIL, we are led to a small conference room, and a few minutes later, Asher is brought in by a correctional officer. He is wearing an orange jumpsuit with white socks and shower shoes and his face is a constellation of purple bruises. One eye is swollen shut. I stand up as the CO closes the door. "What happened?" I manage, throwing my arms around Asher fiercely. He winces as the officer knocks on the glass insert in the door and shakes his head. Reluctantly, I let Asher go, and he sinks down in a chair. He keeps looking over his shoulder, as if he is expecting someone to sneak up from behind.

"Asher," I repeat. "What happened?"

There is a hardness in his gaze. "Where *were* you?"

It feels like a punch. "They wouldn't let us in. We tried, Asher."

"When do I get to leave?"

My throat tightens around the truth—I don't know. This morning, the last bank turned me down for a loan. Because I had already mortgaged the property to expand my beekeeping business, and I haven't paid back that loan yet, I am apparently a financial risk.

Before I can admit this, Jordan slides into a chair across from Asher. "Who did this to you?" he asks.

I reach out to touch Asher's hand, but he pulls away. "I have a cellmate. Ken."

"Your cellmate beat you up?"

He shakes his head. "When I first got here, I was . . . really scared. There's nowhere you can hide—even in the cell, the toilet's right there, the sink, everything. Everyone's always watching. It's not like you get a choice about anything—like where you go or what you eat or even when you want to turn off the lights—and I was just expected to *know* all this. Ken was cool about it. He ignored me when I couldn't stop crying, and when I finally did, he told me that he'd help me out. I didn't ask what he was in for, because I figured that wasn't what anyone in here really wants to talk about, and I was just really happy that someone had my back. He told me stuff, like how to put you on a visitors' list, and when I could go to the canteen, and who smuggled in cigarettes if I wanted to trade stuff for them. Things like that. He also told me who to steer clear of."

Asher rubs his thumb in a groove on the wooden table. The cuticle has been bitten to the quick. When he was little, that was a nervous habit; I used to have to put apple bitters on him to make him stop. Seeing it now makes it hard for me to breathe.

"At dinner the first night, Ken showed me how to get my tray and where to sit. We were by ourselves, which was fine with me, and then another guy came over and asked if Ken had found a new little boy to"—here Asher glances at me—"fuck. I told him to leave us alone, and the next thing I knew, I was at the bottom of a pile of fists and . . ." His voice trails off, and he waves a hand in front of his face. "Ken, as it turns out, is in for kiddie porn, which is like the lowest of the low in here. The reason he was so nice to me is because everyone else knows not to have anything to do with him. Because if you're his friend, you're fair game."

Jordan's jaw is so tight I can hear his teeth grinding. "I'll take care of this. I promise." He pulls out a notebook and a pen and sets it between his hands on the table. "But first, I need to talk to you about your case. Anything you tell me is confidential. What we say in here, no one talks about with anyone outside of this room. Understand?"

Asher nods.

"Second, the reason your mother is here is because she asked to be." Jordan looks Asher in the eye. "But *you* are my client. Which means ultimately, it's your choice."

Asher's eyes flicker over my face, and whatever he sees takes the hard edge off his mouth. "I . . . I'd like her to stay," he says.

This time, when I reach for his hand, he lets me hold it.

"You're being tried as an adult, because you're eighteen. That means I'm going to treat you like an adult. I'm not going to bullshit you, and I'm not going to sugarcoat what you're up against," Jordan continues. "You've been charged with first-degree murder. That means if you are convicted, you're in prison for life."

I swallow hard.

I'm not the client.

"What?" Asher wheezes. "Life?"

"*If* you are convicted," Jordan repeats. "And we are going to do our best to make sure that does not come to pass."

Asher sets his jaw. "I just want to tell you exactly what happened—"

"And I don't want to hear it."

"You . . . what?"

"Here's how the legal system works," Jordan explains. "If you don't tell me what happened, but I manage to convince the jury that the reason you did not murder Lily is because you were actually in Tokyo competing in the Olympics—then you're free. It doesn't matter if you were not competing in the Olympics. It doesn't matter if you have never been to Tokyo. All I have to do is create reasonable doubt for the jury—plant the seed that *maybe* you weren't in Lily's house doing what the prosecutor said you did. As long as you have never told me otherwise, I can spin any story I want in court. I just can't put into evidence anything that contradicts what you have told me . . . and I can't put you on the stand to say something I know would be a lie." He gives Asher a moment to process this. "So . . . *judiciously* . . . tell me what happened the afternoon you went to see Lily."

They are speaking in code, but it is a code that Asher seems to grasp. "She wasn't in school that day," Asher says. "She was sick and stayed home."

"How did you know Lily?"

"She was my girlfriend."

"Exclusively? Were either of you involved with anyone else?"

"No."

"For how long?"

"Since September," Asher murmurs.

Asher, in that moment, is gone to us. He looks down at the table, but I know he is seeing Lily, feeling the loss of her.

Jordan clears his throat. "So you went to her house . . ."

"Yeah. She wasn't texting me back."

"Because she was sick?"

Asher lifts a shoulder. "And because we were sort of in a fight."

"About what?"

For a moment, Asher doesn't respond. "I arranged for her to see her father. She hadn't been in touch with him for a long time, and I thought I was doing her a favor . . . but she didn't think of it that way. She was angry that I set up a meeting without asking her first."

Asher and I do not talk about my life with Braden. We have never specifically discussed the reason I left. Once, I asked him what he remembered about his father—trying to figure out what he had absorbed from his vantage point in a high chair: the window shattering after a book was hurled; the deadly quiet of disappointment; the sound of a slap. If Asher did recall any of that, he lied and said he didn't. Either way, really, it was a blessing.

But this. This admission, that he had tried to broker a relationship between Lily and her estranged father . . . was it because he didn't have one with his own? Was it some twisted transitive property of loss—that Asher felt this part of his life was missing, so he tried to fill the empty space for Lily?

"What do you mean she was angry?" Jordan asks.

"She stopped talking to me. For five days. Maya told me she was sick; I didn't even know."

Jordan's eyes dart toward the door of the conference room, where the correctional officer is again peering through, and I quickly remove my hand from where it rests on Asher's for emotional support. "So you went to Lily's at what time?"

"Around three-thirty? Three forty-five? It was after school."

"Did she answer the door?"

Asher raises his brows. "Is that supposed to be a trick question? Obviously she didn't. The door was open a little bit, so I went inside and called her name. I turned the corner and she was . . ." His eyes fill with tears, and he swipes a hand across them. "She wasn't moving."

"What did you do?" Jordan asks.

"I think I shook her," Asher says, his voice a hush. "I tried to wake her up. I carried her to the couch, and that's when I saw the blood under her head." He's given up wiping away his tears; they stream down his cheeks, meeting at the point of his chin. "I loved her. I loved her, and now she's gone, and everyone thinks it's my fault and they're not even bothering to figure out what the fuck happened to her—"

Jordan puts his hand on Asher's forearm. "Calm down, Asher," he says. "I'm going to make sure the jury understands all of that."

Asher nods. He turns his face toward his shoulder and wipes it on the orange jumpsuit, leaving a wet streak. "I get to tell them, right?"

"Tell who?"

"The jury."

Jordan closes his notebook. "We're going to have a lot of time to talk about strategy while I'm building your case." He slips his pen into his pocket. "Now. Do you have any questions for *me*?"

Asher sniffs once more and lifts his face, swollen and battered, to Jordan's. "Yeah. When do I get to go home?"

Smoothly, Jordan replies before I have to confess my own short-comings. "Your mom's figuring that out," he says, and Asher fades a little bit, like a photograph left out in the sun. "But you *will* be safe in here. I swear to you."

Jordan stands up, and so do Asher and I. This time, Asher reaches for me. I barely touch his shoulder, and he does not smell the way he usually does. The soap is sharper, the shampoo foreign. His face is buried in my hair. "Mom," he chokes out. "Don't go."

When Asher went to nursery school, he cried and clung to me at the door. His teachers promised me this was not extraordinary, and that the worst thing I could do was stay. What they did not know was that I felt just as vulnerable as Asher did. He was, in a way, my lucky charm; although it wasn't foolproof, Braden was less likely to fly off the handle when our son was in the room. But Asher would be at nursery school four mornings a week. My shield was missing.

Now, *he* is the one holding *me*. I pull Asher closer, and repeat what I said fourteen years ago. *Let's both be brave,* I whisper.

THE VERY LAST time it happened was a Sunday. Asher was six, playing in his room with a Brio train set we had scored at a garage sale. Braden sat on the couch, trying to find the Michigan football game on cable. "Why the hell would ESPN show East Carolina over that?"

He had just finished a long shift and was drinking a Sam Adams, the neck of the bottle noosed between his thumb and forefinger. His nine-hour surgery had ended with the patient dying on the table; he'd had to deliver the news to the widow. I was as sensitive to his temperament as a mood ring: I had managed to keep Asher quiet while he took a nap; when he woke, it was to pancakes fresh from the griddle. "Well," Braden said, tossing the television remote to the far end of the couch. "So much for this afternoon."

"We could take a drive," I suggested. "Maybe visit Jordan and Selena." They had just had baby Sam and moved into a new home in Portsmouth.

"I get one day off every two weeks," Braden said. "I don't really want to spend it with your brother."

"I could take Asher," I told him. "So you can relax."

"Wow," he said, shaking his head. "You really want to get away from me that badly?"

I leaned over the couch from behind and kissed him upside down. "Never," I said, but Braden had already dug himself a pit and was settling there.

"The first free day I have I want to spend with my wife," he muttered, "and she picks her brother over me."

"You're being paranoid."

"You're being a bitch."

By now, I knew better than to engage. I took a deep breath and turned away, intending to find Asher.

It happened so fast. Braden's hand snaked out and grabbed my ponytail, pulling so hard at the roots of my hair that my eyes teared. I cried out as he twisted his fist.

You should always wear your hair like this, Braden had said to me once, when we were flushed and tangled in bed, my ponytail dancing over his chest like a paintbrush on canvas. *You look so damn beautiful.*

So I always did.

I steeled myself for what came next, trying to make myself small as Braden loomed over me. But then something soft barreled into my leg. I looked down to find Asher launching himself against Braden. *Stop, Daddy,* he said, beating his fists against his father's belly, trying to save me by doing to Braden what Braden was doing to me.

ON THE WAY out of the jail, Jordan stops at the office of the superintendent. He walks right past the secretary, headed to the inner sanctum. "You can't go in there," the secretary says.

"Ask me if I give a fuck," Jordan tosses back. He opens the closed office door. From where I'm hovering, near the secretary's desk, I watch the superintendent look up with surprise.

"Who the hell are you?" he asks.

"Jordan McAfee. I'm representing one of your inmates. I assume you're aware that Asher Fields was assaulted."

The man shrugs. "That happens in here, sometimes, to murderers."

"*Alleged* murderers," Jordan corrects.

The superintendent comes around his desk. He's as tall as Jordan, and they stand toe-to-toe. A pissing contest. "Surely you realize, Counselor," he says, "that there's a pecking order in the correctional system."

Jordan doesn't blink. "If it happens again, and I speak theoretically, I would assume it's not about the pecking order but about negligence on the part of your correctional officers. Which, as you know, is quite a liability."

The superintendent stares at Jordan for a long, charged moment. Then he turns to his secretary. "Move Fields to a different cell," he says.

Jordan nods, turns, and walks out of the superintendent's office. I follow him out of the jail, holding my shit together until we are outside, in an afternoon that feels heavy with the threat of snow. Then I start sobbing so hard that I can't breathe.

I find myself braced by Jordan's arm. "Easy, Liv."

"That . . . is . . . my *son* in there," I gasp.

"I know."

"What they did to him—"

"Won't happen again."

I round on him. "*You don't know that.*"

Asher is not the killer that the prosecutor and the media and, *Christ,* everyone seems to think he is. But if he has to stay in that jail—if he has to adapt to protect himself—whoever he is when he comes out will not be who he was when he went in.

For eight years I had stayed with Braden. It wasn't until the day I saw Asher hit his father that I understood I had to leave. I had dismissed what Braden did to me, but I could not dismiss what he might do to Asher. Who Asher might become.

"I have to get him out," I say.

A muscle ticks in Jordan's jaw. "You know how."

With the exception of wired child support and alimony payments, Braden and I have no interaction; he is legally forbidden from contacting me. But that does not prohibit *me* from contacting *him*.

Braden now lives south of Boston with his new family, far enough away that a northern New Hampshire boy being arraigned for murder might not have made his local news. If I ask him for bail money, he will give it to me. But he will also insist on being involved in Asher's case, in Asher's life.

"Anything but that," I say to Jordan.

He sighs. "Let's get you home."

ON THAT SUNDAY, twelve years ago, Braden had been so surprised by Asher's tiny, focused fury that it diluted the charge of the moment. Braden turned sweet and solicitous, suggesting we watch a Disney movie as a family; stroking my hair and whispering an apology; making love to me that night as if I were a sculpture he was shaping with his own reverent hands. The next morning, when Braden left for the hospital, I kept Asher home from school. I told him we were playing a game: we had to find our favorite things—clothes and shoes and books and toys—and see how many we could fit into a trash bag. Then we drove to Jordan's, seeking refuge, and he found me the best divorce lawyer in the state.

I don't know what would have happened if I had not left my marriage. I may not have been here today to even wonder about it. I do know that Asher saved me then. And that I will save him now.

It's only been two days, I tell myself. I will figure something out. I will not let Asher be damaged enough to become a man whose anger calibrates him. I moved heaven and earth once to make sure that didn't happen; I can do it again.

But in the furthest crease of my mind is a whisper: *What if I'm already too late?*

LILY ⬡ 3

Three weeks before

I think there is a reason they call it *falling in love*. It's the moment, at the top of the roller coaster, when your heart hangs in your throat. It's the time between when you jump from the cliff and when you hit the ocean. It's the realization that there's no ground beneath your feet when you miss a step on the ladder, when the branch of the tree breaks, when you roll over and run out of mattress.

Here's what they do not tell you about falling in love: there's not always a soft landing beneath you.

It's called falling, because it's bound to break you.

TEN DAYS AFTER I tell Asher, he still hasn't spoken to me. No texts, no calls. He is careful to always pass by me in school in the company of someone else, so that we do not have to be alone. So that he can focus his attention on someone, anyone, else.

Ten days since he stared at me, as if the words coming out of my mouth were knives meant to hurt him, when in fact they'd cut me to ribbons when I spoke them.

Ten days since I made the biggest mistake of my life.

It's not like I haven't experienced what happens when you pull back the curtain and let someone see the ugly cranks and gears that make you *you;* the part that you're still ashamed of; the part you wish you could erase from existence.

It's not like I haven't been here before.

I just thought, maybe, Asher was different. I thought in the equation of our relationship, who I was before we met might count less than who I am now.

In other words, I am an idiot.

Every time I see him at school, it's like there's this invisible force field between us now. When he *does* catch my eye, he looks wary, as if he can't trust me. Why should he, when I didn't trust him from the start?

But.

As far as I know, he hasn't told anyone else what I told him, either. And I *would* know. This kind of juicy bullshit runs through a school faster than a virus; I'd have noticed the side glances by now, and Maya would *one hundred percent* have demanded details. Asher may not have liked me keeping secrets from him, but he's keeping mine for me.

On the days when Asher doesn't have hockey practice after school (because he's had it at some ungodly predawn hour) we usually would hang out together. I'm trying to be respectful of his space, but there is an Asher-size hole in the fabric of my day and I think it's only a matter of time before everything else unravels, too.

I tell Maya I'm going to the library to study after school and suffer her doe-eyed glance of pity. Since our conversation at the fire tower, she knows something is wrong between Asher and me. "Do you think he's breaking up with you?" she had asked breathlessly, when I told her that Asher was still apparently thinking about things.

No, I'd said, and that was the truth. Asher may have said a lot . . . and there may have been a lot more he *hadn't* said yet . . . but so far I had not heard *It's over.*

And even though I knew better than to hope, it felt like a pilot light inside me.

Maya instantly positioned herself as an expert on Asher, ready to dissect every word and syllable and expression to tell me what it really meant. But somehow, I wanted to keep that all to myself, even if it was terrible to remember. I didn't want to share it, because what if that was all I had left of him?

Instead of going to the library like I'd told her, I pass right by the building and walk all the way to Asher's house.

I knock on the door, but no one answers, so I let myself in.

Asher's told me they never lock the door. His mom isn't even sure they still have an actual key.

It's an old farmhouse, which means that the floorboards creak under my weight and there are weird nooks and crannies that hold things like an antique icebox and a grandfather clock and a milk door where bottles used to get delivered. The interior smells of pine, beeswax, and faintly, of Asher. "Hello?" I call up the stairs, wondering if he can hear me.

"Down here!"

It's Olivia's voice. I find the door to the cellar and walk down the narrow steps. The first time Asher had taken me down here—ostensibly to play Ping-Pong, actually to make out—I told him it was the perfect place to commit a murder. *You could hack me into pieces and put me in the freezer,* I told him.

That, he said, *would be a waste of resources.*

I hear a hammer tapping lightly. It's ten degrees colder down here, and that's saying something. Asher's mom has covered the green acreage of the Ping-Pong table with stacks of pressed wax, two little jars of nails, and what looks like an Ikea nightmare of wooden slats.

"Oh, Lily, hi," she says, smiling. "If you're looking for Asher, he's not here."

I try to read her face, to see what Asher might have told her. From the easy smile and the way she naturally assumed that it was normal for me to show up searching for her son, I am guessing that he's mentioned very little. Olivia might not even know that we haven't been speaking.

"Right," I answer, trying to figure out what to do next. Not that I had a game plan, really, for what I would do if Asher *were* here. Talk *at* him . . . again? Force him to talk to me?

"He's still at practice," Olivia says. She is wrestling four of the slats into a rectangular wooden frame, tapping nails into the corners to form right angles. She glances up at me. "But you know that."

"Yes," I admit, because on some level of consciousness, I did. "I came to talk to you." I realize as I say it that this, actually, is true.

I really, really like Olivia. She's funny and smart and amazingly badass, when you see her hauling thirty-pound supers of honey all over the place or dipping her bare hands into a buzzing hive. I've never seen her wear a stitch of makeup, and she always manages to look natural and fresh, even when she's sweating inside her bee suit. But I think what I envy the most about her is how easy Asher is in her company.

"Well, okay," she says. "What's up?"

I open my mouth and nothing comes out.

Olivia stops hammering and looks at me. "I could use a hand," she says. She passes me one of the rectangular frames and picks one up herself. "I'm making frames for next year's hives."

She lifts a sheet of wax from a stack—paper thin, with wires vertically embedded in it every few inches. Then she hands me one, too. "Slip the foundation into the groove at the bottom."

Maybe I'll find the words if I'm busy doing something with my hands. I try to settle the entire wax sheet into the thin groove, but it's bendy and harder than it looks. "See these two little holes?" Olivia asks, pointing to the side of her own frame. She picks something out of the second jar—it looks like the world's tiniest tuning fork—and pushes it through one puncture in the side of the rectangle, its tines falling on either side of the wax sheet. She does this on the opposite side, too. "Go on," she urges.

I pick up the little fastener and thread it through the hole in the wood. The wax is so soft that one of the tines catches in it and rips it. "Oh, crap," I say.

"The bees'll fix it. Technically, we could give them an empty rectangle and they'd fill it with honeycomb." Olivia grins. "I just want to make life a little easier for them."

We settle into a factory line—Olivia building the rectangles and anchoring the wax foundation into place; me inserting the pins to hold it steady. A stack of finished frames grows on the far end of the Ping-Pong table. "Did you know playing Ping-Pong activates your brain more than any other sport?" I say. "The American Museum of Natural History researched it."

Olivia doesn't look up from her work. "Did you come here to talk about Ping-Pong, Lily?"

I shake my head.

"I'm guessing you didn't come here with a burning desire to make frames for beehives, either," Olivia adds.

"No, that was just an unexpected perk," I joke. "It's about Asher." I hesitate, trying to figure out how much to tell her. "We're sort of not speaking to each other."

I stare down at my hands, but I can feel her gaze climbing over me. "Did you have a fight?"

"Not really," I say. I pick up another empty frame, so that I don't have to meet her eyes. "He said he needed some time, and I'm trying to be really patient." Finally, I look up at her. "I think that's why I'm here."

Olivia raises an eyebrow. "I don't know if I'm the best person to give relationship advice," she says.

"But is this something he does a lot? I mean, if he needs to shut me out, I get it. But I also need to know it won't be permanent. Not before I have a chance to convince him not to, anyway."

My cheeks flush, and Olivia's eyes are narrowed, bridging the gaps between what I've been willing to tell her and what I wouldn't say over my dead body. I pick up the tool I've been using and pinch a tiny nail between my fingers. I push it through the wedge.

"When Asher's upset," Olivia says slowly, "he does that sometimes. Pulls away."

"I know," I reply. "I mean, I've seen him after he loses a game. It's like he's trapped in his own head, reliving it."

"Yes, but I mean for the bigger things, too. I'm not sure what Asher's told you," Olivia says delicately, "but his father and I didn't have an amicable divorce."

Asher has told me more, I'm sure, than Olivia realizes. I know her marriage was abusive.

"When Asher was around fifteen, he wanted to get in touch with his father. I understood on some level—he wanted a male figure in his life, and he probably had this golden idea in his head of playing catch or pond hockey, and Braden telling him that his biggest regret was not having Asher around. But I know Braden—far better than Asher ever did. That fairy tale wasn't ever going to happen. Asher was just going to get hurt." She seems to taste and discard words before she chooses her next ones. "I thought . . . Braden had exceeded his quota for that."

I realize in that instant why I like Olivia so much. Because she, too, has so much to hide. But out of solidarity I play dumb.

"I told Asher flat-out that I would not let him see his father, and that he was still young enough for it to be my decision, and not his." Olivia lets out a long breath. "He stopped speaking to me for two weeks. And two weeks is a long time, when you're the only people in a household."

I know that, too. I pick up the tool and thread it with a nail.

"Here's the important part, though. Asher got over it." Olivia shrugs. "One day, he just started talking to me again, like he'd never stopped. Even though he never reconnected with Braden."

I think about the time Asher brought me to meet his father, the way his eyes danced back and forth between us, letting me in on his secret. I push harder on the tool, not trusting myself to look at her.

Olivia reaches across the table and places a cool hand on my arm. "Lily?" she says. "I think he'll come around."

As she says this, the tool slips and the nail shoots through the double layer of wood, piercing my finger. A bead of blood wells at the top of it. For a second, I cannot tear my eyes away.

"Oh my God," Olivia says, springing into action. "I'm sorry! I didn't mean to startle you!" She scrambles, looking for something to stanch the blood, which is now dripping off my palm. She finds a clean cotton rag and presses it against my finger.

"It's okay," I tell her, although it is not, and likely won't be. Asher didn't come around about his father. He didn't realize the wisdom of his mother's point of view. He sees his goddamned father every month, and Olivia is completely unaware.

So what does that mean for me?

"I'm sorry. I've got to . . ." I back away from the Ping-Pong table. "Thank you, for, you know, talking to . . ."

I have to get out of here. This was obviously a mistake.

I fly up the stairs with Olivia calling after me, and run through the house and out the front door. My finger bleeds the whole way home.

HERE ARE SOME unlikely things that have fallen:

1. Blood, from the sky in La Sierra, Colombia, in 2008. Their local priest said it was a sign of sin.
2. A cow, which crushed a fishing boat in Japan in 1997. No one believed the crew who reported it. Then it turned out the Russian Air Force confessed that the crew on one of its cargo planes had kidnapped a cow, hoping to have fresh beef for dinner. The cow, however, wanted none of that, and when it got unruly it was tossed out of the hold at thirty thousand feet.
3. Hundreds of dead starlings in Somerset, England, blanketed a lady's garden in March 2010. No one knows why, or where they came from.
4. Me. Dizzyingly, irrevocably, head over heels. For him.

THERE ARE TIMES when I think I've been playing a role forever. When I was little, I learned quickly what adults expected of me, even when it felt like I was wearing shoes three sizes too small. When I was bullied, I pasted a smile on my face and told my parents I loved school. When I was sad, I rarely let my mother see me cry. If there was an award given out for acting your way through life, I'd win, hands down. So when I get home from Asher's house and collapse on the floor next to Boris, it takes me a hot second to realize I've broken character.

My mother comes into the living room still wearing her uniform. "I thought I heard you come in," she says, frowning at me. "Are you all right?"

There are circles under her eyes. I wonder if she hasn't been sleeping, too. I wonder if it's because she knows *I* haven't been sleeping. "I'm fine," I say.

"Where were you?"

I debate what to say. "I was at Asher's," I finally reply, which is actually the truth.

My mother squats down next to us and pats Boris's side. Her hand is a few inches away from mine, as if the fur is a conduit for candor. A lie dogtector. "You know you can talk to me," she says. "About anything."

It occurs to me that we are living in a time loop, destined to replay this scene over and over. This isn't the first time she's said those words to me, and it's not the first time that I've tried to figure out how to ease her anxiety. She's given up so much for me that I owe it to her to not be sad anymore.

The year I was sixteen, once I got out of the hospital, she watched me like a hawk. I didn't blame her; if my child had tried to die I'd probably have done the same. She was careful with her words, parsing them out like coins for beggars, and she kept looking at me like I was breakable and fragile, when in fact, to my great disappointment, the opposite was clearly true.

I managed to smooth my face into the stillest of ponds. To smile when I thought she wanted me to smile. To pretend that the worst had already happened.

My mother pretended along with me and then one day she just lost it. *You're not the only one who's forgotten how to be happy,* she said, and that—finally—woke me out of my stupor. I couldn't sacrifice myself; hell, I'd *tried*. I couldn't drag her down with me, not after she had given up so much already. So I asked my therapist to help me build a ladder to crawl out of the pit.

My shrink told me that if I couldn't remember how not to be sad, I had to fake it till I could make it. She suggested setting a goal as a distraction. If I were busy chasing a rainbow, I guess, I wouldn't have time to wallow in the swill of my own emotions. So I told my cello tutor I wanted to learn Schubert's *Arpeggione* Sonata.

It's one of the hardest pieces for the cello. Like, Yo-Yo Ma hard. It's a classic combination of stamina, grace, and so much emotion that if you play it right, it actually sounds like the instrument itself is crying. In terms of goals, it's like setting your sights on lassoing the sun.

I don't know if you're quite ready for that, my tutor had said tactfully.

But let's be real. When you've already failed at killing yourself, anything else you might screw up seems minor.

To my great surprise, my therapist's advice worked. I practiced that sonata so hard my fingers blistered. It's a duet with piano, so I downloaded a track and played to it until the notes followed me into my sleep. I spent hours cradling the cello, perfecting the runs and the crescendos.

I didn't realize that my cello tutor had, on the sly, told my mother he was concerned—that the odds of a teenager, even a talented one, mastering this piece were extremely slim. He knew, of course, why I'd been hospitalized. And he didn't want to be a party to the reason I relapsed.

Three extraordinary things happened because of that sonata. The first was that, actually, I aced it. My tutor brought in a pianist from a local conservatory to accompany me, and I took my cello in my arms and the room fell away. When I finished, twenty-four minutes and seventeen seconds after I'd first touched my bow to the strings, my hands were shaking and tears streamed down my face.

My mother came to stand in front of me. She put her hands on my shoulders. *Lily,* she said. *You can do anything.* But it wasn't a command, this time. It was a stunned understanding. She looked at me like I wasn't a ticking bomb, but instead, an inspiration. *Maybe we both can do anything. I can get a new job. We'll move east.*

That was the second extraordinary thing that happened: the satisfaction my therapist (and my mother) had promised me would come with achieving an impossible goal ... didn't. I had played a challenging cello piece . . . okay, great. I had apparently roused my mother's courage . . . awesome. But I was still the same person, and therein lay the problem.

If we move, I'm still me, I told my mother. *Just in a different location.*

The third and most extraordinary thing of all was that after the concert, when I broke down in front of my mother—when I finally lost the will to keep up the act—she didn't fall apart, like I'd expected. She didn't try to cheer me up or tell me that I was wrong to think I was a shattered thing that could never be put back together.

She didn't actually tell me anything, for once. She *listened.*

It is the only time in my life when I let down my guard and didn't regret it. It's why I had thought maybe it could be like that with Asher, too.

That night when I was sixteen, my mother and I stopped pretending *we were fine, everything was fine.* A couple of weeks later, we had a new plan. I felt something so foreign inside me that I couldn't even name it—like I was carbonated, like if you shook me just a little I'd explode. I couldn't define it as hope, not even when it was coursing through me.

It came with its own energy, though, and so I reached for my cello again and began to play my favorite parts of the sonata. I usually avoided looking at my wrist, at my scars, but this time, I focused on them and realized my body was more than something I was trapped in. I saw a strong backbone, a big heart, hands that made this cello sing.

Now, almost three years later, my mother and I *are* east. I'm a very different person than I was during those dark days. Or so I like to think. It seems way easier to slip back there than I imagined, like when you think you've traveled miles and you check and realize that you've only gone a couple of yards.

"Lily?" my mother says now.

I pull my attention back to her, to the present. "Sorry. Just tired," I reply, pinning a smile on my face, because I owe it to us both.

.   .   .

MAYA HAS DECREED that boys suck. I mean, I could have told her that, but I listen to her rant anyway. "So you remember Camper Man," she says.

Maya works part-time at a local newspaper, in the Classifieds department. Three afternoons a week, she sits at a phone bank after school and tries to convince people who are placing ads that, for a small additional fee, putting a banner across the top that says CREAM PUFF or NEW LISTING will make their ad jump out from the hundreds of others on the page. Never mind that she gets a bonus every time they say yes.

"Yesterday, he admitted to me he sold the camper the first week he placed the ad." Maya looks at me across the acreage of her bed. "And that he just kept renewing it because he liked my *voice*."

"Are we feeling this is romantic, or creepy as fuck?" I ask.

"He asked me out."

"Maya," I say, wondering when I turned into my own mother, "you cannot do this. You know nothing about him—"

"Actually, I do, because I have his credit card information, and I googled him. Turns out he is forty. *Forty*, Lily. How disgusting is that?"

"Does he know you're eighteen?"

"I'm not done. When my boss found out, he fired me. *Me!* Even though I wasn't the one who asked anyone out. Then my moms asked why I didn't go to work yesterday and I told them the truth—"

"*Why?*"

"Because I couldn't think fast enough!" Maya explodes. "And now I'm grounded." She flings herself backward on the mattress. "Okay. Now I'm finished. My life is over because an elderly man with very bad taste in recreational vehicles fell in love with my smoky voice."

"I'm . . . sorry," I say. Sometimes talking to Maya is like walking a rabbit on a leash. "How long are you grounded?"

She leans on an elbow. "I refuse to be. I'm throwing a party and you're going to help me."

"Maya, your parents are not going to let you throw a party if you're being punished."

"Yes they are," she counters, "because this Friday we are hosting the Banerjee First Moon Fest."

"What the fuck is that?"

"A menstruation party," Maya says. "We are celebrating womanhood and only womanhood and not only will my lesbian mothers condone this, they will probably cater the food."

I am not so sure. Maya's parents are notorious for being easily upset. Last year, when Maya brought home some of Asher's mom's honey, Sharon had a meltdown because it was a *bee product* in a vegan household.

Plus, there's the obvious.

"You are throwing a period party," I clarify.

"Come on, Lily. It's about time we got something out of it that's more than cramps."

This is how, two weeks after Asher stops speaking to me, I find myself hanging streamers to transform Maya's living room into a living womb. We have stuck maxi pads to the windows; Maya's mixed up some god-awful red punch. Her mothers are so excited about her celebrating the female reproductive system that they've all but canceled her grounding and have made plans to go out so that Maya can have the house to herself and her girlfriends.

She's texted about fifteen girls from school—some I know from orchestra, and some I've never met. Everyone thinks the theme is hilarious. One of the first girls to arrive dumps a bottle of vodka in the punch. An emo playlist beats through the speakers like a pulse. Within a half hour, that tight knot in my belly that's been there for two weeks begins to unwind; it turns out a party without guys is like a quiet sigh. No one is checking out their reflection in the window; no one is hooking up in a dark corner. We are just women, draped over couches and pillows, feeling safe. We don't have to talk about the things that hurt us, because we've all been there before.

I like this, I realize. I like being part of the crowd.

I drink the punch and my head gets pleasantly fuzzy. Maya passes around her phone, showing off Camper Man's profile pic. "On Facebook," she underscores, "because he's *old*."

Maybe this is how it will be, if Asher never speaks to me again. When my star falls from the sky, I will land in the arms of a posse like this. *We get it,* they'll say. *We've got you.*

Sisterhood, I think, *is underrated.*

That's what is running through my head when, just after 10:00 P.M., half the men's hockey team crashes our party. Dirk comes through the door first, holding tomato juice and more vodka. "Bloody Marys," he announces, grinning at Maya. "Am I doing it right?"

"You're disgusting," she says, but she laughs. Others who had been slouched and lounging are sitting up now. Sucking in their stomachs, finger-combing their hair. Preening.

I grab Maya's arm. "I thought this was just girls," I whisper.

"Can I help it if they want to learn about the female body?" She laughs. Meanwhile, there's a buzzing around me: *Who texted them? Not me. Not me. You?*

Then Asher walks in. He looks around at the streamers and the tampons taped to the ceiling, his mouth quirking. Maya throws her arms around his neck. "You made it," she says, and I realize who told them to come.

Then he sees me, and any amusement on his face is wiped away.

Dirk has insinuated himself in the middle of a love seat between two girls. He doesn't fit, and that's the point. Everyone laughs and it sounds like champagne.

Asher turns on his heel and heads for the door before I can reach him, but Maya grabs his arm. "Asher, wait."

His eyes are dark as tar. "You told me," he says to Maya, "that Lily wouldn't be here."

Doubt flickers over Maya. "You've been a fucking wreck. I just want you to be happy, Asher." She tilts her face up to his. "You know that's all I want, right?"

Asher shakes her off, quick and firm. He walks out the front door.

Maya looks at me. "Don't be mad," she says.

I don't hate her, but that doesn't mean I trust myself to speak to her yet. I push past Maya and walk into the kitchen. The punch bowl is there, and a platter of samosas that Deepa made for us. I reach for a clean plastic cup.

"If you're thirsty . . ." a voice says, and when I spin around, it's Dirk. He shakes his hair out of his eyes and waggles the vodka bottle he's still holding. "I don't mind sharing."

I run the tap water. "I'm good."

"Don't sell yourself short," Dirk replies, caging me at the sink with his arms on either side of me. His words fall onto my neck. "You're *exceptional*."

"Four syllables," I say. "For you, that's a big one."

"You have *no idea* how big." He grins. "But if you'd *like* to . . ."

I turn around and shove him with all my strength. "I would not."

He holds up his palms, backing away. "Relax. Jesus. It was just a joke."

"I don't even know why he's your friend," I mutter.

Dirk tilts his head. "I don't know, Lilz. I think Asher and me are tighter right now than Asher and you."

Usually what comes out of Dirk's mouth is utter bullshit, but this is true. Abandoning my cup on the counter, I walk out of the back door and into the quiet of Maya's backyard.

It's freezing, and I don't have a coat. After about five minutes of shivering, I go back, hoping that Dirk's left the kitchen by now, but the door has locked behind me. Wrapping my arms around myself, I walk briskly to the front of the house instead.

Asher's sitting on the curb, under a streetlight that is gazing at him.

He doesn't move a muscle, not when my footsteps are close enough to hear; not when I sit down on the curb with six inches between us.

His hand is curled over the concrete, and so is mine. If I stretched out my pinkie I would touch him. Under the glow of the streetlamp I realize that his knuckles are scraped up and bruised.

"What happened to your hand?"

He shrugs dismissively.

"Ash," I whisper. "Talk to me. Please."

He shakes his head. He will not look at me.

"When you won't tell me what you're thinking . . . it *kills* me."

He makes a small sound in the back of his throat. "Tell me about it, Lily."

Then he stands up. I close my eyes, still shaking with the cold, anticipating the sound of him leaving me. Instead, I feel him draping his coat around me. "You'll freeze," I say, looking up at him.

"I'll live." He pulls his keys out of his pocket, and heads toward his old Jeep.

Do not listen to anyone who tells you a broken heart is a metaphor. You can feel the cracks and the fissures. It's like ice splintering under your feet; like the cliff crumbling beneath your weight.

"Wait," I call out, standing.

Asher doesn't turn, but he stops walking.

My voice is an eggshell. "Do you hate me?"

Finally, *finally*, Asher looks at me. His eyes soften. "I don't hate you," he says. "I hate that you didn't trust me enough to tell me the truth."

I open my mouth to argue, but I can't. He's right. I didn't trust Asher. And it has everything to do with the way I've been treated before, but not by him.

He gets into his Jeep and drives away.

Maybe it's ten minutes later, maybe it's an hour, I don't know. But I'm still on the curb crying when Maya finds me. "I've been looking all over for you," she says. "Lily, I'm sorry. I should have told you I invited him."

I wipe my eyes with Asher's sleeve. "It doesn't matter."

"Do you hate me?" Maya asks, and a shudder runs through me— the same words I asked Asher.

"No," I exhale, and she sits down beside me and wraps an arm around my shoulders.

"Then come back inside."

I shake my head. "I think I'm going to go home," I tell her.

"You *are* pissed at me . . ."

"No, it's just—" I do not want to tell her about Asher; I do not want to relive what he said. So instead I seize on the first excuse to pop into my head. "It's my period."

She laughs. "Oh my God. A self-fulfilling prophecy."

I shrug. "I'm not really in the mood for a party now."

"Cramps?" she says, sympathetic. "I hate when it feels like I'm being turned inside out."

Exactly, I think.

TWO WEEKS AFTER Asher stops speaking to me, I wake up to the sound of rain striking the windows of my bedroom. Except it isn't constant. It isn't even raining.

I pick up my phone: 1:33 A.M. I hold my breath, waiting, and hear it again. Not rain.

I pad to the window and peer into the dark and see the moon of Asher's face.

Scrabbling to open the window, I feel the night spill onto my bare feet. Asher's crouched on the slope of the roof, peering up at me. "Jesus," I whisper. "What are you doing?"

His lips twitch. "Trying not to fall." He cuts his glance toward the tree he must have climbed. "Can I . . . can I come in?"

I nod, reaching out for his hand until he gets a good solid grasp on the windowsill and pulls himself into my bedroom. He is wearing dark jeans and a black hooded sweatshirt, which he yanks away from his face. I swallow, folding my arms across my thin T-shirt and cotton shorts.

Instead of telling me why he's here, though, Asher prowls like a jungle cat through my room. He trails his fingertips over the top of my dresser and picks up my hairbrush. He takes a ring and slips it onto the tip of his pinkie before he sets it back down in a little ceramic dish that was a gift from my mom, which reads: DAUGHTERS ARE SOMEBODIES, NOT SOMEBODY'S.

My heart is like a series of sonic booms. Finally, I can't take it anymore. "Did you come here to break up with me?"

Asher turns, surprise scrawled all over his features. "Do you really think that?"

"I don't know," I admit. "I haven't exactly been privy to your inner thoughts lately."

He sinks down on the edge of my mattress. "I told you I needed a little time." He looks at his hands, clasped between his legs. "It wasn't what you said. It was that you were afraid to say it to me."

I sit down next to him. I wonder if I should turn the light on. "I didn't know you well enough."

Asher just raises his brows at that, and I feel my cheeks burn.

"I need to know something," he says, and I nod, steeling myself. "Is there anything else you haven't told me?"

The thought of my father skitters across my mind, but I shove it away. He is dead to me, and that is a truth in itself. "No," I swear.

"You're sure?" Asher presses, his mouth curling at the corner. "You don't have a secret baby being raised by an aunt in Iowa? You're not, like, a Russian spy?"

"*Nyet*," I say.

"Nothing but the truth?"

"Nothing but the truth."

He brushes my hair back from my face, tucking it behind my ear. "I love you, Lily," Asher whispers. "I don't care about your past. It doesn't make a difference to me."

"But if anyone found out," I say slowly, "it *would* make a difference to *me*."

He knows what I am asking: for a promise.

He holds my hands in his and lifts my wrists, pressing his lips to each of them in turn, even the scars I have kept from everyone but him. "Found out what?" he murmurs, and then he kisses me.

Asher has kissed me before, of course, but it's never felt like this— like there is no seam between us; like I am transparent to him. I surge closer, trying to slip under his skin. His hands thread through my hair and his breath feeds me.

When we finally break apart, fighting for oxygen, Asher kisses my forehead. "Now what?" I whisper into his neck.

His smile is a brand. "It's a goddamned long way down."

I'm smiling, too. I feel like I'm smiling at the cellular level. "It would be incredibly rude then, for me to ask you to leave."

Asher kicks off his sneakers. "You're not one to be impolite."

"Never." I yank off his sweatshirt.

"Manners are the framework that society is built on," Asher says, shimmying my T-shirt up over my ribs.

"Did you make that up?" I ask. "Or is that an actual saying?"

"Do you really care?" Asher asks, and then we fall back in a tangle into my sheets.

My body has never been anything to be proud of. There have been times, obviously, when it only caused me pain. But as Asher peels off my shorts and flattens his hand on my belly, as his mouth coasts from my collarbone to my sternum and lower, I am thinking of none of that. If the last time—my *first* time—was when Asher created a map of me, then this is the trip where he revisits the highlights: Remember when we . . . ? Remember how this . . . ?

When I feel his breath fall between my legs, my thighs press together. Instinct, maybe. Embarrassment. But when Asher lifts his face, the whole world is in his eyes. "Don't hide from me," he begs, and I open like a rose.

I'm so, so tired of hiding.

Then Asher inches up, poised in the cradle of my hips. He slips on a condom and slowly pushes into me. The whole time, he keeps his gaze on mine. He's seeing me, all of me, and there is not an iota of disappointment or disgust. He stares at my face, at my body, like it's perfect. Like I'm a one-of-a-kind wonder meant just for him.

I tear my eyes away. I look down at myself and, for the first time in my life, I am able to see what Asher sees. *Yes,* I think, *a miracle. That's what I am.*

OLIVIA ● 4

A few months after

I t is amazing how quickly the abnormal becomes normal. It is like how, after my father's death, life closed up around the loss like a puncture wound, and how I became accustomed to driving five hours each week to take care of his hives. How my knight removed his shining armor to reveal a monster, and I pretended not to see. And now, how patterning my weeks around the days and times I get to see Asher in jail is the way I now organize my calendar.

Sometimes I go with Jordan, who has set up a makeshift office on my kitchen table. He spends most of the week with me, building Asher's case. Selena mostly stays in Portsmouth during the week to take care of their son, but sometimes brings Sam up for the weekend, so Jordan can see him, or leaves him with her mother when she has to be up here doing investigative work. When Jordan and I visit Asher together, I get to see him in a private client-attorney room; I get to touch his hand or hug him, even if I have to do so out of the near-continuous glance of the correctional officer posted outside the door. When I visit Asher alone, I am just another mother with a sad story and an incarcerated child. He sits in a round room with a panel of phones; I am on the outside of the Plexiglas, holding a receiver to my ear, trying not to listen to the conversations or tears of the women beside me.

When I visit the jail with Jordan, we talk about Asher's case. But when I visit alone, we talk about anything but that. I memorize the sports page of the paper: *The Bruins beat the Trojans, eighty-eight to seventy-four,* I say, and Asher laughs. *A for effort, Mom, but one, that's basketball. Two, it's college, not pro. And three, no hockey score is remotely close to that high.* He asks how his own team is doing, if they beat Berlin. He talks about the things he misses: mint-chip ice cream, snow, sleeping in total darkness, even (surprisingly) his English class. He shows me sketches that he has done, pencil on sheets of white paper, of a doe with a fawn, a dragon, the view from his room at home. There is one of Lily, too, which I take home with me and put in a frame beside Asher's bed.

When I can't visit Asher, I write letters to him. And he writes back to me.

In every letter and at every visit, Asher asks me when he is going to get out of jail, and I think my heart can't possibly hurt any more than it already does.

Until the day he stops asking.

ON SATURDAYS, I have a table at the North Adams Farmers' Market. In the summer and fall, it's a glorious outdoor space, filled with music and shrieking children and vendors selling cheese, grass-fed beef and lamb, lush organic produce, chocolate milk as thick as cream. In the winter, though, we strip to the essentials and cram into the VFW hall. I sell honey I bottled in the fall, and beeswax candles, and body butter. There are times I don't sell a single jar, so I just carry a milk crate with a smattering of products in from the parking lot, leaving the reserves in the back of my truck.

Today, I am feeling hopeful. There's a January thaw and those who haven't wanted to make the trip outside for a nonessential item like a candle or homegrown tea are in the mood to wander a little. I sit at my booth, smiling pleasantly as people walk past. But unlike other years, no one approaches me.

I tell myself that I'm being overly sensitive. But when I ask the vendor beside me to watch my table while I duck into the bathroom, she hesitates before she nods. As if she doesn't want to be seen doing me a favor.

I'm in the stall when two girls come in, and I hear only snippets of their conversation:

—heard that he's in there for, like, ever—
—they took his MVP trophy out of the case—
—yeah the honey lady—
—he's got to be guilty, or he wouldn't still be in there, would he?—

I open the stall door and find them at the row of sinks, applying mascara. "Ladies," I say tightly. "Just for the record, the way our legal system works, you're innocent until you're proven guilty. And that doesn't happen until the trial, which doesn't happen until months after you're arrested. Maybe you'd know that if you spent more time in civics class and less time making yourselves look like baby prostitutes." I feel a sharp blade of shame for picking on adolescents. But I'm overripe with rage, a plum that's split its skin. I wash my shaking hands and dry them. "Instead of *honey lady,* I'd rather be called *Asher Fields's mother.* Have a great day."

I sail out of the bathroom.

What a bitch, one of them says.

For the rest of the market, I watch other vendors get swarmed, while I am ignored. One husband pauses, reminding his wife she said she needed honey. "Not *that* honey," the woman murmurs, and she drags him away, as if misfortune is contagious.

When the market closes at 1:00 P.M., I pack up my crate of unsold wares and carry it to my truck. The sun is deceptive, a false taste of spring. It even smells sweeter outside, or so I think until I open the gate of my truck and see the remainder of my stock—dozens of glass bottles of honey, every last one smashed.

· · ·

THE CONVERSATION BETWEEN me and Detective Mike New-comb is noticeably strained when he comes to take my statement about the vandalism. In addition to the honey, my tires have been slashed. I text Jordan and ask him for a lift, but Selena is the one who steps out of the car.

"That your ride?" Mike asks.

"My sister-in-law."

He runs his hand through his hair. "I would have driven you home."

"Isn't that consorting with the enemy?"

He has the grace to look embarrassed. "You're not my enemy. Neither is your son, for the record." Mike shakes his head. "It's my job, Liv."

I look at the ruined mess in the back of my truck. "And that was mine."

He nods. "I'll find the girls."

I can't prove it's them, but they are the most likely suspects, given our conversation.

"And then what?"

Mike frowns. "You can press charges, if you want."

I shake my head. "I don't. I just . . . put the fear of God into them, or something."

He stares at me for a long moment, as if I'm a puzzle that is miss-ing a critical piece.

"We done here?" Selena interrupts.

Mike nods. "I'm sorry about this, Olivia." He gets into his un-marked car and drives away.

Selena squints after him. "Why do I know that dude?"

"He went to school with me. Now he's a detective," I say. "The one who arrested Asher."

"Riiiiight," she replies. "He was at that celebration we came to when I was pregnant with Sam. The one where white people throw themselves a party because it took two weeks for them to hear the Revolution was over."

"Yeah. Adams Day."

Selena shakes her head. "You all ever heard of Juneteenth?"

I get into the car and tell her what happened as we drive to the farmhouse. We arrive just as Jordan pulls up. He grabs Selena and kisses her deeply.

"What was that for?" Selena asks.

"I'm having a shitty day," Jordan says. "It needed balancing."

"What happened?"

"I had a meeting scheduled with Maya Banerjee," he says, and I turn, surprised. I wonder why he hadn't told me this before. "I guess Maya wanted to talk to me because Asher's one of her best friends."

"That's true," I say.

"Well, her *other* best friend is dead," Jordan finishes. "Every time I asked her a question, she started to cry. One of her moms ended the interview before I ever got started."

"I could try to talk to her," I suggest.

"That's called tampering with a witness," Selena says. "So, no."

Jordan yanks at his tie, loosening it so it hangs off to one side. "Is it too early to start drinking?" he asks, starting toward the house.

"Not for a Saturday," Selena offers cheerfully.

I fall into place behind them, thinking of Maya, of things that are over before they begin.

Just before we enter the house, Jordan turns. "Liv," he asks, "what happened to your truck?"

SOMETIMES, DURING THE attorney-client meetings, I stop listening to Jordan's endless run of questions and concentrate instead on how Asher is changing. It's not just the physical—his skin is pasty and pale, his body whipcord thin instead of muscular. It's the way his gaze darts around the room, like he is looking for the exit. How he always takes the seat where he can face the door. It's the curtain that drops behind his eyes when I ask him anything about being in jail.

I know he has been moved to a new cell; I know that he hasn't been beaten up again—at least not in the places I can see. I think that he has new scars, but they are deeper. And unlike the bruises that were on his face a month ago, I am not sure they will ever fade.

"Do you know Abby Jeter and Tanya Halliwell?" Jordan asks.

That grabs my attention. "Jordan," I warn.

He ignores me, staring at Asher. "They're a year behind me in school," Asher says. "I know them, but I don't *know* them. Why?"

"They were questioned about some vandalism involving your mother," Jordan says.

Asher turns to me, and I can tell that this has shocked him. "*What?* What happened?"

"It was nothing," I assure him, as Jordan says, "They smashed up a few bottles of honey."

"Jesus. I'm sorry, Mom. You shouldn't be ..." Asher shakes his head. "I didn't think about all that," he says softly.

"Technically, Abby and Tanya didn't do the dirty work," Jordan adds. "It was a kid named Danny Barbello?"

"Yeah, Abby's boyfriend," Asher says. "People used to bet on how long it would take for him to wind up in juvie." As soon as the words fall from his mouth, he reddens. "Go figure."

Jordan leans back in his chair. "Your friend Maya is worried about you."

"She always is."

"Not enough to talk to me, though. Her mom pulled the plug on our interview when she started to cry."

"Her parents are superprotective," Asher says. "Back in eighth grade when we did a school trip to Washington, DC, they flew down and stayed in a hotel a half block away just in case."

Jordan taps his pencil on his notepad. "Well, if we can't get Maya to talk to me, then we can't depend on her as a character witness for you. Is there anyone else you can think of from school who might testify about you and make you sound like you're the Second Coming?"

"Dirk?"

"Um, no," I interject.

"How come you don't like him?" Asher asks.

"How come you *do?*"

Jordan watches this volley. "Anyone else?"

"Coach Lacroix," Asher says immediately. "He's my hockey coach, and I'm captain for the second year. In the summers, I teach little kids at his hockey camps."

"You've played since you were, like, five?"

"Yes, but I've been on varsity since I was a sophomore, except for the month last winter when I got benched."

"How come?"

"There was this thing that happened at midterms," Asher says.

I think back to the phone call I got from the principal. The moment I came to find Asher outside the main office, his head bowed, his elbows resting on his knees. How, when he looked up at me, it wasn't remorse in his eyes but a burning anger.

"Some jocks broke into the math department and stole a trig exam and paid a bunch of brainiacs to create an answer key," Asher explains. "Then they sold it."

"You were involved in this?" Jordan asks, stunned.

"I was blamed by association," Asher says tightly. "Because I was on the hockey team."

"So what happened?"

"I got suspended for a month."

Jordan turns to me. "You didn't fight it?"

Asher meets my gaze, and in that one look, we have an entire conversation.

I have to tell him, Asher.

But it wasn't fair.

Life rarely is.

Do you think I don't know that?

"Hello," Jordan interrupts. "What the hell is going on?" He looks at me. "This isn't a drill, Olivia. If Asher was complicit in something like this, it's bound to be dragged up by the prosecution. You need to tell me *everything.*"

"When Asher was questioned by the principal, he said he wasn't involved in stealing the exam. Dirk—the friend he mentioned earlier?—was the one who did that. But some of the other guys on the team said that Asher was the one who came up with the idea."

"*What?*"

"It's not what you think, Uncle Jordan," Asher says quickly. "I wasn't, like, trying to mastermind anything. It was a joke. We were in the locker room talking about how our math teacher refused to grade on a curve and made the tests impossible and everyone's GPA was tanking because of it. I said applying to college would be a hell of a lot easier if we could fix that, and the other guys ran with it. I never meant for them to actually *do* it."

"The end result is that you got suspended," Jordan points out, "which is not great."

"I don't understand why a school suspension I was railroaded into a year ago has anything to do with *this*," Asher says.

"People in your school think you lied. And if your coach is one of them, he can't be a character witness, either."

"Then I'll do it myself. Just put me on the stand," Asher says.

"Look. The whole burden of this trial is on the State. They have to prove everything. We need to be able to rely on the fact that they don't have enough evidence of the crime of murder to justify it sufficiently to a jury. When it's our turn to put on evidence, what we really need to do is to pick holes in what *they* have presented. We can disprove their entire case without ever having you testify."

"That makes no sense," Asher argues. "Who could prove better than me that I didn't do it?"

"We don't have to prove *anything*. Having you on the stand could actually come back to hurt us. You can be asked almost anything about your relationship with Lily—conversations you had, messages you sent, fights you got into—anything about your background that is even *slightly* heated, if not violent. You think you were unfairly blamed for that cheating scandal?" Jordan says. "The prosecution would make that look like a walk in the park."

"But I'd be telling the *truth*," Asher insists.

Jordan meets his gaze. "Remember when I said that if I can convince the jury that the reason you're innocent is because the night Lily died, you were in Tokyo training for the Olympics? I don't have to prove it. I just have to raise the *possibility* of it. But if you take the stand and you contradict what I've said, or if you refute anything that the State has evidence you said at any other time . . . then you look like a liar. And that is a *huge* risk. Because juries tend to think that people who lie about little things are equally likely to lie about big things—like killing someone." A muscle ticks in his jaw as he looks from Asher to me. "Any other surprises you'd like to lay on me? Have you defaced federal property or maybe been arrested for grand theft auto?"

"Jordan," I say. "The cheating thing . . . it was just a misunderstanding."

"There is no *just* anymore," my brother says, and I wonder if he intended for me to hear both meanings of the word.

SELENA SHOWS UP at the house as I am putting away Christmas decorations. The holiday was, needless to say, a bust this year. I visited Asher at the jail. I never even put up a tree. But I also never took down the greenery on the mantel and banister or the Christmas lights on the porch, pretending to myself Asher might be home in time to see them.

"Jordan didn't tell me you were coming today," I say. It's a Wednesday, and she rarely comes during the week. "What about Sam?" I wind a rope of fairy lights around my arm. I am getting inextricably tangled in a web of my own weaving.

"He's with my mom and . . . Here, sweet Jesus, before you strangle yourself." Selena drops her purse on the floor and holds out her arms like two goalposts, allowing me to wind the lights around them like we are playing cat's cradle. "Jordan and I are partying tonight. Dinner and drinks, baby."

"Ooh-la-la," I say. "What's the occasion?"

I slip the rope of lights from her hands. "The anniversary of my surgery," Selena says.

It's been nine years since her hysterectomy. It was a major surgery, with the ovaries being removed, too, and there was some kind of complication that kept her hospitalized longer than she should have been.

"Jordan swore to me when I was sick that if I pulled through he would treat me like a queen, and we'd celebrate every year. We were going to spend it in Aspen, but . . ." She shrugs.

"God, I'm sorry," I say. "You two are completely upending your life for me."

"Don't be stupid, you're my sister," Selena says. "Besides, Aspen's a zoo this time of year. And I'm pretty sure that Dunk's Beef-n-Burg is *not*."

"At least make him take you to the Mount Washington Hotel." I bend down, coiling the lights on top of the other decorations, and when I straighten, Selena is staring at me.

Not *at* me, actually, but *into* me.

"Come with us," she offers.

"No thanks. The last time I accompanied Jordan on a date I was seven and my babysitter canceled and he brought me to an R-rated movie where he proceeded to make out with a girl and I learned four new swearwords."

I pick up the lid of the Rubbermaid box and attempt to snap it in place, but it has warped and refuses to fit. "Dammit," I mutter, yanking the plastic top off and hurling it like a discus across the room.

Selena puts her hand on my arm. "Hey," she says gently. "What's wrong? Other than the obvious, I mean."

I brush away the sudden tears in my eyes. "The more I listen to Jordan, the less I think Asher is going to get a fair trial."

Selena presses her lips together, as if she is going to say something she doesn't want to.

"What?" I press.

"Nothing."

"Selena."

She sighs. "At least your son is going to *have* a trial. If Asher looked like my Sam, he might not have even made it to that point. The cops who came into the house and found him sitting there might have just shot him, instead of arresting him a week later." Selena's gaze is an odd combination of pity and jealousy. "What's shocking to you isn't that the justice system is flawed, Olivia. It's that you were naïve enough to believe all this time that it *wasn't*."

Just as I'm feeling as if I've been slapped, Selena wraps her arms around me.

"It's a lot to take in," she admits. "I've had my whole life to learn it, and you've had five seconds. But maybe while you're counting all the ways this could go wrong for Asher, you can also count all the ways it's already gone *right*." She pulls back, holding my shoulders. "Let's go find you a dress," Selena says. "It's date night for three, and I'm not taking no for an answer."

IN THE END, we do not go to the Beef-n-Burg to celebrate Selena's anniversary. Jordan instead suggests we drive forty-five minutes south to Lyme, to a much fancier restaurant called Ariana's, which is nearly empty on a Wednesday night in January. This comes in handy, since he wants to discuss Asher's case. "The prosecutor's office has an open-file discovery policy," he explains to me. "That means I can make an appointment, come check out the whole case file, take notes, whatever. That way we don't have to file motions back and forth. So, today was my first appointment. Some lackey let me into the conference room with the file. The cause of death, based on the medical examiner's report, is intracerebral brain hemorrhage, caused by blunt force trauma to the head."

My breath hitches. "You mean Lily was *hit*?"

"Not necessarily," Jordan says.

"She could have fallen down the stairs and smacked her head on the stair treads," Selena jumps in.

"That's good, right?" I ask, looking between them. "Isn't that the kind of thing you're always talking about, with reasonable doubt?"

"It would be," Jordan agrees, "if Asher's fingerprints and DNA weren't all over Lily's bedroom."

"I was with him during the police interrogation. Asher said he wasn't in her bedroom," I say.

Jordan looks at me. "He was, Liv."

I can feel my cheeks burning. "Aren't you supposed to be on his side?"

"If there's physical evidence, there's physical evidence. Asher may have an explanation for it, but he *was* in her room." He pauses. "He was dating her for three months. The real question isn't whether he was in there . . . but why he lied about it."

Selena, ever the peacemaker, jumps between us, signaling for another bottle of wine. "Even if Asher and Lily had a fight, Lily could still have tripped and fallen down the stairs all on her own . . ."

"Which is not first-degree murder," Jordan finishes, "but manslaughter." He meets Selena's gaze, and they nod slightly. I do not understand the legal rationale behind it, but I know manslaughter is accidental death, not intentional. That this is their backup plan, should all else fail.

"Anyway," Jordan adds, "I tried to have a follow-up conversation with the medical examiner, but he's a part-timer in the ME's office and was working in the hospital and couldn't talk. Guy's busier than a mosquito at a nude beach." He smiles at Selena. "He offered Monday afternoon, but it's down in Concord."

"Monday afternoon's visiting hours with Asher," I point out.

"Which is why I am hoping my brilliant, beautiful investigator can do the interview for me."

"Your brilliant, beautiful investigator will be at Sam's school for the parent-teacher conference you said you couldn't make because of visiting hours at the jail," Selena says.

"Ah, damn," Jordan says, as the waitress hands him the first sips of the new bottle of wine to taste. "I'll have to hound the guy again and reschedule. God, I thought I was done with parent-teacher conferences after Thomas. Not to mention diapers, chicken pox, acne, and driver's ed." He lifts his glass. "You were smart to stop after one kid, Liv."

I pick up my wineglass and drain it entirely. "Cheers," I say.

.   .   .

I HAD TIMED it perfectly, but in the end, circumstances beyond my control ruined my best-laid plans. There had been an accident on the Mass Pike and the doctor had been two hours late to work; everything was backed up as a result. After hours in the waiting room, it was finally my turn. As I lay on the table, staring at a ceiling light overhead, I wondered why no one bothered to clean out the dead flies that had accumulated inside the fixture. Given how many women had this view, you'd think someone would have noticed.

I knew that Jasmine, the teenager who lived next door and babysat for us, would stay even if I came home late. She would never leave Asher; she was mature enough to know that something must have come up because I was punctual to the *dot*. Timeliness had been, quite literally, beaten into me. My worries stemmed from the fear that the quadruple bypass Braden was performing today would end early and he'd get home before me and wonder where I was.

My eyes filled, and the nurse holding my hand leaned closer. "Almost done," she said.

She looked like rising dough. White and round and kind. She looked like the kind of person you could fall into, and have a soft landing.

I heard the suck of the tiny vacuum pump, felt the tug in my abdomen, and the doctor's gentle hand on my thigh. "You," he said, "are no longer pregnant."

This time, the tears spilled over. The nurse squeezed my hand more tightly. I'm sure she had seen this before; the surge of emotions, the pain of loss laced with relief.

But I wasn't crying with regret, or out of fear of Braden's retributions for my absence. These were tears of joy.

Braden would never know that I'd come to this clinic.

And I would never bring another baby into that house.

"YOUR HAIR, FROM Lily's bed," Jordan says, staring at Asher. He had begun the visit by listing the physical evidence in the case file, as I watched Asher flinch with each item. "Your fingerprints on her dresser. And the statements you made to the police saying you'd never been in her bedroom. Care to explain?"

"I didn't say I was *never* in her bedroom," Asher offers. "I wasn't in it *that day*."

"Are we splitting hairs now about semantics?"

"No. I mean, I sneaked out to Lily's *sometimes*. I climbed a tree and went into her room through the window." He slides his glance to me. "I would spend the night."

I blink at Asher, certain I have misheard him. I would have known if he snuck out of our house. Every morning, when I knocked on his door to make sure he was awake, he grunted. And there he was at breakfast, without fail.

That doesn't mean he didn't sneak back in.

"The entire night?" Jordan asks.

"I'd leave before the sun came up. Then I'd go back home."

"So your mother never knew," Jordan says, a statement.

A streak of color stripes each of Asher's cheeks. "No."

"How often?" Jordan presses.

"Maybe a half dozen times. But *not* the night before she died."

"When was the last time you were in her room?"

"About a week . . . before," Asher says.

"Did Lily's mother know you were there?"

Asher raises a brow. "I climbed a *tree*."

"Did you have sex with Lily while you were in her room?" Jordan says, and I suck in my breath at his bluntness. He turns to me wryly. "You sure you still want to be here?"

I stare at Asher, who looks away. "Yes," he admits.

"Starting when?"

"The first time was in October."

"Did you have sex every time you stayed with her?" Jordan asks.

Asher shifts in his chair. "Do you really need to—"

"Yes, Asher, I do," Jordan snaps.

"Then yes, I guess so."

Jordan rubs his hand over his face. "God save me from teenage boys."

"*You* were a teenage boy," I murmur.

"Did Lily ever indicate that she felt pressured, or didn't want to have sex?"

Asher's face flushes scarlet. "Only the first time."

"Jesus, Asher," Jordan says. "What does *that* mean?"

Please, I pray silently, *don't let him have forced her.*

"Lily got really . . . strange afterward. She wanted to do it— I swear she did—but I thought maybe she'd had second thoughts. She stopped answering my texts and phone calls, and she avoided me in school. She finally admitted she needed some time to think things through."

I think back to what Asher has said about the days before Lily's death; how she didn't respond to his messages and didn't want to talk to him. So this makes two times, then, that she kept him at arm's length. And he'd done the same to her, I knew.

"Eventually, she told me the truth," Asher says, worrying the cuticle on his thumb. "She was afraid our relationship would be different after we had sex. I promised her that it wouldn't change anything."

"How long did you get the silent treatment?"

"About a week. I was freaking out."

"Because you thought she would break things off?" Jordan asks.

"Because she tried to kill herself once," Asher says flatly.

What?

I imagine all the times I saw Lily and Asher tangled together, being silly and giddy and stupid . . . *How lucky they are,* I would muse, *to not be weighed down by the world.* But Lily wasn't carefree; she just wanted to be seen that way. I had not known Lily was suicidal; she clearly wanted to keep that private.

"Do you know when she attempted suicide?" Jordan asks.

Asher hesitates. "Sometime before she moved here. I don't know the details; she didn't like to talk about it. I was the only person she actually told."

"Do you know . . . how?"

Asher shakes his head. "But she had scars on her wrist."

I think back to Lily's clothing. Most recently she'd worn long sleeves when she was at our house—but it was winter. I try to remember her harvesting honey—what was she wearing that sweltering September afternoon? A T-shirt, I think, but she had bright friendship bracelets ringed on both wrists. She always sported a scrunchie there, too. To pull back her hair? Or to hide scars?

"So you kept having sex with Lily," Jordan says. "In the bedroom you told the cops you hadn't been in."

Asher glares at Jordan, tamping down his frustration. "I didn't tell them that . . . I said I wasn't in her bedroom *that night* and I wasn't. Why is this even—"

"Because it *is*, Asher," Jordan interrupts. "Because these are the kinds of things the prosecution will do. This is why I can't put you on the stand. You lied to the cops, and you lied to me."

"I told them the truth! The detective didn't ask me if I'd *ever* been in her bedroom. He didn't ask me if I'd slept with her." His voice climbs a ladder of frustration. "You're supposed to be the *one* person who's on my side. Why are you being such a dick?"

"Asher!" I cry.

Jordan flattens his hands on the table and leans toward Asher. "Because if I'm a dick to you now, then you won't come across as one in court."

"Why don't you just leave?" Asher bites. "*I* would, but my lawyer hasn't managed to get me out of here yet."

Jordan slams his notebook shut. "You know what? You're right. We both need to cool off. We'll pick up again next week."

Jordan is up and banging on the door to be let out before I rise from the chair. The CO holds the door open, waiting for me to follow. "Asher," I say quietly.

"Just go, Mom," he murmurs, so tired that the words can barely carry the distance between us.

I know better than to engage Jordan until we are settled in the car, driving away from the jail. "Did you know Asher was having sex with Lily?" he asks.

"I assumed . . . but we didn't really talk about it."

Suddenly I remember the week that Asher got moody and distant, snapping at me no matter what I said or did. Was that early November? I heard the crash, and found Asher in his room cradling his fist, the sheetrock smashed, looking just as stunned as I was by the violence he had wreaked.

You think you know someone, Asher said to me (by way of apology? explanation?) when I found him with plaster dust snowing over his feet. *But you really don't know them at all.*

Until this moment, I hadn't remembered Asher's words. But now, I wonder if they referenced Lily. If they had anything to do with her suicide attempt; with sex.

My throat is suddenly dry as dust. I picture Asher's knuckles, scraped. I think about the force a punch would have to have to break through a wall. "Jordan?" I ask quietly. "Do you think Asher could have . . . hurt Lily?"

I cannot bring myself to say the word *killed*.

Jordan's eyes slide to mine before refocusing, hard, on the road before him. "If I ever hear you say that again," he replies, "you're never coming to another meeting."

ONE OF THE first dates I had with Braden was to see a zombie movie. He loved them—the good, the ridiculous, the big budget, and the ones that looked like they were shot by teenagers in basements. The Danny Boyle film *28 Days Later* was, in his opinion, the gateway to all things zombie. Although I told him that I had not slept for weeks after seeing *The Shining,* he promised me that this would be different, because I was seeing it with him.

We sat in a packed theater, fortified with Goobers and popcorn. As we watched humans infected with the virus attack others, Braden leaned closer to me. "I would kill you myself before I let them get you," he whispered, and he kissed the spot on my neck that always made me shiver.

.   .   .

BEES SURVIVE WINTER by forming a cluster around the queen, baseball-size in subzero months and beach-ball-size in the early spring, generating heat to about ninety-five degrees. When the snow melts in the spring, I remove the insulation from my hives, in preparation for them to start flying.

January has bled into February, which has seeped into March. I've measured time by my bees, because every day looks the same, now—endless trial preparation, punctuated by visits to the jail.

One day, when the weather starts to turn, I adjust my bee veil and start with Adele's colony, blowing a little smoke at the entrance and beneath the cover. Ten frames are snugged together in the hive body, with bees crawling all over them.

I don't see the queen, but that's okay. You don't actually have to see her to recognize evidence of her work. If Adele's healthy and laying eggs, they will look like commas in their brood cells. A queen lays different sorts of eggs in different spots in the honeycomb. A larger drone cell will get an unfertilized egg, which will become a male bee. A regular-size cell gets a fertilized egg, which will become a worker bee ninety-nine percent of the time.

It takes twenty-one days for a worker bee to go from egg to adult. Twenty-four for a drone. A queen takes sixteen days, and then she will go on her maiden (and only) mating flight. She flies into the sky, releasing pheromones to let the drones know it's their lucky day. The ones who fly fastest and highest get seven minutes in heaven, so to speak. A drone turns the tip of his abdomen inside out to expose his penis, and shoves it into the queen's sting chamber. When he ejaculates, you can actually hear it.

Once his sperm is in the queen, his penis snaps off, staying inside her. He falls to his death as another drone hooks up with her. At the end of this orgy, when the queen goes back to the hive, she has enough fertilized eggs inside her to last a lifetime.

I have not been on a date in eight years.

After Braden, I couldn't imagine being with another man. It took four years for me to agree to go out to dinner with the divorced son of one of my mother's friends. He was smart and pleasant, but I kept thinking he wasn't very tall and that he didn't seem to get my jokes and by the second course I realized I was comparing him to Braden.

I slept with him, though. Not because I was attracted to him, but because I wanted Braden to not be the last. The whole time, I was thinking about queen bees, and how a new drone will literally push his predecessor's genitals out of the way to make room for himself.

If I was thinking about this during sex, obviously, it wasn't particularly *good* sex.

That night I dreamed about making love with Braden. How he had once asked me what my favorite part of myself was, and how I had said, *The dip of my waist.* He'd placed me on the bed, turning me to my side, running his hand over that curve repeatedly, learning the way I loved myself.

The sad truth is that I am more like that queen bee than I'd like to think. I had one run at passion, and that's probably all I'll get for the rest of my life.

The sadder truth is that in spite of all the moments my marriage was a hellscape, there were other moments I was cherished.

The saddest truth is that even *while* Braden was hurting me, I forgave him.

I gently slide the frames back into place in Adele's hive, using a spacer tool to make sure they're evenly set, and cover the top. Her colony looks just like it is supposed to at this time of year.

Beyoncé's colony, next to this, looks much the same, but this time I am lucky enough to see the queen surrounded by a coterie of attendants.

Then I open Celine's hive, the one I repatriated after the bear attack in December. That was the day, I realize with a shock, that Lily died.

There is no hum from the hive when I open the top. The frames are cold and stiff. As in the scene of a massacre, every single bee is dead, heaped in the bottom of the box.

I expected this. I knew the colony that had absconded after the bear attack would never make it through the winter.

But that doesn't make it hurt any less.

.   .   .

AS SPRING UNFOLDS, Jordan's preparation of Asher's case moves into high gear. Selena has found out which judge is assigned—Rhonda Byers, a fifty-something Black single mom who put herself through law school and who has a reputation for being no-nonsense. Jordan has gone back and forth on whom he will call as a witness for the defense. I will testify, of course, but in the end he also chooses Coach Lacroix. The coach didn't know Lily and will be able to present Asher as a good student, a good person, an empathetic athlete who teaches kids during the summer—all pros. The con is that the prosecution knows about the cheating scandal and will bring it up on the cross-exam, and once that area of Asher's character is revealed they are entitled to bring up anything that might show another, less flattering side of him.

He doesn't have to say the real reason he added the coach: because a defendant who has only one witness—his own *mother*—is in pretty sad shape.

We have talked about alternative scenarios—from other visitors to the house (Asher has no idea) to alibis (Asher doesn't have one, since he *was* at Lily's house and, prior to that, was driving there) to accidents that might have befallen Lily—any red herring Jordan might be able to introduce as an alternative theory to stick in the jurors' minds. Jordan has also gone back to the prosecution for another look at the discovery, returning with transcriptions of texts from Asher's and Lily's phones. For the past three hours, we've been in the conference room at the jail, painstakingly going through Asher's conversations with Lily—and we've only now reached the day of her death.

"This was sent at eight A.M.," Jordan says to Asher. "*Are you okay, I heard you're sick.* You sent this to her, even though you two were arguing?"

Asher is sprawled in his chair, his head lolled back. He looks thinner than he did a week ago, and there are deep purple circles beneath his eyes. "*Especially* because of that. I wanted her to know I was still thinking about her."

Jordan shuffles through the text printouts. "The second message was sent at ten-fifteen A.M. . . . three question marks?"

Asher shrugs. "She still hadn't written back."

"*I'm really worried about you.* Eleven twenty-one A.M.," Jordan reads. "One-fourteen P.M. *Please, just give me a chance to talk.* Three thirty-one P.M.: *THIS ENDS NOW, I'M COMING OVER.*" He whistles softly. "All caps."

"That was the last text I sent," Asher says.

"Pretty fucking ominous. At least that's what the prosecution is going to say."

"It wasn't meant as a threat," he counters. "I just wanted to be face-to-face with her. I knew I could explain everything, if she'd just see me. But she never wrote back."

"Yes, she did."

Asher shakes his head. "Well, if she wrote it . . . I never got it."

Jordan frowns and starts shuffling through the printouts. "These messages were on your phone. Here's a thread with your mother . . . here's Maya. Dirk." He flips a page. "Who's Ben Flanders?"

Asher picks at the skin on his thumb. "Just a guy I play hockey with." He grabs another stack of papers from the table. "Look. Here. These are the texts that Lily sent to *me*. The last one was seven days before she died."

Jordan pulls a page free and places it beside the one Asher is still holding. "This is the printout from *her* phone—of her replies to *you*. There's a message that looks like it was typed out underneath your last text to her . . . but never actually sent."

Asher leans over, reading—for the first time—Lily's final message to him. "*Don't bother, it's over.* It's over . . . ?" he repeats, his voice hollow. He turns, tears bright in his eyes. "Do you think . . . was she breaking up with me?"

I reach for him. "No, Asher . . . she didn't send it. Maybe she was mad, or upset, but that doesn't matter. What matters is that she changed her mind."

Jordan starts pacing, thinking out loud. "If you had received that text from Lily and still came over, it looks like you were angry. Like you went there in a rage because you didn't accept that she was breaking up with you. I'm a hundred percent sure that's what the prosecution plans for the jury to see—a guy who was thinking, *If I can't have you, no one can.* But if you never *got* Lily's text . . ."

"Then the prosecution can't make that argument," I finish.

"And they certainly can't use it as a motive for murder." Jordan grins. It is the first time I've seen him actually get excited since he's started building Asher's case. "I'm going to file a motion to exclude that evidence."

"That's good for us," I say. "Right?"

"It is if we win the motion."

I look at Asher, but he is picking at the cuticle on his thumb, lost in thought. I want to comfort him, to tell him I know how it feels when you think someone you love has betrayed you. But I also know that if anyone had said that to me, when I was married, I would have been mortified by their pity.

"There's one more thing we have to talk about, Asher," Jordan says, drawing his attention. "We have a plea offer from the prosecutor."

My head whips around to stare at my brother. He did not tell me that he'd gotten a plea offer; he did not even tell me the prosecutor had been in touch. I am about to lace into him for this when I remember, months ago, what he told me: I am not his client.

"A plea offer?" Asher says. "What does that mean?"

Jordan sits down across from him again. "You're currently charged with first-degree murder, which carries a potential maximum penalty of life in prison. What the State has offered is for you to plead guilty to the crime of manslaughter . . . and in return, they'll ask the judge for a sentence of no more than fifteen years. The judge can certainly sentence you to *less* than that after the presentence report, which will look into your background and the circumstances of the case and—"

"I might have to spend fifteen years in jail?" Asher interrupts.

"Well—"

"I might have to spend fifteen years in jail for *just finding her?*"

Jordan does not break eye contact with Asher. "I know this isn't what you were hoping for—"

"You cannot possibly be recommending this, Jordan," I say, finally finding my voice.

He does not even acknowledge me. "It is my job to tell you what the prosecutor is offering, and it is a limited offer. A trial is a crap-shoot. You don't know what you're going to get when you try a case in front of twelve strangers. The State's theory of the case is that you had a fight with Lily, it got physical, and she ended up dead at the bottom of the stairs as a result of you knocking her around." I flinch at the words. "We don't know the backstories of any of the members of the jury. For all we know, they've all been victims of abuse. Or they may have other biases against you. Getting them all to agree on something—like your innocence—is difficult. This, at least, is defi-nite." Jordan clears his throat. "Sometimes when the judge is aware a plea deal has been offered and a defendant doesn't take it and a trial occurs, the judge moves to the maximum sentence if the defendant is found guilty."

"Well, isn't that life without parole anyway?" I counter. "What more could the judge possibly do to him?"

Jordan ignores me, looking directly at Asher. "I can't tell you to take the AAG's offer, but I *can* suggest you sleep on it. We have ten days to respond."

After that, there's really nothing left to say. Asher is taken back to his cell. Jordan and I leave the jail.

I do not speak to my brother on the drive home, or for the rest of that day.

WHAT I REMEMBER about the night Asher was born was how Braden pulled into the fire lane outside of the emergency depart-ment, leaving the car there with the keys in it as he carried me inside. I remember my belly, tight as a drum; and the unbearable pain in my shoulder from where it was dislocated. I remember bargaining with a God I did not believe in: *If my baby is okay, then you can let him hurt me forever.*

Braden didn't leave my side. He held my free hand as my shoulder was popped back into its socket; he brushed my hair off my face when the contractions came. I remember him demanding ice chips, Demerol, attention. Nurses and residents would jump at his command. *Yes, Dr. Fields. Anything you need, Dr. Fields.*

When the baby's heartbeat dropped precipitously and I was rushed to the OR for a C-section, I thought that I was being lied to. I was certain that I was bleeding internally; that I was dying. *Save my baby*, I thought, even as Braden insisted on paging the *head of OB/ GYN* instead of one of those *butcher OB residents*, who *didn't do real surgical training like I did.*

I was caught in an in-between world. I wasn't a mother, but I wasn't not one. I wasn't a patient, I was a doctor's wife. I was in the hospital to have a baby, but I was also there to take care of my own injuries.

When Braden slowly migrated below the drape to observe the surgery, the timbre of the room changed—everyone a little sharper, a little more precise and focused, now that a brilliant cardiothoracic surgeon was holding them accountable for his wife and child.

Not a single person would ever have guessed that the reason we were in this OR, a full month before my due date, was that he'd shoved me down the stairs.

NO GOOD NEWS comes after midnight. The last time I was dragged out of bed in the middle of the night, it was because of Asher's arrest. This time, it is my phone, jarring me out of the soft sponge of sleep. I fight my way to consciousness, still groggy when I answer. But when the rushed voice on the other end starts to speak, I have never been more alert.

In Asher's bedroom, Jordan and Selena are tangled in a quilt. Jordan leaps up as the door flies open. "It's Asher," I blurt out. "He tried to kill himself."

By the time Jordan and I reach the jail, it is after 1:00 A.M. We've spoken with the sheriff, and I've tucked away the few details he has given us. Asher broke apart a safety razor. His cellmate saved his life by calling for a CO when he saw the blood dripping from the top bunk. He's been to the infirmary and bandaged up. He will be put on suicide watch in an individual cell—with frequent bed checks and no sharp objects allowed.

I refuse to leave until I can see him myself. Now, as we wait for Asher to be brought to us, Jordan and I sit on opposite sides of the table in the attorney-client conference room. Adversaries.

"Liv," Jordan says gently.

"Don't," I bite out. "Don't you say a goddamn thing, Jordan. This is your fault."

"*My* fault?"

"Yes. You kept drilling at him and drilling at him like you didn't even believe in him. His own lawyer! And then to offer him fifteen years in a plea deal—"

"Technically the prosecutor offered the plea deal."

"Shut up," I hiss. "Stop being a goddamn lawyer and just be his goddamn *family*."

Before he can respond, the door opens, and Asher is led inside.

My eyes fall to the tight white bandage on his wrist, and the two thinner, red hesitation marks above it. An involuntary moan bubbles out of me and I throw myself at my son, wrapping him in my arms as he clings to me. I see, through the window in the door, a correctional officer watching us. *Do it*, I think fiercely, meeting his eye. *Dare to ask me to let go.*

He turns away discreetly.

"Asher." I draw back, settling my palms on his cheeks. I don't even know what to say. I can't ask him why; I know. I can't tell him things will get better; they may not. I can't do anything but grieve with him for what he's already lost, and will never get back.

I settle for the truth that vibrates inside me like a tuning fork. "You are the thing that matters most to me in this world," I whisper.

His face is streaked with tears, his eyes red and raw. Although he is in a clean jumpsuit, pink stains remain on his neck and his arm where the blood was wiped away, like ghosts still haunting the scene of a tragedy.

For a moment, I let myself feel the full fury of how horrible the past three months have been . . . and the new knowledge that they could have been even worse, had Asher succeeded. Even if every jar of my honey was smashed; even if I had to leave town because of the rumors; even if I lose every cent appealing Asher's conviction—it would still be better than moving like a wraith in a world without him in it.

If your only child dies, are you even still a mother?

As if she is standing before me, I imagine Ava Campanello at her daughter's funeral.

I must make a sound, because suddenly Asher is the one trying to comfort *me*. "I'm sorry, Mom," he muffles against my neck.

"No, Asher, *I'm* sorry."

"Let's both be sorry," he says, and to my surprise, a laugh hiccups out of me, and then out of him. It feels so terribly wrong, like a sunflower growing from scorched earth.

He sinks away from me, exhausting himself into one of the chairs. I sit beside him, still holding his hand. I need that contact, skin to skin. I need to know I can feel his pulse against mine.

Asher scrubs his bandaged hand down his face. "I felt like I was suffocating," he confesses. "Like someone was holding a pillow over my face. I started thinking, why not just get it over with faster." He shrugs. "If fifteen years in prison is the best-case scenario, then I'd rather be dead. If that was the only choice I still had left, I figured I'd take it."

I hear a throat being cleared. Until this moment, I've completely forgotten Jordan is here. "I don't usually advocate for making mistakes," he says, coming closer. "But in this case, son, I'm really glad you messed up."

Asher raises his eyes, cold. "You're not my father."

"No. But I should have been a better father *figure*," Jordan admits. He looks from Asher to me. "Fuck the plea deal," he says.

. . .

THE NEXT MORNING, Selena is fighting off a cold. "I know this is far from the most pressing issue today," she says, "but do you have any DayQuil?"

I shake my head and hand her a jar of honey. "This is better," I say.

The medicinal power of honey is well documented—it's antibacterial, so has been used in treating wounds. In dressings, it helps clean pus or dead tissue, suppresses inflammation, and promotes new skin growth. A 2007 study at Penn State suggests that it is more effective than dextromethorphan in treating a cough. Irish labs have shown that it combats MRSA infections. Manuka honey kills the bacteria that cause ulcers and is used to preserve corneas for transplants.

Just about the only thing honey can't fix is the kind of sickness that gets into your head, robs you of hope, and lands you in the jail infirmary after you try to kill yourself.

Jordan bustles into the kitchen as Selena is swallowing a tablespoon of my honey. He is wearing a full suit, and I am taken aback until I remember that today is the dispositional conference. In New Hampshire, the parties in a lawsuit meet before the trial, in the hopes of having a meaningful discussion and resolving a case. The judge leads it, and nothing said there is admissible in court. "I'm going to refuse the plea deal and we'll set a trial date. I also want the judge to seal my motion to suppress Lily's unsent text and have the hearing in a closed courtroom. I already texted the prosecutor and gave her a heads-up. If there's a trial, we want it at the Superior Court in Lancaster and not farther away, and if there's any mention of this in the media, it taints the potential jury. If neighbors down the street read that there was an unsent text that said something important, they'll remember it. If the judge doesn't allow that into evidence, then the potential jurors would never have heard about it." He peels a banana and crams it into his mouth, speaking around the bite. "Gina and the judge have one goal in common with us—we want a fair and impartial trial without having to change the venue because we can't find jurors who are fair and impartial."

Selena swallows another spoonful of honey. "Gina's going to agree, because it's in her best interests to have the trial happen in Coös County. It's going to blow up her career as an AAG."

As they trade information about the conference, I pour coffee into a travel mug and reach for my purse. I come around the butcher block island in the middle of the kitchen, and at the same time, both Jordan and Selena fall silent. I see them take in my pencil skirt and silk blouse, my blazer and heels. "Why do you look like a sexy librarian?" my brother asks.

"See you later," I say, completely ignoring the question as I turn and leave.

WHEN I GET to the parking garage for Mass General, I pull into a spot and sit in my car for fifteen minutes. My hands are shaking, and I cannot catch my breath. Even though I know I was the one to request this meeting, even though I know that I will be in a public setting, I still feel like a deer creeping into the lair of a tiger.

But this is not about me, not anymore.

I take a deep breath and get out of my car. My palms are wet and I dry them on the wool of my skirt—an outfit I pulled together from the back of my closet. I can't remember the last time I wore something like this; my usual uniform is a pair of jeans and a sweatshirt, and I am usually covered in honey and propolis. But I needed armor today, and as flimsy a layer as this is, at least it's something.

The office is on the third floor. There's a half-moon of a desk with three secretaries behind it, and several rows of serviceable chairs in the waiting area. I clear my throat and walk up to one of the women. "I'm Olivia McAfee," I say. "I'm here to see Dr. Fields."

The secretary scans her computer. "What time is your appointment?"

"It's a personal meeting, not a medical one," I say, babbling.

She looks at me, giving nothing away. "Why don't you take a seat?"

So I do. I leaf through a magazine so old that the model on the cover has shoulder pads in her dress. Twice, I find myself on the edge of my chair, poised to leave and pretend I never came. And twice, I remind myself that I have spent twelve years getting stronger. That to be afraid is to give Braden power over me.

Again.

A few minutes later, the secretary calls my name. I am led past examination rooms and a nurses' station. The secretary opens a wooden door with Braden's name on it. "Dr. Fields," she says, and she steps back so that I can enter.

The room has lush navy carpeting and a wall of mahogany book-shelves. A massive desk sits in front of a window that shows a crawl of traffic below. On its surface is a stack of file folders, coded with bright tabs.

Braden is sitting behind the desk, wearing a white doctor's coat. His black hair has a few streaks of silver in it, but that only highlights the planes and angles of his fallen-angel face. His eyes are a cold, glacial blue. He is smiling.

I am shaking so hard my knees knock together.

The door closes, and I feel the room pushing in on me. Even as my heart beats at the bottom of my throat, I try to tell myself that he will not touch me, not here, not when anyone can hear us or see me leave this space in a condition different than when I entered. I re-mind myself that in public, Braden was unfailingly perfect.

His eyes move from my face to my shoes, before coming back to meet my gaze. "Liv," he says, just like he used to, a purr in his throat, a syllable that sounded like *love*, which is all I ever wanted from him. "I've got to admit—your text was a surprise."

I had messaged him at 3:00 A.M., after I got home from the jail. I told him I needed to see him. I did not tell him why.

"Thank you for making time to see me," I manage, the words bal-anced like glasses on a tray. I glance at the chair opposite the desk. "Can I . . . ?"

"Of course, sit down." His mouth quirks up on one side, just like Asher's does. "But you don't have to be so formal. I mean . . . it's just me."

What he means is: *We used to sleep together. I used to be able to play your body like it was a symphony.*

What I hear is: *When you've slapped someone so hard you draw blood, why stand on ceremony?*

"You look great." Braden smiles wider. "Still beekeeping?"

I nod. "Still fixing hearts?"

Still breaking them?

We have, of course, communicated. Through lawyers, during and after the divorce. For all that my marriage was a mess, I have never faulted Braden for his responsibility to Asher. Every month his alimony check and child support are deposited into my bank account without fail. Sometimes, they are all that has kept us fed.

If anyone is at fault for being less than transparent, it's me.

On the window ledge behind him I see a photograph of a woman and twin boys. I knew that Braden had remarried; but seeing that feels like falling through a frozen pond—like I can't breathe, like the light on the other side of the ice is a whole different world.

I force my attention to Braden again. "I need your help," I say. Every syllable is a knife.

I start at the beginning, walking him from Asher's relationship with Lily to the day he found her unresponsive to the suicide attempt last night at the jail. While I talk, I clench my hands together in my lap. I explain everything as if it has happened to someone else, some other mother, some other boy. As if I've had the privilege to watch from a distance.

When, finally, my words run out, I glance up at him. His face is pale and a vein throbs at his temple.

"Braden?" I murmur.

"You didn't think," he says, dangerously soft, "that this was something I should have known about *four months* ago?"

I feel dizzy and nauseated. I *did* think about it. But I didn't want to hand Braden the reins again.

"What the *fuck,* Liv?"

On the guttural punch of the curse word, I can't help it. I flinch.

Braden and I both go absolutely still. "Olivia," he whispers, breaking.

"I am sorry," I say. "You're his father. I should have told you."

How easy it is to fall into the habit again.

"*He* should have told me," Braden mutters, picking up the phone
on his desk. "I need to get him a better lawyer."

"He's got a good lawyer," I interrupt. "Jordan."

Braden puts the receiver back and raises an eyebrow. "They don't
let surgeons operate on a family member," he says.

"But if they did," I counter, "you'd do everything you possibly
could to save him, wouldn't you?"

He concedes the point. "What do you need?" Braden asks.

I clear my throat. This is where I have to tell him I am a failure;
that—like he used to say—I couldn't afford my home/car/life without him. "His bail is a million dollars. I need a hundred thousand to
get him out. I tried to get a loan; I even tried to second-mortgage the
house. I was turned down by seven banks." I swallow hard. "I don't
want Asher to spend another night in jail."

In the few seconds that I sit with my head bowed, twelve years
unwind. I hold my breath, waiting. Knowing that every ask has a
cost. Hoping that this time when Braden looks at me, he won't see a
reflection of his own frustration. That this time, he'll just see . . . me.

I don't realize he's come around the desk until I feel the heat of
his hand on my shoulder. "Done," he says.

BY THE TIME I drive back to New Hampshire, the judge has agreed
to a closed courtroom to hear Jordan's motion to exclude, and she has
also agreed that the motion can be sealed. This is good news, but it
pales in comparison to the phone call I receive just as I cross the
limits of Adams. "Mom?" Asher's stunned voice says. "They said I . . .
I can leave."

Silently, I thank Braden for whatever he did to make bail so
quickly. I am at the jail fifteen minutes later. Asher steps outside,

looking dazed and wary. He is wearing the clothes that he came here in—sweatpants pants too warm for this April day. He holds a sheaf of papers. I fold him into my arms, too relieved to speak at first. "Let's get you home," I say, and I lead him to the truck.

But as soon as we step off the sidewalk into the parking lot, the sun strikes his face. He stops walking, tilts his face to the sky, and bursts into tears.

In the car, he worries the edge of the bandage at his wrist. "How did you do it?" he asks. "How did you get the money?"

"It's not important—"

"It is to me."

I glance at him. "Your father."

His eyes widen, and he looks out the window, watching the watercolor run of scenery. "Did he know?"

"He does now," I say.

"What did he say?"

I bite my lip, wondering why Asher is so concerned about the feelings of a man who has not been part of the last two-thirds of his life. "He said you shouldn't be in jail," I answer. To redirect the conversation, I nod at the papers on his lap. "What's all that?"

"Paperwork for my release," Asher says. "And a couple of letters from Maya."

"She wrote you? That's nice."

He shrugs. His face remains turned out the window. Without its blanket of snow, New Hampshire is reawakening. "It's green," he murmurs. "It wasn't green when I left."

When we enter the farmhouse, it is decorated. In the mudroom, Selena has strung a makeshift banner, letters sharpied on printer paper that spell out WELCOME HOME. She and Jordan are waiting just inside the door.

Selena smiles wide and holds out her arms for Asher to walk into. "Tall people unite," she says, the same refrain with which they've greeted each other since Asher was fifteen and hit the six-foot mark.

Asher pushes his mouth into a smile. "Hey, Aunt S."

She holds him by his shoulders, cataloging the length of him, including the bandage, which her gaze skips right over. "You look fine," she pronounces, and she smiles too hard.

Jordan claps Asher on the back, and he pivots immediately, his hands raised in protection.

Jordan's demeanor slips, but he tugs a friendly grin back into place. "Glad you're back," he says. "Did they give you the conditions of release?"

Asher hands the paperwork to Jordan, who reads it out loud. "Judge says you can't leave your property except for medical reasons or court appointments, no visitors . . . you can communicate verbally and electronically with your mother, me, and anyone else I approve."

"Whew," Selena says. "For a second, I thought I wouldn't make the cut." She laughs, and Jordan laughs, and Asher and I smile. But we're all working too hard to act normal, like we are struggling to stay upright in a wind tunnel while pretending it's a gentle breeze.

As we walk into the heart of the old Colonial, Selena tells me that she and Jordan have relocated from Asher's room to my mom's old room, and that there are fresh sheets on his bed. He turns, his face tight and drawn, as if he's expecting me to give him a direction. "Maybe you want to change in to fresh clothes?" I suggest.

He nods. "Yeah. A shower. That sounds good."

We watch him climb the stairs and when the water in the bathroom starts running, all three of us exhale heavily. *Why isn't he happy to be home?* I wonder, and it isn't until Jordan answers that I realize I've spoken aloud.

"The people I've known who've been in jail only want to get out. But when they do, they're shell-shocked. Being incarcerated, you feel like time's standing still. On the outside, you realize that the whole world moved forward without you." Jordan puts his arm around my shoulder. "Give him a little while, Liv. He'll come back to us."

I don't know what I expected, actually. That Asher would not want to let me out of his sight; that he'd have a thousand questions about the months he had missed; that we would sit at the kitchen table and play Scrabble or look at old photos? The truth is that even before he was arrested, Asher was a teenager. He spent most of his time in his room, on his phone or his computer, or with Lily. The Venn diagram of our relationship intersected at meals and was limited to a brief recounting of how his calculus teacher was pulled over for a DUI during the weekend or whether Carniolan bees are hardy enough to make it through a New England winter. Having Asher out on bail would not roll the calendar back to the time when he was a little boy.

Selena and Jordan pretend they have something pressing to do, but I know they are giving me privacy while I help Asher settle in. After the water stops running through the pipes, after a full hour has passed with no sign of Asher, I go upstairs and knock on his bedroom door.

He is sitting on his bed, his hair damp and tousled. He's wearing jeans and a yellow T-shirt and he is trying, unsuccessfully, to tie a new bandage around his wrist.

"Let me help," I offer, sitting next to him. Our shoulders bump as I unwrap the gauze to start fresh, and the wound from his suicide attempt is fully visible. It's angry and red, clenched with stitches. Quickly, I cover it with clean gauze and secure it with a layer of adhesive bandage tape. "All set," I tell him, but I don't let go of his hand.

I realize that he is not looking down at his wrist, like I am. He's staring at the drawing he did of Lily when he was in jail, now in a frame on his nightstand.

"Oh," I say. "I hope it was okay to put it there."

"It's nice," Asher murmurs. "It's been almost four months, you know, and I still can't really believe she won't ever walk through that door."

I feel my throat tightening, and I don't want a day that should be a celebration to lose its joy. So I squeeze his hand and say, "You must be starving. What do you want for dinner? Sky's the limit."

Asher looks up at me, his brows drawing together.

"Filet mignon . . . chicken and dumplings . . . lasagna . . . we could barbecue . . . ribs, burgers . . . or maybe you want vegetables? A stir-fry? Or both." I laugh. "Or all. You pick."

I realize too late that with every option I've offered Asher, he seems more and more stricken.

"I ... um ..." Asher shakes his head, and heat rushes to his cheeks.

I realize when it's been months since you have had a choice, you forget how to make one.

"How about I make one of your favorites?" I gently suggest, and Asher nods quickly.

In the end, I cook steaks on the grill, with a tossed salad and honeyed carrots—fresh, simple food I imagine doesn't exist in jail. I fry bacon and cut up chives and set out bowls of sour cream and shredded cheddar, making a baked potato bar. When Asher was little, that was his favorite meal, and maybe going back to simpler times will make him feel more at home.

But Asher doesn't come down to dinner. When I go upstairs to tell him it's ready, he is fast asleep, and I do not have the heart to wake him. The portrait he drew of Lily, I realize, isn't on the nightstand anymore but next to him, on the bed. I turn off the light and close his bedroom door gently behind me.

Jordan assures me that there's nothing physically wrong with Asher. "The kid probably hasn't had a decent night's sleep in months," he says. "You know it never gets completely dark in jail, at night." He distracts me from worrying about Asher by telling me that the hearing for the pretrial motion has been scheduled for tomorrow in superior court.

"Do you think you'll win?" I ask.

"Well," Jordan says, glancing at Selena. "You'll get to see, firsthand. Asher has to be there, Liv."

"I don't think he's ready for that," I say. "My God, Jordan, he tried to *kill* himself."

"I know," Jordan says. "And I want the judge to see that bandage." He looks at me across the table. "You'll sit behind him, the whole time. You're his emotional-support person. No one's going to argue against that." He softens his gaze. "He doesn't have to say a word. He just has to be present."

Eventually, I agree, and I leave Jordan and Selena to do the dishes while I go upstairs to check on my son.

Asher is still asleep. But the door of his bedroom is now open, and the light in the hallway has been turned on.

BECAUSE IT IS a closed courtroom, there are only a handful of people present: me, Asher, and Jordan; Judge Byers; the prosecutor, Gina Jewett; a court clerk; and a bailiff. Asher is wearing the same suit he wore to Lily's funeral. Before we entered, Jordan adjusted his cuffs—making sure Asher's bandage peeked out from the edge of his jacket.

Judge Byers is an imposing woman with ombré locs and finger-nails that each end in a sharp bedazzled point. She focuses a laser gaze on Jordan as soon as the hearing is called to order. "Mr. McAfee," she drawls. "What a coup to have you in front of my bench. I'm a little surprised that you wanted this motion to be in a closed court-room instead of chasing the publicity that came after Peter Hough-ton's trial."

There's no mistaking her sarcasm, but Jordan flashes her a daz-zling smile. "So glad you're a fan, Your Honor," he says.

She snorts. "Well, welcome to Lancaster, or as I like to call it, *not Portsmouth*. Let the record reflect that the State is being represented by Gina Jewett, and the defendant, Asher Fields, is here with his at-torney, Jordan McAfee. We are holding this hearing in a closed courtroom because of the inordinate media interest in this case." As the stenographer tries to keep up, the judge's gaze falls on Asher's wrist. "The defendant has his mother here for support. Mr. McAfee, this is your motion to suppress, so please proceed."

Jordan rises. "Your Honor, pursuant to the State's discovery rules, we have viewed all the evidence that currently exists in the AAG's file in this case. As part of this evidence, there were texts sent back and forth between the victim and my client, who were involved in a relationship. Naturally, there were many text messages exchanged;

however, what we are moving to suppress is merely one text message that remained on the victim's phone unsent, which was thus never received by my client."

It strikes me that I have never seen my brother in his natural element. He speaks so fluidly that it's mesmerizing. It's like seeing a tiger—already impressive even seen at a zoo—transform into a wild predator when it is released into the jungle.

"The State's theory of the case," he continues, "is that this was a volatile relationship, there was a physical altercation, and the victim is now dead. They are suggesting my client caused that death. Part of what they'll attempt to prove is that my client was enraged by the victim's breaking off the relationship, as evidenced by the text typed on her phone. But this text was never received by my client, and thus has no value whatsoever as evidence of his alleged rage . . . or any other emotion. You can't get upset about something you have never seen or heard about. In fact, for all we know, it might not even be relevant to the *victim's* state of mind. She never sent it . . . and we don't even really have proof that she herself *typed* it."

Jordan sits down beside Asher, and the judge turns to the prosecutor. "Ms. Jewett?"

"Your Honor, this may indeed be the only time I agree with Mr. McAfee, but he is spot-on in our theory of the case. Statements made by the victim, whether in person or by text or over the phone, influenced the defendant's state of mind and his actions and also reflected the victim's fear and her desire to distance herself from the defendant. Therefore *all* of the texts—just like all the actions and communications in a relationship—need to be admitted. In particular, Your Honor, the final text response to this string of texts sent on the day of Lily's death is a crucial one. The defendant sent a message, all caps, saying *THIS ENDS NOW, I'M COMING OVER*. Lily's typed response was *Don't bother, it's over*. The text was typed midargument with the defendant; there is no evidence of anyone else being present; it is on the victim's phone. In order to weigh the importance of certain facts, the jury needs all the circumstances surrounding the argument before, during, and after. This text is the very meat of the evidence that occurred *during* that fight." She looks at Asher coolly. "Thank you, Your Honor."

The judge gets up from the bench and starts walking. Not far—just behind her desk—pacing back and forth. I am pretty sure she's taken off her shoes.

Jordan leans toward the prosecutor. "What's she doing?" he whispers.

"She's a former courtroom attorney. Says she thinks better on her feet," Gina Jewett says under her breath. "Just go with it."

"Ms. Jewett," the judge says, pausing with a hand on the back of her plush black chair. "Does the State have evidence that the text in question was sent from the victim's phone?"

"We know it was typed on her phone, Your Honor. We do not know if it was sent."

"The police and the prosecutor's office have Mr. Fields's phone, isn't that correct?" Judge Byers asks.

"Yes, Your Honor."

"Is there any evidence that on Mr. Fields's phone the text *Don't bother, it's over* was received?"

The prosecutor clears her throat. "Not as of yet, Your Honor."

"Not in four months?" the judge clarifies.

Jordan huffs a laugh. "Cellphone service here is bad," he says, "but it's not *that* bad."

Judge Byers cuts a glance in his direction and he stops chuckling.

She slips back into her chair and looks down at the motion in front of her. "Fiske," she says, and the bailiff blinks at her.

"Your Honor?"

"Why didn't you bring me a maple creamee?" she asks.

The bailiff frowns, baffled. "Ma'am?" he says.

"I have been deeply craving a maple creamee from Tuckerman's Dairy Barn all morning. I woke up thinking of that maple creamee; I ate my egg whites wishing they were a maple creamee; one might even go so far as to say that visions of maple creamees will dance behind my closed lids when I go to sleep tonight. So, Fiske, I ask again, why didn't you bring me a maple creamee?"

"I . . . didn't know you wanted one?" he says, unsure. "I can get you one now . . . ?"

"That won't be necessary," Judge Byers says. She turns to Gina Jewett. "I may deeply covet a maple creamee at this moment. I might even be willing to trade my firstborn for one. But as long as this communication remains in my head, uncommunicated, there is no logical punitive measure I can take for Fiske not having acted upon an unexpressed wish, unless he is gifted with ESP, and if he were, he would have had the good sense to call in sick today. This court is being asked to rule on admissibility of one final text found on the victim's phone. But there is no evidence who typed it into the phone, no evidence that it was ever sent from the victim's phone . . . and there *is* evidence that it was never received by the defendant's phone. Thus even in consideration of the prosecution's theory of the case, there is no reason to think that this particular text sheds any light on the circumstances surrounding the relationship of these parties, or what happened to the victim. The court finds that it would be more prejudicial than it would be probative of any issues of the case." She tips her head, acknowledging Jordan. "The motion to suppress is granted."

The surge of winning, of something finally going *right*, floods through my limbs. I find myself on my feet, hugging Jordan from behind. As the hearing is adjourned, he untangles my arms from his neck, and I see he isn't nearly as jubilant as I am. "What's wrong?" I ask. "Isn't this good news?"

"Liv," Jordan says, "we just got through the gate, but we still have the marathon to run." He offers a tiny, grudging smile. "Pace yourself."

WHEN I WAKE up in the middle of the night, I slip out of bed and cross the hall to peek in on Asher. It's not that I am expecting him to have nightmares, but I also cannot get over the simple ease with which I can check. It's why, as Jordan and I drove him home from the superior court, I kept glancing in the rearview mirror to spy on Asher in the backseat. It's why, when he sequestered himself in his bedroom, I found multiple reasons to knock on his door and ask him a needless question: *Have you seen my phone charger? I'm doing laundry, do you need anything washed? What are you reading?*

Without his phone or his laptop, there is little for Asher to do— so mostly, he's stayed in bed with a book. He can't even borrow my computer, because it's against the rules of his release from jail. I don't think this is a bad thing, actually. I'd rather he not read what has been said about him online.

The hall light is on again. I tiptoe, so that I don't disturb Asher's sleep, and peer around the edge of his open door. His bed is empty.

The bathroom is unoccupied, and I find myself flying down the stairs with my heart pounding, wondering where he could be. I think about his bandaged wrist, the pond in the apple orchard, the shotgun we keep in a safe downstairs in case we need to scare off bears or fisher cats.

I tear the front door open so hard it explodes against its hinges, smacking into the outer wall of the house, and I see him.

A pale white T-shirt that glows beneath the moon, like he's already a ghost.

He's sitting on the porch, looking toward the strawberry fields, his back to me.

"Mom," he says, without turning. "Sorry I woke you."

I walk toward him, shivering in the cool night air. "How did you know it was me?"

"You smell like honey," Asher says. "You always have. Once, in jail, we got packets of really shitty honey with our toast for breakfast, and I almost jumped out of my skin because I was so sure you were there."

I sit down cross-legged beside him. "Bad dream?" I ask.

Asher's mouth twists. "I don't dream anymore," he says.

"Then what woke you up?"

"The quiet," he says ruefully. "In jail, someone is always yelling. There's instructions being called over the loudspeaker. And it's either way too hot or freezing cold, and you don't get to adjust it." He shrugs. "I don't know why I came out here. I guess because I *could*."

I look up at the night sky. "Do you remember how you used to think that you could make stars? You'd come out here with a flashlight and turn it on and off and tell me you couldn't go to bed until more of them floated into the sky."

"Yeah," Asher says. "Then again, I also thought that after the dinosaurs died out, grass grew over them to make hills." He stares out at the hives we can't see in the dark. "The fields are so much bigger than I remember. It's weird, what happens to memories, when they're all you have."

I hold my breath, hoping he'll say more.

"When I first got to jail, I'd wake up and think I was having a nightmare," Asher confesses. "But it was real, and I'd get so fucking sad. Now, when I wake up in the middle of the night, I'm home in my own bed . . . but I'm still so sad I can't breathe."

His bandage gleams in the dark. "Why, Asher?" I whisper. "You're back."

For the first time since I've come outside, he looks at me. "For how long?" he says.

LILY ◆ 4

Four weeks before

"Lily?" says Maya. "Are we going to do this or not?"

We're in the basketball court at Adams High, which is where the fencing team practices. Everyone else is already back in the locker room except us, and to be honest I'd be happier if this day was over.

It has been a week since Asher walked out on me, a week since we've communicated, a week since the trapdoor opened up beneath me and I fell into the void.

But I agreed to stay late because Maya wants to know how to do a flèche attack. So here we are, with me giving fencing pointers, when what I'd really rather be doing is lying in my bed at home eating a whole sleeve of Oreos and crying.

"Sure," I say. "*En garde.*"

She points her sword at me, and I point mine at her, and I raise my other hand in the air. "Okay, step one," I say. "You extend your sword arm forward. That's the easy part. But don't square your shoulders." I pounce in slow motion toward her, and let her sword hit my shoulder. "See?" I take a few steps back, and then drop my left shoulder back. "If you do it like this, you're coming at your opponent obliquely, right? So there's less of you to hit."

I can't see Maya's face behind her mask, but she nods.

"Step two, keep your body low. The whole point of the flèche is the sudden surprise of it—I mean, it's meant to scare people. It's like you're charging against all these assholes, and you just want to stab them. You're suddenly changing the rules, like, all at once everybody who thought you were someone they could just ignore, now they have to take notice, cause you're showing them you *matter*."

"Um. Lily?" says Maya, the point of her sword slowly dropping toward the floor.

"And as you make the flèche, you yell at them like a *banshee*." I pull my shoulder back, lean forward on my right knee, and then charge toward my friend with my sword drawn.

"AAAAAUUUUGHHHHHH!"

I crash into Maya and she falls backward, and I fall down on top of her. I'm still screaming.

"Jesus," says Maya. "Hey." She pulls her mask off. I pull mine off. I cover my face with my hands. Tears seep into my white gloves. I just sit there going to pieces while Maya sits with me.

"Lily," she says. "What the fuck is going on?"

"Nothing," I say, but it's clear that whatever is going on is the opposite of nothing.

IF YOU ASKED ME, I'd tell you I'm a fundamentally happy person, someone whose heart is capable of big leaps in the air. Which is a weird thing to say, actually, considering how much of my life I've spent depressed.

It's not just that so many shitty things have happened to me, it's that for the longest time I didn't know how to make my life better.

Finally, as if I were someone discovering a secret door in a secret garden, the future revealed itself to me. But now that I'm here, I still feel the weight of the past. Sometimes it's like my legs have been bound with anchor chains, and I've been thrown off a ship into the cruel ocean, and all I can do is sink.

I guess there are different kinds of depression. There's the kind that just crushes you for no reason, what Mom calls the *clinical* kind.

But this isn't that. This is the other kind, the kind that comes because the things that have happened to you are actually just unbelievably, heartbreakingly sad.

WE'RE STILL LYING on the floor of the gym. "I'm sorry," I say. I don't even want to think about what I look like right now. This is an ugly cry, with snot coming out of my nose and my face red and wet. "What am I going to do?"

"I'm guessing we aren't talking about fencing anymore." Maya looks at me carefully. "You can tell me, you know. If you want."

I nod my head yes. But I can't. Because really, I'm going to go through this twice?

There's a strange calm about Maya. She's what my mother would call an *old soul*. I wonder if growing up as an Asian girl, the daughter of two mothers, in this very white, very straight world of Adams is what's given her a kind of resilience, a kind of wisdom.

"First off, this is about Asher?"

She looks up at the scoreboard over on the wall behind the bleachers. PRESIDENTS 0 VISITORS 0.

Nobody's winning.

"Did you break up?" Maya asks.

"I don't know," I admit, and it comes out in a rush. "We haven't talked for a week! He told me he—needed some time. Things got really—intense."

"Intense," says Maya. "You didn't—? Did you tell him—you *love* him?"

"I told him that weeks ago," I said.

"Really?" says Maya. "And he didn't freak out then?" I shake my head. "Because that's usually been it for Asher. Whenever anyone's told him they love him in the past, he breaks up with them, because he just—"

"Because why?"

Maya looks thoughtful. "I don't know. Maybe it has something to do with his father? Like, he saw what happened to his parents, and he's afraid that something that seems perfect at first is going to turn into some kind of shitshow—?"

I wipe my eyes again. "I told him I loved him back in October. And he said he loved me. He's said it lots of times. It sounded like he meant it."

Maya's eyes grow wide. "He—said that?"

I nod.

"So—" Maya says. "What's going on?"

"He got weird," I say. "After we slept together."

I assumed Maya knew Asher and I had sex, even if I hadn't expressly told her. "This was back in October," she says, not asking me, but stating a fact. "That time you called me to come get you, and you were so upset."

"Yeah. In the tree house. In the woods behind his house."

"You said you didn't want to talk about it," Maya says. "So I didn't press you. But I was worried about you. I'm *still* worried about you."

I wipe my eyes again. "I'm sorry I haven't told you everything. But some of the stuff with Asher has been so private—I didn't want to share it. Even with you."

"It's okay," says Maya. "I get it." She looks thoughtful. "Only now—things are different?"

"I don't know," I tell her. "Maybe it's my fault. I mean, I wanted to sleep with him. It was great at the time. But afterwards—" I shrug. "I wondered if it had all gone too fast. And when I told him I wasn't sure about it—well, Asher didn't take it very well."

"No," Maya says. "He wouldn't."

I feel tears burning in my eyes, but I am determined not to let them fall. "We were so close," I tell her. "But now we might as well be on different planets."

Maya just nods, like she understands.

"Maybe I should just be grateful we had what we had," I say. "I mean, it wasn't like we were going to get married." But even as I say it, as stupid as this is, I have to admit I'd already thought about it, spending the rest of my life with Asher. All at once it had become impossible to imagine any world where we weren't together.

But now that's the world I'm living in.

"Do you think it's possible that the thing I said is true?" Maya asks me. "That it has something to do with his father?"

"Maybe," I say. "But it's more likely it has something to do with me."

"What?" says Maya. "What about you?"

It's insane that I don't have the words for it, that with all the things I know, I still can't explain myself.

She looks at me patiently, waiting for me to go on. What I *want* to do, actually, is pull up the cuff of my fencing jacket and show her the scars. It hurts so much not to be able to tell her the whole truth, the whole long story. But I'm not going there with Maya, not after what happened with Asher. So I just say, "Sometimes I get so sad, it's like, I can't even see. It's like I'm alone, in the dark."

"Lily," Maya says, and she puts her hand down on my wrist. She doesn't know it, but underneath my cuff, right where she's touching me, is the proof. "You're not the only person to be sad. Sometimes I think, if you're not really sad in this world, you're just not paying attention."

She means this nicely, but it's pissing me off, because she really has no idea what it was like. I remember that day. Mom was at work. I didn't write a note.

"Sometimes," I say, "I think Asher likes the bright side of me, you know, the part that knows the names of all the vice presidents and how to make jambalaya. But there are things about me that scare him."

The gym is getting quieter now, as people head for the buses, or out to cars to drive themselves back home.

"Oh, come on," Maya scoffs. "What about you could be scary?"

I open my mouth, but nothing comes out. I can't lose the both of them, not Maya *and* Asher. Which now I know is exactly what will happen if I say one more word.

People always talk about how their love for you is unconditional. Then you reveal your most private self to them, and you find out how many conditions there are in unconditional love.

"I—I—" But the tears just pour down.

"All right, that's it," says Maya. She stands up. "Come with me."

"What?" I say. I stand up, too. "Where are we going?"

"Trust me," she says. "There's something I need to show you."

A HALF HOUR LATER, we are driving through the Sandwich Range Wilderness in her mother's beat-up Range Rover. We are grinding up an access road along a rushing river called Birch Creek. This is not much of a road, more like a pair of tire tracks leading into the dark wilderness.

"So your mom's a park ranger?" says Maya.

I don't really feel like talking about it. "Forest ranger," I say.

"What's the difference?"

The Range Rover does a major bounce over a pothole in the trail. Maya downshifts. We keep ascending.

"Park rangers work for the Interior Department, in national parks. Forest rangers work for the Department of Agriculture, in national forests."

"It's the same job, though, right? Hold on—" We do another lurch as the car plows over a small boulder.

I sigh. "Park rangers are about conservation. Forest rangers are about resource management."

"Resource management. So, like, logging and stuff."

"Logging," I say. "Water quality. Wildlife."

"Wildlife? Like, mountain lions and bears and stuff?"

"Yup," I say. Why are we talking about this? Why does it matter? Why does *anything* matter?

Maya brings us to a stop. She pulls back the emergency brake. "Okay, we're here."

I look around us. I see deep woods: white pines and birch, a few maples now almost completely bare. Red leaves fading to brown lie on the ground. A path leads up a small hummock.

"Where's here?"

"You'll see," says Maya, and she jumps out of the Rover. I follow her, although without much enthusiasm. Maya can see I'm dragging my feet. "Come on," she says.

We climb the path, which rises sharply up an incline. I want to tell Maya that I just can't bother, I don't have the energy. But I keep climbing.

At the top of the hill is hurricane fencing, and a sign, DO NOT ENTER: PRIVATE PROPERTY. US FOREST SERVICE and next to this an emblem similar to the one I've seen so many times on the badge of my mother's uniform, the pine tree between the letters *U* and *S*. But at the bottom of this one is a banner containing capital letters: EN-FORCEMENT.

Next to the sign is a hole in the fencing, which Maya pops through. She looks back at me. "In we go," she says.

"Maya—" I hesitate. If we get busted for trespassing here, my mother and I are both going to be in serious trouble.

"There's nobody for miles." She reaches forward to help me through the hole in the fence. I know I'm doing the wrong thing here, but I do it anyway.

The path leads up to a clear, rocky space, and all around us are the peaks of the White Mountains, the Sandwich Range. We can see lakes and forest, the setting sun sinking over the peaks in the distance.

And right before us is an old fire tower, looking like something out of a horror movie. It has a square lookout up at the top, accessible by a series of metal staircases. There's a heavy metal chain across the bottom of the staircase, and another Forest Service sign: CLOSED. DANGER.

Maya steps over the chain, goes up half a dozen stairs and turns to make sure I'm following her. Which I'm not.

"It says *closed*," I say. "It says *danger*."

"It's fine," says Maya. "I've been here a hundred times. Trust me. It's worth it."

I'm pretty sure no scenic vista is going to be worth the risk of falling through these rusted stairs. But I'm too numb to object to anything. I feel like I'm a piece of driftwood, just floating along on the tide.

Maya goes up the metal steps. She's holding on to the handrail. So am I. I can feel my heart pounding as we go higher and higher. But then, finally, we arrive, and there it is: the great horizon and the vast wilderness and it is all more stunning than it has any right to be. The White Mountains are an ocean of blues and purples surrounding us. Golden sunlight shines down on the lakes and in the valleys between the peaks. There's a huge bird circling in the sky, and as I look closer, I see that it is a bald eagle. I've never seen one in the wild before.

The whole panorama makes me realize how small I am, in the grand scheme of things. How insignificant my problems are when you zoom out and out and out and see the whole of the world.

"Okay," I say to Maya. "I get it."

"No," she says. "You don't. Keep looking."

So I keep on trying to take in the mountains and the lakes and the light. It's so quiet up here. I watch the eagle circling around and around. I feel the wind.

"All right, so it's beautiful," I say, grudgingly. But what possible difference does the beauty of the world make to me?

Whatever is good about nature is something I can never be a part of. I'm tired of being forced to see how great the universe is, actually. It's never done me any favors.

"Lily," says Maya. "Stop looking into the distance. Focus on what's in front of you."

Of all the eye-rolling things Maya has said so far, this is the worst. But I look over her shoulder at the wall of this rusted old tower. In silver paint is a heart, with two names inside it: *Asher + Jeannie.*

But also: the heart has a big X over it, in red paint, and a more recent update: FUCK ASHER FIELDS FOREVER.

"Who's—*Jeannie*?" I ask Maya.

"She was two years ahead of us in school. She and Asher were a thing, sophomore year. Then he dumped her, and she thought her life was over. But she's fine now. Every now and then I hear from her. She's at Columbia. She's gonna be a doctor."

"And you're showing me this—why?"

"To prove that the world goes on without Asher fucking Fields!"

Will it? I wonder.

I run my finger under the ring of the friendship bracelets I wear as camouflage.

I'm not so sure I want it to.

"A year from now you're going to be at Oberlin," says Maya. "Or Berklee, or Wesleyan, or somewhere. I'm going to be at NYU. And Asher, and Adams, and all of this, is just going to be some hazy memory."

That eagle circles over our heads, and the cold wind blows in my face again. "I want that to be true," I say, quietly. "But all I do right now is hurt."

As I stand there looking at the Sandwich Range, Maya puts her hand on my back, and for a single moment I feel my spirits rise. A little.

"You won't always," says Maya.

I hold my arm out straight toward the setting sun, trying to summon my courage.

"Okay." I point an invisible sword at the universe. "*En garde,*" I say.

OLIVIA ⬡ 5

MAY 5–6, 2019

Five months after

May is prime time for bees and beekeepers. But starting tomorrow, I will be in court. Jordan has explained that there's no way to know how long the trial will take—it could be weeks. So on Sunday, I pay a visit to all my colonies to prepare them for my extended absence.

It takes all day, because some of my pollination contracts are an hour from my house. The last colonies I visit are strategically arranged to collect pollen from the fruit trees at an organic orchard. Worker bees run back and forth. Others are busy unloading pollen from the baskets on their legs and packing it into empty cups in the comb with their heads. More bees are building out the honeycomb from the wax foundation so the cups are deep enough to store honey; drones are lazing around. It's like the aerial view of a city, with all the denizens deeply invested in their individual jobs and errands and families, unaware that there's a whole cosmos beyond.

I add an empty super to the top of a hive, so they have space for more honey.

Nectar is produced in waves. Spring wildflowers, the first stop on the supply chain, are replaced by honeysuckle and clover, then apple and pear and peach trees, and—after a July dry spell—finally goldenrod and asters. It takes a dozen bees to gather enough nectar to make a teaspoon of honey, each of them alighting on roughly 2,600 flowers and flying 850 miles back and forth. A worker bee weighs little more than a breath—around 100 milligrams—but she can carry half her body weight in nectar.

One of the bees starts moving in a figure eight, a crazy little rumba meant to tell the others where her food source is. Using the sun as a compass, her moves are a code: the direction of the dance is the route toward the food; the length of the dance is a measure of total distance. Several other bees watch, too, and then fly away, armed with GPS choreography.

This waggle dance is also used when a colony swarms. Some foragers will come back and waggle-dance to describe a new location they've found. The jazziest dances get the biggest response. If more bees are impressed, they join in the waggling. There may be several factions competing in this dance-off, each advocating for a different home, but once one of those groups has convinced about fifteen bees, democracy wins.

People think of a beehive as a monarchy because there is a queen, but in reality, a colony has a hive mind—knowledge is shared, opinions are offered, decisions are made collectively.

I can only hope Asher's jury is as enlightened.

THE MORNING ASHER'S trial begins, his last stitch dissolves. While we eat breakfast in nervous silence, I notice the two matched rows of divots in the unbandaged skin of his wrist. Running down the center is a thin red line. But by the time Asher changes into his too-small shirt and suit, he has covered up the scar with a watch that used to belong to my father.

It makes me think of how Lily always had scrunchies on her wrist, or a collection of woven bracelets. I wonder if Asher's trying to hide his suicide attempt, too.

Or maybe the reason they covered their scars has nothing do with other people's impressions, and everything to do with their own. Maybe Asher can't bear to spend the day looking down at a memory of a moment of weakness.

I used to have sartorial armor, too. Long sleeves in the summer, brimmed hats that hid a bruise on the cheek, high-waisted jeans that covered the purple shadow of a kick to the lower back.

Selena is back in Portsmouth with Sam, so it is just Jordan, Asher, and me driving to the superior courthouse. Jordan keeps giving Asher reminders: *Don't talk, unless you're explicitly asked to. That doesn't just mean in the courtroom, it means outside it, too. Remember, the whole point of a trial is that it's an adversarial process. We're supposed to attack each other, in the hopes that the truth is the only thing left standing after the carnage. I'm going to do the best I can, but there are going to be moments where the best looks like we're losing.*

"Jesus, Jordan," I say, only partly joking. "He'll never get out of the car."

Asher's face is pressed to the rear window. "Actually, that sounds like a solid plan."

I look outside and see news trucks from as far away as Connecticut and New York. A row of reporters is lined up outside the courthouse, with a second row of camera people filming them, a macabre version of an English country dance. When Asher gets out of the truck, someone calls his name and he makes the grave mistake of turning to the sound. Immediately, we are surrounded by media, shoving microphones in our faces and hurling questions like stones in a trebuchet.

"Asher! Over here! Did you do it?"

"Are you sorry?"

"Is the reason you tried to kill yourself because you know you're guilty?"

Asher freezes, trapped in the web of their words. I sidle closer to him as a digital recorder is waved under my chin. "Has your son showed previous signs of violence?" a woman asks.

"No comment," Jordan says, slipping between me and Asher, grabbing both our arms and pulling us firmly into the building.

The court staff takes us straight into the courtroom. Jordan escorts Asher past the bar to a table on the left. At the prosecutor's table, Gina Jewett is already arranging files and notes.

I sit behind Jordan so that I can see Asher's face in profile. "Remember," he murmurs to Asher, "they get to go first. Don't freak out, we're going to have our turn eventually. I'll be sitting here with a poker face. That doesn't mean I don't have questions or emotions inside. You should have the same poker face. If you have a question, or want me to ask a question, use this pad and pen. Do not frantically scribble all trial, though, because it will be distracting as fuck."

Then, to my surprise, he turns around and hands me a blank Moleskine notebook, like the ones he used to record all his notes in during our dozens of meetings with Asher in jail. "In case *you* think of something for me to ask," Jordan says.

I raise a brow, dubious, because Jordan knows my mind doesn't work with the same precision as his. "Be honest. This is just to keep me busy while the grown-ups are working, right?"

"You're going to get angry every time something about Asher is intimated that you disagree with. Every time Gina opens her mouth, for sure. Instead of letting it show on your face, open up this notebook and write something. Anything. Your grocery list. The lyrics to 'Bohemian Rhapsody.' Draw the prosecutor with a sword sticking into her chest. Or all of the above. Whatever calms you down. Because Asher's not the only one that the press will be looking at."

The bailiff, a round little barrel of a man, steps forward. "*Oye oye,* the Superior Court of the State of New Hampshire for Coös County is now in session; the Honorable Rhonda Byers presiding." The judge enters from her chambers, this time with her locs braided into a crown. I check; she is wearing shoes. She sits down at the bench, bangs her gavel, and opens the file.

"We are here today in the matter of the State versus Asher Fields." Turning to the bailiff, she adds, "We have a jury of twelve plus two alternates impaneled . . . can you have them seated?"

Jordan has warned me against this, but as they file in, I try to scrutinize their faces. They certainly do not look like a jury of Asher's peers—they are all at least twice his age. The lady who seems to be in her seventies, with the frizz of white hair and the embroidered sweater—she will be able to see the good in Asher, won't she? And the three middle-aged women—are they mothers? Will they believe what Jordan says, or will they only see Ava Campanello's grief? The man frowning, like he is too harried to waste time on a civic duty . . . will he vote to convict just to get back to his pressing business?

They settle into two rows of seats, blinking out from the nest of the jury box like hatchlings. The judge addresses them, thanking them for their service and explaining how the trial will proceed, and then turns to the prosecutor. "Ms. Jewett, is the State ready?"

"Yes, Your Honor," Gina says.

"Mr. McAfee? Is the defense prepared to proceed?"

"Yes, Judge."

She nods. "Ms. Jewett, you may make an opening statement."

I knew women like Gina Jewett. They were fellow residents, with Braden, back in the day. Their lives were finely tuned machines that balanced how to be the best mother, doctor, *and* partner simultaneously. They held their careers between their teeth like pit bulls guarding a bone, daring anyone who came near enough to challenge their commitment, ability, and sheer balls. They were so busy holding their shit together I think they lost sight of being themselves.

Gina is wearing a tailored blue suit that looks expensive, though I bet she got it at T.J.Maxx and had her aunt hem it. Her hair is a pair of knife edges framing both sides of her chin. She gets to her sensibly heeled feet and steps in front of the jury. "The defendant, Asher Fields, is charged with the murder of his girlfriend," she says bluntly. "The evidence will show that the defendant and Lily Campanello were students at Adams High School who met in September through a mutual friend, Maya Banerjee, and began a typical teen romance. Lily would go to the defendant's hockey games. He went to her orchestra concerts. They went out to dinner, saw movies, studied together. They also had disagreements that became arguments . . . but unlike typical teen romances, those arguments got increasingly violent."

She looks at each juror in turn. "You will hear evidence of how the defendant grabbed Lily in anger and yanked her hard enough for her to cry out. You'll see the bruises on Lily's arms, bruises her best friend noticed, and worried about."

My hands squeeze the notebook Jordan gave me so hard that my fingernails leave little moons on the soft cover.

This is a lie.

This is not Asher.

Asher, who as a little boy had whispered to whitecaps on the Connecticut River during a windy day—*It's okay. You just need to calm down*—because I told him the water looked rough.

"In fact, in the week leading up to Lily's murder, the defendant and Lily had had a heated fight to the point where they were not communicating. No talking, no texting, Lily even tried to keep the defendant away from her at school. He grew increasingly frustrated. He could not bear the thought of Lily cutting him off. And so the defendant texted her in a way that left no doubt as to his anger, and went to her house to teach her a lesson."

As she lists the evidence she is planning to produce, the buzzing in my ears grows so loud that I think I may pass out. I can hear the scratch of the reporters' pens behind me. By tomorrow, everyone who reads a paper or watches the news will assume Asher is the villain. I am guilty of this myself, every time I read a negative movie or book review and decide it's not worth the trouble of making up my own mind. People believe what they are told.

"Ladies and gentlemen," the prosecutor finishes, "this was a volatile relationship that ended with a beautiful teenage girl dead at the bottom of a flight of stairs. For the crime of first-degree murder to be proven, the defendant has to think about the act for only the briefest moment before he commits it. We will prove beyond a reasonable doubt that the defendant knew exactly what his endgame was when he insinuated himself into Lily's house. That the squeaky-clean teen he pretends to be is just that—a sham. Do not let Asher Fields fool you, as he fooled Lily Campanello. He is a violent abuser, a liar . . . and a murderer." She bares her teeth in a smile. "Thank you."

The jury is rapt, having listened to her like she is Moses coming down from the mountain with the tablets. I open up the notebook. I press so hard with the pen that I leave a blot four pages deep.

"Thank you, Ms. Jewett," the judge says. "Mr. McAfee?"

Jordan is a magnet, every pair of eyes on the jury drawn to him. As he stands, he doesn't rush to fill the silence, instead making them hungry for his words. He smiles at them like he is their next-door neighbor, their cool cousin, the candidate you want to have a beer with. "You know, ladies and gentlemen," he says, as if they are mid-conversation. "I've been married for about twenty years now. This morning, my wife nearly took my head off because I put too much detergent in the washing machine."

This is not true. Selena was a hundred miles away this morning, with their son.

"I mean, is there a wrong way to do the wash . . . if I'm doing it at all?" He grins, and so do the men on the jury. "The point is, there are times my wife and I have really nasty fights with each other . . . but you know what? We work through it. You can be in a long, committed, mature relationship and still occasionally get intensely angry with each other . . . yet it doesn't mean you get violent." He claps a hand on Asher's shoulder. "The evidence will show that Asher and Lily were dating. He supported her, she supported him. They had disagreements sometimes—as all couples do—but *he loved her.*"

He strolls toward the jury box. "At the beginning of the week, after a disagreement, Asher gave Lily her space. But he grew increasingly concerned when she wouldn't respond at all. He just wanted to make sure she was all right, and that she knew he was there for her if she needed it because—as I said, *he loved her.* When his friend Maya told him that Lily was sick, he was worried—because when someone *you love* is sick, you worry. So he went over to her house after school to check on her—and he got the shock of his life. The girl he loved was dead when he arrived."

He slips his hands into the pockets of his trousers. "Like every person in our country ever charged with a crime, Asher Fields is presumed innocent. The State must prove every element of the crime of murder in order for you to convict him. And that includes the looming question that the State cannot answer: what happened in Lily's house before Asher got there? It's not up to me, as Asher's lawyer, to produce any evidence to answer that question. It's up to the prosecution. But at the end of this trial, you'll all need to ask yourselves if you are convinced beyond a reasonable doubt that Asher Fields murdered Lily Campanello. You will *not* be." He lifts his palms. "So what does that leave us with? A dead girl, a grieving boyfriend, and an opportunity for all of you to keep a tragedy from becoming even more tragic."

THE FIRST WITNESS for the prosecution is Officer Owen Tubbs, the first responder to Lily's house that afternoon. He is florid and beefy, with a nose like a steamed bun. He is also wearing a full uniform, his badge and shoes shined to high gloss, knife pleats in his trousers. He is sworn in by the clerk, and after he has stated his name and job for the jury, the prosecutor begins her questioning. "What are your general duties as a patrol officer for the town of Adams?"

"I respond to calls from dispatch, I do routine patrols of the neighborhood, and I take complaints when I'm at the police station."

"On the afternoon of December seventh, were you working at the police department?"

"Yes."

"Did you respond to a call at Forty-five Greaves Lane?" Gina asks.

"Yes."

"What time was that call?"

"Four twenty-two P.M. It was a rescue call," Tubbs adds.

"Can you explain what that means?"

The policeman glances at the jury. "Every time someone needs an ambulance, a police officer is dispatched to the scene, too."

"When you arrived at the scene, what did you do?"

"I walked in," the officer says. "The door was open. Paramedics were working on a young woman in front of the couch. An older woman was crying hysterically, and Asher Fields was standing off to the side."

"Was anyone else there?"

"Just a dog," he replies.

"Did you identify the woman the paramedics were with?"

He nods. "It was the victim, Lily Campanello."

"What about the older woman?"

"That was her mother, Ava Campanello."

Gina turns toward him. "You mentioned a third person, Asher Fields. Is he here today?"

"Yes," the policeman says. He points directly at Asher.

"Let the record reflect that Officer Tubbs is identifying the defendant. Did you recognize him at the time?"

"Yes. I was a school resource officer at Adams High last year, and he was a student there."

"Did you have any interactions with Mr. Fields while you were the school resource officer?" the prosecutor asks.

"I was aware that he was suspended for his role in a cheating scandal—"

"Objection," Jordan calls. "Relevance?"

"Sustained," Judge Byers says. She turns to the jury. "The jury will disregard the witness's previous statement."

Gina asks, "Was Lily a student, too?"

"Not while I was working there."

"I see," she says. "What was the condition of the victim when you arrived?"

"Unresponsive. She was on a stretcher, in front of the couch. The paramedics were attempting to revive her."

"Can you tell us what she was wearing?"

"A T-shirt and leggings."

"Any shoes?" Gina says.

"No, she was barefoot."

"Did you notice any bleeding?"

"Yes," Tubbs says. "There was blood on her shirt, and in her hair."

"Did you notice any cuts, marks, or bruises?"

"The paramedics were bent over her, but I did see visible bruises on her face and neck."

The prosecutor approaches him. "Did you have any idea what had happened?"

"Not until I talked to her mother."

"What did Ava Campanello tell you?"

"She had left the house to get ibuprofen for her daughter, because Lily had a fever and had stayed home sick from school. While she was at the pharmacy, Asher Fields came to the house."

"Did you have occasion to speak to the defendant?" Gina asks.

"Yes. He said he had found the victim at the bottom of the stairs."

"What state was the defendant in?"

Tubbs glances at Asher. "He was very upset. He wanted to know if Lily was going to be all right."

"What did you do next?"

"This was a serious injury, a possible death," the officer says, "so we secured the scene like we normally would and waited for the detective to arrive. I told the defendant that the detective was going to need to speak to him and asked him to wait outside."

Gina turns, as if she is finished, but then pivots back just before she reaches the table. "Officer, did anyone else either enter or leave the house the whole time you were there?"

"The detective came. The paramedics and the victim and her mother left for the hospital." He hesitates. "But I guess it was too late."

The prosecutor sinks into her chair. "Nothing further."

On my lap is the Moleskine notebook, opened to a fresh page. I've written *OWEN TUBBS* at the top, and without realizing it, I have drawn a dark line through his name.

Do something that makes you calm, I think.

I start free-associating, writing what pops into my head: *pumpkin seeds, oats, raspberries.* When I glance up, Jordan is standing in front of Officer Tubbs. "Before that afternoon, you hadn't ever had any police contact with Asher, correct?"

"No."

"You were never called to his residence for public disturbance because the music was too loud . . . ?"

"No," the policeman says.

"Never issued him a speeding ticket?"

"No."

"You haven't so much as stopped him for not wearing his seatbelt, have you?"

"No, I have not."

"In fact," Jordan presses, "you've never been to his home at all, have you?"

Officer Tubbs darts a shy glance toward me. "Only to pick strawberries with my kid."

"So with the exception of the afternoon of December seventh, you had no other reason as a policeman to engage with Asher, isn't that true?"

"Well," Tubbs says, "except for when we arrested him."

Jordan's face shutters, and he sits down.

I look down at the notebook. *Almonds. Canola oil,* I add. *And of course, honey.*

TECHNICALLY, MIKE NEWCOMB took me to the junior prom, but we did not stay there. We were late because of the hubcap incident, and by the time we arrived everyone else had decided to drive down to the Seacoast region—where New Hampshire's eighteen miles of beach are located—to get wasted. Neither Mike nor I had a moral objection to that, but he didn't want to drive drunk (even then, he was a civil servant in training). So instead, we went to a fair held in the parking lot of a Walmart three towns over. In my taffeta gown we rode the Ferris wheel and the bumper cars and the Zipper until the pins fell out of my updo and my hair whipped around my face. When he dropped me off, he kissed me good night, and I thought, *I could like this boy.* Two days later I found out that he'd gotten back together with his long-term cheerleader girlfriend, the one he eventually married.

When the prosecution calls him as a witness, he is wearing a suit that fits him far better than the blue tuxedo did years ago. "Please state your name for the record," Gina says.

Jordan twists in his chair as Mike lists his credentials. "Newcomb? Didn't you go to the junior prom with him?" he whispers.

I nod.

"Jesus Christ. Does *anyone* leave this town?"

"On December seventh," the prosecutor asks, "were you on duty?"

"Yes."

"Did you have occasion to be called to the residence of Lily Campanello?"

"Yes," Mike says, "at about four forty-five P.M."

"What happened when you arrived?"

His eyes slant toward Asher. "I saw a kid sitting on the front steps."

"Did you know at the time who that kid was?"

"I did not."

"Do you now?"

"Yes," Mike answers. "Asher Fields."

"Is he in the courtroom today?"

"Yes. He's the defendant."

"What did you do when you arrived at the Campanello household?" Gina asks.

"I went in and met with Officer Tubbs, who brought me up to speed. I looked around the staircase where the victim had allegedly been found and the living room where she'd been moved."

Allegedly. The word sticks in my throat like a fish bone.

I open the notebook on my lap. *Granola,* I write, *made the night before.* My letters are as precise as an architect's.

"The house was neat, tidy, undisturbed," Mike says. "There was a small amount of blood at the base of the stairs, and more blood in front of the couch in the living room."

"Then what happened?" the prosecutor continues.

"I asked Officer Tubbs to secure the scene and to call the station for assistance with canvassing the neighborhood, to see if anyone had seen or heard something out of the ordinary. Meanwhile, I asked Mr. Fields to follow me to the station so that I could take a formal statement."

"Where was his car?"

"Parked in the driveway."

Gina folds her arms. "Can you describe his demeanor at the time?"

"His shirt was bloody, and he was visibly shaking. He appeared to be extremely upset. I suggested," he says, meeting my gaze for the first time since he began, "that he call his mother."

"Did he?"

"Yes. She arrived right away, and I let her sit in on the interview."

I watch the jury carefully as Mike walks through that first meeting—what Asher said. What he didn't.

"Was Mr. Fields a suspect at this point?" the prosecutor asks.

"No. This was a routine, basic investigation."

"And then?"

"I received word that Lily Campanello had been pronounced dead. Mr. Fields and his mother left the station, and I returned to the victim's house."

"What did you find?" Gina says.

"The house was a small Cape, two floors, with a center stairwell. As I said, there was a small amount of blood at the bottom of the stairs and more in front of the couch."

"Based on your experience, Detective, could a small amount of blood on the floor indicate that Lily hadn't been lying there very long?"

"Objection," Jordan calls out. "Leading."

"I'll rephrase," the prosecutor says. "Based on your experience, what is the significance of the smaller amount of blood at the bottom of the stairs, versus the larger amount near the couch?"

"That Lily's body was not at the bottom of the stairs very long; but she was near the couch for a greater amount of time."

"In that case," Gina asks, "would you put the defendant—who admitted to moving Lily—in the house at or near the time of her death?"

"Objection! Speculative!" Jordan says.

Judge Byers glances at the prosecutor. "Sustained."

I look at the jury. I wonder if they can unhear the implication.

"What did you do next?" the prosecutor asks.

"I walked around the first floor," Mike continues, "and then made my way upstairs. There was a master bedroom that was very tidy, and a teenage girl's bedroom . . . which was not."

"You mean it was messy?"

"No, this was different. A lamp had been knocked over and the bulb was broken, so there was glass all over the floor. A nightstand next to the bed was also overturned."

"Was there any blood in the room?" the prosecutor says.

"No."

"Based on your training and experience, what did you conclude?"

"These were signs of a struggle," Mike says. "I called our crime scene technician to photograph the residence and to collect evidence."

Gina lifts up an eight-by-ten photograph. "This is a photograph presented to us by the Adams PD crime scene technician. Does it accurately depict the bedroom?"

She presents several of these photos, which are entered into evidence. "At some point, did you call the defendant back to the police station to take a second statement?"

"Yes, after I got reports back from our forensics team analyzing the evidence in the house."

"Is that normal?"

He nods. "We do it all the time."

"What sort of evidence needed clarification from the defendant?"

"There were prints at the scene that did not match Lily Campanello or her mother. However, they did match Mr. Fields. The police department had those on file because he had worked at a hockey camp, and all the counselors were fingerprinted as a matter of child safety."

"Was there any other evidence that pointed to Mr. Fields?"

"Yes," Mike says. "We found hair in Lily's bedroom that matched DNA obtained with a warrant after his arrest. I asked if he had gone anywhere else in the house, and he said he had not."

"Not even upstairs?" Gina asks.

Mike looks at Asher. "He specifically said he had not been upstairs."

My face flushes hot. Jordan had said this would be an issue, and he was right. I take a deep breath and look down at the notebook. I write: *Bourbon.*

I could use some now.

"Was there subsequent evidence that led you to arrest Mr. Fields?"

"Yes," Mike says. "We had gotten back the phone records from both his phone and Lily's. He sent twenty-three text messages to her the day of her death."

"Detective," Gina asks, "did anything particular about these texts raise your suspicions?"

"The final one, sent by the defendant, at three-forty P.M."

The prosecutor turns and looks right at Asher. "What did it say?"

"It was all caps," Mike replies. "*THIS ENDS NOW, I'M COMING OVER.*"

She smiles. "Nothing further."

I look down at the list of items I've scrawled in the notebook. They are not random, I realize; they are the makings of cranachan, an old Scottish dessert that my mother would cook for us every New Year's Eve. As a child, I always felt so grown-up, being allowed to eat a dish steeped in alcohol. She'd adapted it to use granola instead of oats, bourbon instead of whiskey. While my father took Jordan out to set a brace of fireworks that we'd light at midnight, I stayed with my mother and made parfait cups. It was, and still is, a tradition for me and Asher. A comfort.

Suddenly I understand why *this* is what I've chosen to write.

When Jordan rises and steps away from Asher, it feels like a void in space, a black hole into which Asher might be sucked. I find myself leaning a little closer, as if I could keep him safe.

"Asher told you in his statement that the door was cracked open, didn't he?" Jordan begins.

The detective nods. "Yes."

"Did you bother to process the doorknob for fingerprints, or DNA?"

"No, we did not."

"Which in fact corroborates the statement that Asher gave you, doesn't it?"

"Not necessarily," Mike says. "Doorknobs are tough surfaces for prints. So many people use them during the course of a day that it's hard to get valid results."

"So because it's hard for you to get results, you didn't even try? Is that correct?"

Mike narrows his eyes. "We have historically found it to not be as practical a site for fingerprint testing compared to other spots at crime scenes, so we direct our resources elsewhere."

"But the fact remains that the doorknob wasn't analyzed for prints . . . so someone else could have shown up at the house before Asher arrived?"

"It's possible."

"Did you check to see who that might have been?" Jordan asks.

"Officer Tubbs canvassed the neighborhood, and no one had heard any disturbances. There was no one else of interest. Plus," Mike adds, "no one else's DNA or fingerprints were found in the bedroom."

"Isn't it true that you cannot tell when, exactly, a fingerprint or a piece of DNA evidence was left behind?"

"We do not have that technology, no," Mike replies.

"So Asher might have gone to his girlfriend's bedroom like any other normal teenage boy to hook up with her days or even weeks prior to that afternoon . . . and maybe left behind a hair or a fingerprint then?"

The detective shifts in his chair. "Yes."

"And he told you that he and Lily had been dating since September?"

"Yes."

"So these fingerprints and the DNA that you're building an entire case around in actuality might have been left behind at any time between September and December seventh . . . not as a result of a fight, but as a result of consensual lovemaking?"

"It's possible," Mike says.

Jordan lets this sit for a moment. "When you arrived at the scene, was Lily there?"

"No. She had already been taken to the hospital."

"At some point did you have the chance to examine her clothing?"

"Yes," Mike says.

"Were there any rips or tears?"

"There was *blood*," Mike says pointedly.

"Again, I ask you, Detective—in other cases with struggles and physical altercations, have you seen articles of clothing that are torn or ripped?"

"Yes."

"But again, that was *not* the case here, right?"

"That is correct."

"Excellent," Jordan says. "Let's talk about Asher's clothing. When you brought him to the station for his first interview, did you see any rips or tears in his clothing?"

"No," Mike answers drily. "Just his girlfriend's blood."

"As a detective, you've investigated other fights and disturbances, I assume?"

"I have."

"Isn't it true that people in fights and disturbances often have scratches or wounds consistent with a struggle?"

"Yes."

"Did you notice any scratches or wounds on Asher?" Jordan asks.

"No."

"Did Asher display *any* physical signs of being in a struggle?"

"No."

"You didn't even take the time to photograph his hands that day, did you?"

"No," Mike replies. "At the time, Mr. Fields was not a suspect."

"Ah, right!" A smile breaks across Jordan's face. "He only *became* one when you couldn't come up with anything else."

The prosecutor rises. "Objection!"

"Sustained," the judge orders.

Jordan turns and finds me, lifting his eyebrow the tiniest bit. "Nothing further," he says.

. . .

A YEAR AFTER my father died, when I was still taking care of his hives—a commuter beekeeper—I'd drive more than five hours in a single day so that I could be home when Braden got back from the hospital. But one Saturday each month, with Braden's blessing, I went to the Adams farmers' market to sell honey and beeswax products.

It was October, the best month for farmers' markets. Children ran in dizzy circles around the bluegrass musicians in the little gazebo, booths overflowed with bushel baskets of kale and Gem lettuce and squash, there were samplings of yogurt and locally roasted coffee and goat cheese with lavender. I stood behind my table under a portable white awning, doing a brisk business.

It felt like I had been selling nonstop, so when I realized that my line was down to one customer, I sighed with relief. The sun was in my eyes, and I didn't realize until the man spoke that he was wearing a police uniform, and that I knew him.

"Olivia," Mike said, grinning. "Wow, it's been a while. I didn't know you moved home."

He leaned forward, like he expected me to lean over the table and embrace him, but I didn't, so he covered his gaffe by picking up a jar of honey body butter.

"I haven't. I'm down in Boston. I just come up to help my mom with the hives."

He turned the jar in his hand. "I heard about your dad passing. I'm sorry."

"Me, too." I felt breathless, nervous. With the exception of my mother, who was still battling her own grief demons, I tended to distance myself from people who knew me before Braden. "You in the market for something in particular?"

Mike looked down as if he was surprised to find himself holding a jar. "I don't know," he said, laughing. "I'm not much of a tea drinker."

"I wouldn't suggest drinking that anyway," I offered. "It's body butter."

"With honey?"

"Yeah, it's an old recipe. *Really* old. An ancient Egyptian papyrus from 1550 B.C.E. said honey, alabaster, natron, and salt can beautify the body." I shrugged. "This is a modified version, but maybe Nadya would like it." I remembered his wife, a cheerleader, leaning over a mirror in the girls' bathroom with her Bonne Bell lip gloss.

"Ah," Mike said, flushing deeply. "Nadya. Yeah, she ran off with her personal trainer."

Without missing a beat I lifted a different jar. "The ancient Egyptians also mixed honey with crocodile shit to make a contraceptive paste," I said. "You could send her some with a good riddance note."

His eyes widened. "For real?"

"Yes, about the contraceptive paste," I replied. "But this? This is just lip balm."

He laughed out loud. "And you? You got married to a doctor, right?"

"Yup," I said, instinctively cupping a bandage on the back of my other hand. "Braden. It's great. *He's* great. We live outside Boston."

"So you said," Mike murmured, his eyes narrowing on the gauze. "What happened to you?"

"I burned myself rendering beeswax. You'd think I'd be better at it, after all this time."

It *was* a second-degree burn. But I'd gotten it when I forgot to put sugar in Braden's coffee, and he threw the mug at me.

My hands were suddenly shaky. "Anyway," I said. "It's nice to see you again."

It was, of course, an invitation for him to leave. Quickly.

I knew people saw what they wanted to see, and in my case, that was usually a surgeon's wife. Mike, though, expected me to be the Olivia he used to know, and I wasn't even sure if I remembered her anymore.

Mike picked up the jar of body butter. "Might as well try it. I'm not getting any younger." He reached into his wallet and pulled out a twenty. "Keep the change." His fingers brushed mine as I took the money. "You know," he said gently, "you always have options."

He disappeared into the busy center of the farmers' market. I opened my cashbox and unfolded the bill. In the center was a card for a battered women's shelter.

DURING A FIFTEEN-MINUTE recess, Jordan hustles us into a private conference room. Asher slumps into a chair and loosens his tie. "Are you all right?" I ask. I fight the urge to hold my hand to his forehead, the way I used to check him for a fever. He is not a little boy, and this is not a common cold.

"It's like being in a zoo," he says, and he looks at Jordan. "You didn't tell me that part."

"It gets worse," Jordan says flatly. "You're doing a good job, Asher. You're not letting anyone see you sweat."

Asher snorts at that, lifting the side of his suit jacket. "I'm drenched."

"*They* don't know that." Jordan pats his pocket, looking for his wallet. "I'm going to get a drink. You want anything?"

"Sure," I say.

The door opens into a slice of noise and bustle, and then Jordan is gone.

I sit down in the chair beside my son. "Hey," I say softly.

He flicks his eyes toward me. "Hey."

"Do you want to talk," I ask, "or do you just want to sit?"

I know how hard it must be for him to remain stoic in front of the jury, while he's dying inside. I know, because I am doing it myself.

"I tried to imagine the worst," Asher murmurs. "But I didn't even come close."

"I know—"

"The way they keep calling her a *victim*," he blurts, his face twisting.

My breath catches in my throat. Asher is not even hearing what they say about him. He's still thinking of Lily.

I reach for his hand and squeeze it. "Do you remember the first time you jumped off a diving board?"

He turns to me, his head tilted.

"We were at the Y in Framingham—the outdoor pool. You were four. You had a friend from school who just ran down the diving board, totally fearless, and you wanted to do it, too. But you froze on the end, and you were too afraid to go forward or to go backward, and other kids were yelling at you for holding up their turn and you started to cry."

"Listen, I get the metaphor, but I think being on trial for murder might be—"

"I swam into the deep end," I interrupt.

He rolls his eyes. "And you said you'd catch me?"

"No. I told you the *truth*. I couldn't catch you, because I couldn't stand in the deep end. If you jumped in, everything was going to go dark and weird for a second, and you might get water up your nose, and not know which way was up. But I would grab you if that happened."

"Did I jump?"

"No." I laugh. "You chickened out entirely. But the *next* time we came to the pool, you did."

He smiles wryly. "Is this where I'm supposed to tell you that everything's dark and weird in the courtroom?"

"I don't know, Asher, but I'm still going to tell you the truth. You're brave, and you're strong, and if you don't believe it today, maybe you'll believe it tomorrow."

Asher closes his eyes, but not before I see the tears beaded in the corners. "Thanks, Mom," he says softly.

Jordan opens the door. "Ginger ale or Coke?" he asks.

I KNOW THAT both Jordan and Selena have tried multiple times to pin down Rooney McBride, the medical examiner, and that multiple times, they have failed. Appointments were made and canceled as one emergency or another arose. Selena made it as far as his lab in Manchester, only to find out that his wife had gone into labor and he'd left for the day. He's proven so slippery in fact that he's assumed almost superheroic stature in my imagination, so when he takes the witness stand and is only a middle-aged man with thinning hair, I feel like I've been deceived.

"I'm a hospital pathologist at Manchester Medical Center," he says, his voice reedy. "I've practiced in New Hampshire for eleven years and I'm licensed in New Hampshire, Massachusetts, and Vermont. I'm board certified in anatomic and clinical pathology and cytopathology, and I rotated through the chief medical examiner's office in Concord for training in forensic pathology."

"What does a forensic pathologist do, Dr. McBride?" asks the prosecutor.

"We conduct autopsies in situations where there is a death that resulted from accidents, suicides, homicides, or is not clearly the result of natural causes," he states.

"Did you perform a forensic autopsy on Lily Campanello?"

"I did."

"Dr. McBride," Gina says, approaching him with a handful of paper, "I'm showing you an autopsy report dated December eleventh with your signature, purported to be the autopsy you performed on Lily Campanello. This has also been stipulated to by the defense. Is this the autopsy report you filed with the findings on Lily Campanello?"

"Yes, it is."

The judge admits the report into evidence as Gina gives a copy to the pathologist. "Can you explain, Doctor, what happens at an autopsy?"

"The first step is to review the circumstances surrounding the death of the person—including the police report and medical records, if available. We examine the body to try to figure out the cause of death—not just from the outside, but from the inside—looking at things like the central nervous system and all the organs in the chest and abdominal cavities. Samples of organs and tissue are taken for microscopic examination. The extremities might be dissected and sampled, too. Tissue, blood, and other fluids can be taken for chemical analysis or microbiological cultures. And we do an MRI, a CT scan, and X-rays, if warranted."

"What about toxicology screens?" Gina asks. "Are those run as a matter of course?"

"Yes, to identify alcohol and drugs and if they might be a factor in the death."

"Was a tox screen run on Lily Campanello?"

"Yes," Dr. McBride says. "It was negative for alcohol and drugs."

"Doctor, I'm going to ask you to detail the injuries you found on Lily, starting at the top of her head. What, if anything, did you find?"

"On her scalp was a laceration two-point-five centimeters in length—"

"Let me stop you right there," the prosecutor says. "A laceration, for those of us who aren't medical professionals, is what?"

"A cut or tear to the skin. Her hair was matted with blood. Underneath the skin of the scalp was a palpable smooth mass approximately nine by four by two centimeters. In layman's terms, that's a large bruise. It was on her temple."

There is a soft cry across the room; I don't have to look to know it's coming from Ava Campanello. Instead, I steal a glance at Asher. His jaw is set tight, and his eyes are unblinking.

"There was also a subarachnoid hemorrhage over the right fronto-temporal lobes," Dr. McBride says. "She was bleeding into her brain."

Gina asks, "What about further down on Lily's body?"

"She had extensive bruising on the face and neck, and ecchymoses on the arms and lower legs."

"Which are . . . ?"

"More bruises that are visible in areas of minor trauma."

"Dr. McBride, could you determine which of Lily's injuries were fatal?" the prosecutor presses.

"Yes. The cause of death was intracerebral hemorrhage. That means there was enough trauma to her head to cause a brain bleed and a transtentorial herniation. In plain English: there's blood where there wasn't blood before. Because the blood occupies space, lower parts of the brain are pushed down through a layer of meninges—the tentorium—and press against the brain stem. The brain stem controls respiration and heart rate. If that's not treated immediately, it can cause brain death, and/or a cessation of breathing and heartbeat."

Asher's eyes are closed now, and his chest rises and falls in shallow pulses. I watch Jordan elbow him, and he blinks.

"From what you found in the autopsy, Doctor, could you tell what caused the trauma to the victim's head?"

"Blunt force," he replies.

The prosecutor turns toward the jury. "Would that blunt force be consistent with being hit by someone's fist, or being shoved against a wall?"

"Yes."

"Would it be consistent with being pushed down a flight of wooden stairs?"

"Yes," he says.

"In your expert opinion," Gina asks, "did you determine a manner of death?"

"Homicide," Dr. McBride says.

"Nothing further," the prosecutor replies, and she sits down.

"DR. MCBRIDE," Jordan says, beginning his cross-examination, "you said the injury that led to Lily's death was an intracerebral hemorrhage—a brain bleed. Do I have that right?"

"Yes."

"You've said that you take into account what the police tell you about how the body is found, correct?"

"Yes," the doctor says.

"Isn't it true that the police report told you there were signs of a struggle in the house, and that Lily was alone in that house with her boyfriend?"

"It is."

Jordan narrows his gaze. "So you were already predisposed to think of this as a homicide?"

"Maybe, but the facts of the autopsy also supported it. The under-lying hematoma on the victim's temple and the laceration on her scalp are consistent with the blunt force trauma caused by being hit, or thrown down the stairs."

Asher tries to hide his flinch; it becomes a tiny earthquake down his spine.

"If Lily tripped and fell headfirst down an entire flight of wooden stairs, wouldn't that also be consistent with blunt force trauma?"

"Yes."

Jordan hesitates, plotting his course. "You're not a full-time foren-sic pathologist, are you?"

"No, I'm a contract pathologist. Roughly twice a month, I work at the office of the chief medical examiner in Concord."

"So your specialty *isn't* forensic pathology?"

"I have had forensic training," McBride says, "but my day job is in hospital pathology."

"Your real job is distinctly different from your part-time work, right?"

"In some ways," the pathologist says. "But I've had extensive prac-tice at both."

"So you do forensic autopsies in addition to your day job?"

"Yes."

Jordan nods, impressed. "You're a pretty busy guy."

"I am."

"Lily's autopsy wasn't the only one you did that day, was it?"

The medical examiner shakes his head. "I did four."

"You must have been exhausted!"

He shrugs. "Part of the territory."

Jordan looks at the report. "It says here you started Lily's autopsy at four P.M.?"

"That's right."

"Isn't it possible that you might have been in the unfortunate position of rushing through Lily Campanello's autopsy?"

"No," the doctor says, affronted. "I would *never*."

"And yet, there does seem to be some missing information."

McBride goes beet red. "What?" he says, leafing through the papers. "No there isn't."

"On page two, for example," Jordan says smoothly. "You'll see a blank. Next to *Female genital system.*"

"Oh, no." The doctor looks up, recovering. "That's not missing. I mean, it is, but not like you think."

"Negligence is negligence, Doctor Mc—"

"I looked for the uterus and ovaries, naturally," the medical examiner says, cutting Jordan off. "The possibility of pregnancy as a motive for homicide is always considered in the death of a woman in her reproductive years. There's no record of the organs because the uterus and ovaries were absent."

For the first time since we've come to court, Jordan seems completely lost. "You mean . . . like a hysterectomy?"

"Surgical removal would be one reason for that finding, yes . . . but not in this case." The medical examiner looks from Jordan to the prosecutor. "I assumed you all knew," he says. "The deceased was transgender."

LILY ⬢ 5

Five weeks before

Just be yourself, they tell you. Worried about how you'll come off if you're interviewing for something? *Just be yourself.* Wondering what to say or how to act on a first date? *Just be yourself.* Looking for the words to describe the impossible? *Just be yourself,* they tell you, to put you at ease. As if *just being yourself* is so easy. As if, for so many people, it isn't the very thing that most puts you at risk in this cruel and heartless world.

I remember getting ready for T-ball one Saturday morning, back in Seattle. Maybe I was eight years old? Wearing that little uniform they gave us. Going to the bathroom before Dad and I were supposed to leave the house, and seeing one of Mom's lipsticks on the sink, and just twisting it open and doing my lips and then standing there amazed, looking at myself in a mirror I was almost too short to reach. From the hallway, Dad shouted, "Liam, are you coming?" I tried to get the lipstick off with toilet paper, but it wouldn't come off. Dad, hearing the faucet running, said, "What's going on in there?" I called out, "Nothing!"

When of course it was not *nothing,* but *everything.* Why couldn't I just have come out wearing lipstick, looked my dad in the eye, and said, *I'm here, this is who I am?* I mean, I've heard of all these people who did that, who were brave enough to come out at age six, or younger. So why didn't I have the courage to make myself known? It wasn't as if I didn't know the truth.

But I was years away from being able to find the right words for the thing I felt, years away from even seeing the face of another person like me. All I knew was that, looking in the mirror at this boy wearing a T-ball uniform, whoever I was, this was not it.

I finally came out of the bathroom, and my father looked at me angrily and said, "What's wrong with you?"

I wish I'd known what to tell him, back then. I wish I'd had the courage to say *Not a goddamned thing*.

Instead, as years went by, and I got a better understanding of how deep the trouble was that I was in, I came up with a strategy. If I couldn't live honestly in the world, I figured the next best thing was to do the opposite: to live as if I was invisible.

There are people who think that invisibility is a superpower. That nothing would be cooler than being the Invisible Girl, like in the Fantastic Four. But they're wrong. Invisibility isn't a superpower. It's a curse.

"What is going *on* in that head, Lily Campanello?" says Mom, from across the room. She's drinking a glass of chardonnay, still wearing her uniform. I look up at her.

I've been playing the Schubert *Arpeggione* Sonata by the fireplace, the piece that I learned over a year ago after I'd tried and failed to kill myself (because, as it turned out, I couldn't even do *that* right), the piece that everyone said was too hard for me. I guess I'd finished a moment ago and had just been staring into space, lost in thought.

"Can I ask you a question, Mom?" I say. "Would you rather be invisible—or be able to fly?"

Mom laughs. I love the sound of her laughter. It's like bubbles coming up from a Sparkletts machine. A *watercooler*, they call it on the East Coast. I haven't heard that sound much since we moved.

"Lily, I'm a middle-aged woman. I'm *already* invisible."

In so many ways, Mom acts like her life is over, and it pisses me off. It makes me feel guilty, too—because she's spent so much of her life trying to save me. She got us out of Seattle when my father tried to crush me, and resettled us in Point Reyes so I could do the social transition, and then she homeschooled me when everything went to hell at Pointcrest. She kept me alive after the suicide attempt. She got me to Dr. Powers for surgery. She moved us out here and got the desk job after that. There are times when her whole life has just been bailing me out, time and time again.

I start playing the Schubert once more, and I do fine until I get to the crazy passage toward the end of the first movement. It's like I'm doing cartwheels on a high wire.

I can feel Mom's gaze. She raises the glass of wine to her lips.

When she was twenty-five she became a ranger so she could spend the rest of her life *in the wild*. It didn't pay well, but she always said, *I take my paycheck in sunsets.*

I'm playing so furiously, and so hard, as I think about her, and Asher, and Jonah, and Dad, that all at once the A string on my cello snaps. It's a hard, sharp sound, and I jump about a foot in the air. The sound of the sudden snap resonates and echoes in the body of the cello. I'm glad I didn't get hurt—once before when I snapped a string, it sliced right through my ring finger.

Boris, who's asleep on the floor, raises his head, although it's more likely that this is because I jumped than because he actually heard anything.

"Lily," says Mom, putting her wineglass down.

I go over to the couch and sit next to her and let my head fall onto her shoulder. The ugly tears come in a rush.

"Mom," I say. "Do you hate me?"

"What is this?" says Mom. "Honey. How could I ever hate you?"

"I wrecked your life," I tell her.

Mom pets my hair some more. "Is this about Asher?"

"No," I tell her. "Yes."

Mom thinks about what she wants to say. "He hasn't been around for the last week," she says carefully, running her index finger around the lip of her glass. I was hoping she hadn't noticed.

Boris sighs. It's hard sometimes not to think that dogs can feel your emotions, the same way deaf people can hear music through the solar plexus. There have been times when Boris seemed to know what was going on in my heart better than any human, although this happened more often back when my old dog was young.

Sometimes I miss those days.

Not often.

"I always thought I'd choose flying," I say quietly. "But now I'm not sure."

Mom keeps stroking my hair. She knows damn well I'm not talking about *flying* flying. But if we're going to talk about sex, we're going to have the conversation in code, or not at all. "I think there are a lot of misconceptions about flying," she says, already speaking the language.

Boris puts his head back down.

Mom pulls back from our hug and looks me in the eye, wipes the tears off my cheeks with her thumb.

"Flying's overrated," she says.

It absolutely breaks my heart to hear her say this.

"Did I tell you? I had to rescue some hikers today," she says.

I wonder why we are talking about this. Now.

"I thought you were doing the paperwork on the—bobcat habitat—thing—?"

"The Lynx Analysis Units," she says. "Yeah. But these hikers got into trouble, and the chief sent me in. I mean, there were rangers closer to them than I was, but you know how he likes to give me the worst jobs. Just to make sure I know how much he resents my being forced on him."

I do know about this. The chief thinks that Mom has an attitude because she used to be Park Service. This is a distinction that no one cares about except for the chief. Because he wanted to be Park Service, but he failed the test.

"You should have seen these two. Peak baggers up from Boston, hiking the AT in shorts and T-shirts. In November. No rain gear, no hiking boots, dead cellphone batteries. They got drenched in the downpour, started shaking with the cold—they'd have got hypothermia if a through-hiker hadn't found them and called HQ. I wrapped them up in thermal blankets, gave them some soup from a thermos, got them down okay, but jeez. You wouldn't believe the situations people can get themselves in by not looking ahead. By not being prepared."

She looks me in the eye, hard. "Or maybe you would."

Suddenly I understand why we are talking about this, and what she is trying to tell me. That when I make a decision, I have to understand what the consequences are.

The thing is, there are consequences no matter what I decide now, but I'm not sure which ones pose the biggest risk. Let's say I tell Asher, *Listen, I'm trans, I know I should have told you before we slept together, but I didn't so I'm telling you now, because I just want to be honest.* The consequence of that might be that he gets angry, that he flies off the handle, that—well, who knows what he'll say? He is a gentle, gentle spirit—but I have also seen him angry, and I have worn his bruises.

Transgender people get murdered all the time in this country. They don't get murdered because they kept their identity private. They get murdered because someone else finds out the truth. Incredibly, some courts still allow the gay panic defense—or the trans panic defense—to justify the killings. As if killing another person because they're trans is somehow understandable. *Well, we don't approve of murder, but really, considering the circumstances . . .*

On the other hand, let's say I *don't* tell him, that I decide there's no reason for him to know because the past is past, period, full stop. I was never a boy anyway, not in my heart, not in the ways that matter most. Does not telling him *everything* mean I'm lying to him? Is it really lying if all you're doing is keeping your mouth shut, about something that's nobody's business anyway?

I don't like either of these scenarios.

There's another one, of course, in which Asher says, *It doesn't make any difference to me, and I love you.* That's the one I want.

I'd like to say that the Asher I know will react this way. But do I really know him? What if he has a private self, too? Actually, if you think about it, how could he *not* have a private self?

Is there anyone worth knowing who doesn't have something about themselves that is theirs, and theirs alone?

My mother is staring hard at me. "Is there anything you want to tell me?"

There is so much I want to tell her. But I can't stand the idea of her worrying about me anymore. Her sacrifices and help have brought me as far as she can. I'm the one who has to figure out what to do next. I'm the one who has to live with the consequences of my choices.

I'm picturing the conversation. *Asher. There's something I have to tell you.*

Are you okay, Lily?

I want to tell him, *Fuck yes,* I am fine. In fact, I am wonderful. I am not a mistake. I am a miracle. Can't you see?

But people never see who you are, all they can see is who you *were.*

I stand up. "I'm going down to Edgar's," I tell my mother.

Mom looks surprised. "I have no idea who that is."

"Edgar's. The music shop. We've driven past it a hundred times. I need a new A string."

She drains her glass, plays with her long braid with one hand. In that single moment I get a glimpse of the younger woman she used to be, the girl who got her forestry degree at Syracuse and headed off to the Olympic National Park in Washington, at age twenty-five, thinking her life was about to begin.

"When you get back," Mom says, "I will be here."

I PULL INTO a parking spot on Pierce Street. As I step into the sunlight the bells from St. Clement's are tolling. As I pass by I can see on its sign that today is All Souls' Day.

All Souls' Day is the day when a mystical portal is supposed to be open between the land of the living and the dead. It started because, in the eleventh century, a traveler was shipwrecked on an island that contained a chasm. He could hear sounds coming from it, and believed they were the cries of lost souls in purgatory. Hearing them wail, he decided we need to pray for everyone who's trapped. When he was rescued from the island, the idea spread from there.

I've always liked the name. Like it's a day for *everybody*. Is it Just *Some* Souls' Day? No, stupid, it's *All* Souls'.

I'm not very religious, but I know there is something bigger than I am, bigger than all of this. What *is* this thing? I absolutely do not know.

FIVE THINGS ABOUT THE BIBLE

5. The only part of the New Testament I can quote from memory is Luke 2:8–14, and that's because it's the part that Linus recites in *A Charlie Brown Christmas*.

4. Actually, I sometimes think there is something very Jesus-like about Charlie Brown—his heartbreaking patience, his endless suffering.

    You have to admit the show would have a very different ending if, after he and Linus bought the sad little Christmas tree, the other kids in the Peanuts gang came after them with a hammer and some nails.

3. The thing that contains the burning incense in a Catholic church is called a *thurible*. The rising smoke is supposed to symbolize the prayers of believers rising up to heaven. The word *incense* comes from a Greek word. Originally it meant *sacrifice*. It's no wonder one of the Magi brought it as a gift. Gold and myrrh were powerful presents, I'm sure. But the king who brought frankincense to that child knew full well that the world would take its toll.

2. My least favorite Bible verse is the one about Balaam and his talking donkey. Because, honestly, who could possibly take that seriously? If your donkey started talking, I promise you that you wouldn't say you'd hit him and tell him he was being a bad donkey, like Balaam does.

    Instead, you would probably exclaim, *Hey, I have a talking donkey; I'm gonna be rich!*

1. I keep trying to be an atheist, but it just won't take. In spite of how much garbage there is in the Bible—like all the instructions on how to treat your slaves, and how women should pretty much accept that

we're destined to be the property of men—there is still something about faith that I cannot let go of. I do not know what this world is, but I know that it contains miracles that I cannot explain, and the love that people have for each other is the biggest mystery of all.

AS I GET out of the car, I feel another memory trying to surface, something triggered by the sound from the steeple. It's something buried so deep it takes a while to form.

I'm remembering a nursery rhyme about the churches in London. It rises in my heart suddenly, the whole thing, and goosebumps prickle my arms. Because the person who used to sing this to me was my father. I couldn't have been six years old. But I'm remembering being in his arms. Back when he loved me.

> *Oranges and lemons*
> *say the bells of Saint Clement's*
> *You owe me five farthings*
> *say the bells of Saint Martin's.*

I open the door to Edgar's Music. It reminds me of other music shops I've been in, except airier and messier—it's like being in someone's cluttered living room. There are chairs and a potbelly stove. A guy with a beard is sitting on a stool playing "Wagon Wheel" on a Martin. On the right wall are Fender Strats and Telecasters, little white price tags dangling on strings tied to the tuning pegs. There are amps toward the front—Peaveys and Rolands. Toward the back are the drum kits—snares and floor toms and hi-hats.

Over at the counter a large woman with a bad perm is talking to a customer, and the two of them are laughing, like they are old friends. The customer grabs his bag and says, "Dig ya later, Lizzy!" and the woman says, "Take care, Len," and looks happily at him as he heads toward the door.

Then her gaze falls upon me, and I freeze.

Because Lizzy is clearly a transgender woman.

Obviously I have a well-tuned trans-radar, compared to most people, but you don't need *t-dar* to know this woman's history at a glance. Lizzy has big hands, an Adam's apple, a large frame, five o'clock shadow, the works. She looks at me with a big smile, her face welcoming and bright. "And how can I help you, young lady?" she says, in a voice that is both low and unashamed. It's like she's well practiced in being herself. And in taking exactly zero shit from anyone.

My heart is pounding in my chest. "I need—a cello string?"

"A cellist," she says, impressed. "Any special string, or you want me to pick one at random?"

"The A string," I mumble.

"One A string, hold the mayo," she says, with a laugh, and she turns her back and starts rummaging around in a set of drawers behind the counter.

Outside, I can still hear the bells of the church pealing away.

When will you pay me?
say the bells of Old Bailey.
When I grow rich,
say the bells of Shoreditch.

There's a growl from behind the counter, a sound I'd expect more to come from Boris than a woman my mother's age—or older—and now she turns back to me, looking slightly sorry. "I don't have the individual strings anymore. I thought I did, but all I have are the sets." She puts two different packages on the glass countertop. "I've got the Red Label Super Sensitive for $45.99, and the D'Addario Helicore for $134.11. Plus the tax. You can take your pick."

I'm still trying to find my voice. "I don't know," I say, haltingly. "I mean—"

"Yeah, it's a choice," she says. "You have to ask yourself the question we all ask ourselves." She looks at me hard.

"What's—that question?"

"Are you Super Sensitive?" she says, with a grin. "Or are you a

Hella-core!" And now she laughs, deeply, as if she has just said something hilarious.

The guy with the Martin is still singing. *Hey, hey, Momma rock me.*

A little bell rings as the door to the store opens, and a dude with a ponytail and a Charlie 1 Horse cowboy hat ambles in. He has a loose walk, like he's high.

"Yo, Lizzy, what *up*?" he sings.

"Hey, Johnny," says Lizzy. "It's good to see you!"

The guy playing "Wagon Wheel" stops playing. "Hey, John," he says.

Johnny takes a look at me and raises one eyebrow. "And who do we have here?" he says. "New girl in town?" He looks down at the counter. "Cello strings. You play cello, honey?"

"Yes," I say. I point to the cheaper set. "I'll take these."

"You *are* Super Sensitive," says Lizzy, approvingly. "I knew it."

"Is she taking good care of you, honey?" says Johnny. I nod, and hand Lizzy fifty bucks. "Cause if she's not, I can take good care of you." He pushes his cowboy hat back on his head. "You need taking care of?"

"Let's back off, Johnny," says Lizzy, all business. "All right now?"

"Aw, I'm just—"

"I said back off." She looks at him intently, and Johnny backs off. It's clear nobody messes with Lizzy in her own store. There might be different rules out in the world, but in Edgar's, Lizzy's word is law. It's kind of amazing, how fearless she appears to be. Because a lot of the trans people I've seen seem a little apologetic, like they're somehow begging the world for permission just to be themselves.

And what I fear—what I know—is that sometimes I'm like that, too, because I'm afraid to lose my invisibility.

"Jeez, somebody took some *bitch pills* today," Johnny says, heading toward the back of the store. The "Wagon Wheel" guy starts playing again—this time it's "Dear Someone," by Gillian Welch. He sings it softly, as I stand there at the counter, my head still spinning. *I wanna go all over the world, and start living free . . .*

"Sorry about him," Lizzy says, handing me the change and the strings in a small brown bag. "Drummers, you know. They get frustrated because they can't play a real instrument."

Lizzy's makeup is really bad. Her eyeliner wobbles all over her eyelids, and she's wearing way too much mascara. I kind of want to point this out, to help her. But she isn't the one who needs help.

"What—do you play?" I ask her.

"What do you think?" says Lizzy. "The cello, of course."

"Do you really?"

"Well," Lizzy says, modestly. "Not much anymore. We have a little trio that plays weddings, bar mitzvahs."

"Thanks," I say. "How long have you— Has this store been here a long time?"

"Twenty-three years," says Lizzy, thinking it over. She gestures to the inventory. "My empire!"

"It's your store?" I say. "You're—Mrs. Edgar?"

Her face lights up with a big smile. "You *are* new in town, aren't you."

"I am," I say. "I just moved here in August."

"Cause you'd know, otherwise. Everybody knows. I was Edgar, now I'm Elizabeth. You know."

"Right," I say, and I can still feel my heart beating.

"What's wrong, honey?" says Lizzy. "You never seen a trans woman before?"

From outside, the bells come again.

When will that be?
say the bells of Stepney.
I do not know,
says the great bell of Bow.

"I've known—a couple," I tell her.

"Isn't that something," says Lizzy. "Used to be, I was the only one around. Now we're everywhere. The world's gotten to be a little bit better place, bit by bit."

"Have people been . . . nice to you?"

She laughs, like this is a funny question. "Nice enough. So. What's your name?"

"Lily." I want to say: *I'm trans, too. You and I are sisters!* But is this really true? Are we sisters?

"Hey," says Lizzy. "Are you okay?"

"I'm fine." I walk toward the door, my heart pounding.

"You come back anytime. People like us, we got to stick together!" she calls after me, and I'm gripped with fear that what I think is hidden might be apparent to Lizzy.

I'm not the only one in the world with *t-dar* after all.

"Cellists, I mean," she says, as I head outside.

All I wanted to do was to be like everybody else and have a normal life. And it's not like my being trans is some terrible secret: it's a wonderful thing, really—at times I've thought of it as a gift. Not being openly trans—whatever that means—hasn't been some crazy plot of mine to deceive people; it's just been the fact of living every day. Because I was lucky enough to get on puberty blockers, and do my transition young, people think I'm cis, they think I'm just like they are. Is it really my responsibility to out myself over and over, for the rest of my life? What is it, in the end, that makes me different from cis people at this point in my life—besides *history*?

Still: it's different when you're in love with someone. Maybe the whole point of being in love is that you tell each other everything. Even when you don't know what the consequences might be.

I climb behind the wheel of my car. The bells of St. Clement's have fallen silent.

Asher, I text. *Can you come to my house tonight? I need to see you.*

IT'S QUARTER TO TWELVE, and I'm lying in my bed holding a book that I am not reading. I have one light on, the Hello Kitty lamp I've had since I was six years old. The book I am not reading is *The Princess Bride*, which they made into a movie. I remember my mother reading it out loud to me while I was recovering from surgery a year and a half ago.

There are so many things I love about that book, but the thing I love most of course is all the sword fighting. It was seeing that movie when I was little that made me want to start fencing. I love when the Man in Black and Inigo Montoya are fighting all over the rocky terrain, and Inigo is so amazed by Westley's virtuosity. *Who are you? I must know!* he says.

Get used to disappointment, Westley replies.

There's also the business about Westley pretending to be the Dread Pirate Roberts. It makes me think about the way people assume identities, about all the masks we wear, and how often people assume you are exactly what you appear to be.

There's a thing called *passing,* which is not only about transgender people but about everybody. It has to do with the way the bigotry and meanness of the world get parceled out, based on how you might, or might not, look or act like everybody else. The way there's a particular kind of anti-Semitism that gets leveled at people who "look Jewish," whatever that means. African Americans with darker skin sometimes are on the receiving end of more bigotry than people whose skin is lighter. Gay men who "act gay" get treated one way, those who *pass* as straight get treated another. It's a whole pyramid of bigotry, with people who most resemble the dominant culture at the top, and people whose difference makes them stand out at the bottom. It's inconceivable, if you think about it, the complex ways people have come up with for being horrible to one another.

Inconceivable. *You keep using that word. I do not think it means what you think it means.*

As a trans girl, I pass without much effort, thanks in part to the random luck of genetics, and also thanks to my mother getting me on puberty-blocking hormones when I was twelve. My body loved estrogen, too, which is mostly because I'm shaped like my mother, big up top, slim hips. And once surgery was done, what was there to make me stand out as different from other girls my age? The thing Dr. Powers had promised me—that "even your doctor won't be able to tell"—turned out to be true.

How my surgeon managed to magically make a vagina and clitoris and labia out of nothing more than superfine sugar and marzipan I can't tell you. But I know everything looks and feels like it's supposed to. There's a statement someone in my support group once used—*The plumbing works and so does the electricity.*

So what makes me different, at this point? A Y chromosome that you can't even see? Is that really the thing that determines the truth of the world? I mean—I can't get pregnant, so there's that.

But a lot of women can't get pregnant. And, as it turns out, there are even some women who have something called androgen insensitivity disorder, which means they have a Y chromosome and never even know it.

I don't think it's an invisible chromosome, or the inability to get pregnant, or anything else, that makes people so cruel to transgender folks. I think what they hate is difference. What they hate is that the world is complicated in ways they can't understand.

People want the world to be simple.

But gender isn't simple, much as some might want it to be. The fact that it's complicated—that there's a whole spectrum of ways of being in the world—is what makes it a blessing. Surely nature—or god, or the universe—is full of miracles and wild invention and things way beyond our understanding, no matter how hard we try. We aren't here on earth in order to bend over backward to resemble everybody else. We're here to be ourselves, in all our gnarly brilliance.

Which is why I feel so ashamed to be in hiding. I ought to be standing in a spotlight on a stage, shouting *I'm trans and I'm proud, everybody shout my name!* I mean, it's not like there aren't trans and nonbinary students at Adams High. I remember how amazed I was, that first week of school, to see Caeden Wentworth stand up in assembly and tell everyone about the Rainbow Alliance. Oh, I knew that there were plenty of people in that room who didn't get it, or who couldn't tell you the difference between a transsexual and the Trans-Siberian Railway, but mostly people seemed glad to be in a place where a nonbinary person like Caeden could just be themselves. There are lots of other queer students at Adams High. Sometimes it seems like over the course of my own transition, the world has gone from a place where trans stuff was exotic and incomprehensible to, you know, just one more way of being human.

So why is it that instead of joining the Alliance at school, I acted like this had nothing to do with me? Why—instead of making friends with Caeden and Gray and Ezra and all the other queer and trans and enby students—did I wind up going out with Asher Fields, the co-captain of the hockey team, a poster boy for cisgender straight men? Is it just internalized transphobia? Is my love for him actually a weird way of hating myself?

Inconceivable!

The thing is, I already know what it's like to be outed, to live in a world where everyone knows the most private things about you. Nobody ever threw me a Pride parade.

Time and time again, I got exposed against my will, and the consequences were terrible. It happened at Pacific Day School in Seattle. It happened at Marin-Muir. It happened at Pointcrest. Each time, it was worse. Even at Pointcrest, where—thanks to Dad—everyone found out about me, and they tried to turn me into the diversity poster child—even there, I wound up humiliated and tortured. That last time, at the Valentine's Day dance my junior year, was the end of the line.

The day after that dance, while Mom was at work, I filled the bathtub with water, and I got a knife from the kitchen and turned on the sharpener. I can still hear the sound of the blade as I pulled it against the spinning sharpening stone. I can see the light reflecting off the steel. I can feel the quiet of the house.

I patted Boris on the head as I made my way up the stairs. "Goodbye," I told him. "You're a good boy."

Which was more than I could say about some people.

We won't tell anyone, Mom said, afterward, when we were getting ready to move east. *What's past is past. From now on, it's just you and me.*

It was a great plan, but there was one thing we hadn't counted on. We never considered what would happen if I fell in love.

There's a gentle tap against my window. I look up.

He's here.

. . .

I CAN TELL, from the way he stands awkwardly at the foot of my bed, that he doesn't know what to do next. Asher Fields, who does everything with sureness and grace, is completely at a loss. He looks at me with what can only be described as hunger and hope, all braided together, but he doesn't want to come any closer until I give him a sign that it's what I want.

God, I love this boy.

I take a step forward and press myself so close to him that it is like we were carved out of the same piece of wood. I feel like wax, molding to him everywhere there is heat.

He drops his coat on the floor, and we wrap our arms around each other and we kiss like we're on the deck of the *Titanic*. "Thank God," he says. "I missed you. I missed you so much."

"I missed you, too," I say, and we kiss again and I wish I could slip underneath his skin, but he pushes me back until he can look into my eyes.

"Are you okay?" he asks, just like I thought he would.

"Yes," I tell him, and I am—there's a way in which I feel more like myself when I'm with him than when I'm alone. Maybe deep down I always thought I did not deserve to be loved by someone like Asher. But then again, the thing I feel is not only about him. It's about being part of the world. There is so much ahead for me and I want to put my arms around all of it.

"I was afraid you had—second thoughts," he says. "After we—"

"No," I tell him. "I mean yes."

He's listening to me very carefully. "Yes you have second thoughts?" he says. "About me?"

"Yes I have second thoughts about myself," I say.

"Lily," he says, sitting down on the bed. "Talk to me."

"I—" I feel my throat close up. "I don't know how."

He reaches over and holds my hand. "Then I'll wait till you figure it out," he says.

I squeeze his hand back, and I'm feeling the tears welling up, but goddammit I am not going to cry. I think about Lizzy in the music store, how she was herself and how, amazingly, that was enough. That was perfect.

"If what you want," Asher says, "is to go back to the way things were before, we can do that. I'm sorry if we—if *I*—rushed things. I love you. I don't want you to feel—"

"Stop," I tell him. "Asher. Being with you ... *being* with you," I underline, "made me feel like I've never felt before."

He takes this in, and he breaks into a big smile. Dimples. I think, fleetingly: *Fuck it, I can just keep my mouth shut and everything will just stay like it is.*

"Then ... why?" he asks. "I've been losing my mind. I thought—" He looks down, as if he's afraid to say it out loud. "I thought you changed your mind. About us. About *me.*"

That almost breaks me. Because my body may be different, but the one part of me that has never changed is my mind. "Asher, I love you," I rush to explain. "I love you so much that even using those words is like saying 'the ocean's just water.'" I swallow. "But there's something I have to tell you."

He sits. Waits.

"Lily?" he asks gently.

"I'm scared," I whisper. "I'm afraid that once I tell you, you won't ever look at me the same way again."

Asher shakes his head. "Nothing you could say would change how I feel about you. Do you understand? What we have, you and me—I don't know. It's—"

"Holy," I say.

Asher thinks it over. "Okay," he says. "I wasn't going for *holy,* but sure. *Holy* works."

"I feel like no one's ever known me the way you do," I say.

"I feel that way, too," says Asher.

"We've been honest with each other," I tell him, and he nods. "Except that there's something about me you don't know."

"You're scaring the shit of out me," whispers Asher. "Just say it."

The room is so quiet.

"Just say it," he says again softly. He rubs his thumb in small circles on the back of my hand.

It's the kind of quiet like when a conductor is standing in front of an orchestra, holding a raised baton, and you're just waiting for the music to begin.

"I'm trans," I say.

He takes this in, sort of. Then Asher smiles again. "Very funny," he says.

"It's not a joke," I say, a little too loudly, and I think about how Mom is asleep down the hall. What would she think if she knew that Asher was here? What would she think if she knew I was telling him everything?

"You're—what?"

"I'm trans," I tell him. "I should have told you, before we started going out, before we had—"

"You're trans," he says. "You mean, like—you want to be a *man*? Seriously?"

Oh, Asher.

"No," I say. "I mean—when I was born, people thought I was a boy. I looked like a boy, I had the body of a—"

He's looking at me like a bloodhound who's heard someone call his name in the distance. A little bit curious, but mostly confused.

Now he lets go of my hand. "You're saying—"

"I'm trans," I tell him. "Or—I used to be. Before surgery—"

"You had *surgery*?" says Asher. His face is pale, and there is no longer any part of him that is touching a part of me. "So, when we had sex, you were—"

"Me," I interrupt. "I was me. I'm exactly the person you've always known. The person who loves you."

"But I-I . . ." His voice trails away.

He's thinking really hard. It looks like he's gnawing on a bone, like he's trying to get to the bottom of something, but it keeps slipping away. Then, all at once, I can feel a wave of disappointment washing over him. "Jesus, Lily." He looks up at me, and repeats my name. "Lily," he says slowly, like he's pulling on a sweater that doesn't fit.

Asher stands up. He walks over to the window, the same one he came through not ten minutes ago, then he walks back to me, staring at me hard, like he's looking for something he couldn't see before.

"But what, Asher?" I say again.

He shakes his head. I can't tell if he can't figure out what to say, or if he's trying to keep from saying something he will regret. He makes a fist, then his hands go slack.

"I have to think," he says.

Everything inside me turns to ice. "Please," I beg. Tears are in my eyes, but it doesn't keep me from seeing what's happening. What I *knew* would happen.

He opens the window.

"Asher—" I cry, walking toward him. "If you have to think, think *here*. Stay *here*." I reach out my hand to keep him from leaving and that's when it happens.

He flinches.

Like my very touch is poison.

It feels like he's flayed me down to the bone, and it shows on my face. "You've known about this your whole life," he says. "I've known for ten seconds. I need . . . I've gotta think." He steps out onto the roof and he jerks his chin, the kind of goodbye you give someone you barely know, someone who is an acquaintance. Not someone you've moved inside; not someone who loves you, whom you love.

Loved.

A second later Asher is climbing onto the branch of the tree outside my window.

He didn't even close the window behind him.

From town I can hear a church bell tolling. It's the spire of St. Clement's. It's midnight. The cold wind freezes my face and I listen to the bells chiming in the distance—*ten, eleven, twelve.*

And just like that, the day of All Souls is done.

OLIVIA ⬡ 6

Five months after

The courtroom is so quiet that, for a heartbeat, I can hear the crawl of my own blood. And then, in the next, everything explodes. The gallery erupts in a rush of sound and shock, the attorneys struggle to speak over each other, and Judge Byers is banging her gavel.

I ignore all of it. I look at Asher, whose face is pinched and white. His eyes are closed and his hands are clasped on the table. It looks like he is praying.

Or begging for forgiveness.

"All right . . . all *right*!" the judge yells. "I will remind you we are in the *middle* of a trial and if you cannot handle yourselves you will be removed from my courtroom." She turns to Jordan and the prosecutor. "Mr. McAfee, proceed."

Jordan's mouth opens and closes around empty air. Finally he says, "No further questions at this point, Your Honor. But . . . we reserve the right to recall the witness."

Gina clears her throat. She looks like she's smacked into a wall—a little dazed. "Your Honor," she says. "We have no objections to the defense recalling the witness."

"I didn't ask you, did I?" the judge snaps. "This is a good stopping point. Idris Elba walking into my courtroom right now couldn't convince me to finish out the afternoon." She turns to the jury. "We're going to recess for the day. I reiterate my admonition to you—do not read any media, do not talk about the case with anyone, not even the people who share your bed, and come back tomorrow at nine A.M. Court is dismissed."

The bailiff takes the jury out, and the judge retreats into her chambers. Asher is now staring blindly in front of him, like the empty-eyed marble bust of an old philosopher.

I am in no rush to stand up, or go anywhere. I can't imagine what the media gauntlet will be like, once I step outside these doors.

Gina jams papers into her leather briefcase. Jordan grabs her arm and turns her to face him. "Why didn't you tell us this?" he demands under his breath.

She yanks herself away from his grasp. "You're assuming I *knew*."

The prosecutor exits through the double doors of the courtroom, and immediately I hear the roar of questions rise over her like a tide. Jordan turns to us, waving me through the little wooden gate that separates the gallery from the table where he and Asher were sitting. "Don't say a word," he says, and he leads us through a side door into a hallway. At the end of it, I can hear Gina saying something to the press, and with her in the spotlight, we are able to sneak off in the opposite direction.

Jordan pulls us into the conference room we were in earlier. He slams the door behind him, sits down at the table, and opens his briefcase. "We'll stay here till the media gets bored and goes away," he says, as he takes out the autopsy report, scouring it like he is expecting it to burst into flames in his hands. "How the hell did we miss this?"

I know the answer to that.

No one was looking for it. People see what they want to see.

Asher picks at the cuticle on his thumb. There's color in his face again. He opens his mouth and then closes it, as if there is so much inside of him to say that it's jammed up in the back of his throat. He seems unsettled.

But not surprised.

I shove that thought away so hard that I feel dizzy.

Jordan spears his hands through his hair, making it stand on end.

"Okay," he says, giving himself a pep talk. "Okay. We will figure this out."

I clear my throat. "Is it . . . really that big a deal?"

My brother pins me with a glance. "Yes. And here's why Asher's case just got progressively worse: It's a lot easier to blow holes in a case that is basically a glorified version of *boy meets girl, boy and girl argue.* Plenty of couples fight without killing each other. What Gina Jewett couldn't offer a jury, until ten minutes ago, was *why* Asher got so mad that he would commit murder. But now, the prosecution has motive. They're going to say Asher found out Lily was transgender, felt duped by her, and then killed her in a fit of rage. Trans panic. It's in the news every goddamned day."

Asher looks up. "But I—"

"No," Jordan interrupts. "Don't. Do *not* tell me whether or not you knew Lily was trans. As long as you say nothing about that to me, I can build your defense on the belief that you were never told. And if you were never told, you had no motive to kill her."

Asher very slowly wilts toward the table, pressing his cheek against it, as if all the will to fight has gone out of him.

WE WAIT LONG enough for the press to have dispersed, and then before heading to the car, I tell Jordan and Asher I'm going to use the bathroom. The ladies' room at the courthouse is on the far side of the building, but I don't pass a single person in the hall the entire way there. I use a stall, flush, and step out to wash my hands.

Standing at a sink a few feet away is Ava Campanello.

I have not seen her in the months since Lily's funeral. She is stick-thin, her dress hanging on her shoulders and swallowing her body whole. She looks up.

"Ava," I say, hoarse.

She jerks her gaze away from mine, scrubbing at her hands with the vengeance of Lady Macbeth. Then she turns, reaching for the tongue of paper towel curling from the dispenser.

I am rooted to the floor, trapped by the loss of Lily and the potential loss of Asher. If things were reversed—if Asher had been the one to die—would I so badly want to find a scapegoat, a way to burn the world down, that I'd think the worst of Lily? I can't imagine how badly she hurts, how she can hold herself together. I would never presume to know Lily as well as Ava did, but I still cannot see myself believing the worst of her.

I would never presume to know Lily as well as Ava did.

Jordan might not have known Lily was trans. Gina Jewett might not have known Lily was trans. But Ava *did,* and she chose to say nothing. Not even to the prosecutor, who would have interviewed her at length before moving ahead with this trial.

The question is . . . why?

It wasn't to protect Asher, for sure. Was it to protect Lily?

Or was it because this secret wasn't Ava's to tell?

"Asher isn't a murderer, Ava," I force out. My voice is wobbling so much it is unrecognizable. "You must know that."

Sometimes, in a hive, you find brood cells shaped like circus peanuts, where potential new queens are being raised to replace an old or weak one. Most beekeepers say the first queen to emerge will sting the others still in their cells to kill her rivals, but I prefer to think that she caucuses: running around the hive, shaking hands and kissing babies and leaving her pheromones all over the place. As later queens hatch, they have to challenge her candidacy. It's about persuasion, consensus. Not everything is solved with violence.

Ava doesn't turn around, but her shoulders stiffen. "Things aren't always what they seem to be," she says, and then she is gone.

I run the water in the sink and wash my hands. Then I splash some over my face. Finally, I go back to the conference room where Jordan and Asher are waiting. "It's about time," Jordan says. "What the hell took you so long?"

I force a smile. "Coast is clear," I announce.

He gives us our marching instructions, in case we are ambushed en route to the truck, but it is unnecessary—the reporters have slunk back into whatever holes they came from. Our vehicle is in the far corner of the lot, baking in the afternoon heat. An oak tree stretches its arms over the truck, casting long shadows on the flatbed. Asher climbs into the backseat, but before Jordan can open the passenger door, I put my hand on his arm. "Jordan?" I ask softly. "Do you think Asher knew?"

The sun glints in his eyes, illuminating a flash of sympathy. "You better hope like hell," Jordan says, "that he didn't."

BRADEN AND I met on a blind date that included neither him nor me. I had been set up by a co-worker. Her fiancé's former college roommate worked in the Clinton White House and had suggested we meet at The Tombs in Georgetown. I hated going to Georgetown; it was crowded and full of frat bros and decidedly out of the loop of the Metro—but I decided to give him the benefit of the doubt, because who wants to be the woman who nitpicks over the meeting spot? When I got to the bar, I was ten minutes late because of traffic, but I figured maybe he was late for the same reason. I didn't want to start a tab, so I asked for a glass of water and sat down next to a man nursing what looked like whiskey, neat. I noticed him in the way that single women notice men—sizing him up for general douchiness—and marked his athlete's body, his cashmere sweater, his ringless left hand. "You wouldn't happen to be Henry?" I asked.

"Uh, sorry, no." He smiled politely at me and turned back to his drink. When he was otherwise absorbed, I slid a glance in his direction again, this time taking in the black gleam of his hair, the electric blue of his eyes. The groomed stubble on his jaw, which somehow on him looked honest, instead of cultivated.

He kept checking his BlackBerry. I checked my watch. I finished my glass of water, and asked for another, this time with lime.

When the bartender brought it, the man beside me raised his empty glass, signaling another. I started to wonder if I had messed up—gotten the date wrong, or the time. My missing date had five more minutes, and then I was going home.

Beside me, the man lifted his new glass and took a sip. "Please don't spontaneously combust," he said, staring straight ahead.

It startled a laugh out of me. "What makes you think I'm angry?"

"I can feel the temperature creeping up," he said, pulling at his collar, and then he turned.

If I thought he was handsome before, he was *devastating* now.

"I'm Braden," he said. "And you are?"

"Waiting for a blind date," I replied.

"I figured." He lifted a brow. "How late is he?"

I glanced at my watch. "Thirty-five minutes," I said.

Braden huffed out a laugh. "I've got you beat by fifteen."

At that, I nearly fell off my stool. "You were stood up, too?"

He lifted his glass, clinked it to mine. "I have an idea," he said, leaning closer. "Let's egg their houses. I'll stand watch and then you can return the favor."

I smirked. "I have no idea where he lives."

"Right. The blind part of the date."

"They'd have to be blind," I said, "to not show up for you." My hand flew to my mouth. Did I really just say that out loud?

He was grinning at me, his eyes bright. "Thank you," Braden said. "I think."

"Guess I've had enough to drink," I muttered.

"Yeah, two glasses of water and I'm under the table, too."

Suddenly a hand squeezed my shoulder. I froze, thinking that it must be my date and that the greeting was a little aggressive. Braden had stiffened, too. A very drunk woman wearing a necklace of plastic penises and a sash that said I'M THE BACHELORETTE had wedged herself between us from behind, draping her arms around us both. "Sorry, sorry," she slurred. "The bartender's been totally ignoring me."

"Go figure," Braden said.

The bartender came over. "Six CoronaRitas," she ordered. Braden looked at me over her head, and I met his glance, and we both hid a smile. But she intercepted the glance, only then seeming to realize that she was cuddled between us. "Oh my God," the bachelorette sang. "You two are the cutest couple. I'm gonna buy you a drink, too."

"We're good," Braden assured her, at the same time I said, "I'm not drinking."

Her eyes grew huge. "You're pregnant!" she announced, like she'd just deduced the theory of relativity. She looked down at my stomach. "How far along are you?"

Before I could tell her she was hugely mistaken, Braden said, "Three months. But we want the gender to be a surprise." He reached for my hand on the bar and laced his fingers with mine. His skin was warm and dry and between our palms it felt like we were holding a secret.

"Name it after me, no matter what," the bachelorette said. "Brenda." Then she disappeared, having gathered up a tray of giant frozen drinks with beer bottles upended in them.

"That escalated quickly," I said.

"Considering the fact that we're expecting, I should probably know your name."

"Olivia," I told him. I squeezed his hand, a pulse, and started to let go, but he wouldn't let me.

"Would you like to go somewhere for dinner?" he asked. "Maybe toss out some potential baby names? We're *obviously* not going with Brenda."

He took me next door to 1789, a restaurant far too chic for my pocketbook. I learned, over dinner, that Braden was a resident in cardiac surgery; I told him that I worked in the panda enclosure at the National Zoo. He was delighted—he'd never met a zoologist before. He leaned forward, elbows on the table, and asked me to tell him something he didn't know about pandas. "Well," I said. "What do you know?"

"They eat bamboo."

"A lot of it," I confirmed. "They cost five times more to keep in a zoo than any other animal. Also male pandas do handstands to pee to mark their territory."

"What about the female pandas?"

"They ovulate only a couple days every year, and a baby panda is one nine hundredth the size of its mother."

We were eating steak and drinking wine I could not afford on my salary, and Braden was gorgeous and charming and so attentive to me that it took me an hour to realize how rarely I'd been on a date where the man seemed to care more about my answers to questions than about hearing himself talk. An hour had passed, and I still knew little about him.

"Your turn," I said, as he ordered a second bottle of cabernet. He'd grown up in Virginia and went to UVA, then medical school at Vanderbilt. His grandfather had died of a heart attack, which is why he became a cardiac surgeon. "Tell me something I don't know about hearts," I asked, turning the tables on him.

"What do you know?" he parroted.

"That they can be broken?"

"Actually, that's true," Braden said. "Broken heart syndrome is a lot like a heart attack symptom-wise, but it's caused by emotional trauma instead of heart disease." I realized that, through this entire dinner, he had never taken his eyes off me; he had never looked at his phone to see what happened to his original date. He treated each word out of my mouth as if it were a drop of water, and he was a desert.

It was making me more drunk than all the cabernet in the world possibly could.

We were still talking four hours later, when the restaurant closed down and kicked us out. It was pouring, and there were no cabs in sight.

"Well," I said. "This sucks."

"Does it?" The corners of his mouth turned up. "I thought every woman wants to be kissed in the rain."

I looked at him, matted and drenched, the most beautiful man I'd ever seen. Certainly the most beautiful man who had ever made me feel like I was the only planet in his universe. "This one does," I said, and then I was in his arms.

When he finally hailed a cab and dropped me off at my apartment building, I asked him if he wanted to come inside, and he shook his head and kissed my forehead. I was tipsy enough to not realize, until he was gone, that although he knew where I lived, I didn't have his number or his address. I figured that would be that; the best date I'd never had.

The next morning, when I got to work at 6:00 A.M., there was a helium balloon tied to my staff locker—CONGRATULATIONS ON YOUR BABY!

A note was tied to the ribbon. *Are we having a boy or a girl?* There were instructions to be ready at seven, at my place, with my response and whatever I'd wear to a picnic in Rock Creek Park.

Back then, I thought Braden's directives were romantic, not controlling.

Back then, I thought it was sweet that he asked me out with that question.

Boy or girl?

Back then, I thought the answer was simple.

ARISTOTLE WAS THE one who said the largest bee in the hive was the leader of the colony, but because of the time he lived in, he made the assumption it was a king. Even though scientists subsequently saw that same monarch laying eggs, cognitive dissonance allowed them to still assume it was a male, because female rulers just . . . *didn't exist.* In the 1600s, when a Dutch naturalist, Jan Swammerdam, dissected a queen bee and found ovaries, it was the final proof that the "king" bee was actually female.

In college zoology classes I learned there are plenty of animal species that change sex. It's called sequential hermaphroditism. Clown fish are all born male, but the most dominant one becomes a female. Wrasses work in reverse, with a female able to transform her ovaries into testes in about a week's time. The slipper limpet, when touched by other male limpets, can become female. Male bearded dragons can change sex while still in their eggs, if exposed to warmer temperatures. Spotted hyena females have what look like penises and have to retract them into their bodies for mating. Coral can go from male to female or vice versa. Common reed frogs spontaneously change sex in the wild.

In other words, it's perfectly natural.

Yet it occurs to me that while I studied this phenomenon in animals, I never really considered what it was like for humans.

A change of sex occurs, in the animal world, when it is beneficial to the continuation of the species.

I think about Lily, and her suicide attempt, and consider that you could make the same argument.

I want to ask Asher if he knew. If he talked to Lily about this. But I am afraid to hear that answer.

What I know about transgender women comes from the media—from seeing and hearing Caitlyn Jenner and Laverne Cox and Chelsea Manning and Janet Mock. I haven't really thought about what it means to be trans . . . because I have had the luxury of *not having* to think about it.

But I'm thinking about it now.

WHEN WE GET back home Asher and Jordan head to their rooms. I find myself pacing around the house. I put a kettle on the stove for tea, then stare out the window at the fields, so green and verdant it nearly hurts to look at them. The windows are open, filling the house with the smells of grass and warm earth.

In the mudroom, my bee suit is hanging on a hook. I stare at it for a little bit, thinking of the day last fall when Lily helped me make the frames for this year's hives. I remember at that moment thinking that if I'd had a daughter, I would have wanted her to be like Lily.

But Lily had been born a son, too.

The kettle in the kitchen begins to whistle, which is good, because it breaks me out of my spell. I find a tea bag, pour the water in the cup, and watch the steam rise. I sweeten it with honey.

If I am being painfully honest—is this a terrible thing to say?—I have not really given any time to understanding what it means to be transgender. I don't actually *know* any transgender people. (Or is it *trans*? Is *trans* the same as *transgender*? Is a *transsexual* the same thing, or something different?) I know about clown fish and slipper limpets, but somehow not so much about humans.

There is one transgender person in town—Edgar, who is Elizabeth now. The man—no, the woman—who runs the music shop. I've seen her here and there—Adams is so little that you run into everyone sooner or later. People seem accepting of her, but I can't say that when I see Elizabeth I especially think of her as a woman like me. She seems—Jesus, I hate how this sounds—like a work in progress? Like a subcategory of *woman*? But even saying that makes me feel like I'm judging, when I don't mean to.

Still. When I first heard through the rumor mill that Edgar was now Elizabeth, I wondered, why go through all of that? Why not just make peace with the body you have?

I lift the tea bag out of the cup, wrap the string around the spoon, and squeeze it. Then I throw the bag in the trash. I remember the day Asher called me from the police station. *Mom, I think Lily's dead.*

There are a lot of times I don't particularly like being female. Like, for instance, the first day of my period, every month of every year, since I was eleven. The way men look at my breasts instead of my face. The times I've been slightly psychotic about my appearance, my figure. The assumption that I'm "the weaker sex" instead of a beekeeper who can lug a forty-pound box across several acres without breaking a sweat. All the times I've had to live up to the standards of men—and had to remind myself that those standards are bullshit.

I hate that being female is equated with being frail, and yet, I'm proof of it. I'd let myself become Braden's victim because of messaging I'd received my whole life: that it was my job to take care of my husband, that if something was wrong it was because I'd somehow failed at my job. I'm ashamed to admit it, but there were times—even as a feminist—when I bought into seeing that as my role.

For all these reasons, and others I haven't even thought of, life as a woman isn't exactly a party. I cannot imagine a man actively choosing to give up that winning ace.

So . . . what made Lily decide she wanted to be a girl?

Maybe that's the wrong word, *decide*. It's not a thing you'd do on a whim, like changing your hair color, or learning Italian. But it's impossible for me to imagine feeling so off-kilter with yourself you'd crave such radical change.

Then again, I remember when I was married, how I would step out of the shower and wipe the steam away on the mirror and think, *Today is the day I see someone strong.* But every time, it was always just broken, spineless me.

I had wanted this cup of tea to settle me, but the more I think about all of this, the more restless I become. I walk up the stairs with the teacup in my hand, and I knock on the door to Asher's room. When he doesn't answer, I open it. He's lying on his bed with his eyes closed and his headphones on. From the sound of his breathing I can tell he's asleep.

On the wall not far from his bed is the hole he punched that day last fall, and which he never did get around to fixing. He was going to get to it during Christmas vacation, he said. But by then my son was in jail.

Well, I said, *I hope whatever's pissed you off is worth what you're going to spend repairing that.*

Now I stand there in the doorway with my cup of tea, examining his room in the same way I once looked at the dioramas in the Smithsonian. Here: the bedroom of the adolescent *Homo sapiens,* with the specimen in a state of repose.

I want to wake him up and tell him, *Asher, it's going to be all right, I swear to God,* and that *I understand.* But what if it's not all right? And what if I *don't* understand?

Moments later, I'm back in the mudroom, putting on a light jacket. I get in the truck and start driving into town before I even realize where I am headed.

If you want to understand something, you first need to accept the fact of your own ignorance. And then, you need to talk to people who know more than you do, people who have not just thought about the facts, but lived them.

I can't even call Elizabeth an acquaintance. I know she has a job, and a store to run, and a life that doesn't involve educating me; that for her I am at best an annoyance and, at worst, an audacious imposition from someone privileged. She owes me no time, no answers, no tutorials.

But ten minutes later, I pull into a parking space in front of Edgar's Music.

FROM FAR AWAY, we would look like two women pausing to watch the sun set. The sun dissolves into the ribbon of the Cobboscoggin River as Elizabeth and I stand with our hands on the railing. On the opposite bank are the ruins of the old paper mill, shuttered these last twenty years. A cold smokestack points into the sky.

Elizabeth is smoking a cigarette. "What an eyesore, huh," she says. She takes a deep drag, and then blows it all out in a thin blue cloud. "My father worked on the log drives, back in the fifties and sixties." She shakes her head. "The Cobboscoggin used to be jammed with timber. My old man spent a lot of hard days with his pike and his ring dog."

We've been here for about five minutes now. When I approached her counter at the music store, she made it clear she wasn't all that thrilled about talking to me. I'd introduced myself, but she interrupted me. *I know who you are,* she said, coolly.

The store—which had been filled with the sounds of people playing guitars and strumming basses—fell silent. *Please,* I said to her.

Ms. McAfee, she said, thoughtfully. *I don't need to please you.*

She turned away from me. I backed off, not sure what to do. But then, halfway to the door, I stopped. *My son is not a bad person,* I said.

Elizabeth put her hands on the glass countertop before her, a case containing harmonicas and maracas and tambourines. *I know all about your son,* she said.

No, I told her. *You don't.*

We stood there for a long moment, like cowboys in a gunfight, just eyeing each other. Then I walked out the door. A bell rang softly.

I stood in downtown Adams, wondering what to do next. Wondering why I'd come here, and what I'd expected.

Ms. McAfee, said a voice behind me.

She was standing there in a yellow jacket, a pink skirt. The look of suspicion was gone from her eyes, succeeded now by something more like curiosity, or pity—a look I'd seen before, years ago. A look that made me feel even smaller, even more foolish. *You're right,* she said. *I don't know your son.*

"What's a ring dog?" I ask her now, as we stand by the river, and she crushes the cigarette butt beneath her heel.

"It's like a peavey," she says. "A hook for rolling logs over." She smiles. "My father's house was full of antique tools. All the things he'd need for undoing the jams on the river."

"Maybe I should get one," I tell her. "I'm in kind of a jam myself."

She thinks this over. The sun is just about to disappear behind the hulking silhouette of the old mill. "I know what it's like to have assumptions made about you, without anyone bothering to get the actual facts. That's why I am standing here, giving you the benefit of the doubt, although the nightly news suggests that your son murdered a trans woman," Elizabeth says.

"Thank you for talking to me," I say.

"I met her," she says. "That girl, Lily. She came into my store one time, to buy cello strings."

I don't know why, but this catches me by surprise. "Did you talk about"—for some reason I can't bring myself to say the words out loud—"what you have in common?"

"Ah," Elizabeth says. "You mean how we're both"—she leans closer, lowering her voice—"Capricorns?"

My face floods with heat. "I just thought, since you were both . . . born male."

"I was *not* born male," Elizabeth says. "I was born a *baby*. I spent my whole life fighting my way to the truth." She glances at me. "Lesson one: AFAB and AMAB. Assigned female at birth, assigned male at birth. Or better yet, trans man. Trans woman."

"So you were both born," I correct, quieting my voice, "*transgender.*"

"Lesson two. It's not a curse word, you can speak up. And lesson three—you know what they say: if you've met one trans person, you've . . ." She smirks. "Met one trans person. What's true for Lily might not be true for someone else."

I nod, filing this away. "Did you get the—" I say. "Lily had—"

"The *operation*?" Elizabeth says.

I can tell from the expression on Elizabeth's face that I have asked the wrong question.

"See, that," she continues, "would be an example of something that's none of your fucking business."

"I'm sorry—" I say. "I didn't mean—"

"What difference would it make to you, if I told you I'd had it—or I'd not had it? Some people don't want the surgery. Other people can't afford it."

"Lesson four," I accept, and nod.

"Jesus, I cannot believe it's 2019 and I'm still talking about this bullshit," she mutters. "We're all different, and we all experience gender in different ways—even if we all fit under that umbrella of being trans. As opposed to *cis,* which is what you call someone who's *not* transgender. So *trans* is to *cis* like *gay* is to *straight*. With me so far?"

Lesson five, I think. "So you can be trans—and straight, too?"

"Being gay or straight," says Elizabeth, "is about who you want to go to bed with. Being trans—or cis—is about who you want to go to bed *as*." She lights up another cigarette. "If you got a bunch of transgender people together, you might hear them arguing about what it all means, or what the most important thing about it all is. There are *cross-dressers*—often straight men who dress as women as part of fantasy, or escape. There are *drag queens* and *kings,* who think of gender as a performance, an art form. There are *nonbinary* people, or *enbys,* who see gender as a spectrum—which it is—and want to express themselves anywhere along that spectrum as an act of freedom. Sometimes people call that *genderfucking* or *genderqueer*. If you hear someone say, 'Reject the gender binary!' you're probably hanging around with a genderqueer person. Some of us *like* Caitlyn Jenner"—she smirks—"and some of us can't stand her. Some folks are like me, and have a deep sense of who they are, and want to do a medical transition. Some don't. Sometimes people know it from when they're children, like Lily. Other times, the light switches on a little later. I know transsexuals who've transitioned in their seventies."

"Transsexuals?" I repeat.

She grimaces. "Well, someone my age uses that word. But it's kind of going out of fashion, to tell you the truth. Because that word makes it sound like it's all about sex—which it's not. It's about fitting into the body you live in."

I wonder if it would be like being forced to wear size two clothes when you are a size twelve. You wouldn't be able to move comfortably. You'd always be aware of the fact that something pinched. There would be wardrobe malfunctions and embarrassment when you thought people were looking at you oddly. You'd be thinking constantly about taking off the outfit just so you could *breathe*.

But if you're trans, that too-tight ensemble never comes off.

"When did you know?" I ask.

"I was ten. But I never came out until I was forty-five. Now I'm sixty-seven. It'd have been better, maybe, if I came out when I was young. Like Lily." She finishes her smoke and crushes the cigarette beneath her shoe. "I'd probably have been a lot happier. Although, who knows?" She gives me a piercing look. "Maybe I'd have gotten killed. Like she did."

"My son did *not* kill her," I say, a reflex.

"You know this because . . . ?"

"Because I know Asher."

She glances at me. "Just like you knew Lily?"

There's a truth to those words that makes me freeze. People tend to see the default that is presented, instead of the complexity of the truth: the gamine teenage girl, the charming cardiac surgeon.

The innocent son.

Elizabeth shrugs. "*Somebody* killed her," she says, and the way she says this gives me chills. Because if it wasn't Asher—then who? "Dozens of transgender women are killed every year. Especially trans women of color. And that's only the ones we hear about. So many others are killed and thrown away, like their lives meant nothing, like this wasn't someone's child, someone's friend, someone's lover." She looks at me carefully, uncertain whether she should go on. "A lot of the time, it's the people who are supposed to love these women who get violent."

On the day I married Braden, if someone had told me that my prince would become a monster, I never would have believed it. I would have said no, that is not the direction in which the fairy tale goes. But there is a vast canyon between who we want people to be, and who they truly are.

We fall into silence as the sun disappears behind the ruined paper mill. For a moment it's a lot darker, the park falling into shadow. Then the sun bursts through windows on the mill and lights everything up again with the colors of goldenrod and rust.

Elizabeth looks at her watch. "I can't be away from the store much longer," she says. Code for: *We're done here.*

"Can I ask one more thing?" I say. "Did you know Lily was trans?"

"That's not the right question," she replies. "The right question is, why would anyone care?"

"My *son* would care," I say. "If he knew, I mean. You really think it doesn't matter? If she kept such an important thing secret from him?"

"Maybe," Elizabeth says, "you need to think about the difference between what is *secret* and what is *private*."

I want to tell her that those are the same things, but maybe they're not.

I think about my history with Braden. Is what happened between us a secret, in the way that the nuclear codes are secret? Or is it private, in the way that—painful as the facts are—this is history that belongs to me, and is mine to reveal?

Elizabeth leans forward on the railing, balanced on her elbows. "Ms. McAfee, do you know what made me come out here to talk to you?"

"To . . . help me understand?"

"No," she says. "Because I have a son, too."

I blink, surprised. "Does he go to school here, in Adams?"

"He'd be in his late twenties by now," Elizabeth says, looking toward the distant bank. "But I haven't been allowed to talk to him for over fifteen years. His mother told him I was dead."

"But—" I falter. "You're not dead."

"Depends on who you ask." Her gaze falls upon the slowly flowing river. "To be trans in this world means being at risk," she says. "That's true whether you're out, or not. Everybody in this town knows my story, and people are mostly nice. Not everybody, but mostly. Because they know me. But when I leave town, when my trio plays at somebody's wedding or something, people take one look at me and figure it out. I mean—I'm six foot four, I weigh nearly three hundred pounds, my voice—" She looks a little sad. "Well, I'm not exactly a soprano. You should see the looks people give me when I walk into a restaurant. It doesn't take more than five, ten minutes before everybody's whispering, elbowing each other in the ribs, *Hey, check out the freak show.*"

If I were in a bar and Elizabeth walked in, I'd probably look up at her. I'd probably draw all kinds of conclusions about her that had little to do with the truth.

"So why *wouldn't* Lily keep her business to herself?" asks Elizabeth. "She was exactly what she always wanted to be: a pretty young girl. She didn't go through the whole transition in order to have an asterisk next to her name, a footnote: pretty young girl *but* . . . She wanted to be herself. Is that really so hard to understand?"

Wife, I think. **Battered.*

"If you choose to carry that asterisk," Elizabeth says, "you get it coming and going. There's all the shit you catch for being trans. And then there's the shit you catch for being female. Sometimes, when I'm walking home by myself at night and I hear footsteps on the sidewalk behind me—when I'm driving a car alone, getting tailgated by some asshole . . . I don't really remember what it was like to not feel vulnerable in the world."

I have a sudden flash of my bee suit hanging from the hook in the mudroom. I like it because it's part of the job of caring for the hives, because it says *beekeeper* in the same way that a turned-around collar says *priest*. But I also like it because, while I'm wearing it, I feel invincible, like no harm can possibly come to me.

It's not a feeling a woman gets very often, whether she's trans or cis, or anything else.

From down the sidewalk, we hear a pair of voices approaching. Two teenage girls from the sound of them—but then I think: *What does it mean to* sound *like a girl? Is it pitch? Is it resonance? Is it the words themselves? Is the whole idea of sounding like this or that something we all just came up with at random, in order to separate people from each other?*

The girls pass us now, talking to each other, and whispering. They're about Lily's age. Or they're the age Lily was. Before she died.

"I'm sorry," I say.

"For?"

"Ambushing you?" I offer. "Not bothering to know all of this, before today? Take your pick." I shake my head. "I just wanted to understand Lily better."

"You just have to open your heart," says Elizabeth.

"I think my heart's pretty open," I say defensively, but even as I say it, I wonder: *Is this true?*

"Ms. McAfee," says Elizabeth. "Maybe you could . . . open it *more*?"

At this moment, the girls—now receding down the walkway along the river—burst into laughter.

"Did you *see* that?" says one girl.

"Oh my *God*," says the other.

How similar does someone have to be to you before you remember to see them, first, as human?

We don't say anything as we ascend the path back to Temple Street. A few pedestrians pass us by. This time I am aware of the looks Elizabeth gets from strangers. Some of them look at me, to see if I am like her.

Something in me wants to tell these people, I *am* like Elizabeth. I *am* like Lily. I am like a lot of women in the world who choose to conceal something; who live in fear of what might happen, if the exact wrong person ever found out.

LILY ◈ 6

Six weeks before

I'm looking in the mirror when I hear the screams. All the hairs on my arms stand up because whatever this is, it is *bad shit*. "Mom?" I rush out of the bathroom and fly down the stairs. There's a scary moment where I'm afraid that I'm about to tumble down the steps and kill myself.

"Mom?" I shout. I know she's in trouble. "*Mom!!!*"

And there at her desk she sits: holding a mug of coffee, wearing a huge grin. The screaming grows more intense. "Come here," she says, delighted. "You have to see this!"

On her computer there's a video of two wildcats standing in a forest clearing, face-to-face, yowling.

"Watch," says Mom. One lynx climbs atop the other, its claws sinking deep into the dark blond fur of the other. *Rrraaroooww! Rrraaroooww! Rrraaroooww!*

It's the lynx equivalent of *Stop! Don't stop!*

Mom pauses the video, then pushes her chair back from her desk contentedly. "I shot this yesterday on Bald Mountain," she says proudly. "Isn't it *awesome*! You never get to see this, *never!*"

"Why do they make that—sound?" I ask. "I thought somebody was dying."

"It's pent-up *kitten energy*," says Mom happily. "They were having a dispute. Finally, they—you know. *Reached an understanding.*" She looks at me. "You look nice," she says.

"Asher's picking me up," I tell her, and even as I say this, I can hear his Jeep pulling into the drive.

"Again?" Mom says pointedly.

Yes, I think. *Isn't it amazing?* But I head out the door without answering her. She has already started the video again. From the living room comes the sound of wildcats screaming.

Asher gets out of the car to open my door of the Jeep. *He was raised well,* my mother would say.

He's been like that for two weeks now—so attentive that he seems to know when I am cold, hungry, or tired before I even realize it myself. He has been charming, funny, self-deprecating—the perfect boyfriend. And he's touched me like I'm made of glass. I know he is still intent on proving to me that his outburst at the fencing meet was an anomaly, but I already know that. Whatever it was that made Asher so possessive there hasn't resurfaced. If he's trying to convince anyone now, it's himself.

We are supposed to be going to brunch, but I realize, as he starts driving, that something is off. He's drumming his free hand against the gearshift, and he seems lost in his own head. "I was thinking maybe we could go somewhere . . . else."

"Sure," I say. I don't care what we do, as long as I'm with him.

But my answer doesn't seem to put him at ease. "Is everything . . . okay?"

"There's something about me that you don't know," says Asher.

"Okay," I say slowly.

I cannot imagine that whatever's making him nervous is something that would affect how I feel about him. Because, of course, there are things about me I haven't revealed, either.

I want him to tell me, because I want to know everything about him. I want to know what makes him tick. But whatever age of honesty this ushers into our relationship, it won't be *I'll tell you mine if you'll tell me yours.*

Because I love Asher, but not enough to risk everything.

I am just falling, falling deep into the Sea of Asher, and I want to see everything, even the murk on the ocean floor. But it's not going to go both ways.

"You have to promise not to tell anyone."

"I promise." I wait for him to spill the beans, but he doesn't say anything. Then he drives past the town line. "Where are we going?"

"To Massachusetts," he says. "We're going to see my dad."

"Your dad?" I know that Olivia is a single mom, like mine. I know his parents are divorced. But in all the time Asher and I have been together, he has never spoken about his dad.

"That's the secret," he says. "That I see him once a month. At the Chili's in Leominster." He lets this sink in. "My mom doesn't know."

"Why not?"

We drive in silence for a little bit. "You could say they parted on— bad terms. It was pretty ugly."

"Uh-huh," I say.

"I didn't see him for a long time," says Asher. "But just about a year ago, I stalked him on Facebook. I sent him a message, and he answered. We went back and forth, eventually decided to meet. I hadn't seen him since I was six. I guess I— Well, it's not like I forgave him for everything. But I was curious. It was like there'd always been this hole in me, and I wanted to know what it would be like if I ever filled it up."

"What's he like?"

"You'll see," says Asher.

"That sounds ominous."

"No, no," says Asher. "He's excited to meet you."

"He knows I'm coming?"

"Oh yeah," says Asher. "I told him all about you."

That makes me glow inside. "What did you tell him?"

"Fishing for compliments?" Asher jokes. "That you play the cello. That you know the names of all the state capitals. That you can recite *The Princess Bride* from memory."

"Yeah?" I say with a smile. "What else did you tell him?"

"I told him I love you," he says. "And that you're the most important thing in the world to me right now."

And just like that, I'm completely slain. I want to kiss him until neither of us can breathe anymore and we die like that, asphyxiated by joy. But my throat closes up and I've lost my ability to talk, so instead I unbuckle my seatbelt and I lean my head on his shoulder and curl my arm across his chest.

Outside, the trees are orange and yellow and red and everything is on fire, as if we are the only two people in the world and the whole universe is blazing around us.

"I'm glad you found your dad," I say finally.

"You said," Asher asks carefully, "that your father died, when you were little?"

I pull back from Asher, refasten my seatbelt. It makes a sharp *click*.

"I don't want to talk about it," I say.

ASHER'S FATHER IS handsome, charming, funny, and larger than life, but there's something so practiced about it that I feel like it's a show. He puts down a ten-dollar tip on our thirty-dollar breakfast. From the way he puts down the bill you can tell he wants to make sure Asher and I have noticed, but also that he wants us to be sure that we didn't think he *wanted* us to notice.

"Dad, that's thirty percent," says Asher.

Our waitress, a curvaceous young woman named Tiffany, comes to pick up the check. "Well, she's worth it," says Mr. Fields—or Braden, as he insists I call him. He winks at her, and she blushes.

"Thank you, *Doctor*," says Tiffany, and I can tell from this that Tiffany's waited on Braden before.

Braden watches her walk away, then turns to Asher, his eyes twinkling. "And thank *you*, Tiffany." It's the kind of code traded between men—a semaphore for *She's hot, amirite?* I remember, a long time ago, when boys used to say that kind of thing in my presence, back when they thought that I spoke their secret language, too.

He looks at the receding Tiffany again, and for a moment his eyes narrow, like he's a lion zeroing in on a wildebeest. Then he smiles.

"Summer between high school and college," he says, "I had a job waiting tables. I never forgot how much it meant to me, somebody giving me a good tip."

"You waited tables?" says Asher. "I've never heard this story before." My heart breaks for Asher a little. He is so, so thirsty for stories about his father, especially ones that took place when Braden was the same age Asher is now.

"Lenny's Clam Shack, Newport News, Virginia. The only place in town that was open past eleven at night. It'd be quiet as the grave and then suddenly the place was packed. At dawn we'd all go out on the beach and watch the sun rise."

"Did you ever take Mom there?" Asher asks.

There's the shortest pause as Asher's mom gets mentioned. "No," he says. "We didn't meet until I was a resident." Braden looks at me, smoothly changing the subject. "Asher says you're a musician? You're hoping to go to a conservatory?"

"Yeah, maybe," I say. "But I don't know. Sometimes I think it'd be better if I went to some liberal arts college, and just majored in music. If I go to Oberlin, or Peabody, or Berklee, I'm afraid all I'll do is practice and I won't have time to do anything else."

"I get that, Lily," he says, looking thoughtful. "I was so focused on premed in college I never got to do a semester abroad, or play club sports, or act in a play. I wish I had, sometimes. I was the lead in my high school musical."

"Seriously?" says Asher, surprised again. "What was the show?"

"*Oliver!*" says Braden. "I was Fagin."

"*I'm reviewing,*" I sing to him, "*the situation . . .*"

"*Can a fellow be a villain all his life?*" he sings back to me, and laughs.

"All right, you two," says Asher. "Break it up."

"That's such a great show," I say. "You know what's weird, Lionel Bart wrote that one perfect musical, and that was it."

Braden shrugs. "There's a lot of people who just have one great work in them, though, aren't there? The guy who wrote *The Music Man—*"

"Meredith Willson," I say.

Braden narrows his eyes at me. Is he pissed I keep one-upping him? "Sounds like you know a lot about musical theater, Lily."

"She knows a lot about *everything*," Asher says, squeezing my hand. Braden gets out his pager, stares at it for a second like he's worried, then he gets out his phone, and stares at *that*. After about ten seconds, he puts them both away.

"Well," he says, and that's how we know it is time to leave. "I'm going to hit the men's room before I go back."

Asher and I wait in the booth. From speakers in the ceiling I can hear the sound of Miles Davis playing "Straight, No Chaser." It's the classic sextet, with John Coltrane, Cannonball Adderley, Red Garland, Paul Chambers, Philly Joe Jones.

Asher looks at me wryly. "What do you think of him?"

"Smooth," I say. "He's *real* smooth."

"Surprised?" says Asher, and I detect what sounds like pride in his voice, although I didn't mean it as a compliment.

I look down at my hands, braced around a cup of coffee. I'm wearing a shirt with three-quarter-length sleeves, and a gray cuff bracelet to hide the scars on my right wrist. I saw Braden eyeing it earlier, and I wonder if he suspected. He is a doctor, after all.

From my vantage point in the booth, I can see Braden come out of the bathroom. Instead of returning to the table, though, he crosses to the cash register and starts talking to our waitress. There's a strange intimacy between them that I can detect all the way across the room. He takes one of her hands, and gives it a squeeze. His eyes are fixed on her, like a lighthouse illuminating a ship at sea. Then he slips a card into her hand. He glances over and sees me and for a moment his expression looks weird again, like I've clearly witnessed something he didn't want anyone to see.

Braden strolls over to us.

"Ready to head out?" he says.

We get up from the table and follow him into the crisp October light. The Chili's borders a small park, and as we stand there an acorn pings off the windshield of Asher's Jeep and rolls toward Braden

Fields's feet. He picks it up and puts it in my palm, like the heavens have presented him with a gift, and in his generosity he's decided to pass it on to me. "Here you go, Lily," he says. "Take this home and plant it. Someday you'll have an oak tree."

"Thank you," I tell him.

"Did you ever hear the story about the man who asked his gardener to plant a tree? And the gardener complained that the tree was slow growing, and wouldn't mature for a hundred years. And the man replied—"

"*There's no time to lose then, plant it this afternoon,*" I say.

For a moment Braden gives me that look again, like he's annoyed with me. Then he smiles. "Right," he says.

Braden grasps his son's shoulder and gives it a squeeze. "See you next month," he says to Asher. He leans forward and kisses me on the left cheek, and then on the right one, European style.

A few moments later, Asher and I are headed north again, through the screaming colors of fall. We don't say anything for a while. I guess I'm waiting for him to start, and he's waiting for me. Finally, Asher says, "So?"

I say, "So."

"What do you think of him?"

I turn to him and blurt out, "Did he cheat on your mom?"

"What?" Asher asks, surprised. "Why?"

I don't want to tell him what I saw, but I don't *not* want to tell him, either. I shrug. "I didn't get the greatest vibe from him."

To my surprise Asher doesn't answer right away. Is this because he doesn't think his father is sketchy? Or because he does, and he was hoping I wouldn't pick up on it?

"When I told you things were bad between my parents before the divorce," says Asher, slowly. "What I didn't say was . . . how."

"What do you mean?"

"I'm pretty sure he hurt her," says Asher quietly. "It's not like she talks about it. I mean, she goes out of her way to *not* talk about it. But, like, we left in the middle of the night, when I was a kid. And I remember her wearing turtlenecks and long sleeves when it was hot out. And sometimes, when I come up behind her and she's not expecting it, she cringes. It's all these little things, that add up."

As Asher tells me this, I'm thinking about the bruise I had on my arm from where he grabbed me too hard after the fencing meet.

"If he hurt your mom," I ask, "why do you want to be part of his life?"

"He's still my *dad*," Asher says, defensive. "I mean, I get why my mom would want nothing to do with him ... but whatever I am is partly because of him."

I imagine Asher as a young boy, trapped between his arguing parents. For a horrible moment I remember the young child *I* used to be, as my own mother and father fought with each other. About me.

"What's his new family like?" I ask. "He kept mentioning his wife and ... some boys?"

"Shane and Shawn," he says. "Twins, eight years old. And his wife is named Margot. She's a nurse."

I want to say, *Well, that will come in handy.* We don't say anything for a while. I notice that Asher has begun to drive faster. "Do they look like you?" I ask him, finally. "The twins?"

"I don't know," he says. "Every time I'm supposed to go over there, something comes up. One time, their dog got—what's that thing when their stomach gets twisted?"

"Gastric dilatation-volvulus," I say, remembering the time that Boris got it after swimming all afternoon in the Pacific.

"Whatever," says Asher. "Another time one of the boys got sick."

"So you've never met them," I say.

He's driving really fast now. We're up over seventy on a little two-lane road. A sign says WELCOME TO NEW HAMPSHIRE. LIVE FREE OR DIE.

"No," says Asher, his face reddening. "Go on, say it."

But we both know I don't have to.

"You think he pities me." On the far side of the turn a minivan flashes his lights at us, and honks.

"I don't think he pities you," I tell Asher. "I think he's playing you."

"Yeah, like you know anything about him."

"I know enough, Asher," I say. "I've got eyes."

Asher honks back at the minivan. "Asshole," he says. "Can you believe these fucking assholes?"

"Can you slow down?" I ask him. "You're scaring me."

"Well, you're pissing me off!" he shouts. Asher is driving faster and faster now: eighty, eighty-five miles an hour. There's another curve ahead of us.

"I said you're scaring me!" I shout at him.

"You're going to tell me how to drive now?" he says. "Is that it? Cause I know you're an expert on fucking everything."

"All right, stop the car!" I yell at him. "Goddammit, Asher, fucking stop! You're going to get us killed!"

Asher is now driving close to ninety. He looks at me with a wild smile, like he is actually enjoying the fact that I'm frightened. Which I am. And his driving like this isn't the thing that scares me the most. What's worse is the fact that Asher has suddenly turned into a stranger.

"Please stop!" I shout. I can't believe that now he's got me begging. "Please, Asher!" I'm clutching the handle on the Jeep's ceiling.

"You don't know everything, Lily, okay? There's some shit that's so dark you can't possibly imagine it, ever! You couldn't even if you tried."

"Stop the car!" I yell at him. "Goddammit, Asher, just fucking *stop!*"

But he doesn't. We must be doing close to a hundred. In a panic I reach over and grab the wheel, but Asher flings me back with his right arm and I feel myself crash against the window on my side. I cry out in pain as I bounce off the glass, but it's not really the pain that makes me cry. The thought flickers through me: *I'm going to have a bruise on my shoulder, a bruise given to me by the boy I thought I loved.* Asher jams his foot down on the brake and now—*finally*—we screech to a stop, bumping and skidding all over the road. A car comes around the curve before us, its horn blaring all the way. We just sit there on the shoulder, in a hot, angry silence.

"Fuck you!" I shout at him. "What is *wrong* with you?"

"Me?" he says. "You think *I'm* the one who's got a problem?"

"I don't even know who you are right now," I say.

Asher doesn't look at me. His jaw is clenched so tight I think he might break a tooth. He pulls out, driving the speed limit. "That makes two of us," he says.

WHEN I WAS six years old, my father took me out of kindergarten one day and brought me to the circus—Ringling Bros. and Barnum & Bailey. I remember the smell of the popcorn and the sparkling leotard of the lady on the high wire and how very big the elephants were. It was just the two of us; Mom must have been out on the Olympic seashore that week. I remember being a little frightened by how many people were in the arena. I remember his arm around my back.

But most of all I remember the man who was shot out of the cannon. He had a big handlebar mustache, striped shorts, and a white muscle shirt with a red star on it. His head was shaved bald, and it reflected the glare of the spotlight that lit him up. There was a drumroll as he was hoisted by the acrobats into the muzzle. He waved to the crowd, as if saying farewell, and then he disappeared into the barrel of the cannon and a moment later there was an explosion and a puff of white smoke and that man with the star on his chest soared through the air. Then he landed in a net on the other side of the arena and everyone clapped, and I looked at my father and said, *Will he do it again?* and Dad explained no, it was a onetime thing. A moment later a woman rode into the ring standing on two white horses, one foot on the back of each steed, and I forgot about the human cannonball for the rest of the night, at least until the moment when, full of popcorn and snow cones and hot dogs and soft pretzels, I lay my head down on my pillow, and my dad kissed me on the forehead and said, *Remember today, Liam. Life was good today.*

I fell asleep thinking about what it might feel like to be shot out of a cannon. To fly through the air. For days I wondered about the moment at the top of the arc, the moment when the human cannonball was suspended between the explosion that had propelled him toward the ceiling and the long fall back to earth. I imagined being immune from gravity. Being that free.

I remember asking my father one morning, as I ate my Alpha-Bits, if I could be a human cannonball when I grew up. He laughed and said, *You can be anything you want to be, Liam.*

Years later, after I'd tried—and failed—to kill myself, I remembered that man with the star on his chest. This was when I was starting to wake up in the hospital. I hadn't seen a tunnel of white light or heard angelic voices calling me, or any of that. There was a black space, and then there was the room, and my mother was sitting in a chair by my bed, and I closed my eyes and disappeared. It was like that for a long time, like I was at the top of my arc, between the explosion that had launched me skyward, and the long fall back to earth, and everything that lay ahead.

Eventually my eyes were open long enough for my mother to say things that I understood. *You're okay, Lily,* she said. *You're safe, and I love you.* There were bandages on my right arm. I'd lost a lot of blood.

The first thing I said, when I got around to saying anything, was *Where's Dad?* Mom looked really confused, and then she looked hurt, and then tears filled her eyes. Because of course, we'd left Seattle years ago. I found out later my father didn't even know what I had done.

But in my head, I was sure we'd only been to the circus a couple days before. He'd kissed me on the forehead and told me never to forget that day when things were good.

When I got out of the hospital a few days later and we went back to the Point Reyes cabin, I tried to make sense of what had happened to me. Not cutting my wrist, of course—that was still all too clear. So was saying goodbye to Boris, climbing the stairs, filling the tub. I knew I had listened to the water running, had thought about leaving a note, but couldn't think of anything to say that would make it all less terrible for my mother. I remembered putting on the Barber Adagio for Strings and how, when the tub was full, I took off all my clothes and lay down in the water.

That part I could make sense of. What was incomprehensible to me was the Valentine's Day dance the night before: getting picked up by my friend Jonah in his mother's Prius, for the date that had come out of nowhere.

Until he asked me to the dance, I'd thought Jonah was never going to talk to me again. He'd been so ugly to me. But then, out of the blue, he'd asked me to the dance, and given me a sheepish apology, too. *You just have to give people time,* he'd said, and gave me a look. I should have known that it was a look of malice.

But I so wanted to believe in the goodness of people.

There was a mirror ball in the gym. The music: "Can't Stop the Feeling!" by Justin Timberlake, "Cold Water," by Major Lazer, "One Dance" by Drake. The expression on Jonah's face, all night long, like he knew something I didn't. *Here,* he said at one point, handing me a can of Coke. *Have something to drink.*

It was weird seeing everyone all dressed up. Students there acted like vegan hippies, but at the dance it was clear how much money they all had. In their tuxes and their gowns, you could see the people they were behind their masks, the people that they'd grow up to be, little carbon copies of their parents.

My friend Sorel came up to me at one point and said, *Lily, you have to get out of here. I'm not kidding. You think these people are your friends, but they're not.*

All I could think was *Actually the person who is not my friend is you.*

I'd come out to Sorel a few months earlier. She'd said I was the *bravest person she'd ever known.*

Then she betrayed me, by telling everyone else that I was trans.

She'd spilled the beans the semester before, fall of 2016. The school, which was supposed to be so progressive, turned me into the diversity poster child. I had never wanted that; all I'd ever wanted was to fit in, to be left alone.

Jonah and I danced to a few of the early tunes, but then he vanished, leaving me standing alone and awkward. I started feeling really strange, like time was speeding up and slowing down.

I thought about that Coke that he had given me, and wondered whether anything else was in it. My co-captain from the fencing team was there. Boyd looked like he'd been inflated with helium, he was so large. His voice echoed strangely in the dark space, and it was hard to understand him. When I walked, it was like wading through hot tar.

Then Jonah appeared out of nowhere. I could tell from his eyes he was wasted. *I've been looking all over for you.*

We went out on the dance floor. The DJ put on a song by Aerosmith. Jonah spun me around, and I saw all the faces of the people I went to school with, all my friends, watching us, smiling.

She had the body of a Venus, Lord, imagine my surprise.

The tiny sparkles of light from the mirror ball revolved around the dance floor. *Dude looks like a lady.*

Then there was a drumroll, and somebody said, *Now! The moment you've all been waiting for. The crowning of the Valentine's King and Queen!*

There was a spotlight, and Jonah and I were standing in it, and everyone was applauding. *Lily O'Meara, come on up here!*

I felt giddy, airborne. I couldn't believe that Jonah and I were going to be crowned. Sorel was wrong about these people. They knew the truth, and it did not matter to them! It had been a long, hard road, but I'd come into my own at last.

Come on, Jonah, I said. *They want us!*

Not us, Lily, he said. *Just you.*

I'm not sure how I got to the front of the room. But I remember them putting the crown upon my head. And then the sash: VALENTINE'S KING AND QUEEN.

Even now I'm not sure if they were trying to humiliate me on purpose, simply because they were all cruel fucks—or if, in some twisted universe, they thought that crowning me king *and* queen was supposed to be a joke I was in on. *We're not laughing* at *you, we're laughing* with *you!*

It didn't feel like they were laughing with me, though, when they cued up "Dude (Looks Like a Lady)" on the speakers again.

It didn't feel like they were laughing with me when the tears poured down my face and I rushed off the stage and through a side exit into the parking lot.

It didn't feel like they were laughing with me when I ran head-long into a crowd of people who yanked off my crown and tore off my sash. I struggled to get away from them but someone—*it was Boyd, from the fencing team, but how could it be Boyd?*—had me in a headlock. I heard fabric tearing. They pulled off my shoes. They tore my dress. Then they grabbed my panties and cheered, like they were playing Capture the Flag. I lay on the pavement, naked from the waist down, while everyone stood around laughing like my body was the funniest punch line they'd ever heard.

I don't know how long I stayed there on the asphalt after they left. I lay on my back looking up at the sky. There were no stars.

Then Sorel was there. *I'm so sorry,* she said. *I tried to stop them. I really did.* In slow motion she picked me up and got me into her car. I didn't say anything.

In the morning I woke up in an empty house. Somehow, word hadn't gotten back to Mom, and incredibly, she'd just headed off to the national park to do her job, same as any other day. There was a note on the kitchen counter: *Have a muffin! Back by supper!* There was a little heart at the bottom of the note.

Oh Mom, I thought. *You tried so hard.*

I grabbed a paring knife from the butcher block. Boris raised his head and cocked his ears. *Are you okay?*

No, Boris. Actually. I'm not.

As I climbed the stairs, I had a last, fleeting memory of that human cannonball at the circus. My father's hand upon my back. *You can be anything you want to be, Liam.*

I would never know what it felt like to fly. But I knew all about what it was like to come crashing back to earth.

.   .   .

IN THE DAYS after I got out of the hospital, my dreams were dark. I'd find myself wandering through underground caves, hearing the dripping of water, every once in a while seeing a shaft of light falling from a distant crack overhead. I'd search those caves, looking for a way out, but I just got more and more lost. Now and again I heard the sound of footsteps behind me, and from this I knew that I was not alone in my tomb.

I saw a social worker while I was in recovery, a sweet woman named Deirdre, who, as I quickly found out, had a strategy for keeping me alive, which wasn't to get me to see the whole world through a different pair of eyes, but simply to get me to agree not to make another attempt before the next time I saw her. Mom, of course, wanted to solve all my problems, but Deirdre seemed to understand that if anyone was going to solve my problems it was going to be me. We did agree that I wouldn't have to go back to Pointcrest, and that I'd finish eleventh grade by homeschooling. Mom took an indefinite leave from the Park Service and stayed in the house with me all day. But what could she do besides make chicken noodle soup and look worried? I sat myself down in front of the Akela Homeschooling video tutorials, but my heart wasn't in it. The chirpy instructor just droned on and on about cosines and the Missouri Compromise and *As I Lay Dying*. All I could think about was that dance, and Jonah, and Boyd, and all those people I'd thought had been my friends.

I thought about the crown they'd put on my head.

Eventually I stopped the Akela videos and just spent a lot of time flipping through this old encyclopedia we had. It had been published in 1953. I read about Vice President Richard Nixon. I read about the Suez Canal. I read about this new planet, Pluto, which they'd discovered only twenty-three years before. I didn't keep up with the other stuff I was supposed to be learning, though—chemistry and pre-calc. It was weird, because I'd always loved school so much: it was the one thing I was good at. But now, for the first time in my life, I just thought, *What's the point? Everything comes to nothing in the end.*

The worst of it was the day I made one last-ditch attempt at doing the reading for the AP Psychology course. There wasn't any mention of trans or nonbinary people until I got to a chapter titled "Abnormal Psychology." I checked the title page, thinking, well, maybe this, too, was a book that hadn't been updated since 1953. But it had been published in 2005, just a dozen years before.

Abnormal? I thought. *I'm tearing my heart out, trying to find my way. And all you've got for me is* abnormal?

In time my wrist healed; I started playing cello again. Mom tried to act like I was getting better. But all the knives and razors in the house had been hidden away, along with all the prescription medicines.

The dreams got darker, a little more each night. I was lost in the dark, chasing after flickering shafts of light. I'd hear the footsteps behind me. Then I'd turn. I'd see the silhouette of a man, hunched over, drawing closer. *Lily,* he'd say. *I'm waiting for you.*

THERE'S A TAPPING on my window, and I sit up in bed, terrified. Lightning flickers, and rain hammers against the glass. In the light I see that shadow, and I see that he's here now, come for me at last.

He taps again. *Lily. It's me.*

The lightning flickers once again, and in the flash I can see that it's Asher.

I get out of bed and open the window and he steps into my room, soaking wet. "What the fuck, Asher?"

"Sorry," he says, whispering. He's wearing a backpack. "I didn't mean to scare you."

I look at the clock. "It's almost 1:00 A.M.?"

"I had to see you," he says. I close the window. Outside, the rain rushes into the gutters.

"What did you do, bring a ladder?" I ask him.

"I climbed up the tree onto the roof," he says.

"I'm not even sure I'm fucking talking to you right now," I whisper, although I want to yell it.

"I know," Asher says. Then, again, more softly: "I know." He takes off the backpack and unzips it. There's a bouquet of flowers inside, late-season mums and black-eyed Susans from his mother's farm. "I picked these for you," he says, a little embarrassed, and it's in his awkwardness at this moment that I actually recognize the boy that I love. And not the hotheaded asshole who scared me half to death in the car today.

"What happened today?" I ask him. "I felt like I was driving around with some stranger."

Asher looks at the bed. "Can I sit down?"

I think about it. "No."

"Please?"

I sigh. "You're wet."

He nods. "I know."

"Wait," I say, and I slip out into the hallway and into the bathroom, where I grab one of the towels. While I'm there, I steal a glance in the mirror. A frightened girl looks back.

I head back into the bedroom, and Asher's sitting down on the bed, after I told him not to. The flowers he gave me are lying on the pillow.

He dries himself off with the towel, then he looks at the floor. "I got mad," he says. "Because you were telling the truth."

Asher saying this to me makes me feel like I've been stabbed with a sword—because of course, the question of whether and when to tell him about my private truth is the one thing that is starting to really mess with me.

"Was I?" I ask quietly.

I sit down next to him. "When you said you didn't know who I was ... and looked at me like that—" His voice cracks. "I only saw that look once before in my life. On my mom's face." He pauses for a moment. "I don't have many memories of my parents together. I remember them fighting, the sound of their voices. But most of all I remember that look—the look of someone who sees that the person who's supposed to look out for them is actually the person who's putting them in danger."

The rain is still hammering against the windowpane. Lightning flickers in the distance. Fifteen seconds later, thunder rolls. Which means that the storm is three miles away: you count the seconds, and then divide by five.

"When we drove off this morning," Asher says. "I told you there was something about me you didn't know."

I nod. Lightning flashes once more.

"It wasn't what I thought," he says.

"What do you mean?"

"I mean, it wasn't that I see my father once a month at the Chili's. The secret is—it's that I'm afraid I'm more like him than I want to be."

"Asher," I say, wrapping my arms around him. Thunder rolls in the distance. I hold him for minutes, maybe even hours. I know I ought to be warier of him at this moment, that I shouldn't so quickly forgive him for what happened in the car on the way home. Because that was some bad shit. I'm never going to forget what I saw in him today, what I understood he was capable of doing.

But it's up to me right now to decide whether I believe him when he says he's sorry.

And I do. Because I know better than anyone the power of second chances. If that makes me an idealist, I'll admit to that. It's not that I'm not angry with him anymore. But at the same time, even more than the anger I feel is the desire that I have to do whatever I can to take away his pain.

I rub his back and kiss his hair. It smells like rain. After a while he pulls back and we look each other in the eye. Both our faces are wet. "I'm sorry," he whispers. "I'll never hurt you again. I promise."

"I love you," I tell him. "All of you. Even the dark parts."

"I love you, too," he says, and our faces draw close together and we kiss and we kiss and we kiss.

He is so tender, and so gentle. I think, *Asher Fields is nothing like his father.*

There's a lightning flash, but I never hear the thunder. The storm is moving off. The rain is still falling, but it's lost its fury.

"What's your biggest secret?" Asher says.

I open my mouth, but nothing comes out.

"Lily?" He can see I'm struggling.

"If I tell you," I say, "you have to promise never to tell anyone, ever." I hear his own words from this morning echo in mine.

"I promise," Asher says.

I can feel the truth rising in me. I can almost hear it spoken in this quiet room. I so want to tell him. But then I remember Jonah, and Point Reyes. I'm actually shaking now, because I can't imagine telling him, and I can't imagine not telling him, and I don't know how I'm going to survive going on like this. Even after everything I've been through, I'm *still* torn in half.

But then Asher puts his hand on my wrist. "I think I know," he says, and he gently pulls off my gray cuff bracelet.

Even in the dim light of my bedroom, the scars are still visible.

"I told you I got these in a car crash," I say. "But I didn't."

"Oh, Lily," he murmurs, and from the way he says this, I can see he's really shocked.

"It was a year and a half ago. Valentine's Day." I feel the tears coming as I remember. But I also feel a sense of fear, because even if I give him more of the truth, it's not all of it, and he deserves to know *why* I tried to kill myself. And that's what I can't tell him.

He traces the scars that travel horizontally across my wrist: one, two, three. He waits.

"There was a dance," I murmur, aware that my mother is just down the hall; and that saying it out loud makes it come alive again: all those cruel faces, the laughter. Aerosmith. Sorel, whispering, *You think these people are your friends, but they're not.*

How can I explain this all to Asher? If he had been there, would he have been among the crowd that put me in a headlock and then tore off my clothes?

No, that's impossible. He'd have defended me. Yet if that is true: how can I *not* explain this all to him?

"I'm not good at talking about it," I confess. "I was in the hospital for a while." If I can tell him just a few true things, maybe it won't be the same as lying. "After the dance—no, *during* the dance, some people—"

"You don't have to tell me anything you don't want to," says Asher, and he holds me tight. And all at once, I shudder, and I'm sobbing. In a year and a half, I've never cried about it, not like this. All this time I've had to keep it in, prove to Mom that I was strong enough to get through surgery, to get through the move, to get through everything. Prove it to everyone, including myself.

Except that I'm not strong. I'm exhausted from living this life.

As I'm weeping it occurs to me that no one's ever put his arms around me and protected me like this before. For the first time, I almost do feel safe.

"There was a fight," I say again. "After the dance. I got hurt." I take a deep breath. "I got hurt by people who I thought were my friends. Instead they—" I swallow. "They tore my dress off in a parking lot, and laughed. Everybody was there. Even the boy who'd been my—"

Asher takes all this in. He looks me deep in the eyes. "I'm not him," he says. Then he says it again. "Listen to me. *I'm not him.*"

The rain has almost stopped. Water drips onto the roof outside my window.

"I never went back to school," I told him. "And I didn't go back last year, either. I finished up eleventh grade at home. That's why I'm a year older than everyone. I had a lost year."

I'm not telling him what else happened during my lost year.

"I'm really glad," Asher says. "That you didn't succeed."

"Me, too," I tell him. "Me, too."

Our kisses feed into each other and I have two sensations at once. The first one is the feeling of finally occupying my body exactly in the way I always dreamed: because what's even the point of having a body, if not to be able to choose to give it away to someone you love?

And the other sensation is both this feeling's twin and its opposite: that I am not a body at all, that I am floating free above myself like the human cannonball, and that after a lifetime of being chained to the earth by my own flesh I am unbound.

"I want to tell you something else," I say.

A car goes by the house, and the wet tires make a shushing sound against the pavement. There is a long, long silence while I try to find my nerve.

Then I say, "I changed my name."

"Really?" says Asher.

"My mother's maiden name was Campanello," I say. "But my father's name was O'Meara."

"O'Meara!" he says, and he sounds delighted. "All this time, I've been going out with an Irish girl? And I never even knew?"

"Half Irish," I tell him.

"Wow. You went from O'Meara to Campanello! So many more letters. It must have been painful!"

He smiles, like he's made a hilarious joke. But I want to tell him, *You have no idea.*

Asher can tell I'm thinking something, because he looks at me seriously. Maybe he's remembering the way I shut down the conversation today when he asked me about my father. I whisper, "Actually, it *was* painful."

"Well," says Asher, holding me tight. "I love you no matter what your name is."

"Why?" I ask, because no one, except my mother, has really loved me before, and I'm pretty used to thinking of myself as someone who is impossible to love.

What is it that Asher can see in me that everyone else is blind to?

"Because you're the only one who gets me," he says.

"That's how I feel," I tell him.

He tips his forehead to mine. "I wish," Asher whispers, "the world was just the size of you and me."

"Maybe it can be," I say.

My hand slowly, slowly slides down toward his pants. And then, the most incredible thing of all happens.

"Wait," he says, and I am wondering if Asher, or any boy, ever, has ever said these words before.

"Wait?" I say.

"Let's do this the right way," he says.

"This isn't the right way?" I ask. I think of those wildcats in my mother's video, and the sounds they made.

"Our first time should be somewhere . . . we don't have to whisper."

I feel like I'm surfing on an ocean of feelings: disappointment, but also relief. Because in addition to being psyched I'm also more than a little afraid. "Tomorrow," he says. "I'll find a place. We'll make it a night to remember."

I want to tell him that I'm going to remember *today*, actually.

We kiss for a long time, and then he grabs his now-empty backpack, goes to the window, and steps out onto the roof.

"Good night, Juliet," he says.

"Good night, sweet prince."

And just like that he climbs down the tree and into the night. I go to the bed and pick up the flowers he gave me. I bury my face in the blossoms.

IT WAS A little more than three months after what I'd started calling the Valentine's Day Massacre, two weeks after I'd played the impossible Schubert sonata, two weeks after I'd successfully risen from the dead.

Two weeks after I'd realized that even though I'd done all this, I was still trapped.

Mom and I walked down the long stairs that led to the Point Reyes Lighthouse—more than three hundred steps down the rocky cliff. Mom went first, carrying a picnic basket. She was wearing her Park Service uniform, complete with the Smokey the Bear hat. I was wearing a long black skirt and a black tank top.

The stairs were lined on either side by a short hurricane fence. It was there to protect the fragile, dry landscape, but it also protected people like me, who, if the fencing were not there, would be sorely tempted to take off over the cliffs and plunge into the cruel, seething water below.

I hadn't wanted to go. Mom had said she had a surprise for me. I told her I didn't want any more surprises. She'd said, *I have to show you something*. Then she'd added, *Please?*

It had taken about forty-five minutes to get there. On the way, we'd pulled over to look at the sea lions, hundreds of them all splayed out on the beach below like giant blobs of jelly. I'd been surprised by the smell of the sea lions, too, how strong it was, a thick stink of brine and fish and sand. Some people don't know the difference between sea lions and elephant seals. They're both pinnipeds, but sea lions are really, really, really huge. They walk on their flippers, unlike seals, which wriggle on their bellies.

Eight months earlier, I'd stood there with Jonah and he'd kissed me for the first time. It was before Sorel told everyone.

We got to the visitors' center at four o'clock. There, a ranger named Rudy waved at Mom. "This must be your daughter," he said.

"Rudy, this is Lily," said Mom, and Rudy winked at her. Just then I noticed the sign at the top of the stairs that said: LIGHTHOUSE CLOSES AT 4 P.M.

"The sign says it's closed," I told her.

"I know what the sign says," said Mom.

The lighthouse was a small tower with a red roof and a glass dome. Next to it was an equipment cottage—like a little white barn that also had a red roof. We walked into the lighthouse and passed through its lower chamber, filled with displays on the light's history. We climbed the stairs to the next level, where they keep the original clockworks and a Fresnel lens. "Just a little further," said Mom, and we spiraled up a tiny set of metal stairs to the top of the tower, even though there was a sign that said STAIRS CLOSED.

The top of the lighthouse tower had round glass walls and a spectacular view of the Pacific Ocean. On the floor was a checkered tablecloth and a candle. I realized that whatever this was, Mom had been planning it for a long time.

"Have a seat," she said. It was a small space, not much bigger than the tablecloth itself. We were bathed in light, surrounded by the sound of crashing waves and the cries of seagulls. Mom lit the candle, then opened her picnic basket and took out two plastic wine-glasses.

"When I was a little girl, my mother had a ritual," she said. "Every year on my birthday, she took me into New York City and we had lunch at the Waldorf. We wore matching dresses. We had our hair done. We got mani-pedis."

It was a little hard to imagine Mom getting a mani-pedi, but I just nodded. "Sounds like fun," I said.

"Yeah, that's the thing," Mom said. "I *hated* it. Even when I was seven years old, I hated it. I always hated dresses. I hated people messing with my hair. I hated the Waldorf. Most of all, I hated the fact that this was what Mom thought I wanted, that she was so clueless. It was like being reminded, year after year, that she had no idea who I was."

She had my attention now.

"The year I turned sixteen I told her I wasn't going to do it anymore. Mom was heartbroken. She said something like *But you love going to the Waldorf!* I had to tell her, *No, what I love is camping in subzero temperatures and tracking brown bear. What I love is fishing for brook trout in the spring when the ice is first melting in the streams. What I love is standing up to my ass in a swamp so I can watch a snapping turtle lay its eggs.* She took it hard. I should have told her years before that, but I guess up until then I hadn't realized that the whole time, the only reason I was doing it was because I knew it was so important to her."

She poured some white wine into the glasses, and then raised hers. "We're here," she said, "because I want to propose a toast."

"Okay," I said, although it was pretty unusual for her to be serving me wine. "What are we toasting?"

"We are toasting my daughter," she said. "Who at last I think I understand."

We clinked plastic glasses, and I sipped the wine. It was sweet.

"What is it you understand?" I asked her.

"I've been talking to Dr. Powers," she said. "Do you know who she is?"

Of course I knew who Monica Powers was. She ran one of the best transgender medical clinics in the country, in San Francisco.

I went very still, afraid to hope. "What have you been talking to Dr. Powers about?"

"About you," she said. "About surgery."

My mouth fell open. "There's an age limit. You have to be eighteen."

"Dr. Powers accepts clients as young as seventeen, if they've been on hormone blockers and been living successfully as themselves in the world. Which you have."

I thought about my suicide attempt, and in what possible universe this counted as *living successfully in the world*.

"You said—you said that surgery was the bridge you couldn't cross. That you'd help me with the hormone blockers, and getting me on estrogen—but that surgery was too—"

"I think the word I used was *unnatural*." She put her wineglass down. "I was wrong." She looked out the windows of the lighthouse at the blue ocean. "I've spent my whole life studying nature, educating people about it as well as protecting it. I guess that's what I thought I was doing—protecting you from making a mistake, and trying to educate you about the world. But all this time, I had everything backward. The person I was trying to protect wasn't you, it was me."

"Mom," I said. "You've done everything for me—"

"Everything except really see you," said Mom, and there were tears hovering in her eyes, and the fact that she was going to cry *while wearing her ranger uniform* made it even worse. "It's like my mother taking me to the Waldorf."

"What are you saying?"

"If you want to have the surgery, you should have the surgery, and have it *now*. If we get on Dr. Powers's wait list, you can be treated this fall. You take next year off from school, recover from surgery, and finish eleventh grade at home. I was talking to a friend of mine who works for the Forest Service, in the White Mountains. They have three retirements coming up. If I can pass the Forest Service exam, I can land one of those jobs. And you can really begin living your life."

The crashing of waves and the crying of gulls was coming from outside, but I could feel the shudder under my own ribs. From her picnic basket Mom pulled a Hope Cake, a recipe she made for me sometimes when she wanted to lift my spirits. On the top, in icing script, was written CONGRATULATIONS.

And underneath this: IT'S A GIRL.

I swallowed hard. "Mom," I said. "I have one question."

"What is it?"

"Where are the White Mountains?"

IN THE MOVIES, sex just happens. With one arm, everything is recklessly swept off of a kitchen table; or the man just hoists the woman aboard in some swiftly moving freight elevator; or they collapse on a giant bed in a room filled with flickering candles. But if you're Asher and me, it can't just *happen*. It takes planning, and strategy, and cunning. Asher wants it to happen in a place where we don't have to worry about being discovered, by our moms, or by strangers, or by anyone else. But he also wants it to be somewhere special. Our first time shouldn't be in the back of the Jeep, or on a blanket in the woods, or—God forbid—anywhere near those buzzing beehives of his mother's. It can't be in our bedrooms because Ava or Olivia might walk in, and it can't be outside where anyone could see us, and it can't be anywhere on the campus at school because the only thing worse than our parents walking in would be our teachers. Or Maya. Or Dirk.

And it's not just a question of *where* and *when,* it's also a question of *how.* Asher has asked me about birth control, and I told him the truth—that I'm not on the pill, although I didn't tell him why. He said he'd get condoms, and I almost wanted to tell him that I can't get pregnant and not to bother—but then I thought about STDs and realized that, no matter how special what we have is, this is definitely not Asher Fields's first trip to the candy store.

I haven't told Asher that it's my first time. I wonder if he knows.

I wonder if him knowing that it's my first time makes a difference to him.

I wonder what it will feel like.

I wonder, most of all, whether he's going to be able to tell.

Dr. Powers had told me that when all was said and done, "even your doctor won't know the difference unless she looks very, very carefully." The few times I've gotten out a mirror and checked out *the unit,* it seems like that's true. Also, I'm pretty sure Asher's not going to be doing an *inspection.* For all I know, everything's going to be under blankets, and maybe we'll have the lights out? I'd like that, I admit, just so I don't have to worry about all of this. But another part of me thinks, *Dammit, when do I get to stop hiding?* I *want* to see Asher's face. I *want* to see his body. I want to see *everything.*

People think that being trans is about sex. I suppose for some, it is. But for me, sex was the last thing I was thinking about. I want to be alive and I want to be joyful and I want to be on fire, I want to be so human it makes the ice in my water glass melt. So, sure: I love sex—or at least the idea of it—and I want to experience every last sensation I can ever feel. But none of that was ever what was driving me to become myself. For me, being trans was always more about the heart than any other organ. If I were, like, some disembodied spirit, a ghost that blew around on the wind, I would still be female. If I were a head in a jar, I would still be female. If I were just a piece of forgotten music played at night on a viola da gamba, I would still be female. All along, the only thing I ever wanted was for the thing I felt in my heart to find its home in the body in which it ought to have been nestled from the beginning.

So it's ironic that, now that I finally have all of that, having sex with the boy that I love turns out to be so complicated. I guess sex is *always* complicated. But only for me does giving myself up completely to someone else threaten to resurrect the person I used to be.

To tell you the truth, what I'm afraid of isn't that Asher's going to be able to tell anything by looking at me. No, what I'm afraid of is that he's going to be able to tell because of how I act.

I don't actually know *how* to be with a man.

The only thing that makes me less nervous about all of this is that every woman, the first time she sleeps with a man, doesn't know, either.

Maybe, against all odds, my biggest problem is that—I'm normal?

Everybody is always still trying to learn, day after painful day, how to be themselves.

I can't wait.

ASHER SAID WE were going to have sex the day after he snuck into my room, but on Sunday he texted me and said he needed more time to figure it all out, and so by the time I finally get the text that says *CAN I GET YOU NOW* it's a week later, Saturday afternoon, and between the equal portions of fear and excitement I've been feeling, this week has taken about nine thousand years to go by.

But there is the honk in the driveway, and I am floating down the stairs like I have wings. Mom is up on Bald Mountain tracking wildcats again, so I am spared having to explain where I'm going.

We go to Asher's house, and after he parks in the barn he takes me to the fields behind the house, just along the edge, where it meets the thick forest filled with naked maples and the birches with their papery white bark. We walk hand in hand to the base of an old tree. There's a rope ladder hanging down, and high above our heads is the base of an elaborate, if slightly decayed, tree house. The rope ladder leads to a trapdoor in the middle of the floor.

"I'm going to go up first," says Asher. "I'll tell you when to come."

He kisses me, and then he ascends the ladder. At the top he puts one hand on the trapdoor and swings it open. A moment later, he disappears into the dark above me.

In the distance I can see Olivia's beehives, arrayed in a semicircle. I think of all those fluttering wings.

"Okay," calls Asher.

The rope ladder is harder to climb than I expected, but between my fencing muscles and my absolute eagerness to reach him, I climb up the rungs in seconds. My head pops into an old wooden chamber, with a window in each wall. Light slants through the window that faces the fields. Asher reaches over and helps me up. Then he pulls up the ladder and closes the trapdoor.

The tree house is filled with romantic touches—a soft knitted blanket on the floor, a half dozen flickering candles all around, a yellow lantern hanging from a beam overhead. There's a little platter of chocolates. There's a cooler and two wine goblets. There's a pillow with a yellow silk pillowcase. There is soft music playing from a boom box in one corner—it's the Yo-Yo Ma and Kathryn Stott album *Songs from the Arc of Life*.

It's the music that most touches me, because it shows me once again that Asher *knows* me. "Wow," I say, at a loss for words. "Look at what you did."

Asher puts his arms around me, and it begins, so slowly that I never have the sense of moving from the time before sex to the time while it is happening. It is like the quiet part of Aaron Copland's *Appalachian Spring*, all those strings just hovering so softly and sweetly that it's almost impossible to know when the music has stopped, and when it is just a memory of itself. We spend a long time just holding each other in the yellow light, kissing each other on the neck, kissing each other on the lips, kissing each other on the ears. His hands cup my breasts and he looks down at me with amazement, like I am a goddess risen out of the sea, and the love in his eyes makes me think, *Well, the hell yes, that's exactly what I am.* I unbutton his flannel shirt, carefully, thoughtfully, taking in each new wonderful revealed inch of him—that athlete's chest, the tight muscles across his stomach. He lowers his arms and his shirt falls to the floor, and I raise mine, and he pulls my shirt off over my head and he reaches around back and my bra comes undone and then I reach down for his pants. I touch him and he feels wonderful in my hand, like something raw and living that has just forced its young head above the wet earth.

Then he takes a step back, and says, "Careful," and I know he's telling me he wants this to last. We lie down upon the blanket on the floor, and I rest my head on the pillow, and Asher reaches over with one hand and grabs the little plate of dark chocolates. They're Ghirardelli squares, made in San Francisco, and I smile because I remember passing the Ghirardelli factory on the way to Dr. Powers's last year. For a moment I wonder if the memory of California is going to sweep me out of this moment, but instead it just rises toward the ceiling like smoke and dissipates and I eat that chocolate square and it is so incredibly good and dark and sweet.

Asher eats one, too, and now he has a little melted chocolate on the corner of his mouth. I kiss it off. "You melted a little," I tell him.

"You did, too," says Asher, drinking me in. "You got a little down here." He puts his hands on my nipples and he lowers his face to my breasts and licks me gently and I can feel the stubble on his chin brushing against me. "Look at that," he says. "There's a little more down here." His lips move slowly and softly down my rib cage, kissing me as he goes, until after what seems like a couple of centuries he arrives between my legs and he parts me like the petals of an orchid and I can feel each exhalation of his warm breath upon me.

"I'm the luckiest person who ever lived," he says, looking up at me, "to be with you."

He doesn't say a whole lot more, but he keeps kissing me and I keep feeling his breath and I feel so close to him, so much a part of him I can't quite tell where he stops and I begin. The thing that I was afraid of was that I'd be standing outside of myself while we were making love, that I'd float above myself and view the whole experience as if it was happening to someone else. But instead I feel the opposite, like I am now something more than myself, like Asher and I have become a single being whose only purpose is to feel the love we feel. I'm wet as a harbor seal now, and Dr. Powers's distant promise to me echoes deep in my memory: you'll be *sensate, mucosal, orgasmic.*

"Lily," Asher murmurs. "Are you ready?" All I can do is nod. He reaches somewhere for a condom. Asher moves on top of me and slowly and gently he slides into me and just like that he is something that has always been part of me. He is looking into my eyes and I am looking back into his and I think, distantly, *I'm not only me, now. I'm also Asher. That's why I can feel all his faith in me.*

When I come it's like being tumbled onto a beach by a monster wave, and I cry out in a voice I hardly recognize. Asher, hearing me, finally lets himself go. A minute or two later, he collapses on top of me with his face resting on my chest, and I know he is lying there listening to the sound of my heart pounding like the kettle drums in the *molto vivace* movement of Beethoven's Ninth.

Molto vivace means *very lively*.

Then he raises his head and snuggles up next to me, holding me in his arms. "You all right?" Asher asks, quietly. I want to say *Fuck yes I'm okay*, but I still can't quite talk, and I realize that tears are rolling down my face. So instead I just nod.

His hand skates over my shoulder, down my spine. "I love you," he says.

Looking over at the window I notice the light that was slanting at such a sharp angle when we first arrived is now falling closer to a straight line. It makes me wonder how long we've been up here, and what has been happening in the world while we've been in the tree house. I would not be surprised to crawl back down the rope ladder and find that twenty years have passed.

"That was"—I whisper—"my first time."

Asher's arms tighten around me. "I thought it might be. You're—okay?"

I smile against his neck. "I feel like I just fell out of an airplane."

He thinks this over. "You mean—in a good way?"

"I mean in a good way," I tell him. "Was I—" I know I shouldn't ask him, but I have to know. Did he notice anything? He couldn't tell, right? "Was I okay, too?"

"Oh my God," he says. "You're perfect."

Asher gets up and takes a bottle of wine out of the cooler. He stands with his back to me, and the sight of his lovely ass and the muscles in his back is breathtaking. I hear a crack as he twists the top off the wine bottle. Then there's a soft *glug glug glug* as he pours the wine into the plastic goblets.

When he turns to face me, I almost gasp at the sight of him. He is everything.

"This," I tell him, "is *some fucking tree house*." I glance around. "I like the ship's wheel. I can see you standing there as a kid. Sailing your ship across the ocean."

He sips his wine. "You can sail it, too. We'll go everywhere and never come home."

"I wish," I say quietly.

"Me, too." He kisses the top of my head. "Instead of having to go back out into the world and all its bullshit. I don't ever have to pretend with you."

I choke on my wine a little bit, and Asher looks at me, worried. "Are you okay?"

That statement, *I don't ever have to pretend with you,* is a sharp slap. Because it reminds me of everything I *haven't* shared with Asher. I'm naked in every way but the most important one.

"Hey," he says. "What's wrong?"

"Nothing," I say.

I want to tell him everything because it shouldn't matter. It *doesn't* matter. What possible difference does it make?

But if it doesn't make any difference, why am I so afraid to tell him?

The sad truth is that I've seen what people do when they know. Jonah told me he loved me, too, not so long ago. Jonah, who held my hand and kissed me as we stood by the ocean watching the sea lions. Jonah, who not long after, tore my dress in two, and left me lying in a parking lot.

At this moment I remember something from the dance that I had buried deep. After the attack, as everyone headed back into the gym, Jonah was the last one to go. *Did you think this was real?* he asked. He looked down at me, bleeding on the pavement, and laughed. He said, *That's what you get.*

That's what you get. That's what you get. That's what you—

"I have to go," I say, suddenly, standing up.

"Wait, what—?"

"I just . . . I have to go."

Asher frowns. "Did I say something wrong?"

"This was a mistake," I say, and Asher reels back like I've punched him.

I pull on my clothes as fast as I can, and I open the trapdoor and throw down the rope ladder.

"Lily, please," he calls, scrambling down behind me. He isn't even wearing a shirt. "Talk to me."

I hit the ground and start running through the woods. I don't know where I'm going exactly, because I can't get back to my house on foot. But I don't care. I can't believe how stupid I was. I can't believe how stupid I am.

Asher is running after me. He's faster than I am. I feel him getting closer, and closer, and then he grabs my right wrist, the one with the scars. I didn't wear the cuff bracelet today. I didn't think I had to.

"Jesus . . . what is going on?"

"Let me go," I yell at him.

"Whatever it is, we can figure it out," he says. "If you feel like we moved too fast, we'll go slower. I'll do whatever you want."

"I want to go *home*," I say, but he doesn't let me go.

"I can't read your mind," Asher presses. "Talk to me, or I'll—"

"You'll what?" I shout at him. "You'll give me another bruise? You'll smack me around like your father?"

With this, his jaw drops open, and he lets go of my arm, and I turn my back on him and run through the woods. He doesn't follow me. I keep on going until I get to a small clearing. All around me the arms of the trees are twisted, bony-fingered, accusing.

I pull out my cellphone. Maya answers on the first ring.

"It's me." My voice breaks, and I start crying. It occurs to me I don't really know where I am. I'm lost, so lost. It's amazing that I ever dreamed for one second that I might be found.

"Stay where you are," says Maya. "I'm on my way."

THE MORNING MOM drove me to Dr. Powers to finally have my surgery, I knew it wasn't the defining moment of my life—I'd had so many defining moments before that. But I did believe that at long last, I'd soon see in the mirror the person I had always, *always* known myself to be.

Surgery was early; we'd left Point Reyes before dawn to be at the hospital on time, and by the time we got to San Francisco, the city was coming alive. I saw the tourists down on Fisherman's Wharf. I saw the sea lions gathered on Pier 39. I saw Treasure Island off in the distance, beneath the Bay Bridge, and I thought about how all the years we lived in Point Reyes, I'd never been there.

Later that morning, I was wheeled into the OR. The walls of the room were green tiles. I saw Dr. Powers behind her surgical mask and her glasses, her smiling eyes reassuring me that everything was going to be okay. Her nurses and residents and fellows swarmed around her, and there was an anesthesiologist, too.

"And how are you feeling today?" asked Dr. Powers.

"I feel *alive*," I told her. "I feel happy."

She nodded. "We're going to take good care of you," she said, and then she glanced up at the anesthesiologist, who was threading an IV feeder port through a vein on top of my right hand.

"Hi, Lily," he said. He was a dark-haired man with strong arms. He was wearing blue scrubs. "I'm Dr. Strauss."

"The Waltz King!" I said, thinking, of course, of Johann Strauss, who wrote "The Blue Danube" and "Tales from the Vienna Woods," and all those corny old songs in three-four time.

If he knew what I was talking about, though, he didn't let on. "I'm going to give you the anesthetic now," he said. "Can you count backward from one hundred for me?"

"Okay," I said. I took a deep breath. "*Einhundert, neunundneunzig, achtundneunzig—*"

"German?" said Dr. Powers. Her eyes twinkled.

"I thought I'd count it . . . ," I said, but I could feel the drug welling up in me, turning everything into saltwater taffy. "Like they did in old Vienna . . ."

"English is fine," said Dr. Strauss. "Just relax. Put yourself in our hands."

From the corner a machine beeped, and it occurred to me that what it was measuring, and what I was hearing, was the sound of my own heartbeat. *How wonderful it has been to have been alive,* I thought. *How wonderful, and how sad.*

When I wake up, I thought, *the world will be different.* In that new world, I would never be sad again.

"A hundred," I said. Everything was so slow, so soft, so tender.

"Ninety-nine."

I thought about Jonah, and I tried to forgive him. A little.

"Ninety-eight."

I thought about my mother, and how much I loved her, and how lucky I was to be loved by her. I thought about the day we had descended the long stairs to the lighthouse together.

"Ninety-seven."

I thought about my father taking me to the circus. How the man with the star on his chest rose into the air on a puff of white smoke. How he sailed, unchained, toward the heavens.

"Ninety-six."

OLIVIA ◆ 7

Five months after

My dream is so real. When Asher sits down on the edge of my bed, I roll to my side, the mattress dipping. He's wearing a suit that used to belong to my father, and he is barefoot. His mouth has been sewn shut with red thread.

He wants to tell me something, but he can't, and he grows increasingly frustrated. Then there's a flash in his eyes, as he figures something out. He pulls a piece of paper from his breast pocket. It is an index card, a yellow one, the kind my mother used to write her recipes on. There is a list on it with three names: my father, Lily, Asher. The first two are crossed out.

I wake up bathed in sweat, fighting for air. Through my window the horizon is a ribbon of blood. This time of year, the chatter of blue jays and chickadees usually wakes me at dawn, but it's earlier than that, the quiet seam between night and daytime. I push my hair back and stagger into the bathroom, washing my face and pulling on a robe before I slip downstairs.

I put the water on for coffee, then toe on my sneakers so that I can walk to the end of the driveway to get the morning paper. I am afraid to see what it says, after yesterday's bombshell in court. It's already old news—the 11:00 P.M. local television broadcast covered it—but that doesn't mean it will hurt any less to see it in black and white.

I don't make it to the end of the driveway, though.

The second I step outside, I see the wide wall of the barn where I process my honey. On the weathered boards, someone has written in vivid red paint a single word: MURDERER.

Inside the house, the teakettle whistles. It sounds like a scream.

A HALF HOUR LATER, when the sun is still pouting and bleary-eyed, I stand in front of the barn beside Mike Newcomb. I've put on jeans and a tee and long cardigan, but the detective is already suited up for work. His trousers are pressed, badge clipped to his belt. His shirt is starched, the pocket still glued against a layer of fabric. I remember how, when Braden got dressed, I'd slip my hand inside his dry-cleaned shirt pocket for the sheer satisfaction of feeling it peel back.

Although our shoulders are nearly touching, there is a distance between us.

Mike runs his hand through his hair, still damp from a shower. I wonder if he usually goes to the station this early or if—as the only detective in this town—he is subject to calls at all hours of the day and night. The two policemen who came to the house first have already left, photographs in hand. But there wasn't a smoking gun—or in this case, a spray can. Whoever did the damage is long gone. "I don't know, Olivia," he says. "It *could* be the same kids who vandalized your honey. But . . ."

He lets his voice trail off because I know the rest of the sentence: I have a lot more enemies, now that Asher's officially on trial.

"We'll do what we can," Mike says. "I'll check the hardware stores nearby to see if anyone bought red spray paint recently. Maybe we'll get lucky. But don't get your hopes up. A lot of times, with defacement of property like this—the perps are long gone."

I nod and fold my arms. "I better go. Court starts—"

"At nine. I know," Mike finishes. He jerks his head in a tight nod and starts down the driveway to his car. I turn and walk up the porch steps.

I am about to open the front door when he calls my name.

He's standing in front of his car, hands fisted at his sides. He hesitates, but then he meets my gaze. "I'm sorry," he says. "About this. About . . . all of it." He scuffs his boot at the gravel of the driveway. "You don't deserve it."

I watch as he drives away. If he was so sorry, I think uncharitably, he shouldn't have testified against my son. But at the same time, I know he was doing his job. Just like I'm doing mine—protecting Asher.

I think back to my conversation with Elizabeth yesterday at the river. *Am* I protecting him? Or am I trying to convince myself Asher needs protection?

When I go back into the house, Jordan is in the kitchen cooking an egg. He slides his eyes toward me, and then clenches his jaw and flips it over easy.

"You're still mad at me?" I ask.

He'd heard the commotion of the police car arriving, and came outside in a robe to find me talking to the officers. Quickly sizing up what had happened, he pulled me aside. "Why did you call them instead of waking me up?" he had asked.

"I'm sorry, did I miss the part where you went to police training?"

Pissed, he had stormed into the house again. Now, I lean against the counter, watching him cook. "Was I supposed to just let this go?" I ask him. "Maybe if I get lucky, they'll *burn* down the barn tonight."

"Had you bothered to ask me, I would have told you not to involve the police. Your detective isn't going to find whoever did this."

"He's not my detective," I say. "And last time I checked, Jordan, this house still belonged to me. If someone vandalizes it, I'm not just going to pretend it didn't happen."

He bangs the spatula down on the stove. "Well you should," he snaps. "There is nothing you can do, Olivia. And there's nothing the police can do. It's part of the process."

"*What* is?"

"Being tried in the court of public opinion." He stares at me. "Even if Asher's acquitted, that doesn't mean people won't whisper behind his back for the rest of his life. And behind *yours*."

Suddenly I understand. Jordan isn't mad because I involved the police. He's mad because he couldn't protect us from this.

"You don't have to take care of me," I say softly. "I'm a big girl, Jordan."

He snorts, and I know what he's thinking: *How'd that work out for you before?*

Jordan turns back to the stove. "You should eat something. It could be a long day."

"I will. I just want to make sure Asher's up first." I pause at the kitchen doorway. "Jordan?" I say, waiting till he turns around. "Thanks."

As I head to the staircase, something catches my eye through the pane of a window. Across the strawberry field, Asher stands on a ladder, a bucket balanced on the top of its frame, a car sponge in his hand. I watch him scrub at the red paint, smearing the letters slowly and methodically. He muddies it into a broad dark stain, until it's not an accusation but a slurry of shadow on the side of our barn, like a swarm of bees that cannot find a safe place to land.

BY THE TIME we get to court, it feels like I've already lived an entire day. Today Ava Campanello will be the first witness called, and Jordan has already explained to me that she has to be treated with kid gloves by both the prosecutor and himself, because no one on that jury wants to see a grieving mother suffer even more.

I try to remember everything Asher has told me about Ava as I watch her being sworn in. She is a forest ranger, which as it turns out is less Smokey Bear and more scientific, involving tracking something—wildcats, maybe? I remember Asher glowing over the fact that Lily knew how to start a fire using flint and pine needles and that it was good to know if he was lost in the wilderness with her, he'd survive.

I can see Lily in her mother. The high cheekbones, the set of her shoulders, the dark pools of her eyes. As Ava settles herself, she focuses her gaze right on me, which is unnerving. It's like Lily is peeking out; like I am trapped by the gaze of a ghost.

The reporters are silent, puppies who know that, at the slightest provocation, they will be banished from the table before they get a treat. Judge Byers has made it clear that she is not in the mood for any bullshit, which has only ratcheted up the already charged atmosphere in the courtroom. Yesterday, there were empty seats on either side of me; today both are occupied. I have no idea who these people are. They could be media, they could be Ava Campanello's coworkers, they could be Lily's cousins for all I know. I can feel them both staring at me when they think I'm not looking, but their curiosity is tangible. My hands reflexively curl around the Moleskine notebook sitting on my lap, and I focus my attention on Ava.

"Can you state your name for the record?" the prosecutor begins.

"Ava," she says, but the word is rusty. She clears her throat, like running water through a pipe. "Ava Campanello."

"And you are the mother of Lily Campanello, the murder victim in this case?"

"Yes." She is already fighting tears.

Gina hands her a box of tissues. "Ms. Campanello, we know this is hard for you, and we appreciate your willingness to be here and to answer a few questions about your daughter. If you need to take a break at any time, please just let me know." Her voice is soft, changing the landscape of her questions. "When did you and Lily move here?"

"This past summer."

"So Lily started high school in September?"

"Yes. Adams High," Ava says.

"Was Lily involved in any extracurricular activities at school?"

"She plays in the orchestra." A cloud crosses her face. "*Played*. She *played* in the orchestra. And she . . . was a fencer."

"Fencing." Gina's brows rise. "For those of us who've never done it—like me—you mean the sport that involves swordplay, with a foil. What did that require from Lily in terms of physical conditioning and athleticism?"

"You have to be light on your feet, have good fitness, and good balance."

"So was Lily a strong, coordinated teen . . . or would you define her as clumsy?"

"You have to be *really* coordinated to fence. And attentive. You have to always be planning your next move. Lily . . . was one of the best on the team."

"And regarding the staircase in your house . . . would it be fair to say Lily had gone up and down it hundreds of times since your move?"

"Yes."

"Is it fair to say she navigated the stairs hundreds of times without incident?"

"Absolutely," Ava says.

The prosecutor pauses, and I realize that all of these questions have been the easy ones, the breadcrumbs leading Ava off the main trail onto a darker, thornier path. "Ms. Campanello," Gina says, "we've heard the medical examiner, Dr. McBride, testify that Lily was transgender. Can you tell us a little about Lily's transition?"

Color heats Ava's cheeks. I feel the two strangers bracketing me now blatantly staring at me, and I think that maybe I am just as flushed as Ava is.

"Lily was born biologically male," Ava says. "I can't really remember a time she seemed to feel comfortable being referred to as a boy. By the time she was three or four, she was identifying with little girls."

"Wait, what do you mean by *identifying*?"

"Well, for example, the first time I took her to the ocean, her bathing suit was a pair of swim trunks, and she didn't want to get out of the car. She said she was naked and needed a bikini top like the other girls."

The first time I took Asher to the ocean, he was eight. In New Hampshire we have only a miser's portion of it, so he had learned to swim in lakes instead. He stood at the edge, hands on his hips, and asked me where the letters were. ATLANTIC OCEAN, he explained. Like on the map.

"Tell us about Lily's middle school experience," Gina says.

"Lily was expressing her female identity more and more . . . and it really upset her father. As a result, he insisted on sending her to a private school that was all boys—where she had to wear a coat and tie every day." My mind casts back, remembering how Asher had told the detective that he and Lily had fought about her dad. Was this why she was estranged from him?

"How did that go?"

Ava smiles a little. "She found ways to rebel. She grew her hair long and she wore nail polish—and got bullied for it. One day, after a particularly bad incident, Lily's father told her he was going to make life easier for her." She hesitates. "He buzzed her hair into a crew cut. By the time I got home from work, Lily was catatonic."

I steal a glance at Asher. I want to know if this is news to him, or if Lily shared this pain in her past. But as Jordan requested, his face is stony and impassive. One fist is curled tight beneath the table, my only clue.

"What did you do?" Gina asks.

"I took her and left. In the middle of the night with a suitcase full of clothing. We drove to a cabin my family owns, near San Francisco. A few months later, when her hair grew back and she wasn't quite as fragile, I enrolled her at a private school called Marin-Muir. After eighth grade she went to another school called Pointcrest. She was living as a girl. She dressed like one. She identified as one. To everyone but the school administration, she *was* one."

"Had Lily had surgery by then?"

"No," Ava says. "She asked, but I thought she was too young to have that conversation."

"Did something happen to change your mind?"

"Yes. Lily's father showed up unannounced, and outed her to her friends. At first, it seemed like they were accepting. But then she was assaulted and humiliated by them in a very public way." Her lips flatten into a tight line. "Lily became suicidal," Ava says quietly. "And I realized I'd rather have a live daughter than a dead one." She wipes beneath her eyes with a finger.

I think about Asher revealing Lily's suicide attempt to Jordan and me. How, at the time, he felt privileged to be the one she'd confided in.

"What happened next?" the prosecutor asks.

"I pursued surgery options for Lily."

"Did your husband know?"

"Yes."

"What was his reaction?"

"He was furious. He acted as if this was something being done to *him*. Eventually I had to get legal permission for Lily to have surgery without him signing off on it."

"Was Lily aware of this? How did it make her feel?"

"She felt rejected. She felt like he hated her."

I stare at Asher's profile, again. Two of a kind, him and Lily. With mothers who protected them from their fathers, giving enough love to spackle over the hate.

"Ms. Campanello, is there a reason you didn't tell the State that Lily was transgender?"

She shifts, straightening almost imperceptibly. "Is there a reason I *had* to?" Ava asks. "Lily was a girl. A girl who fell in love," she adds, "with the wrong boy."

THIS IS HOW I told Braden we were having a baby: I had fallen asleep in the middle of the afternoon, and I didn't respond to the daily AIM message he sent from the hospital, just checking in to see how my day was going. He came home midshift, wild-eyed, slamming the front door against the wall as he burst through it, yelling my name. I jerked up off the couch, too surprised to do anything but stand like a willow in the face of his storm. *Do you have any idea how worried I was? I thought you'd been in an accident. Why didn't you answer my message?*

When I told Braden I had been asleep, he grabbed my wrists hard. *You're lying to me,* he accused.

I'm pregnant, I blurted out. I had taken an over-the-counter test the day before, and I was waiting for a blood test to be sure.

Braden's mood changed like the wind. He let go of my wrists, his hands sliding up my shoulders with a feather-light touch. *A baby?* he said. *Yours, mine?* A smile broke over his face, and he kissed me as if I were made of air and light.

He called the hospital and said he wouldn't be in for the rest of the afternoon. We talked about names—he liked Violet and Daisy and I teased him about having a whole bouquet of babies. He made love to me as if he was claiming an uncharted territory. Later, I sprawled across Braden with my ear pressed to the drum of his heart. *You know what this means,* he said. *As long as that baby exists, you and I are inseparable. We're literally fused together in its genetic code.*

I woke up to Braden tucking the duvet around me and kissing me on the forehead as he slipped out of bed to get ready for work. But I pretended to be asleep, so I didn't break the spell.

IT'S TRUE THAT for years, I hid the fact that Braden abused me. Part of it was because I bought into the gaslighting, the constant barrage of abuse. Part of it was because I was bewildered and embarrassed that I had reached this point—as if I could no longer mark the spot where I stopped being an intelligent, confident woman. And part of it was because, in spite of everything, I loved him more than I had ever loved anyone else—and I thought that meant that I might be able to change him.

What made me finally willing to reveal the violent underbelly of my marriage was fear—not for me, but for Asher. I would have killed myself to keep him safe, but I also knew that if I was dead, I couldn't protect him. So I left, and I told my parents and Jordan the truth. I got a restraining order, I got counseling, I got a divorce. I started over.

If I had never had Asher, though, I might still be married to Braden.

There are some secrets that I think we are willing to take to the grave for the people we love. It's why, I think, Ava Campanello did not tell anyone in Adams that Lily was trans.

The prosecutor has shifted her line of questioning. "When did you first meet the defendant?" she asks.

"Lily invited him to dinner when they started going out. It was September," Ava replies.

"What were your impressions of him, at first?"

She turns to look directly at Asher. "I liked him," Ava says flatly, her words at odds with her expression. "He was polite to me and he looked at Lily like she was the Eighth Wonder of the World."

"Do you know if Lily and Asher were intimate?" Gina asks.

A flush steals across Asher's cheekbones.

"I don't know," Ava admits, her eyes filling with tears again. "I assume they were."

"Why did you assume that?" Gina gently presses.

"Because she was so happy." Ava breaks down. "I had never seen her so happy."

I open up my Moleskine notebook. I can feel the eyes of the strangers on either side of me, and I curl my hand so that they cannot see what I'm writing.

Gin. Lemon juice. Honey.

I close my eyes. I imagine every cocktail you can make with honey, boiling it down into a simple syrup. I imagine sitting on the porch on a hot Sunday afternoon, with nothing better to do than drink one and listen to the hum of the bees collecting nectar. I imagine Asher coming up the porch steps, sweaty after a run, grinning at me.

Got extra?

I will when you're twenty-one.

Lily Campanello will never be twenty-one.

I close the notebook.

"Ms. Campanello, I'd like to walk you through the day of Lily's murder. We've heard that she was sick. What were her symptoms?"

"She had a fever, and felt weak. She stayed home from school."

"Did you stay with her?"

"Yes, I called in to work and told them I needed the day off. Her fever spiked, and we had no Advil in the house, so I ran to the pharmacy to get some."

Gina nods. "What time was that?"

"A little after three o'clock."

"When you left, who was in the house?" the prosecutor asks.

"Just Lily. And Boris, our dog."

"How long were you gone?"

"An hour or so."

"When you returned," Gina says, "what's the first thing you noticed?"

"Asher's car was outside. And the front door was open," Ava responds.

"What happened next?"

"I went inside," Ava says. "Asher was on the living room couch, holding Lily. She was bleeding. And . . . she . . . she wasn't moving." Her voice fades away until it's only a hush that hangs over the room, like the air after a thunderstorm.

"I only have one more question, Mrs. Campanello," Gina says. "Did you and Lily ever have a conversation about whether she should tell Asher that she was transgender?"

"Yes," Ava admits. "I encouraged her to tell him . . . but she didn't want to."

"Why not?"

"Because she said he would hate her for it, like her father did." Ava swallows hard. "She said that if that happened . . ." She looks directly at Asher. "If that happened, her life would be over."

The prosecutor lets that settle. "Nothing further," she says.

DURING THE FIFTEEN-MINUTE recess that the judge calls, Jordan spirits Asher and me into the conference room we used yesterday. He doesn't sit down, instead just paces and hovers like a coach during halftime. "Okay," he says, as if he needs to convince himself. "She gets the sympathy vote, period. We accept that, and then we dismantle it as best we can when it's time for the defense to put up our case."

Asher is even more quiet than usual. "I liked Lily's mom," he says.

"The first time I met her, we talked about how there are signs on New Hampshire mountains that say the summits have the worst weather in America. We joked about whose job it was to verify that, and what they'd done to get demoted." He rubs his hand down his face. "She told me that once, Lily put herself in time-out because she didn't want to clean her room and she assumed she would have wound up there anyway. And that when Lily was really little, she had an imaginary friend—a striped spider named David." Asher shakes his head. "Who makes up an imaginary spider and names it David?"

Being in court this morning has already taught me that Ava Campanello is a better mother than I am. She had a child turn out to be someone she didn't expect, and for all intents and purposes, she not only supported her but had her back against the judgment of the rest of the world.

On the other hand, I now have a child who may turn out to be someone I didn't expect him to be, and all I want to do is reverse the clock to the moment before I doubted him.

JORDAN HAS AN older son, Thomas, from his first marriage, but I was still pretty young when he was born, so it wasn't until Sam arrived that I saw my brother play the role of a parent. I remember watching him coo to his baby when Sam was colicky and Selena had given up in exhaustion. I had seen Jordan argue and tease and fight and brood and even fall in love, but I had never seen him gentle all his rough edges before. Sam usually fell asleep in less than five minutes when Jordan soothed him; he never stood a chance against my brother's soft voice and even softer touch.

It's the same way, now, that he approaches Ava on the witness stand. "Ms. Campanello," he says gently, "I am very sorry that you have to be here today. I have only a handful of questions to ask you." She nods, a quick jerk of the chin. "Back in September, you knew Lily and Asher were dating?"

"Yes."

"And you knew they were getting very close?"

"Yes."

"Back then, you felt like Asher was good for Lily, didn't you?"

Ava eyes him warily. "Yes."

"In fact, only a few short months ago, didn't you think Asher showed great concern and consideration for your daughter?"

"Yes, I did."

"Isn't that why," Jordan says, "you suggested that Lily confide in Asher that she was transgender?"

"Yes."

"And you've stated that Lily resisted telling Asher, right?"

"That's correct."

Jordan slips his hands into his trouser pockets. "Most parents aren't around for most conversations between two dating teenagers. Assuming that you weren't present for every conversation between Asher and Lily, you really have no idea whether or not Lily ever *did* confide in Asher that she was transgender . . . do you?"

"No," she says.

"Thank you, Ms. Cam—"

"But my daughter is dead," Ava interrupts. "So I can make a pretty damn good assumption."

Jordan steps backward. "Nothing further," he murmurs.

THE NEXT MORNING, when I walk by Asher's bedroom door and knock to make sure he is awake and getting ready to leave in time for court at nine, he doesn't answer. I knock again, and when there's only silence, I open the door. His sheets are tangled, as if he's recently been buried beneath them, but he is nowhere in the room.

He is not downstairs in the kitchen, or in the living room, or sitting on the porch with a cup of coffee. He isn't in the basement or the barn. By the time I get back to the house, I nearly collide with Jordan in the hallway. "Whoa," he says, grabbing my shoulders. "Where's the fire?"

"Asher's missing," I say bluntly, and Jordan hesitates in the act of tightening his tie.

"Missing," he repeats. "What do you mean?"

"What do you think I mean?" I ask, my voice rising in pitch and volume.

"He can't leave," Jordan says. "It's a bail violation. Is his car here?"

"Yes, but I have no idea when he left. He could have walked all the way to town by now."

"Well, we have to find him before the cops do, or he could get locked in jail for the rest of the trial. Where would he go?"

To Lily's, I think immediately, and realize at the same time that is exactly where he *isn't.*

"Maybe he just went for a walk to clear his head," Jordan says charitably, but at the same time, he grabs the keys to the truck from the bowl near the front door. "I'll drive around and look for him. You stay here. Whoever finds him first, texts."

I cannot say out loud what I am thinking, so I wait for Jordan to leave the driveway before I run downstairs to the basement and with shaking hands open the gun safe that holds the old .22.

The gun is still inside, propped as it's been since it was last used, five or six years ago.

I am so relieved that my knees give out, and I wind up sitting in front of the open safe with my heart racing. It was only a couple of weeks ago that Asher tried to kill himself and failed.

But just because the gun is here doesn't mean he's not thinking about suicide.

I close up the safe, scramble the combination, and hurry back upstairs. The house is still, silent. Outside, a light rain has started to fall.

I run through the litany of terrible possibilities in my mind as I wonder where he might have gone. The apple orchard, with its thick branches? I grab my phone in case Jordan texts, and run along the fields, calling Asher's name as I head to the woods that separate my property from the orchard. I step into the soft sponge of pine needles, looking for broken branches or footprints or any kind of evidence that Asher was here.

Suddenly a bird bursts out of the brush, a grouse startled by my arrival. To be fair, I'm just as scared as it is, and I cower as it flaps away in a blur of feathers. But when I'm crouched like that, my face is turned up, which is how and why I notice the tree house.

My father built it for Jordan when he was a boy, and I inherited it when Jordan got too old to bother with it. Eventually, it was passed down to Asher when we moved back to Adams. He played there with Maya in elementary school. Now, it is camouflaged, its wood the same streaked gray of the tree trunks surrounding it.

"Asher?" I call, my hands on the rope ladder.

It's faint, but audible. "Up here."

With a relief that floods me from heart to fingertips, I scramble up and poke my head into the tree house. I am assailed by a wave of nostalgia—my initials and Jordan's on the beams, and Braden's (something he did when I showed him the hideaway, which completely pissed me off, because this was *my* place, not *ours*), the ship's wheel I added for Asher, the smooth knot in the wooden beam that I used to pretend was a button that could transport me to Bangladesh, to the moon, to the future—to anywhere but Adams, New Hampshire.

Asher is lying on his side on the floor, wrapped tight in a rust-colored afghan my mother crocheted sometime in the 1970s. His bright hair sticks out from the very top, like the tip of a paintbrush. "Asher?" I say quietly. I put my hand on his shoulder.

He doesn't turn.

"It's time to get ready for court."

Slowly, like a man four times his age, Asher sits up. The afghan is caught around his shoulders. I reach for it, thinking to fold it and put it aside, but he turns ferally, grabbing at the wool. "Stop," he snarls, and I am so surprised that the afghan drops between us.

On his knees now, he gathers it like an armful of flowers. He buries his face in the mess of it. "It still smells like her," Asher says.

With the light drizzle outside striking the corrugated metal roof and the leaves of the trees, it feels like the whole world is weeping.

"You should leave it here," I tell him. "It's raining." What I mean to say is: if that's all you have left of Lily, do not expose it to the elements. Keep it safe, keep it hidden.

"I'll wait at the bottom of the ladder," I add. As I make my way down, Asher tenderly doubles up the afghan, a captain folding a flag for the family of a fallen soldier.

I HAVEN'T SEEN Maya Banerjee since Lily's funeral, but I can tell as soon as she takes the stand that she is a nervous wreck. On the one hand, Lily was her best friend, and she wants to honor her memory by helping the prosecution. On the other hand, doing so means dragging her *oldest* friend through the mud.

As soon as she sits down, she locks eyes with Asher. *Hi,* I see her mouth.

I feel hope flutter in my chest. Maybe this will not be the slam dunk the prosecution thinks it will be.

Somewhere behind me are Maya's moms, here to lend her emotional support as she testifies. Neither came up to me before court was called into session. Deepa looked at me, whispered something to her wife, and when I returned their gazes they both found something on the floor to stare at that must have been utterly fascinating.

Maya is wearing a blue blouse and a pleated skirt. She looks young and conservative, a parochial school girl. I wonder what the jury would think if they knew that as a sixth grader, she coated a lab table with hairspray and tried to light it on fire with a Zippo. "Were you a friend of Lily Campanello?" Gina asks.

Maya nods.

"You're going to have to speak up," the prosecutor coaches.

"Oh," Maya squeaks. "Yes."

"But you're also a friend of the defendant, right?"

Maya takes a deep, shuddering breath. "Yes," she says.

"I imagine this is scary for you, Maya," the prosecutor says, "but it's really important."

Scary for Maya? I think.

"I know," Maya. "I just want to help."

"That's good," Gina says. "Why don't you tell us how you met the defendant?"

"Asher and I were in school together. From second grade on. We've been friends ever since."

"Did the two of you ever have a romantic relationship?"

Maya shakes her head. "Asher says I'm the sister he never had."

"How and when did you meet Lily?"

"She was a new student at school this year," Maya says. "We met at orchestra practice. She was smart and funny and into the same things I was; we were friends right off the bat."

"How did Lily meet Asher?"

Maya's mouth twists. "It was the first week of school, after orchestra. I was hanging around waiting for Asher, because he was giving me a ride home. Dirk—he's a hockey player, like Asher—started hitting on Lily. She wasn't into it at all, but Dirk wasn't getting the hint, and then Asher showed up. He took one look at what was going on and said that he'd already asked Lily out so Dirk would get lost. It was a lie—Asher hadn't even met Lily yet—but then they actually went out, and from then on, they were exclusive."

"Their dating relationship from September to December . . . was it copacetic?"

Maya blinks at the prosecutor.

"Was it problem-free?" Gina corrects.

"Oh," Maya says. "Mostly? I mean, they fought sometimes. And there were other times that one of them wasn't speaking to the other."

"Were there any particular instances where you thought maybe their relationship wasn't a healthy one?"

Maya looks at Asher and bites her lip. "This one time, we were at a sleepover at Lily's. She was changing into a T-shirt to sleep in, and I saw bruises all over her arms."

My throat goes dry.

The prosecutor lifts an enlarged photograph from her table. "I'm showing you State's Exhibit Seven. Can you tell me what this is, Maya?"

"A selfie we took that night. Me and Lily. You can see what I mean about the bruises."

They are dotted up Lily's left arm, four on one side, one on the other. The exact sort of marks you get when someone grabs you hard and shakes you.

I would know.

"Maya, did you ever see the defendant being physically aggressive toward Lily?"

Jordan is out of his seat like a rocket. "Your Honor, there has been no evidence to suggest that the defendant is responsible for those bruises, and the prosecutor is asking that question as if to draw a direct line."

Judge Byers flicks her eyes toward him. "Overruled."

How different would my life have been if someone—my mother, Jordan, Selena—had seen the handprints that Braden left on *my* shoulders, *my* throat? If instead of just believing what he wanted them to see, they'd looked a little closer?

Had Lily been wearing long sleeves because she was hiding the scars from her suicide attempt, or was it to hide the evidence of violence? Was she protecting Asher like I used to protect Braden?

Like I'm trying to protect Asher now?

"I saw Asher grab Lily by the arm once. They were having an argument because she was talking to another guy at a fencing match. She tried to walk away from Asher, but he wouldn't let her leave. And she told him to stop because he was hurting her."

Suddenly Asher leaps to his feet. "That is not," he seethes, "what happened."

The jury swivels in unison toward him. Jordan grabs his suit jacket and yanks him back down to his seat.

"Maya," Asher cries. "What the fuck are you *doing*?"

Jordan grits out, "Quiet," as Maya looks at Asher, tears filling her eyes.

But Asher is like a volcano that has been stewing at the core, and now that fire is unstoppable. He jerks himself free of Jordan, his words tumbling fierce and hot. "That's not what happened. She's lying—"

"*Shut. Up,*" Jordan snaps, squeezing his arm.

"Please control your client, Mr. McAfee," the judge says, "or I will have the bailiff do it for you."

Once, Braden called me into the kitchen, fuming. The dishwasher was open midcycle, water pooling on the floor. *I told you this is not how you load a dishwasher,* he said, gesturing to the white china on the rack, which was arranged at odd angles. *But you never listen.* In fact, we had never discussed how to load the dishwasher. Before I could say anything, he picked up a plate and—holding my gaze— dropped it so it shattered on the floor. I jumped out of the way, but Braden grabbed another one, and another, until I stopped flinching when they dropped and all our dinnerware was in shards at my feet. *What a mess,* he said, as if he hadn't been the one to make it.

A slow, satisfied smile unfurls across Gina's mouth. "Mr. McAfee," she asks, "do you need a few minutes to calm your client down?"

"We're good," Jordan says tightly, and that's how I realize that Maya's testimony was not about Lily, or friendship, or bruises. It was about getting Asher to explode, while the jury watched.

WHEN ASHER AND Maya were in second grade together, they were classroom reading buddies, T-ball teammates, and best friends. I remember their teacher telling me during a conference that Asher and Maya were inseparable. That at recess, they had to be reminded to let other kids play with them. It seemed like Asher was always at Maya's house or vice versa. Sharon and Deepa and I used to joke about planning their wedding. About Romeo and Juliet endings, minus the double suicide.

I bet Shakespeare wouldn't have seen this one coming.

After Gina Jewett takes her seat again, the judge turns to Jordan and offers him the floor. He sits at the table next to Asher for a moment, tapping his fingers against the surface, as if he's trying to wrap his head around the right line of questioning. "Hi, Maya," he says finally, offering her a smile. "You're doing great."

She returns the smile. "Thanks?" she says nervously.

"You've known Asher for almost your whole life, right?"

"Since he moved here when we were six."

"When was the last time you saw him?" Jordan asks.

"At Lily's funeral."

"I bet that was really hard for both of you."

"Yeah," Maya says.

"Did Asher seem upset that day, to you?"

"He seemed . . . numb," Maya recounts, and then she squares her shoulders, as if she is defending her own statement. "But he gets like that sometimes."

"Like what?"

"When he's really emotional . . . he kind of turns inside himself, instead of letting it show on the outside."

"This must seem surreal to you," Jordan says. "That we're in this courtroom. That Asher's on trial. I mean, you're one of Asher's best friends, aren't you?"

Maya stiffens. "I was Lily's best friend, too."

"Hm. And as Lily's best friend, she told you things she didn't tell anyone else, right?"

"Yes."

"So you knew she tried to commit suicide before moving here, I assume?"

"Wait," Maya says. "What?"

Jordan's brows rise. "Oh, she didn't tell you that?"

"No." Emotions chase across Maya's face: surprise, hurt, betrayal.

"She didn't tell you she was transgender, either, did she?"

"No."

"Because she didn't really want anyone to know, right?"

"Objection!" Gina says.

"Withdrawn," Jordan replies. "Nothing further."

Maya looks stricken as she steps out of the witness box. She turns to Asher at the last moment, guilt written all over her features. Behind me I hear the rustle of Sharon and Deepa as they exit the gallery to get their daughter.

Gina rises partly out of her seat. "Your Honor," she says, "the prosecution rests."

THE BAILIFF TAKES the jury out, and I watch Asher's hands tighten into fists beneath the table. I wonder if he thought, like I did, that the State's evidence would go on for days, weeks. If he is nervous, now, about what Jordan will do next.

"Judge," Jordan says, "I move to strike the evidence as insufficient to support a verdict."

"Thank you, Mr. McAfee," Judge Byers says. "Ms. Jewett?"

"Your Honor, the State's case has sufficiently proven every element of the crime of murder. And in fact, now we've even thrown in a motive."

"Thank you for that . . . embellished argument," the judge says drily. "The defendant's motion is overruled. There is sufficient evidence to proceed with the trial, and we will return tomorrow at nine A.M. with the defendant's evidence, if they so choose to present any." She bangs the gavel, and the hum of noise in the gallery increases as reporters crowd one another at the doorway to file their stories and to get into position to ambush us as we exit the courthouse.

Like yesterday, however, Jordan draws us back into the conference room. "What was that?" I ask. "Did she really do a shoddy job presenting her case?"

Jordan shrugs. "Oh, no. She's got plenty. That's just what the defense *always* does at this point—try to discredit the State's evidence. I mean, there's always a chance a judge will fall for it." He sits down at the table across from Asher and me. "Gina's connected all the dots for the jury: Asher killed Lily in a fit of trans panic after she told him the truth. Maya gave proof of earlier violence—"

"I never hurt Lily—" Asher interrupts, but Jordan talks right over him.

"—and finally, thanks to Asher's little outburst in court, the jury got to witness firsthand what it looks like when Asher flies into a humiliated rage."

Once, when Asher was little, we had chickens. I came out of the coop to find him holding a chick headfirst in its water bowl. *It's thirsty,* he said. I took it out of his hand, this tiny, lifeless thing. *Why isn't it moving, Mommy?* he asked.

It drank so much, I told him, *it needs a nap.*

I'm not sure which one of us I was shielding—him, for making an honest mistake; or me, for wondering how he could not have felt the struggle of those tiny bones, that gasping beak, and not let go.

"Clearly," Jordan is saying, when my attention drifts back to him, "we're not putting Asher on the stand . . . especially now."

Asher's head snaps up. "Wait. I never get to tell the truth?"

"No," Jordan says. "You don't get to say anything. You let me do the talking."

Asher's face reddens. "But all I did was *find* her. I showed up when she was already dead. Why can't I just *say* that?"

"Because the State is going to twist your words. Just like they manipulated you today, when you *weren't* on the stand, to grace the jury with an Oscar-worthy performance of frustrated fury. Except if you're a witness, it's a thousand times worse. Once you're in that box, I can't prevent the prosecution from asking all kinds of questions you do not want to answer."

I can practically feel the steam rising between them, so I intercede. "If Asher can't speak up for himself, who will?"

"Selena is at this very moment picking up from the airport the doctor who performed Lily's gender affirmation surgery," Jordan says.

"How does that help Asher?"

"I don't know, yet," he admits. "But I think the more educated the jury is, the more chance we have of them believing Asher's innocent. We'll put Coach Lacroix on the stand. And you." He meets my gaze. "Who else is better qualified to vouch for his character than his own mother?"

I have a flash of Asher's small, chubby fist clutched around the limp chick, holding it up to me like an offering.

"Who else?" I repeat, and I wonder if the question is rhetorical.

BY THE TIME we get home, Selena has arrived, and she and Jordan immediately disappear into their makeshift office in the dining room to go over the testimony of tomorrow's last-minute expert witness, Dr. Powers. There is a message on the phone from Dirk for Asher (which he isn't allowed to answer, per the judge's bail orders) and one from the post office for me, telling me my bees have arrived.

I am thrilled to have a task, a responsibility that distracts me. I do not want to believe Asher could ever be the villain he's been painted by the State to be. But when I let my guard down, I have to admit that what is so exhausting to me isn't just their depiction of Asher. It's the struggle to keep *my* version of him sacrosanct.

The post office is a few minutes away from closing by the time I park my truck in front of it. The pound of bees the postmaster hands me (moving faster, actually, than I've ever seen him move before) are about four thousand in number, shipped from an apiary in New York, in a box made of wood and mesh. The cage is heavier than you'd think, and hotter. I drive it back home, to rehouse the bees in Celine's old hive.

I go to get my bee kit in the mudroom and hesitate. I can hear Jordan and Selena in the dining room, but Asher is likely upstairs. I walk up and knock on his door.

Asher is sitting on his bed with his sketch pad. He closes it quickly when I enter, but not before I see the curve of a jaw and a fall of dark hair. "Hey," I say, and he jerks his head in greeting. "You okay?"

He shrugs. "I'm great, except for the murder charge and the fact that I never get to tell my side of the story."

I lean against the doorjamb. "I have to go out to the hives. Do you want to come?"

"Do you need help?"

"Not really," I say, and I just wait, holding his gaze.

He puts the pad down beside him. "Okay," he agrees.

I carry the smoker and my veil, while Asher lugs the crate of new bees. We walk along the edge of the strawberry fields. "What's going to happen to the fruit?" he asks.

Strawberries are perennials, and we run a brisk pick-your-own business in June, thanks to the pollination of my bees. It feels like a lifetime ago when I mulched the plants last November, before . . . everything. By now, I should have raked away the straw; I should have removed the winterizing row covers as soon as the plants blossomed. But the crop has been the last thing on my mind. "Next year," I say, "we'll just plant twice as many."

It's an optimistic way of saying that this year, the fruit will likely die on the vine.

Asher hasn't brought a veil, so he lights up the smoker while I open the hive that used to belong to Celine and her bees. It's empty and still, a stark counterpoint to the other bustling colonies. He sits down in the tall grass, watching me as I suit up and crouch beside the box of bees.

Package bees are harvested bees and a queen from a different hive that specifically raises queens. In the middle of the cluster is a can of sugar syrup, to tide the bees over during the shipment, until they can collect nectar for themselves. The queen is fastened to the top near the syrup in a little cage, with a couple of attendants to take care of her; I can hear her piping, like a toy trumpet. Some of the new bees have not survived the trip, but only a handful.

"How come you haven't asked me?" Asher says.

My hands still, and then I smoke the sides and top of the crate. "Asked you . . . ?"

"Whether I did it."

I look at him through the veil. My heart is pounding so hard I am sure he can hear it. "Do I *need* to?"

Asher rolls his shoulders. "I know why Uncle Jordan doesn't want to talk about it," he says. "But I figured you would."

You figured wrong, I want to say. *Since that would mean I doubt you, and I don't.*

But the words don't come.

I peel off the queen cage so I can set it aside. Then I overturn the crate and dump the bees into the empty hive. They explode around my face in a cloud of agitation. "There is nothing you could say to me," I tell him, carefully picking my words, "that would make me love you any less."

Asher stills. "That's what I said to her."

Is it a veiled confession? Did she tell him?

Did Asher hold up his end of the bargain? Or did he let Lily— and himself—down with his reaction?

Does it even matter?

If Asher were to confess to me that he was fighting with Lily and things got out of hand and she wound up dead, I would still defend him.

That's different, a tiny voice curls in my head. *That's an accident.*

I just do not believe that Asher has managed to hide a white-hot rage for eighteen years without his control ever slipping.

Then again, things have come easily to my golden boy. School, sports, friends. Girls. Maybe he has never felt so mortified that he needed to strike out, until now. "I don't think I ever knew how . . . lucky I am," Asher muses.

I could argue with that, based on his fraught early life with his father, a messy divorce, a hand-to-mouth existence in a rickety farm-house.

"No one's ever thought the worst of me before," he says, and he picks the queen cage up from where it is balanced against the side of the transport box. "Now I kind of feel like this. Boxed in. Like I've got nobody."

I take the little wooden coffin from his palm and set it between two of the frames in the hive. "You've got me," I say. As I wedge it tightly, I hear myself ask, "Did you know . . ."

I turn to find the sun crowning Asher, an afternoon prince. His eyes meet mine for a moment, hesitating just long enough for me to take the coward's way out.

"... these come with a candy plug?" I blurt, adjusting the queen cage.

"Yeah," Asher says, letting me change the subject. "When I was little and you told me that, I tried to lick one."

"It's not that kind of candy," I say.

"So I discovered."

Since the queen hasn't been raised in the same hive as the bees shipped in the box, she's unfamiliar to them. As the worker bees chew through the thick fondant at one end of the cage, they become used to her. The candy plug isn't a barrier meant to restrain the queen; it's a barrier meant to protect her from attacks, while the colony decides whether or not they will accept her.

I find myself thinking of Lily. Were the fences she built meant to keep others out, or to keep herself in?

There is no set of rules that dictates what you owe someone you love. What parts of your past should be disclosed? Should you confess you are trans? Alcoholic? That you had a same-sex relationship? An abortion? That you were abused by the person you trusted most in the world?

When, if ever, is the right time for that conversation: before your first date, before your first kiss, before you sleep together?

Where is the line between keeping something private, and being dishonest?

What if the worst happens? What if honesty is the thing that breaks you apart?

"What's her name?" Asher asks, drawing me out of my reverie.

I cover the new hive. I've been thinking of Billie Eilish, but maybe not every queen needs to be a pop diva. "Lily?" I suggest.

I sit down next to him in the field, as stragglers from the crate fly to the entrance of the hive. We watch the sun go down, until the horizon burns like the coil of a stove. "She would have liked that," Asher says.

LILY ⬡ 7

Two months before

I am eating apple pie with cheddar cheese melted on top of it when I find out that the thing I thought existed only inside of my head is actually real. And I couldn't be more excited. Or more scared.

Tonight Maya and I went to see the hockey game—hockey in Adams, New Hampshire, kind of being like football anywhere else. Our school mascot is the Presidents, which is ironic when you think that the only president from New Hampshire was Franklin Pierce, and that his three claims to fame are that he was a drunk, he completed the Gadsden Purchase, and he once ran over an old woman with his horse and was arrested for it while still in office. We were playing the Jefferson Patriots, and the bleachers at the school's hockey rink were packed. Maya screamed her head off after every goal (Asher scored three of the five). It's kind of amazing to see the players skating so fast, almost like ballet dancers except every last one of them is huge. But it's a violent beauty. Dirk, the goalie, got himself put in the penalty box twice for roughing. In the last period, Asher wound up in the penalty box, too—for slashing.

Afterward we went to the party, which was, of course, at Dirk's house. This was pretty much the bloodbath you'd expect (Dirk drinking an entire can of Foster's lager through a giant funnel as the other hockey players shouted, *DIRK, DIRK, DIRK*). But instead of hanging out with the hockey bros, Asher spent most of the night sitting on the front porch talking to Maya and me. There we were, the three of us in the warm evening, crickets chirping, the moon shining down. I saw other girls watching us, enviously. Many of them were from the women's soccer team, which is called—aspirationally—the Lady Presidents. Some even barged in on our conversation to openly flirt with him, like Maya and I weren't even there. But every time, Asher politely dismissed them and picked up the thread. It was hard to square the fierce athlete I'd seen tearing up the ice an hour or two earlier with this thoughtful, quiet boy who seemed to listen to me talk the way I'd listen to a favorite cello piece.

When I was telling a story about Point Reyes, he asked about the Pacific Ocean—*How is it different from the Atlantic? Isn't it weird to put your ankles into water that you know is also touching Australia, and China, and Vietnam?* I told him about the sea otters and how they tie themselves in kelp when they sleep so they don't float away, and he said he heard that they float around linked together like a giant jig-saw puzzle and had I ever seen that? Later, he and Maya talked about growing up in Adams, and then they started singing the praises of the A-1 Diner's house special, apple pie with steamed cheese.

I said, "Steamed cheese?" I didn't know what that was, but it sounded a little gross. And the two of them started swearing left and right about how I had to have some *now*, and the next thing I knew we were in Asher's red Jeep Rubicon—Maya up front, me in the back—on our way to get a slice.

They were chattering about people I didn't know yet and mo-ments I hadn't been around to share. I know I have only been in Adams a little while, but watching Maya and Asher in the front seat was like seeing two circles of a Venn diagram overlap, and realizing I was somewhere on the outside.

In the diner booth, I sit next to Maya, Asher opposite us. They watch me lift a bite of the pie to my lips. The cheese has been melted in a little copper tin and then laid on top of the crust with a spatula. It is a little bit sweaty, and very gooey, and frankly, sort of nasty.

But surprise: it's ridiculously good. It's hot and tart and sharp. "Okay," I say to them. "You were right. It's great."

"Another convert," says Asher.

"It's good that you like it," says Maya. "Because this is kind of it for Adams. There's ice fishing, there's hockey, and there's steamed cheese."

Asher has ordered a cup of coffee, and the waitress now puts it down on our table. He adds two sugars to it, and some milk from the creamer. This surprises me—he doesn't look like someone who'd drink his coffee sweet. He doesn't even look like someone who drinks coffee. I wonder why that was my initial impression. I also wonder what to do with this surge of curiosity that nearly buckles me, to know not just how he takes his coffee but what pets he had growing up and if cilantro tastes like soap to him and which TV shows he can quote from memory.

Asher sips his coffee and then he looks at me thoughtfully. "Do you miss California?"

I think about the village of Point Reyes Station, the Bovine Bakery and the little bookstore. I think about the ocean, and the walk down the steps to the lighthouse. But I also think about Jonah, and Sorel, and everything that happened at school. "It's okay," Asher says, intuitively. "I wasn't trying to dig around. I'm just curious about anywhere that isn't here, you know?" He raises his coffee cup to his lips. "It's hard not to think about California sometimes, when you have five months of winter."

"Correction, six months of winter," says Maya.

"I'm excited to see snow," I tell them. "I've never seen it before."

Maya laughs. "We can help you see some snow." She turns to Asher. "Remember that time when we were nine, and we made the snow fort that looked like a castle?"

I feel a pang of jealousy. I've never had friends like that. Maya and Asher have an unbroken line of history.

Asher puts his cup down in his saucer and glances out the window. He doesn't reply to Maya, like he's lost in his thoughts.

"The winter's fine," he says, turning back to us. "The hard part is the spring—March and April, when you really want it to get nice out, and instead it just keeps snowing."

"And driving during Mud Season is a competitive sport," Maya adds.

We laugh and we eat our pie and look out at the quiet Main Street until Asher finishes his coffee. I imagine driving here during Mud Season with Asher and Maya, six or seven months from now, watching the snow finally melt.

I also have a quick flash of next summer, meeting here for apple pie with cheese one last time before we're off to our various colleges: me to Oberlin or Peabody—and Asher and Maya to wherever it is they want to go.

Something else I don't know about him.

"I'll be back," says Maya, and she walks the length of the diner and disappears into the tiny bathroom.

"Lily," says Asher, "I have to ask you something." He says it almost fiercely; I'm afraid he's about to tell me something terrible.

Asher lowers his hand onto mine. "I wanted to ask if you'd ever want to go out sometime. With me."

I am hoping I don't look too shocked. But I've been taught by the world to think of myself as forever undatable, that anyone who ever expresses the smallest bit of affection for me is either someone who is just lying in order to taunt and hurt me; or, even worse, someone who *does* like me, but only because they don't know everything. And the moment that they *do* know everything, all their love will turn to ash.

So the first thing that comes out of my mouth is "Are you sure?"

But then his face ripples into this big, broad smile and it is everything I can do not to pass out face-first into my empty pie plate. "I *am* sure," he says.

"But what . . . what about Maya?"

His eyebrows raise, like the idea of Maya as a romantic partner is something that has never seriously occurred to him. "She's not the one I'm asking," he says.

"Yes," I tell Asher. It's the softest thing I've ever said. But Asher squeezes my hand. He heard me.

"Well, well, well," says Maya, now standing at the side of our table. "What do we have here?" Asher does not let go of my hand.

"I asked Lily out," Asher says.

Maya's mouth opens, and then she snaps it shut. She looks from me to Asher, and then smiles like she orchestrated this whole thing. "I was wondering how long it would take you two to realize the obvious."

"Was I that easy to read?" says Asher.

Maya rolls her eyes. "Asher, you just spent a whole night sitting on a porch talking about sea otters when you could have been doing funnels with Dirk. Do you really think I thought that was because of *me*?"

"How much do you actually know about sea otters, Maya?" says Asher. "A lot?"

Maya laughs. "I don't know shit about sea otters. But I know all about *you*." She looks at her watch. "Now can we get out of here?"

"Okay," says Asher. We go out to his Jeep, his fingers along my spine, and Maya gets in the backseat. "You take shotgun," she says to me.

I think about protesting, but Asher kind of nods at me, and holds open the door to the passenger seat, and helps me up into the car. He's got surprisingly good manners, considering that earlier this evening I saw him spend two minutes in the penalty box for slashing.

I'VE HAD ONE BOYFRIEND.

This was the fall of eleventh grade, before everything went to hell. Jonah Cooper and I had become friends as sophomores, and that whole summer we hiked the national seashore, or lazed around the house playing Xbox. He had black hair, freckles. He was lanky, a little bit shy. In the fall and winter he fenced with me, but in the spring he was the pitcher for the Pointcrest baseball team. He had a killer fastball.

In August, when he passed his driver's test, we spent a lot of time cruising up and down the coast. It was nice, after all that time, to have a friend besides Sorel. We went to the Cowgirl Creamery and spent part of the afternoon lying on the lawn sampling all the cheeses: Red Hawk, and Wagon Wheel, and Devil's Gulch. We drove to the Cypress Tunnel, its arching tree branches interlocked overhead. It looked like a portal to another world.

Which, looking back, it was—although not the one that I had hoped for.

On a September day we drove his father's Miata to the seashore, top down. We parked the car and walked down to Wildcat Beach, in hopes of hiking to Alamere Falls. The beach was nearly deserted, and very dramatic—the stretch of sand running between the crashing ocean to our right and the high cliffs to the left. I'd told Mom our plan, and she was insistent that we only do the hike at low tide. One time, in fact, she had to rescue some people who got trapped against the cliff wall, a couple who'd set out at exactly the wrong time, on exactly the wrong morning.

But Jonah and I had the perfect day. We found seashells, and pieces of polished glass, and a creepy doll with no head and all of its clothes washed off, and we made up a whole story about what had happened to the doll, and a cursed little girl who had thrown it over-board after it had started to whisper to her in her sleep.

When we finally got to Alamere Falls, the creek gushed wildly off the cliff and crashed forty feet down. The stream from the falls had cut a winding path into the sand as the water rushed toward the ocean. Mist hung in the air and on our faces.

That was when Jonah took my hand.

I could feel my heart hammering away in my chest. It felt so nice, his hand in mine. I was afraid to move, because it might be a dream. And I was afraid to move, in case it wasn't.

What came next was that he kissed me. Then he kissed me again.

It was sunset of that same day—after we'd hiked all the way back to his car, after we drove the Miata to the other side of the point, after we'd stopped every five minutes to make out some more—that we stood by the Elephant Seal Overlook in Inverness. Below us were the seals. It was just the juveniles on the beach at that time of year, a bunch of rubbery teenagers.

"Lily," said Jonah. "I want this, I do. But I also want to make sure that no matter where it goes . . . we stay friends. Promise me we won't lose that."

I don't want to lose it, either, I said. But I wondered, even then, whether we were making a promise we could not keep.

MY FIRST OFFICIAL date with Asher Fields is a week later: Saturday morning, September 29. What we're doing is a surprise, although he did ask me for my shoe size. I'm a little nervous about this because, of course, I'm paranoid about my big feet. But Asher just said, *Okay, great.* Which makes me suspect we're going bowling. Or, I don't know: tap dancing?

But when Asher pulls into a parking lot, we are not at a bowling alley. We are at the Adams High hockey rink, deserted except for the two of us. I wonder who Asher had to bribe to get in here. Then I realize he probably just had to smile and ask nicely. I can't imagine anyone saying no to him.

When he hands me the skates that are in the trunk of the Jeep, he says size ten women's is size eight men's. "Your skates should be one size smaller than your shoe," he tells me. "Lucky for you I have every pair of skates I've ever owned, going back to third grade."

It is sweet that he brought me a pair of skates that fit, but I hold them out like they are poisonous. Because they're black.

Asher reads my mind. "What, you don't want to wear men's skates?"

The truth of the matter is that I don't. I know it's just a little thing, but all those childhood years wearing the wrong clothes—it pushes my buttons a little. Then I take a look at Asher's smiling face, and I decide that just this once I can get over myself.

And I lace up.

"The first thing you need to learn," Asher explains, as he helps me onto the ice, "is how to fall."

"I'm pretty sure that's the one thing I already know how to do," I say.

"Correction: you need to learn how to fall *safely*," says Asher. "If you're going to skate, you're going to fall. So here's what you do." He lets go of my waist for a second, does something almost like a pirouette so that now he is facing me. His skates go *ksshhh* on the ice. "When you feel yourself going over, bend your knees, put both arms out to the side, and push yourself down onto your ass. You want to try it?"

"I'm afraid to fall," I say, and as I say it I think, *You can say that again.*

"Watch me," says Asher, and he does just what he described, splaying himself down so gently it's like he just lay down in a frosty white bed.

"Okay," I say, and a moment later I'm beside him.

"You," he says, "are an A-plus student. Now: lesson two. Getting back up. Spin so you're on your knees. Then put both hands on your right knee, and push as hard as you can until you stand. Now put your arms out to your sides and get your balance. Ready?" He does it, and now he's standing above me, looking down. Without a pause I get up, too, and he smiles, like he's impressed. "Nicely done. Ready for some baby steps?"

I am absolutely ready for some baby steps, Asher Fields. You have no idea. Or maybe you do. Maybe you're as ready as I am.

Asher tells me that he teaches little kids how to skate during the summer, and that he hasn't lost one yet. He talks to distract me, so I don't look down at my feet. A half hour later I'm actually doing it— gliding around the rink, not gracefully exactly, but without falling constantly. I'm not good at stopping, though. Asher shows me how to do this, too. "To stop, you put your right foot forward and hold it at an angle. You should make a little snow when you're doing it. That's how you know you've used enough pressure."

Which is what I'm trying to do when I wipe out on the ice—not gently like Asher taught me before, but a complete crash where my limbs go in directions they aren't meant to go and the ice knocks the breath out of me. I'm thinking, *Don't cry, don't let him think you're not tough,* and I almost succeed, until Asher skates to me swiftly and gets down on his knees to make sure I'm okay. The bracelet I wear to cover my scars came loose during my wipeout, and as I tug it back into place, I realize Asher is staring at them, and fuck, my tears just spill over. I feel like I have been holding them in for years now.

He helps me sit up. The ice is cold through my jeans. After I calm down, Asher hesitantly touches two fingers to my bracelet. "That looks like it hurt."

"I was in . . . a car accident," I lie. "Two years ago, on Valentine's Day."

I feel awful not telling him the truth, but there is no way I'm going to do that on our first date, or it will likely be the last. What I want right now is not to be reminded of Jonah, or Valentine's Day, or anything that came before. What I want to do right now is put all of that behind me and just skate with Asher.

Asher helps me back onto my feet. This time he doesn't let go, and even though I'm staying upright, I know I'm falling for this beautiful boy, who skates backward as he holds my hands and looks into my eyes.

Then Asher guides me into the middle of the rink, raises one hand, and says, "I'm going to spin you. Go up on one skate, okay?"

"Wait, what?"

"Go with it!" he says, but I'm overthinking everything—my skates, this date, my life, and just like that I crash again, taking Asher down with me. We roll and come to rest in a heap. We are right at the center of the ice, the place where during a game, the ref drops the puck to set everything into motion.

"I think we're ready for the Olympics," I say.

He laughs. "For sure."

"I'm crushing you," I say, wriggling to get off him, but he tightens his arms around me.

"I'm good," he murmurs. His words are little clouds. "Actually, I kind of like this better than skating."

"I like it, too," I whisper, "Asher," and then I lean down, breathless and cold, and press my lips against his. There it is: our first kiss.

After about eight hundred years, he sits up and I move to the side. "I'm turning into ice," he says.

"Let me help you up," I say, and I reach down and then fall on top of him again.

He kisses me again. Against my mouth he warns, "You can get a penalty for that."

"What did I do?"

"Delay of game," he says, grinning. "And hooking."

"Hooking!" I repeat. "What do I get for that?"

"Two minutes in the box," he says. He gets up and pulls me with him, skating us to the far side of the rink, where a little door opens into the penalty box. Asher and I sit down on the bench and fall into each other again.

"I *like* the penalty box," I say, coming up for air.

"Sometimes you get an extended penalty," says Asher. "And have to stay in a little longer."

"What do we have to do to get one?"

Asher's hand falls upon my breast. We are all alone in the giant rink, and the world around us is frozen. He leans in for another kiss. "Misconduct," he whispers.

SIX BEST MOMENTS OF WEEK ONE WITH ASHER FIELDS

6. We are sitting at the top of an abandoned lifeguard stand at the Adams Town Beach on Pierce Lake. In the summer, Asher says, this place is mobbed, but now it's deserted. There's a wooden raft that's been hauled up onto the beach for winter. Leaves are turning orange. A pair of loons float on the lake, and they sound like ghosts: *hoooo*.

   Asher tells me loons mate for life.

5. I am walking down the hallway on my way to lunch with Maya and Asher is approaching from the other direction with Dirk and the hockey bros in formation and he stops and says, "Hey, not so fast," and takes me in his arms and kisses me, right there in

the corridor in front of everyone. Dirk watches, amazed. *Dude*, he says.

4. I make Hope Cakes for Asher on Wednesday night. On Thursday I bring them into school, and we sit in the cafeteria together, just us two. He is supposed to be doing his calculus homework but instead we're holding hands across the table. Other people are staring. We are officially A Couple now. We are eating Hope Cakes. It's like that.

    "Whoa," he says, "these are amazing. What is *in* these?"

    I grab his calculus notebook and write down the recipe on a blank page. Then I hand it back to him. At the bottom I write—*Bake in oven for 40 minutes, or until an impossible thing comes true. Whichever comes first.*

3. We have our first fencing tournament of the fall next weekend, October the 13th, and the team is practicing hard. I swing my sword forward and shift my weight onto my right leg and charge at my opponent, and as I do this, I give off my classic fléche scream: *Aieeee!* And everyone looks over at me, like: *Who's that girl?* I look up into the bleachers, and there is Asher, watching me, with a look that says, *I know who she is.*

2. Saturday is unusually warm, and Asher and I are in the fields behind his house, right near the place where the long grass meets the tall trees. We lie on a blanket drinking iced tea sweetened with his mother's honey. I'm reading *The Invisible Man* by Ralph Ellison, and Asher is sketching. He asks if I can be his model, and I say, *Sure.* I prop myself up on an elbow. *Draw me like one of your French girls,* I say, like Kate Winslet in *Titanic*.

    He smiles and says, *Don't make promises you're not gonna keep,* and I hear myself answer, *I'm not.*

    A moment later my shirt is off, and so is my bra, and I'm looking him right in the eye and I think, *He'll have this picture of me forever, and I am not afraid.*

1. We are at my house after school but Mom is still at work. Boris is on the floor. Asher sits in a chair by the fireplace as I play my cello for him. It's "The Swan," by Saint-Saëns. I think about the legend of the swan, the one that says that the bird is mute for her entire life, until

the moment she's about to die, and then she sings the most beautiful melody in the whole universe, so gorgeous that just hearing it can crack you in half.

It's called a swan song.

When I finally lift my bow from the strings, Asher's eyes are shining. He looks like I feel. "Doesn't it make you sad," he asks, "to play a song like that?"

"It's only a sad song," I tell him, "if there's no one to hear it."

He kisses me and I feel like my heart is going to rise from my chest. Like I will be forever wearing it on the outside.

"I heard it," he says.

ASHER AND I reveal small bits of information to each other like we are trading Pokémon cards. I learn that he is allergic to cantaloupe; he finds out that I am double-jointed. He tells me that he once had a goldfish that lived six years. I tell him I've watched every episode of *The Office* at least eight times. He says once he saw Adam Sandler in a Subway restaurant in Nashua. I admit that I didn't know until a month ago that the division sign was just a fraction with dots replacing the numerator and the denominator. We tell each other the things that have to be whispered, too: that I've moved so much no place feels like home. That he's afraid to tell his mother he wants to go to art school. That I worry my mom has spent so much time worrying about me, she won't remember who she is when I leave for college.

The difference between Asher and me, though, is that presumably, he's telling me the truth, and I am skirting the edge of lies.

When he asks me why we moved so much, I say it was for my mother's job.

When he asks me why my mother worries, I say it's because I'm an only child.

When he asks me if my parents are divorced, I tell him that my father is dead.

It is particularly gratifying to kill him off, if only fictionally.

My whole life begins to orbit around Asher—when I'm with him, I'm enraptured. When I'm not with him, I want to be. Even when I spend time with Maya now, she wants to know all about Asher. I can't tell if she is trying to be a good friend or if it's because that's the only way she can be part of a relationship that is now only big enough for two. But in spite of all of that, I am very guarded in what I choose to reveal to her. Saying the words out loud makes it less special, somehow. I don't want to share Asher with anyone, not even the girl who introduced me to him.

But he wants to share me, at least with his mother. I know that, like mine, his father isn't in the picture. And I know that his mother is a beekeeper, which is weird and a little badass. The first time I meet her, she takes me out to the hives and we watch her bees carrying out their tiny secret missions. I didn't tell her that I'd already been to her farm the week before, when she wasn't home, and that while she was out I took off my shirt in the autumn sunshine and Asher sketched me in his book.

While she taught me Beekeeping 101, Asher put his hand in the back pocket of my jeans, and all I could think of was that he wasn't ashamed of me in front of his mother.

I caught her staring at me when she thought I wasn't looking. "I like this one," she said to Asher, before I left. But I could tell she was thinking, *This boy is the most precious thing I have in the world. You be careful.*

WE ARE SURROUNDED by drifting yellow mist, like the smoke that wafts from a fireworks show. Asher and I are making love and I can smell gunpowder. His eyes are soft and green and *knowing*. That's what tips me over the edge in fact, not the undulating electricity rising in me, but his eyes, those eyes of his, which tell me, *Lily you are seen, and loved.* And then and then and then

Yeah, then the morning sun is coming through the window, slanting onto my pillow, and I open my eyes from sleep. And I remember the big glass of water I drank last night, just before I turned out the light.

It's one of the more arcane delights of being trans, the surprise orgasms that sneak up on me sometimes, if my bladder is full. Dr. Powers explained it to me once; because of the way my parts have been turned inside themselves, a lot of the most tender tissue now rests right up against my bladder. Which means that if I have a lot of liquid to drink the night before I go to bed, as my bladder fills up toward morning I can wind up getting all hot and bothered—*while I'm unconscious.* The result is these orgasms that arrive unbidden in the early dawn. I call them the *Night Visitors.*

Biology sure is goofy, is my conclusion.

As I sit up in bed, a lot of the details of that dream are already disappearing, like dew on summer grass. But the look in Asher's eyes—*that* I remember, maybe because that much was no dream.

He's looked at me that way before, and grinned. And did not disappear.

A FEW DAYS LATER, Asher meets my mom for the first time. Mom picks us up and takes us to Ripley Falls, near Bartlett. Mom is in full ranger mode—showing us all the flora and fauna—but she has her guard up, too, remembering what's happened before. But she *moms* the hell out of him anyway—insisting he put on sunscreen, making sure he has a full water bottle, and so on. Then we're off— this is a trail that she's been on several times, since it's part of the lynx habitat she's researching—but I haven't been on it. Asher is diplo- matic, asking Mom about her work, and for the next one point one miles we hear all about lynx. *The tufts on their ears increase their hear- ing. They can detect a mouse from 250 feet away. Their big, rounded feet can act like snowshoes.*

"Have you seen one yet?" Asher asks. "Since you've been here?"

Mom sighs. "Not yet. But I'm hoping."

Suddenly there is a fluttering of wings as a bird, frightened by our approach, skitters into the air, flies over our heads, and lands on the branch of a white birch. "Oh my God," says Mom, her long braid swinging around as she points toward the bird. "Look! It's a scarlet tanager!" It's an amazing creature—bright red with blue-black wings, and our sudden sighting of it is like seeing some fabulous celebrity walking swiftly from a theater door and into a limousine. The bird, perched on her branch, looks at us nervously for a second. Then it takes off, disappearing into the forest.

Mom looks at us with her mouth open. "Did you *see* that? It's on the SGCN list!"

"SGCN?" asks Asher.

"Species of greatest conservation need." Mom's still standing there stunned, like we just saw Elvis. "They're so beautiful, and so threatened." Her eyes fall upon me.

And then she turns and leads us deeper into the wild.

Later, after we get home, Mom makes us dinner while Asher looks around the house. He goes over to the bookshelves and reads some of the titles—*Silent Spring, The Sun Also Rises, The Stand,* paperback folios of Shakespeare plays, everything ever written by Toni Morrison. I go into the kitchen to see if I can help Mom. She just looks at me with big shining eyes, like she's about to cry.

"Are you okay, Mom?" I ask. I'm guessing she's falling in love with Asher a little bit, too.

"Wasn't that wonderful today?" she says. "Seeing the scarlet tanager?" And I realize it isn't Asher she's all emotional about. It was seeing a rare bird in the wild.

I'm just about to tell her to get over herself when I hear Asher's voice from the next room. "Whoa," he says. I head back to the living room in time to see him holding—to my horror—an old photo album, the one that contains pictures of me as a boy.

"What's *whoa?*" I say, trying to be casual.

"Who's this boy?" Asher asks. "He could be your twin!"

I feel the blood rushing to my face. I'm also remembering the fight Mom and I had, when we were unpacking, about leaving the album out. *Sometimes I feel like I don't have any history,* she'd said.

"That's my cousin," I say swiftly. "My cousin Liam."

"Wow," says Asher. "He looks just like you. Where does he live? California?"

I can tell from the complete silence in the kitchen that Mom is listening to this conversation very, very intently. It's a good question. Where *does* Liam live now?

"No," I tell Asher quietly. "He's gone. Leukemia."

"Jesus," says Asher, chagrined. "I didn't mean to, uh—"

"It's all right, Asher," says Mom, coming out from the kitchen. She takes the album from Asher's hand and puts it back on the bookshelf. "We'll always love Liam. He was a great kid."

THE FENCING TOURNAMENT is at Dartmouth, a school that my mother wants me to go to so badly she's done everything but fill out the application herself. She definitely feels like I should do the full liberal arts thing, instead of going to a conservatory—because it will make me "well-rounded."

That's what she says, anyway. But the real reason she loves Dartmouth is because it's less than two hours away from Adams. "We'd be able to stay close," she says, although I am pretty sure that hanging out with Mom on the weekends is not going to be my top priority next year. What's really clear to me is that Mom hasn't really figured out what she's going to do with her life after I'm finally launched to college. Maybe she'll stay with the Forest Service in Campton, but it seems like a long shot to me.

What I hope she'll do, actually, is through-hike the Appalachian Trail, which she's always said she's wanted to do. That'd be a five-or six-month-long commitment, hiking from Mount Katahdin in Baxter State Park, Maine, all the way down to Springer Mountain, Georgia. People who do it say it's transformative; that they figure out what's missing in their lives, or who they are meant to be. Maybe she'd even meet some other through-hiker, and fall in love.

I'd like that. Knowing she isn't alone.

On the drive down here, in fact, Mom suggested that after the tournament we could hike part of the AT—"just a little day hike," she said. Incredibly, the trail goes right through Hanover, goes right through the Dartmouth campus, in fact. But I'm pretty sure that when the tournament is over, Asher and I are going to try to sneak off to a mini-golf/ice cream place in West Lebanon. Provided we can ditch not only Mom but Maya, who is driving down with Asher to cheer me on.

My coach, Mr. Jameson, is my AP English teacher, better known as Chopper. He's a fearsome character indeed, considering that he's at least seventy. He paces up and down the edge of the piste, watching every move his fencers make. He's such a grumpy old man, but then again, when he picks up a foil during practice to show us how to make a particular move, he suddenly is full of grace and poise.

I win my first three matches: 15–4, 15–8, 15–1. By the time we get to my final match of the day, just after lunch, people are tired. The crowd in the stands is thinning out, but there's still a fair number of folks watching, including what looks like a number of kids from the Dartmouth College fencing team, whom I can identify by their extremely cool matching jackets, decorated with a big green D, a white tree in the middle, overlaid with two crossed swords.

My opponent is a girl named Nancy Seidlarz, who has at least three inches and forty pounds on me, and I can tell from the start that she's going to be tough. I saw her steamroll her last opponent this morning, 15 to 2, and it didn't even take her the full three periods to do it. She gets a touch off of me in the first period, and then another, and then three more.

It's five to nothing when we take the first break, and Chopper comes over to whisper in my ear.

"What's the matter with you?" he growls.

I want to explain to him that Nancy Seidlarz is bigger and stronger than I am, but he's not hearing it. "Use your head," he says. "She's big but she's slow. You can outsmart her. I know you can."

The ref says, *"En garde. Prêtes? Allez!"* Nancy Seidlarz comes charging at me and gets a touch before I even raise my sword to parry.

"Focus, Campanello!" shouts Chopper. "Focus!"

I take a deep breath, and the ref says, "*Prêtes? Allez!*" and just like that I point my sword at Nancy Seidlarz and I scream "*Aiieeee!*" and I flèche her. She is not prepared for this at all, and unless I'm mistaken, she takes a half step backward before I get the point.

"Halt," says the ref, and the place erupts in cheers. It's 6–1.

This point is enough to put me back in the game. In the next five minutes I catch up with her, tie her, and then we trade the lead back and forth. It's 10–10 at the end of regular play. Now we're in sudden death.

The ref conducts the "draw" before we get started, a coin flip which Nancy calls and wins; that means that if neither of us scores in this final minute, Nancy gets the win. It's not a good situation for me to be in, but then, it's not the first time my back's been against the wall.

My whole being is focused on anticipating and outguessing Nancy Seidlarz. With fifteen seconds to go, I get my break. Nancy parries an attack, but she swings her arm out too far to the right, leaving her open and slightly off-balance. That's when I hold my sword forward, move my weight onto my right knee, and then charge at her.

I get the point, and the match. The gym erupts in thunder.

We take our helmets off, and Nancy and I reach forward to shake hands. She takes off her helmet, and to my surprise she just looks at me with generosity and respect. "You're amazing!" she says.

"Isn't she?" answers a strangely familiar voice, and I turn, and that is when all the sound in the room disappears.

"Jonah?" I say.

THE VALENTINE'S DAY Massacre was the final act for Jonah and me, I guess. But things had really ended long before that.

I had been fencing against Hartshorn, not well, but that wasn't the problem. It was because—halfway through my third match—there'd been a disturbance up in the stands. A man was shouting and

swearing from one of the bleachers, more upset with my poor performance than maybe *I* was. The voice was unmistakable.

You can be anything you want to be, Liam.

There in the bleachers was my father, wearing a ratty-looking
raincoat. He had at least two days' beard on him. His voice sounded
like he was drunk.

It was impossible. How could he be here?

Even more rattled, I lost that match, and the next one. I kept
wanting to go up into the stands and say, *What the fuck are you doing
here? Why can't you leave us alone?* I wanted Mom to pull him by the
hand into the parking lot, and tell him to get lost.

But Mom wasn't there that day. She was at the national seashore,
doing research on the tide pools.

Had he driven down from Seattle to see me fence? How had he
wound up so drunk on a Saturday morning? It was the first time I
realized that you can cut someone out of your life, but that doesn't
mean they'll cut you out of *theirs.*

Fuck you, Dad, I thought. Strangely, the anger helped me focus. I
stepped up for my final match and made short work of my opponent.
But I wasn't really fighting a fencer from Hartshorn.

I pulled off my mask as the crowd cheered.

"That's my kid!" Dad shouted, pointing to me. "That's my *boy!*"

Everyone on the team—including Jonah, and Sorel—looked up
at my drunken father, and then at me. "Lily," asked Sorel. "Who *is*
that?"

A security guard was talking to Dad now. Dad was still shouting.
"His name's not Lily!" he shouted. "It's Liam! I should know! I'm the
one who fucking *named* him!"

"I have no idea," I said, and turned to leave the gym.

THAT WEEKEND, Sorel took me aside. "Everyone's been talking
about that guy at the fencing tournament who said he was your father," she said, and she waited, like she knew if she let the time and
silence rise between us, I'd fill it with the answers she wanted.

"I don't know how to tell you," I said.

"I'm your friend," she told me, "and I've got your back. You can tell me *anything*."

I made the mistake of trusting her, and told her I was trans. I told her about Seattle, and how my mother and I left our home in the middle of the night.

"Have you had the surgery?" she asked, and I told her, no, I wasn't old enough. "Maybe someday, though." I started to cry as I told her. "You have to promise me you won't tell anyone."

Sorel just looked at me. "After yesterday, everybody already knows."

As it turned out, Sorel's definition of having a friend's back didn't match mine. Through texts and whispers she made the most private aspects of my life as public as possible. I know Sorel thought she was doing the right thing. *We all have to look out for Lily now! Treat her with respect!*

But *looking out for Lily* wasn't what people had in mind.

Instead, when I got to school on Monday, some kids stared at me with a combination of pity, horror, and disgust. Oh sure, some people tried to be nice. *You're so brave!* they said. But most people just ignored me, like I made them uncomfortable, like I was suddenly invisible.

The only person I *really* wanted to talk to about this was avoiding me.

I finally saw Jonah that morning at his locker. "You," he said, like he couldn't even bear to call me by name.

I wanted to say: *Remember when we were standing by the ocean, and you said,* No matter where it goes . . . we stay friends.

"Can we just—"

"No," Jonah said. "You know, yesterday if you asked anyone in this school who I was they'd say, *Yeah, he's the guy who pitched the perfect game.* But now, you know who I am? The guy who was too stupid to know what was in your pants."

"That's not what matters," I said. "What matters is how we feel. How we—"

"You know how I feel?" Jonah's eyes slid away from me. "I feel like you should go *fuck yourself.*"

He stormed off down the hall, leaving me standing there alone.

Goodbye, Jonah.

"HELLO, LILY," Jonah says. He's wearing one of those jackets with the D and the crossed swords. He doesn't look unhappy to see me, but he does look embarrassed. Then again, the last time I saw him, he was standing over me in a parking lot and my dress was in shreds.

"What are you doing here?" I say.

"I go to Dartmouth," says Jonah. "I'm a freshman."

Of course he is. I'd be a freshman, too, if I hadn't lost a year. Thanks, in part, to Jonah.

"I live here now," I explain. "Well, a couple hours north."

"I wasn't sure it was you until I saw your flèche. I'd recognize that scream anywhere."

Members of the team are swirling around, celebrating. The stands are emptying. Maya waves to me, beaming. But I distance myself from her, and everyone else. I don't want the stain of my old life to spread through my new one.

"Listen," Jonah says. "I just wanted to say—I'm sorry. About what happened. I've thought about you *a lot.*"

I want to tell him, *I've thought a lot about you, too, you bastard.* But there's something different in his face. He seems more mature, maybe a little smarter about the world? Maybe a little bit sadder?

Good, I think. *I want him to be sad.*

"I did a terrible thing," Jonah says. He looks like he's in real anguish.

I remember the moment just before I succumbed to the anesthetic: *ninety-eight, ninety-seven.* One of the thoughts that passed through my mind was the hope that I could find forgiveness for Jonah. It isn't easy to do.

"Yeah," I acknowledge. "You did."

"If I could take it back—"

"Well, you *can't*," I say.

"I just need to know—" he says. "If you're okay. If you're happy?"

It's a simple question, but for me, it's never been an easy one. I want to say, *Yeah, since I got away from you.*

Instead I just nod, and Jonah smiles. "That's good," he says. "You deserve it."

"Well," I say, and I'm unexpectedly moved by this. "Thanks, Jonah."

Someone calls Jonah's name and he twists around, raises a finger to tell them to wait up. "You take care," he says.

He steps forward, opening his arms, and incredibly, I find myself walking into them. Even more incredibly, it feels good, like I am starting to let go of some of the anger that has haunted me all this time. I'm still holding my sword in my right hand, but as my arms wrap around his back, my foil falls out of my hand and I rest my face against his shoulder.

"Friend of yours?" says Asher coolly.

"Asher," I say, pulling back swiftly. My heart is pounding away, because with just a few choice words, Jonah could wreck my life a second time.

"Former boyfriend, actually," Jonah corrects, and he smiles at me, as if he's just set the universe to rights. My jaw drops. *Now?* Now is when Jonah's decided to own up to what he should have back then?

"This is Jonah. From Point Reyes. He goes to Dartmouth now," I explain. "I didn't know he went to school here."

Asher looks from me to Jonah and back again.

"It was great to run into you," says Jonah. "I really am sorry. Really. If you ever wanted to talk—well, maybe you still have my cell."

Asher grabs my shoulder. "She doesn't want to talk to you," he says.

Jonah looks like he's been slapped. He turns his back, and I instinctively reach out to tell him Asher didn't mean that; that he's just never seen me with anyone else, and he is jealous—but before I can reach him, Asher yanks on my arm *hard*, like he's cracking a whip.

"Oww, that *hurts*," I say. "What are you doing?"

"What are *you* fucking doing?" says Asher. "I look down and someone else is hugging you?"

I would laugh at that, if it weren't all so goddamned sad. I have never seen him like this—vindictive, jealous, *alpha*.

"Asher, back off," says Maya, who has made her way through the crowd now, with my mother by her side. They've both witnessed the whole thing. Maya's voice seems like it snaps him out of the spell, and he looks first at her, and then at me.

He drops my arm like it's on fire. "Lily—I—"

My mother steps forward and clamps her arm around my shoulders. "I'm going to take my daughter home now," she says firmly.

I pick my sword up off the ground, and Mom guides me out of the Dartmouth gym.

Asher follows us halfway, dazed, like the beast in a fairy tale who awakens from the curse. "I didn't mean it!" he says.

I know, I think, as tears spill down my face. *So why did you do it?*

THE NEXT NIGHT, Maya comes for a sleepover. She's brought Captain Morgan in a S'well bottle, and neither her moms nor mine are the wiser. We eat sheet cake left over from a forest ranger's office birthday party and watch *Naked and Afraid.* We talk about what one item we would bring with us if we were on the show. I say a knife, because obviously, but Maya says she'd take her oboe, because sometimes on that show you just need something to calm your nerves.

I do everything I can to not think about Asher, who has texted me seventeen apologies.

The truth is, my heart hurts, and not because I can't forgive Asher, although that was some weird shit he pulled off at the fencing match. But it's more like, up to now, everything has been a dream with him, and this is the first time I've had to face the obvious: that it's not a dream, that he's got this nasty jealous streak, and that having a relationship with him isn't only going to be about making out on a lifeguard stand and playing "The Swan."

I'm remembering Jonah, how different he seemed. I guess I

seemed different, too. It was my scream that let him know that I was still me, and still fighting.

When it's time to go to bed, Maya and I change in to our pajamas. I still feel strange about undressing in front of other girls; I think I always will. It's a behavior that was forged in making myself invisible, before, in locker rooms and bathrooms. Maya rips off her shirt and parades around in her panties, shimmying into a satin set of shorty pj's. I shuck off my pants and turn my back and drag my turtleneck over my head, taking care that my cuff bracelets don't come loose, so Maya won't see my scars. I unhook my bra, folding myself forward like a bird tucking in her wings, arms crossed over my breasts until I can pull on a T-shirt. CRANKY FRANKIE'S BBQ, the T-shirt says. GRILLS GONE WILD.

Suddenly Maya throws her arm around me and holds up her phone. "Smile!" she says, and she snaps a selfie.

"I'm getting dressed!" I complain, glancing down at my bare legs.

Maya shrugs. "If we don't post a girls' night in on Insta, did it even really happen?" She starts typing on her phone, but then blows up the picture, squints, and reaches for my arm. She twists it a little, until she is looking directly at the big, ugly bruise where Asher grabbed me. You can see the marks of each of his fingers, and the round blob where he pressed his thumb.

"Oh my God," she says. "Are you okay?"

"I'm fine," I tell Maya. "It's nothing."

OLIVIA ◆ 8

Five months after

Dr. Monica Powers lives up to her name. She is tall and self-assured, and arrestingly beautiful. Her chestnut hair is pulled back from her face in a low twist, and she commands the witness stand instead of being cowed by it. If not for the power suit and the lack of a lasso of truth, she could be the incarnation of Wonder Woman—smarter and stronger than most people, and weary of being underestimated.

"Dr. Powers," Jordan says, "can you tell us what you do for a living?"

"I'm a gender confirmation surgeon at Mills-Peninsula Medical Center in Burlingame, California. I'm on the surgical subcommittee of WPATH—the World Professional Association for Transgender Health. I perform pro bono reversals of clitoral circumcision and genital mutilation in Africa and other countries." Her lips curve. "And I happen to be a trans woman myself."

I know Jordan has flown her in here to be an expert, to educate the jury. I watch them study her with unabashed curiosity. Some look patently surprised, as if the act of seeing a stunning woman and hearing her say she is transgender is already forcing them to reevaluate their opinions.

"What does it mean," Jordan asks, "to be transgender?"

"Trans people are people whose gender identity doesn't match the gender they were thought to be when they were born," Dr. Powers says. "Normally, in the delivery room, a doctor says, *It's a boy!* or *It's a girl!* depending on what reproductive organs the baby arrives with. Most babies who are called boys at birth actually grow up to be boys. Most babies who are called girls at birth actually grow up to be girls. But for some people, what's on the outside doesn't match what is on the inside. They know who they are, and it's different from what was assumed at the moment they were born. A trans woman is someone who lives as a woman right now, but was thought to be a man when she was born. A trans man is someone who lives as a man right now, but was thought to be a woman when he was born." She smiles gently at the jury. "To make this even more complicated, gender identity isn't always either column A or column B. Some trans people don't identify as male *or* female, but somewhere in be-tween, or a combination of both. Sometimes that's called *nonbinary,* or *genderqueer.*"

I think of my conversation with Elizabeth. I can't imagine what it's like to have to educate everyone about your right to exist in the world. I think of her shoulders, rounded as she leaned on the railing at the bridge, while two girls who were lucky enough to be born in the right bodies whispered about her.

Tired, I think. That's what it means to be transgender. Elizabeth must be continuously exhausted.

"So," Jordan says, frowning, "you're saying that just because I have XY chromosomes, that doesn't necessarily mean I'm male?"

"Objection, Your Honor," Gina says. "Relevance? I'm all for Mr. McAfee waving the Pride flag, but this is a murder case."

Judge Byers shakes her head. "I think we can all benefit from hearing this, Ms. Jewett. Mr. McAfee, proceed."

"We were talking about chromosomes . . ." Jordan prompts.

Dr. Powers nods. "There's a difference between sex and gender. A person's sex is the body's biology—what's between your legs and in your DNA. A person's gender refers to what's between your ears. Your own psychological sense of self—who you *know* yourself to be—is called your *gender identity.* If your gender identity doesn't dovetail with your biological sex, you are transgender."

"How does someone know if they're transgender?"

"I like to think about it in terms of handedness," Dr. Powers explains. "If I asked you to sign your name with your nondominant hand, it would feel weird. If I asked you to describe it to me, you'd probably say things like *the pen doesn't fit comfortably in my hand;* or *it's awkward;* or *I have to try hard to make legible something that I can do with my other hand effortlessly.* It feels forced. Even a kindergartner can tell you if they're a righty or a lefty, even if they don't have the words for it. It's also true that while most people are righties, and a smaller sliver of the population are lefties, there are some people who can use either hand with equal facility. Years ago, if you were a lefty, teachers tried to break you into being right-handed. Eventually, someone realized that it's perfectly okay to be left-handed. Right-handed people who don't write with their left hand can still understand that some people might . . . even if they never do it themselves."

She looks at the jury. "This example is a really great way to understand what it means to be transgender. Everyone has a dominant gender identity. It's not a preference, it's not something you can change just because you feel like it—it's just how you're wired. Most people who are assigned male or female at birth feel their gender identity matches that label—they're called *cisgender.* But transgender people know that being in the body they are in feels not quite right. Some know this when they're very young. Some spend years feeling uncomfortable without really knowing why. Some avoid talking about gender identity because they're ashamed, or afraid."

"Why would they be afraid?" Jordan asks.

"When trans people tell the truth about who they are, they face stigma, discrimination, harassment, and in some cases, violence," Dr. Powers says bluntly. "Trans people have been fired for expressing their gender identity. They've been beaten up or thrown out of their homes. Last year, nearly thirty trans people were murdered. This year, so far, another four have been killed."

I glance at Asher, who is staring at Jordan with undisguised confusion. It sounds, from the doctor's testimony, like she is supporting the prosecution's theory.

"It's not just adults who are targeted," she continues. "Imagine you're a twelve-year-old girl in a boy's body, who has started wearing girls' clothing to school, and you are told by your principal that you have to use the boys' bathroom. You might imagine there are some boys in there who are . . . less than accepting. And all you want to do is pee."

"What does it mean to transition?" Jordan asks.

"Transitioning is the period during which a trans person starts to live according to their gender identity, rather than the gender they were incorrectly assigned at birth. It's important to point out that you can be transgender and never transition. It's not one-size-fits-all, and gender expression looks different for every person. For one, it may mean certain clothing, or growing your hair long, or putting on makeup. For someone else, it could be changing your name or the pronouns you use to refer to yourself. Some people change their driver's license or passport to reflect their correct gender. Others undergo hormone therapy, or surgical procedures, so that their bodies reflect their correct gender."

Jordan approaches the witness stand. "Dr. Powers, did you know Lily Campanello?"

"Yes," she says. "I performed her gender affirmation surgery."

"As her doctor, were you aware of the process she undertook to transition from male to female?"

"Yes. Lily followed a fairly typical course of transition. Around age thirteen, a trans female would start taking estrogen and spironolactone, which serve as puberty blockers. Since we typically start puberty at that age, this ensures that a transgender girl won't develop facial hair, voice change, or the growth of an Adam's apple—anything you'd associate with secondary sex characteristics. Following that, some individuals—like Lily—choose to have gender affirmation surgery."

"What is that?" Jordan asks.

"Lily had what is commonly referred to as *bottom surgery*. In scientific terms, it's a vaginoplasty, in which the testicles are removed, and the skin of the foreskin and the penis is inverted—preserving blood and nerves—to form a fully functional and sensitive vagina. The glans of the penis forms the clitoris, with all its nerve endings. There is no cervix, and no uterus, and no ovaries. Trans women do not menstruate or get pregnant."

I think about how, when Braden and I went for our ultrasound of Asher, the technician asked if we wanted to know the sex. She had pointed to the tiny thorn of a penis on the grainy screen. Had Ava Campanello had a similar experience? If so, how had she gone about rewriting that history in her head, in her heart?

I have seen sweet videos on social media of middle-aged parents announcing the birth of their "child"—a middle schooler with braces and a wide smile, who is now identifying as the opposite sex. They've always made me smile, because those kids are loved simply and unconditionally, which is so much better than the alternative . . . the trans teens without parental support, whose obituaries sometimes cross my feed.

But now I wonder if there's more behind the giddy smiles and the winking rebirth announcements of those videos. Does the joy of presenting their new daughter come at the expense of losing their former son?

Has Ava Campanello grieved *twice* for her child?

"Can trans women enjoy a healthy sexual relationship," Jordan asks, "including vaginal penetration with a male partner?"

"Absolutely," Dr. Powers says.

My face heats; this isn't really a dialogue I ever thought I'd hear my brother have. My gaze slides to Asher, and I realize that for him, this is more than just scientific. This is personal.

This is a validation.

His jaw is clenched so tight that the muscles in his neck are strained.

Jordan tilts his head. "Would a male partner be able to tell, from intercourse alone, that a trans woman's vagina was surgically crafted?"

I stare at Asher, who remains immobile, impassive. A cipher.

"Not unless she told him," Dr. Powers replies. "In other words, Counselor: I am damn good at my job."

Asher's eyes drift shut, like he is praying. Or like a prayer has been answered.

"Nothing further," Jordan says.

THERE IS PROOF that the ancient Egyptians made little honey cakes for children as sweets, the way we would make gingerbread men today. I have my own version—one that is a loaf, not a cookie, that has nutmeg and cloves and coffee in it, too. I made it not as a treat for Asher but as a consolation for things that he lost: after getting creamed in a hockey championship game, when a friend moved away, when I spirited him away from his home and his father without advance notice.

When Jordan takes his seat and the prosecutor rises, I distract myself by writing the ingredients in the Moleskine notebook. *Cinnamon, sugar, eggs. Ginger and walnuts.* Easier to do that than to notice that Asher's head is bowed toward the table now, like a snowdrop on its stalk.

Four cups of honey are in this loaf—dark honey, from the second harvest. It's made late in the season, after the nectar drought in July, when the bees turn to goldenrod and sunflowers instead. It's deeper and richer. It tastes like secrets.

I should make Asher a honey loaf, I think, *for loss.*

Of Lily? I wonder. *Or of this trial?*

The prosecutor stands close to the witness stand, her arms folded. "Isn't middle school a little early to start hormone therapy?" Gina asks.

"We don't believe so," Dr. Powers answers. "The trick is to stop puberty in its tracks so we don't have to remove certain physical characteristics . . . but still have enough raw material, so to speak, to work with if the trans kid comes of age and wants to have surgery."

"Lily's surgery was at seventeen, though," the prosecutor says. "She wasn't even of legal age. That's extremely young, isn't it?"

"Honestly, no. It's what I'm now recommending. I look for a combination of physical and emotional maturity in the child. If the surgery is done precollege it also means they have the watchful eyes of their parents to support them through the process and to make sure the aftercare is kept up."

"Aftercare?"

"Yes. Daily dilation of the vagina for six months to prevent stenosis postsurgery."

"You say a man would not be able to tell that his partner was a trans female after having surgery . . . but there are scars, aren't there?" Gina glances at Asher as she says this.

"We've gotten so good at this that the scars are practically undetectable. And postop vaginas undergo metaplasia—the lining adopts the characteristics that a cisgender vagina has. Not even a pathologist would be able to tell the difference."

"Ah, but isn't a pathologist different from a lover, in an intimate setting?"

Heat blooms across Asher's cheeks.

"The surgical scars are hidden in the vulva, in the groin creases. A lot of times they're obscured by pubic hair. If you were looking closely enough, you might ask, *What are these scars?* But something tells me that a teenage boy having sex with his girlfriend isn't being quite so . . . scientific." Dr. Powers shrugs. "A transgender girl could be standing naked in front of you, and you wouldn't see a single visible scar."

"Not a single visible scar," Gina repeats. "Except for the ones caused by her boyfriend beating her up."

"Objection!" Jordan roars.

The prosecutor looks at him. "Withdrawn," she says. And she smiles.

SOMETIME BEFORE ASHER was born, when Braden and I had moved to Boston, we decided to spend his day off at the Museum of Fine Arts. We wandered through the mummies and the John Singer Sargents, but I was drawn to the collection of Monets. There was something about the way impressionist paintings make sense from a distance, but not up close, that I felt in my bones.

It was a lovely, perfect day. Braden was funny and charming and wandered from gallery to gallery with me, holding my hand. When we studied Rodin's *Psyche,* he whispered how much he liked my body better than hers. We sat in front of modern art and tried to decode it.

When we stepped outside, however, it was pouring. We had to run to the T station, and by the time we reached it everything was dampened—our clothing, our outing, our moods. *How did you not look up the weather before we left?* Braden yelled at me. *You should have brought an umbrella. Can't you ever do anything without it turning into a clusterfuck?*

I bent like a willow in the strength of his storm. I knew better than to argue. Instead, I nodded when I thought it was appropriate. I apologized.

I caught the eye of a woman farther down the platform, who immediately turned away.

Braden picked at the soggy mess of his suede bomber jacket. *This is ruined, thanks to you.*

When the train finally came, we climbed on. I sat down next to the woman who'd been watching me, and Braden took the seat across from us. He plucked at his drenched coat. *I hope you're happy,* he huffed.

Beneath the folds of my own jacket, the woman beside me grasped my hand, and squeezed.

DURING A FIFTEEN-MINUTE courtroom break, Jordan sequesters us in the private conference room that has become our refuge. I have to argue with him to let me go to the bathroom. Since my last trip there involved meeting Ava, he doesn't want to take any chances, but I tell him I'm a big girl and can handle the odds. As it turns out, the ladies' room is empty, but there is a line for the water fountain outside it. I wait for the man who is drinking to finish, and when he straightens I realize it's Mike Newcomb.

"Olivia," he says.

"Fancy meeting you here," I reply, forcing a gust of false cheer through my words.

He wipes his mouth, still wet from the fountain, with the back of his hand, and then blushes at his own lack of manners. "Sorry," he says, and I murmur something dismissive, and we do a little stilted do-si-do as he cedes his spot in front of the fountain to me.

Mike slides his hands into his pockets. "How are you doing?"

"I mean . . . ," I say, which is not an answer.

He angles his body so that he shelters me from the eyes of others passing by in the hallway. He smells like fresh laundry. "Has anyone else bothered you at home?" he asks. "Any more vandalism?"

"No," I say.

"I, well, don't have any leads yet," Mike says. "About the barn."

"Right. You probably have a lot on your plate." He's dressed down today—a collared shirt, jeans. He doesn't look nearly as unapproachable as he did on the day he testified against Asher. "Are you here for the prosecution?"

He looks confused for a moment, and then a smile unspools across his face. It changes his features, and all of a sudden I can see the boy who fed me fried dough on prom night, so that I wouldn't stain my dress. "Olivia," he says. "I came here for *you.*"

He says goodbye, and I watch him walk down the hall. When I return to the private conference room, I realize I've completely forgotten to take a drink of water.

COACH LACROIX'S CONCESSION to dressing the part of a witness is wearing his Adams High Hockey fleece vest. He gives Asher a sober nod as he settles into his seat, waiting for Jordan to begin his questioning.

"How do you know Asher Fields, Coach?" Jordan asks.

"Asher's been playing hockey for me since he was nine. First on Peewee leagues, and now at the high school varsity level."

"Do you know Asher as a student as well?"

"Well, yeah. In order to play on a varsity team, kids have to main-tain a 3.0 GPA. Asher's always well above that," the coach says.

"Has he been on the varsity team for four years?"

"No, he was JV his freshman year, but he started on varsity as a sophomore, which is pretty incredible. Great talent."

"What kind of teammate is Asher?" Jordan asks.

"A natural leader," Coach Lacroix promptly replies. "He was voted captain when he was still a junior. First time in thirty years of coach-ing I've ever seen that. He would lead by example, but he also looked after the kids stuck on the bench. He collected underdogs, you know?" He smiles at Asher. "If I had a son, I'd want him to be like that kid."

"Have you known Asher as a community member as well?"

"Yeah. During the summers, he's a counselor at a hockey camp I run for elementary school kids," the coach says. "He's a hard worker, reliable, good with kids. It's my understanding that Asher doesn't have siblings, but you'd never know it from the way he works with little ones."

"Can you give us an example?" Jordan asks.

"Every summer we get a couple of campers coming from the city, through the Fresh Air Fund. Great kids, but they don't even know how to lace up a pair of skates. Asher took them under his wing without being asked to. He taught them to skate, and he looked out for them during free time, and he invited them to sit with the counselors—which is like winning the lottery, for any camper. When the kids went back to the city at the end of August, he didn't just forget about them. He stayed in touch, listening to them when they were struggling, encouraging them to dream big—and to get out on the ice now and then. As far as I know, he's still writing to them." Coach Lacroix turns to the jury. "I've seen a lot of teenagers over the years—and I've seen a lot of Asher in the past ten years—and I can tell you, he's a lot more mature than other guys his age."

"Thank you," Jordan says. "Nothing further."

The prosecutor sits at her table, tapping a pen against an open folder. "Isn't it true that Asher Fields was involved in a bunch of fights while playing hockey?"

Coach Lacroix shrugs. "When you're the best on the team, you get targeted by the opposing team. So yeah, he was involved in some scuffles."

"Isn't fighting in hockey a penalty that hurts the team?"

"Yes but—"

"So he let the team down because he couldn't control his temper?" Gina asks.

"Objection," Jordan calls out. "Relevance?"

The judge narrows her eyes. "Overruled."

The prosecutor stands and repeats her questions. "Like I said," Coach Lacroix answers, "he was usually targeted. He wasn't fighting . . . he was fighting *back*."

The prosecutor turns on her heel, as if the wind has changed direction. "I assume you're familiar with the cheating scandal at Adams High last year, where a group of athletes masterminded a ring that included breaking into the math department offices, stealing an exam, having some A students create a key, and then dispersing the answers to others?"

"Yes."

"I assume you are aware that it was the defendant's idea that set the entire cheating scandal in motion . . . and that he subsequently lied about this?"

"I heard something to that effect."

Jordan rises, his knuckles balanced on the table. "Your Honor, I object to the coach testifying to what he heard—"

"I'll rephrase," Gina says. "Asher was suspended and prohibited from playing on your hockey team for a month. Wasn't the reason because he was implicated in this scandal?"

"Yes," Coach Lacroix replies, "but look, the Asher I know . . . he's a good kid. That stuff didn't line up with the boy I know."

Gina raises a brow. "Looks like there's a lot of stuff people didn't know about him." She flicks a glance at Jordan, poised to object. "Nothing further."

Judge Byers calls for a lunch break, but I have lost my appetite. Dr. Powers did more to validate Lily's life than to clear Asher from being involved with her death; Coach Lacroix—the only witness who's said kind words about Asher since this trial started—had his testimony pretzeled back to him in a way that made Asher look like a liar. I will be the next witness after we reconvene, and I'm already so nervous that I am shaking. I can't imagine this day getting any worse.

Until we slip out of the courtroom and I come face-to-face with Braden.

"DAD?" ASHER SAYS, his eyes wide.

"What are you doing here?" I ask bluntly, as Jordan steps forward to form a human wall with me, separating Braden from my son. Sweat trickles down my spine; I am both furious and frightened and I can't sift one emotion from the other. To my consternation, my hand flies up to the nape of my neck, where my ponytail trails. *You should always wear your hair like this. You look so damn beautiful.*

"What am I doing here?" Braden repeats, as if it is ridiculous to even ask the question. "I'm here for Asher. I would have come at the start of the trial, but I had surgeries that couldn't be postponed." He turns to Jordan, his eyes narrowing just the slightest bit. "Apparently I arrived just in time. Clearly, you need a better character witness."

He exudes power and privilege, a superhero coming to save the day in his tailored suit. But you don't get to be the hero of the story when you're the villain.

"Are you volunteering for the job? Because there is no chance in hell that you will testify," Jordan says flatly. I can feel fury rolling off his skin, and I realize this is the first time my brother has seen Braden since I told him the truth about my marriage. He looks like he wants to punch Braden.

I grab Braden's arm and drag him into the conference room, with Jordan and Asher following. As soon as the door has closed, I turn on Braden. "Just because you paid Asher's bail doesn't mean you get to act like you have a relationship with him," I hiss.

"This isn't about the bail," Braden argues. "And I *do* have a relationship with Asher. I was seeing him once a month, before he went to jail. But of course I didn't *know* that. When he stopped answering my texts—"

The buzzing in my ears is so loud that for a second, I think I am going to pass out. "Oh," Braden says quietly, glancing to Asher and then back to me. "You didn't know."

The prosecutor's voice echoes through me. *You are aware that it was the defendant's idea . . . and that he subsequently lied . . . ?*

"You do not belong in here," Jordan says to Braden. "I'm going to have to ask you to leave."

A familiar expression settles over Braden's face—one I remember from when he was angry and about to lash out, but then realized we were in public. His features smoothen, and he turns to Asher, folding him into an embrace. "I'll be in the courtroom," he says.

When Braden leaves, I sink down at the table and bury my face in my hands. "Uncle Jordan," I hear Asher say. "Can I have a minute alone with my mom?"

I hear the door click shut behind my brother and when I look up, Asher is sitting beside me. "I didn't know how to tell you that I was seeing him," he says. "Remember when Uncle Jordan found texts on my phone to Ben Flanders? That wasn't a guy on the hockey team. That's Dad. I gave him a fake name, so you wouldn't find out."

Ben Flanders. Braden Fields. "Why, Asher?" I ask.

He lifts a shoulder. "I wanted to know why I wasn't part of his life."

My gaze flies to his. "I was trying to *keep* you from being part of his life."

"Yeah," Asher says. "How come?"

I open my mouth to say the obvious: because he is the seed for every terrible thing, every potential abusive trait, that is being said about Asher in this courtroom. But instead, I press my lips together and shake my head.

"I know things were bad between you and him. But that was your relationship—not mine," Asher says. "I wanted to find out for myself what he was like."

You have no idea what he's like, I think. Braden would have made sure of that.

I force myself to speak evenly. "And did you?"

"We met at a restaurant, once a month, just over the Massachusetts border. He wanted to know everything about me. What I do for fun, what I study in school, where I was thinking of going to college. You wouldn't have thought from the conversations that he was an awful father."

I remember a time when Braden and I were dating, when I woke to find the entire bedroom filled with helium balloons. Braden had peeked around the corner of the door, grinning. *It's not my birthday,* I told him. *That doesn't mean,* he said, *that you don't deserve it.*

As fiercely as Braden loved me, he hurt me. If I had known that his love came at such a high price, would I have married him?

The answer is, sadly, yes. Even if someone is violent, or a liar; even if he breaks your heart every time you hand it to him—that doesn't necessarily stop you from loving him. The two are not mutually exclusive.

Listening to the prosecution's testimony has been a refresher course.

I look at Asher now. I wonder if Braden smiled at him across the table in that restaurant and recognized a kindred soul. I wonder if Asher's curiosity in rekindling a relationship with Braden was to discover the source of parts of himself that he could not find in me.

Parts ignited by his relationship with Lily.

When I saw Asher with her, they seemed to be a happy couple.

But that's what people saw when they looked at Braden and me, too.

"He has another family now," Asher says, pulling me back.

"I know."

"I was good enough for the blue plate special once a month, but he didn't exactly invite me over to watch football with my half brothers on Sundays." Asher lifts his face to mine. "I was going to stop meeting him," he says.

I look at him, hard. *Are you telling me the truth?* I think. *Or are you telling me what you think I want to hear?*

Because if Braden rubbed off on Asher during those visits, that is exactly the kind of thing he'd say.

"But then," Asher continues, "this happened."

Lily's death. His arrest. Jail.

"I should have told you," Asher says.

If he had, would I have intervened? Prevented him from going? Did I fear that Braden would tell Asher lies about me?

Or that Braden would tell Asher the truth?

Asher and I do not talk about the fact that I was physically abused by his father. "Do you remember a lot about him?" I ask carefully. "Before we left?"

I hold my breath, waiting for his answer. I don't know if he can recall what it was like in that household; what his father did to me; what he saw. Or what happened the night before we left for good.

"No," Asher says quietly. "That's one of the reasons I wanted to meet him. I can only remember one conversation I had with him, when I was little. *One.* How can you be six years old when your parents split up and not remember more than one conversation?"

Because you bury them so deep so they don't come out to hurt you, I think.

"It was Christmas, and he took me outside," Asher says. "I was really little—so little he was carrying me. He pointed to the sky and he said, 'Right there—there's Santa. Can't you see it?' And I looked and I looked and then, I swear, I totally saw a sleigh and reindeer." He shakes his head. "Stupid, right?"

"Your father could be pretty persuasive," I reply, but I think: *Maybe that's when it happened. When he taught you how to lie.*

THERE IS ONE type of honey you should avoid at all costs.

Mad honey comes from bees that forage on rhododendrons and mountain laurel, and it's full of poisonous grayanotoxins. It causes dizziness, nausea and vomiting, convulsions, cardiac disorders, and more. Symptoms last for twenty-four hours, and although rarely, if left untreated, can be fatal. It has been used in biological warfare as far back as 399 B.C., to make Xenophon and the Greek army retreat from Persia. During the Third Mithridatic War in 65 B.C., citizens of Pontus placed mad honey on the route taken by Pompey's soldiers, and when the enemy helped themselves to the treat, they were easily conquered.

The secret weapon of mad honey, of course, is that you expect it to be sweet, not deadly. You're deliberately attracted to it. By the time it messes with your head, with your heart, it's too late.

A WOMAN'S HEART beats a little faster than a man's, Braden told me the first night we went out to dinner.

Mine is hammering like the wings of a hummingbird.

As I place my hand over the Bible, as I swear to tell the truth, I look into the gallery. Mike Newcomb is sitting on the aisle, his eyes fixed on me. He offers me an encouraging smile.

Braden stands along the back wall of the courtroom, his arms folded across his chest.

I would never be called to testify against Braden if we were still married. There is spousal immunity in the American legal system.

But here I am, being called to testify against Asher.

No, no. *For* Asher.

Well. It will not be the first time I've lied to protect someone I love.

THE NIGHT OF the 1999 Mass General Cardiothoracic Department Christmas party was foul—a cold, sleety rain was falling, as if the weather couldn't make up its mind to segue into snow. Braden had picked out my dress—formfitting to show my figure, but below the knee, so it wasn't tacky—and I'd picked my way through puddles in my heels. It was important to him that I look the part of the surgeon's wife; therefore, it was important to me.

Braden and I were standing in a pocket of conversation about

Y2K and whether in a week's time every computer system in the hospital would crash. Braden had had too much to drink, and he interrupted the attending who was talking about the Y2K bug and how to protect patient records. *I suppose you have a Doomsday bunker, too,* Braden sneered.

He didn't see the look the doctor gave him, but I did. To keep him from doing or saying something else he'd later regret, I reached for his arm, to pull him away. Instead, my gesture made him spill his wine—all over the front of his shirt. He laughed, making fun of my clumsiness, and dabbed himself dry with his napkin.

An hour later, just before I was about to get into the car, Braden grabbed my wrist. *Don't you ever fucking embarrass me again,* he said, and he shoved me so hard that I fell to my knees. He got into the car, locked the doors, and peeled away, leaving me behind.

This was, of course, before Uber. I didn't have any cash; I hadn't even carried a purse, since I was traveling with Braden. I started walking home in the sleet, in my heels and my too-thin coat. Ice settled on my shoulders, in my hair. I couldn't feel my feet.

I didn't realize that a police car had stopped beside me until the officer called out. *You all right, ma'am?*

For just a heartbeat, I thought about telling the truth. But doing so would ruin Braden's life, and I loved him too much to destroy him.

Instead, I started babbling lies. My husband had been called in to perform an emergency surgery, leaving me to get home on my own from a party we were attending. The policeman offered to drive me, but I realized that if Braden saw me arrive in a cop car, there would be hell to pay. So I gave him the address of a house I passed sometimes when I went for a run—a small pink Colonial with a sunroom and a little ivy-covered screen porch that led to the front door. Once, I'd seen the couple that lived there. The woman was kissing the man at the screen door before she left for work.

As the police car pulled over, I prayed that the owners of the house were already asleep. I waved to the officer just before I cracked the screen door and stepped into the strangers' enclosed porch. Aware of the police car with its headlights on, waiting, I fumbled for a light switch, and with shaking hands pretended to insert a key into the front door.

I waved and turned off the light in the porch, as if I'd unlocked the front door and was all set. After the car pulled away, I slipped out the screen door. In the shadows and the sleet, I walked the rest of the way.

WHEN I WAS a little girl, Jordan used to take me to the bus stop. My kindergarten bus came before his middle school one, and as it lumbered up the hill, groaned to a halt, and flipped out its little Stop paddle, he'd hoist my backpack onto my shoulders, pull my pigtails, and say, *Don't do anything I wouldn't do.* It became more than a routine; it bordered on superstition. If Jordan was sick and we couldn't have this exchange, inevitably something bad happened at school: I would be picked last in gym class; my favorite teacher would be absent; the cafeteria would run out of chocolate milk.

Now, Jordan approaches me to begin the testimony we have practiced a hundred times in my kitchen. But he angles his body in a way that allows me to see his face, without revealing it to the jury or the judge. *Don't do anything I wouldn't do,* he mouths silently.

"Please state your name for the record," Jordan says.

"Olivia McAfee."

"How are you connected to Asher?"

I look at my son's face, a ghost of my own. The expression in his eyes is the one he used to have when he was a toddler and I picked him up after a fall—total faith I could make things right. "I'm his mother," I say.

"Tell us a little about Asher in elementary school," Jordan begins.

"He was obsessed with hockey from the time he started playing at seven," I reply. "We have a pond on our property, and he'd skate there when it froze over in the winter. He joined a Peewee league, and on weekends, I'd drive him all around the state for games."

"When did he start volunteering with younger kids?"

"When he was fifteen," I say.

"As the person who knows him best," Jordan asks, "can you tell us about some of the qualities Asher has that make him want to help people?"

My gaze is drawn to Braden. When we were out in social situations and someone asked him why he became a surgeon, he always said he wanted to help people. He would talk about his grandfather, dying in front of him of a heart attack, and how he couldn't turn back time but decided to do the next best thing by making sure someone *else's* grandfather didn't die.

I was married for a year before I learned that he had never met his grandfather, who'd been a traveling sales rep who had a secret second family he went to live with before Braden was born.

When I asked Braden why he didn't just tell the truth, he shrugged. *No one wants to admit they became a cardiac surgeon for the money. I'm only telling people what they want to hear.*

I think about Asher, meeting Braden for breakfast once a month in secret. I remember Asher looking Mike in the eye and stating he wasn't in Lily's bedroom. I think about the cheating scandal Asher swore he hadn't set in motion.

Jordan steps closer to me. "Ms. McAfee?" he prompts.

"Sorry." I look at him. "Asher's compassionate. Empathetic. He's always looking out for someone weaker than he is."

So was Braden, I think. *And I qualified.*

The first time Braden and I slept together, he kissed my temple when he thought I was asleep. *I think I love you,* he whispered. Back then, I melted at the thought of him confessing something so monumental only when he thought I couldn't hear it. Now I wonder if he knew, all along, that I was awake. If, even then, he was that manipulative.

I clear my throat. "I wasn't surprised to learn that Asher stayed in touch with the campers even after summer ended. And I wasn't surprised to hear that he rescued Lily from a boy who was pushing her to go out with him. That's just who he is," I say.

"You're a single parent, aren't you?" Jordan asks.

"Yes. For twelve years."

"What has Asher had to do to adapt?"

"Well, for a really long time, it's just been the two of us. Asher had to grow up fast. I make a living as a beekeeper, and once he was big enough and old enough, he had to help me with the bees, sometimes when other kids were out having fun. He had to fend for himself on days when I was selling honey at farmers' markets. We've learned together how to be carpenters, electricians, plumbers, handymen—because things break on a farm, and we don't make a lot of money. I rely on my son." My gaze softens as I turn to Asher. "His first instinct has always been to take care of me."

Just like that, twelve years have spooled backward. Braden grabs me by my ponytail. I feel hair ripping at the roots as I cower. I wait for the blow.

But there he is: my tiny savior, Asher. His body makes a wedge between us. His small hands beat against Braden. An act of defense.

And also an act of violence.

"Did you witness the relationship between your son and Lily developing, from September through November?"

"Yes."

"How did Asher behave with Lily?"

"He loved her," I say flatly. "He took care of her. He protected her."

If you had asked a witness to describe my marriage from the outside looking in, they would have said the same about Braden.

"He would never have laid a hand on her," I say woodenly.

That same witness to my marriage would have staked everything on this fact, too.

"Thank you, Ms. McAfee—" Jordan says, because when we have practiced my testimony, this is where it ends.

Except I'm not finished.

"—and this is how I know: because Asher's been protecting me since he was six."

Jordan freezes. I can see the warring expressions on his face—he doesn't want to cut off his own witness, but he also wants to keep me from revealing something personal that I might later regret.

My mother, my brother, and my therapist are the only people I've ever told about the abuse. But I am so, so tired of hiding.

And I'm terrified that maybe Lily was, too.

"It's okay, Jordan," I say softly. "I want to do this." I turn to the jury. "When Asher was six years old, he stepped in front of me before his father could hit me. His father had been beating me for years. It wasn't until that day—when I realized Asher could wind up hurt, too—that I got enough courage to leave."

A hushed shock falls over the gallery. The jurors look as if they've been carved of stone.

"I have known abusive men," I say. "I have *loved* abusive men. I have lived with abuse." Beneath my thigh, I cross my fingers.

"I know an abuser when I see one. And I can tell you without a doubt," I lie, "that Asher is not abusive."

THE STORM THAT darkens Braden's face is one I remember well: *You're going to pay for this.* It whisks me back to being a victim, to knowing that when I least expect it, I will suffer for my actions.

I burst into tears. I start crying so hard that I cannot catch my breath. Jordan pushes a box of Kleenex into my hands and puts his hand on my shoulder. The warm weight of it is the only thing holding me together. "Let's take ten minutes," Judge Byers says, and I wipe my eyes. When I look up, Braden is gone.

DURING THE BREAK, after Asher walks into the conference room, Jordan holds me back at the threshold. "You didn't have to do that," he says.

"I was trying to save my son," I answer. "Isn't that what you wanted?"

He grimaces. "Not if it meant sacrificing yourself." He hands me my Moleskine notebook, which he's been keeping for me while I'm on the witness stand. "I'll give you two a minute," he says, and he leaves me to face Asher alone.

I close the door behind me. Asher is sitting at the table, but he looks up when I enter. "I knew," he says quietly.

"I figured." I sit down beside him.

"This makes me even more of a dick for wanting to meet with him, doesn't it?"

"Well," I say carefully, "given how difficult it was for me to get you away from your father, it's kind of hard for me to wrap my head around."

Asher bites his lip. "I hate that he did that to you."

I hate that I let him. "Did you talk to him about it?"

He shakes his head, then looks at me. "Do you think . . . he could have changed?"

I stare hard at Asher. *Is he wondering about his father . . . or himself?*

"I don't know, Asher," I say. "I don't think so."

Asher nods, digesting this. "Do you think he was sorry?"

In this harsh fluorescent light, Asher looks so much like Braden. Not his features, more in his demeanor and the set of his shoulders, the tightness of his jaw. "Asher?" I ask stiffly. "Is there something you want to tell me?"

He glances up, looking wounded.

His father looked at me like that, too.

"Mom," Asher begins.

There is a knock on the door, and I jump. Jordan sticks his head in. "Court's back in session."

Asher leaps up as if he's on fire, as if he's just made a narrow escape. He slips through the doorway, past Jordan. "You coming?" my brother asks.

"In a minute."

I stay seated, my hands knotted together so hard that my fingernails cut into my skin. The cross-examination is coming, but that's not why I dread returning to the courtroom.

It's because whether or not I choose to admit it, some part of me has already found Asher guilty.

. . .

WHEN I STEP outside the conference room, Mike Newcomb is standing awkwardly in the hall. He looks at me, and I feel my cheeks burn with embarrassment. He was in court, too, listening to everything I said. I had been so wrapped up in Braden and his reaction, I didn't even think about who else heard me tell my secrets.

"Olivia." He hesitates. "I'm sorry. I . . . didn't know."

But you did, I want to say, thinking of the time he pressed the card for a battered women's shelter into my hand years ago, at the farmers' market. *Or at least, you suspected.*

He reaches out and gently touches my arm. "Not every man is like that," he says.

GINA JEWETT PROWLS toward me for the cross-examination with a barrage of questions. Although the mother of the victim is treated with kid gloves in court, the mother of the accused does not merit the same consideration. "So you're telling me Asher's never lied to you?"

He hid his father's texts under the name Ben Flanders. He said he didn't go upstairs, though his DNA was found in Lily's bedroom. He said he didn't touch her, though she was bruised.

"Don't all kids?" I say, forcing a smile.

"I don't mean lying about whether he brushed his teeth at night. For example, he didn't tell you about the cheating scandal at Adams High, did he?"

"Not at first."

"When did you find out he hadn't told you the truth?"

"When the principal called," I said.

"Ah, yes. To tell you he was suspended. I assume you also did not know he was sneaking out of the house to spend the night at Lily's?"

I clear my throat. "No," I admit.

I glance at the jury, because I don't think I can look at Asher right now. I wonder how many of them have children.

The prosecutor holds up photographs that have been entered into evidence. Even though I have seen them before from the gallery, it is shocking to have them up close: the picture of Lily and Maya at a sleepover, with bruises ringing Lily's arms; the photograph of Lily's body from the autopsy with purple contusions. "Do you see the extensive bruising on Lily's body in the photograph taken by her best friend, Maya Banerjee?" the prosecutor asks.

"Yes."

"Do you see extensive bruising on Lily's body in the photograph taken by Dr. McBride, the forensic pathologist?"

I swallow. They reminded me of bruises *I'd* had. "Yes," I murmur.

"Objection," Jordan calls. "Are we going anywhere with this? We've established that the witness has twenty-twenty vision."

"Get to the point, Ms. Jewett," the judge says.

"These photographs were taken in October and December. When was your son dating Lily?"

"From September through December," I reply.

"You've heard testimony from Maya Banerjee that your son grabbed Lily hard enough to leave bruises."

"Yes."

"Yet none of this was something you would have normally expected of your son, was it?"

I think about Asher punching a hole in the wall of his bedroom. How I'd opened the door to find him cradling his fist as if he was just as surprised by his outburst as I was. *You think you know someone,* he had said, dazed, *but you really don't know them at all.*

I think about the day Asher was born, a full month before his due date. The pain from my dislocated shoulder was an excruciating counterpoint to the contractions. I remember the nurses twittering dreamily over Braden, because he never left my side. But I knew why he stuck so close: so I wouldn't have a chance to tell them what he'd done to me.

Wait, Asher had asked during the first police interview with Mike Newcomb. *How did she fall?*

Had he planted that seed, so everyone else would see it that way?

My eyes swim with tears; my hands are shaking. "Asher couldn't have hurt her," I manage, wondering if I am trying to persuade the jury, or myself. "You don't know him like I do."

The prosecutor's eyes light. "But by your own testimony, Ms. McAfee, you once loved an abusive man. Isn't it true that you can love someone . . . who inflicts great physical harm?"

Dimly, I hear Jordan object; I hear the judge dismiss him, saying that he opened this line of questioning during the direct exam.

They are waiting for my answer.

It is true that people are not always who they appear to be.

It is true that I lied about the bruises my lover had given me.

Had Lily?

I have studiously avoided looking at Asher, but now I do. Something shutters in his eyes as he realizes my love for him *is* conditional, after all. That I am as much of a stranger to him as he is to me.

Isn't it true that you can love someone who inflicts great physical harm?

There are fault lines in my heart. I stare at Asher, unblinking, as I finally answer the prosecutor. "Yes," I say. "It is."

HERE IS WHAT Asher does not remember, and what I will never tell him: on the day that he came between Braden and me, when Asher clung to his leg like a barnacle, Braden plucked him off and hurled him across the room. There, he struck the wall and crumpled.

For a terrifying moment, Asher didn't move. Then he began sobbing and shrieking. I crawled over to Asher and cradled him, surrounding him with the barrier of my own body, and my life cracked in half: before that moment, and after. I could suddenly see two paths, clear as day.

I thought: *I will not let him hurt my son.*

I will not let Asher become a victim, too.

I would save that boy, even if I lost everything else.

LILY ◆ 8

Two and a half months before

*M*y mother doesn't know about it yet, squeals Mackenzie LaVerdiere, the co-captain of the girls' soccer team. We're in the locker room, and Mackenzie's teammates are gathered around her, looking at her new tattoo, a black butterfly. Some of the Lady Presidents are naked. *She told me I couldn't get one until I'm eighteen, but screw her! It's my body!*

It's really my first time in a girls' locker room. At Marin-Muir I was excused from sports. I have to say the vibe here is really different from the men's locker room—where guys just walked around naked, laughing, talking. Once, a long time ago, I was in the locker room of a public swimming pool in Seattle, and I remember seeing a guy standing in front of a steamy mirror, *shaving,* naked as a blue jay.

That's definitely not the deal in the women's locker room, where most of the girls are more modest, turning their backs to one another as we wriggle in and out of our gym clothes. Over at the mirrors, there's a tight crowd. There are blow dryers and lipsticks, moisturizer and tease combs. One girl from my AP Bio class stands in front of a sink staring at herself for a good thirty seconds, before simply announcing, *Somebody kill me now.*

And then there's Mackenzie and her court. There's an air of confederacy about them as they admire the black butterfly, a confederacy not only of the tattoo but of their own gorgeousness. You can tell they are confident and at home in their bodies, these girls. I see other girls on the outside of their circle casting looks at them, wondering what it must be like, to feel in your nakedness only a sense of pride and command, rather than a sense of somehow being *less than.* There were boys like that, too, in the men's locker rooms I once inhabited, nerds looking on at the muscle boys with envy.

Later, as I walk through downtown Adams, I think about the things I have seen that most men, and most women, don't get to experience. In a way, it's a gift, being trans, and there are moments— like now, walking through this pretty town on a late summer evening—when I am willing to say, *Sure, I'm grateful for it all.*

For the longest time, I wasn't grateful, though.

I remember what it was like to look in a mirror and think, *Somebody kill me now.*

Mom's working late tonight. I told her I'd just walk home. It's a long walk, but I'm feeling expansive, here almost at the end of my second week at Adams High. I go over to the little park that overlooks the Cobboscoggin and sit down on a bench to watch the river flow.

I open my backpack and get out the poetry book we're doing for Chopper. We're starting out with William Blake, the *Songs of Innocence and of Experience.*

O Rose, thou art sick!
The invisible worm,
That flies in the night

In the howling storm:
Has found out thy bed
Of crimson joy:
And his dark secret love
Does thy life destroy.

And all at once, tears rush to my eyes, and I'm sobbing.

When we were talking about the Blake poem today, Chopper looked at us and asked what it made us think about—not what it *meant,* but how it made us *feel.* I thought that was a nice distinction.

Until Dirk raised his hand and said, *She's got an STD!*

Chopper pointed to the door. "Out," he said.

"But, Mr. Jameson—"

"Out," said Chopper, and Dirk got his things and slunk out of the room. Then, with a smile, Chopper said, "Actually, venereal disease is one of the things readers have thought the poem's about. But maybe that's too specific. What else do you think when you read this?"

"It makes me think about a woman who's been made sick," said the girl in front of me. "By a man. Who says he loves her. But mostly, she wants to be alone."

There was a long pause as we all thought about this. "So sometimes," growled Chopper, "love just makes people sick?"

Heads nodded. A *lot* of heads nodded.

"Sick," said Chopper, again. He is positively the gnarliest, most wrinkled teacher I have ever had. But then he looked at us with a strange, gentle expression. "But we keep on looking for it, day after day. Getting our hearts broken. And getting them healed again."

He looked out the window. We all sat there in an electric silence. Chopper looked back at us, and pointed toward the door again. "All right," he said. "*Out.*"

Today was a Granite Day. The schedule at Adams High changes every day, and each schedule has a different name. There's Finch Day (named after the state bird) and Quartz Day (the state gem) and Birch Day (tree). On a Granite Day (rock) we have "Morning Meeting." Today at Morning Meeting there was a presentation from something called the Rainbow Alliance. It's the student LGBTQ group, led by two students named Finn Johnson and Caeden Wentworth.

"We want to welcome everyone back to school," said Finn, who was assigned female at birth but is now nonbinary. Finn uses the pronouns *they* and *them,* binds their top in order to have a flat chest, and seems to delight in subverting all the expectations people have around gender. Caeden is trans, AFAB, but has been on testosterone for two years now and has a short black beard. "We wanted to let you all know what the Rainbow Alliance is doing," said Caeden, "and what we have planned for the coming year."

There are going to be buses to take people to some lectures at Dartmouth this fall—one by Kate Bornstein, another by Janet Mock. There's going to be a drag ball just before Christmas, and weekly drop-in sessions where anybody who wants to can come and talk.

Sitting there in my chair at assembly, all I could think was how remarkable it is that Adams—this tiny, rural New England town— has resources like this. How people who feel the thing that I felt now have something I didn't have—allies, resources, fellow travelers. It used to be that trans stuff was something you had to figure out on your own, like joining a secret underground. Now there are *people to talk to.* It seems like since 2005—the time I first said to myself, *I'm a girl*—the whole world has changed.

But the strangest thing of all is that I do not have any interest in joining the Rainbow Alliance. I don't even want them to know who I am.

What on earth is that *about?* I wonder. Why, after suffering for so long, and in such isolation, would I not want to talk to people who are *just like me?*

But that's the question. *Are* they like me?

Well, of course they are. It makes me ashamed to think this, makes me feel like even now, deep-rooted transphobia and self-hatred must be turning me away from people who, God knows, I could help. I could tell them about what I've been through. I could tell them how it almost killed me. I could tell them about Sorel, and Jonah, and my father. I could tell them what it's like to go from a place where everything about you feels wrong to a place where you finally feel at peace.

But in order to do any of that, I'd have to come out.

And even though I am proud of who I am, proud of having fought against all these odds to become the person I always dreamed of being—it means everyone would know I'm trans.

When all I really want to be—all I've ever *been*—is a girl.

Is it so wrong to want to fit in, and to be left alone? Do I really have to spend the rest of my life as the emblematic trans girl?

But again: that's the question. Is being trans the truth of who I am? Or is it just the truth of who I *was*? Am I even still trans, at this point, after everything I've been through? What is it that makes me so different from other girls my age? Is everything that happened to me before the age of seventeen really going to be the most important thing about me for the next seventy?

Or is all of this just a long-winded way of running from the facts: that I'm never going to be like everybody else, that whatever scars being trans has left upon me, they're pretty much there for the rest of my life, like it or not.

But there are times I don't want to be an outlier. There are times when all I want is just to sit on a bench by a river and read a poem and watch the sun slowly sinking behind the mill.

Like now.

When dusk falls, I put my book in my backpack and head toward home. Streetlights have come on, and I can see people in the A-1 Diner, eating their burgers and their fish and chips.

It surprises me how early it starts to get dark here, but then, as I keep reminding myself, *We're not in California anymore*. I walk down Main Street, past the Catholic church and a music store called Edgar's.

As I draw near the public park—Presidents' Square—I see a dad in a polo shirt, shouting at a little boy, who is sitting on a park bench, sobbing. "I don't want to!" says the boy.

"I don't care what you want," says the father. "Life is not about getting what you want!"

I've stopped on the sidewalk to stare at this exchange, and now the man looks up at me and says, "What are you goddamned looking at?" and I quickly walk on. But the sound of that boy sobbing is like a knife in my heart.

I remember what it was like to be that boy.

And I remember what my father did to me our last night together.

After he cut all my hair off, he'd stormed out of the house, heading down to the bar. My mother came home late and found me on the kitchen floor, right where he had left me. I couldn't move.

She scooped me up in her arms and held me. I sobbed into her shoulder. *I'm so sorry.* I kept saying over and over again.

That was when Ranger Mom kicked into gear. *You don't have a thing to be sorry about,* she said. *You're my child, Liam, and I love you.*

But Daddy said— I paused. I couldn't even bring myself to say it. *But Daddy said—*

You don't have to worry about him ever again, she replied.

She meant what she said. Two hours later we—the two of us, plus Boris—were driving south on Route 5, past Tacoma, past Olympia, past Grand Mound. We stayed that night at something called the Mt. St. Helens Motel, in Castle Rock. Mom tried pointing out the cone of the burned-out volcano, but it was too dark.

In the morning, though, I saw it, the summit covered in snow. "It looks so peaceful," I said to Mom.

"It does," said Mom. "But things aren't always what they seem, are they?"

No, I told her, *they're not.*

We drove all day, past Portland and Eugene and Medford. Mom talked about the national forests in Oregon—Willamette and Umpqua to the east, Siuslaw and the Rogue River–Siskiyou off to the west. I don't remember Mom saying that we'd never return to Seattle, that she wouldn't be going back to my father, that she'd never again guide people through the Olympic National Park, showing them the Hoh Rain Forest or Hurricane Ridge.

What I do remember is a field of flowers near Mount Shasta. We'd crossed over into California in the late afternoon, and stopped for a break at a restaurant not far off the highway. While Mom was in the bathroom, I got Boris out of the car and let him have a pee. There before us was a beautiful field of long grass with a small stream trickling through it. LILY HOLLOW OVERLOOK, said a sign.

Mom came out and found me lost in thought. "Do lilies bloom here in the summer?" I asked her.

"I bet they do," she said. "They're pretty hardy. But they only bloom once a year."

I thought it over. "I think I want my name to be Lily," I told her.

Mom got down on her knees and put her arms around me. I still remember that hug. "That's a pretty name."

"I'm going to be a girl from now on," I clarified.

"Lily," said Mom. "You've always been a girl."

IT TOOK A while before Point Reyes really started to feel like home, instead of just a place where we were camping. Mom's family had owned the house there for decades, and I vaguely remembered visiting it a couple of times when I was really little. But now it wasn't a summer home, a place to stay a couple of weeks a year. Now it was where we lived.

I didn't go back to school that spring, but Mom homeschooled me, and I didn't fall behind. It took until the summer to get things straightened out with the Park Service, but by July, Mom had been officially transferred to the national seashore. I stayed home, practicing cello, exploring this new world with Boris. Mom came home in the evening with fresh fish and vegetables she bought at the farmers' market. In June and July, she brought me bouquets of lilies, too: Pitkin Marsh lilies, and Humboldt's.

That summer was when I had my first consult with a gender counselor, and an endocrinologist. They started me on puberty blockers—a drug called Lupron.

I turned twelve. I bought new clothes.

Mom started introducing me to people as her daughter.

In the fall I started seventh grade at Marin-Muir, a private elementary school that goes all the way through eighth grade. Mom told the principal about me, and incredibly, the principal was supportive. *Maybe you'd be surprised,* she'd said, *to learn that you're not the first trans student we've had.*

I *was* surprised, actually. You spend your whole life thinking that you're the only person who feels the way you feel, only to find out that being trans is not that uncommon, that it is just one more way of being human.

But at the end of that year, I began to feel left behind again as I looked at all of the bodies of my girlfriends, suddenly in flower. It was one thing to be on puberty blockers. It was another to start in on estrogen and spironolactone. Mom had been sanguine about delaying adolescence; but leaping into female puberty seemed, to her, like a whole other can of worms.

But she came around in time. It wasn't like I was suddenly going to start being a boy at that point anyway.

So I started in on hormones. Puberty hit me the way Hemingway once described people going broke—gradually, and then suddenly. It was delicious. And dramatic. And exciting. And, at times, a little bit scary. I was flat as a board. Then I was an A cup. Then a B. By the time I started ninth grade at Pointcrest, I was a generous C. And that's not to mention the hips, which weren't there at all one day, and the next, it seemed, had appeared from nowhere.

It was a miracle, and sometimes just catching a glimpse of myself from the waist up could stop me in my tracks and make me wonder whether I had fallen into a dream.

And yet, at the same time, the sight of myself below the waist was enough to crash me out of that dream in an instant. The secret, which I had, incredibly, been able to keep ever since we fled Seattle, now seemed more dangerous than before.

Because now I was suddenly on the radar of boys and men.

My mother and I spent a lot of time talking about what it means to be a woman, in this world, and at this moment in time, and she was determined that, if her child was going to be female, at the very least she would also be a feminist. I remember being a little irritated by this line of thought. I told Mom it was kind of a hysterical way of defining womanhood—and that there were other identities, too, including nonbinary and gender-fluid ones.

Mom asked me if I knew the origin of the word *hysterical*.

It comes from the Greek and Latin word *hyster,* which means *womb*. In the nineteenth century, *hysteria* was the word men gave to a disease defined as *insanity as a result of being female.* They'd lock women away for it, women who wanted to do things like write books, or study science. Or play music. The prescribed treatment was *rest*—by which they meant having no mental life whatsoever. There's a whole novella about it, in fact, called "The Yellow Wallpaper," by Charlotte Perkins Gilman. It's the story of a woman who's confined to her bed by her husband, a wife who winds up being driven insane by the cure he has inflicted on her.

I told Mom that we didn't live in the nineteenth century, and that if anybody could prove that it was possible to redefine gender, it was me. Mom just said, *You have to be careful.*

Sometimes I wonder if, when she told me that, she was thinking about what might happen to me in the future, or what had already happened to her in the past. What had it been like, being married to Dad, a man who seemed nice enough on the surface, but who turned out to have a heart of stone?

Sometimes I wonder if something bad happened to Mom, maybe when she was young, that made her want to spend her life in the wild, among brown bears and lynx, instead of in civilization, in the teeming world of men.

I MUST HAVE taken a wrong turn after overhearing the fight in Presidents' Square between that father and his son. Or maybe it's just that the flood of memories has got me all mixed up. In any case, now I'm in a part of Adams I've never seen before—a line of closed-down row houses, maybe the homes of millworkers from a hundred years ago. Most are boarded up, but there's a light on in one of them, and one old man sitting on a porch drinking beer.

I can see the river down at the bottom of the street, so I know that I'm going the wrong direction. I turn around and start back the way I came.

From behind me, the man shouts something in a deep, raspy

voice. It takes me a minute to realize he's speaking in French, although it doesn't sound like any French I've ever heard, and I remember some story about the original workers on the log drives all being French Canadian. I look at my watch, and I see it's going on seven o'clock. Mom's going to be wondering where I am.

It's not long after that I hear footsteps behind me. They're soft at first, but I hear them. I stop and look back, and there he is—a man in shadow, about half a block behind me. My heart starts to beat faster.

I walk more swiftly now, hoping that this street is going to return me to the center of town, but the houses are boarded up here, too, even as they slowly continue up the hill, away from the river. I come to an intersection and look up and down this other street—it's old warehouses in one direction, a vacant lot in the other. The footsteps are coming faster now, and I turn around and see the silhouette growing near.

All at once, I know for sure I'm in trouble.

I reach into my purse, pull out my phone, and hit my mother's number on speed dial—all the while walking faster and faster up this street.

The man behind me is getting closer.

The phone freezes for a second, and then I get the message: *no signal.*

My pursuer starts to whistle a song with no particular tune, and it's this, more than anything else, that sends me into full-blown panic.

Ahead of me now I see a bar—there's a neon sign buzzing in the twilight, with the name LE CHEZ. I think about rushing into the bar and asking for help, but there's no way of knowing whether this is a place of safety.

Now there's a car with its high beams on coming toward me, and I put my hand over my eyes as it approaches, then passes. It gets about ten feet down the road before I hear it screech to a halt, and then it shifts into reverse and backs up alongside me.

"Excuse me, miss," says a man's voice. "Are you okay?"

I'm just about to yell at whoever this is, because I've pretty much had all the fuckery I can take for one day, when he says, "It's okay. I'm a detective." I don't believe him at first because he's not in a car with lights and sirens and he's wearing normal clothes, but then he holds up a badge with his name on it: NEWCOMB. I see the holster of a gun, too, strapped on his hip.

I look behind me, and here comes the man who's been following me, a greasy-looking dude with ornate tattoos on each arm, neck to wrist. He looks me in the eye with an expression of what can only be described as pure hatred. "Didn't you get lucky," he whispers to me, and then ducks into Le Chez. As the door opens and closes, it briefly displays a room lit by a lightbulb hanging from a wire suspended above a pool table.

The detective is out of his car now. "What's going on?"

"I'm lost," I say to him, choking on the words. "I don't know how I got here."

Detective Newcomb nods. "How about if I give you a ride home."

I wipe my eyes. "Thank you," I say.

Moments later, we're back on Main Street—it was just a street over this whole time, but because of a bend in the river I've been walking parallel to it, instead of toward it.

"You might want to stay off Temple Street after dark," says the detective. "And stay away from Le Chez, all right?" He pronounces it *La Shay*. "Nothing good happens in there, especially to young women."

"I got mixed up," I tell him, "walking home."

"Easy enough if you don't know your way around."

He asks me my address, and I tell him. We drive toward home in silence for a little bit, except for the crackling of static on his police radio. I look out the window at Adams, all the closed-up buildings, the dark river off behind them.

The detective asks me something that I do not hear. "What?" I say.

"I asked you for your name, miss." He grins. "What do people call you?

I hear a bell chiming from the steeple of a church in town. As I listen to it peal I think about how easy it is to get lost. And how grateful I am at being found.

"I'm Lily," I tell him. "I'm new."

OLIVIA ◈ 9

MAY 9–13, 2019

Five months after

As soon as Gina Jewett finishes her questions, Jordan stands up. "Your Honor," he says, through gritted teeth, "perhaps we could take our lunch break."

Judge Byers agrees to a recess, and the bailiff leads the jury out of the room. Jordan steers me toward a side door. "With me," he seethes. "Now."

I know he is going to lay into me because of my testimony—which, instead of being a ringing endorsement of Asher's innocence, was anything but. Sure enough, when we are in our private conference room, again, with Asher, Jordan spears a hand through his hair and turns on me, wild. "What the *fuck* was that, Olivia? You came across like you were hiding things."

I was. I always will be.

"I was . . . in my own head," I murmur.

"Well, you're the one who put yourself there!" Jordan rails. "I never told you to bring up your relationship with Braden—"

"I didn't know how else to—"

"And once you did, you opened up a whole line of questioning about Asher that—"

From the far end of the room, Asher says, "I need to talk."

But Jordan is in my face, inches away, furious. "You just tanked my defense."

"I thought it would be better—"

"You pay *me* to think!"

"I'm not *paying you*," I yell back at him.

"I need to talk," Asher says more forcefully. He lifts his head from the table, where it has been pillowed on his arms.

"Fine," Jordan snaps, turning to him. "What?"

"No," Asher says. "I mean, I have to talk *in there*. I want you to put me on the stand."

For a moment, we all freeze. "Absolutely not," Jordan says, recovering.

"Look. That jury thinks my own mother doesn't believe me," Asher says.

"Asher," I stumble. "It's not—"

"No," Jordan interrupts.

"Who better to tell them about me and Lily . . . than me?" Asher asks.

"If you get on the stand, the prosecutor will twist your words and ask you all kinds of questions meant to trip you up. Look at what just happened in there, with your mother." Jordan folds his arms. "Asher. It could make things way worse."

"Or," Asher says evenly, "it could make them better."

"Trust me. This would be a colossal mistake," Jordan replies.

"You need to listen to your uncle." I touch Asher's sleeve, but he jerks away.

"You said you're here to advise me," Asher presses, staring at Jordan, "but that I get to call the shots, right?"

Jordan nods, a tight jerk of his head.

"Either you put me on the stand," Asher says, "or you're fired."

"Asher!" I cry.

Jordan's spine stiffens. "I vehemently disagree with this."

For the first time since we have left the courtroom, Asher's eyes flick over me, like frost. "One other thing," he says to Jordan. "If I'm in charge? She doesn't get to be here anymore."

I remember Jordan telling me, months ago, that I could only be privy to attorney-client meetings as long as Asher wanted me there. "Please. Let me explain—"

"Thanks, but I've got it," he says coolly. "I may be a murderer in your eyes, but I'm not stupid."

"Your father—"

"*I am not my father*," Asher roars, standing so fast that his chair topples backward. "And right now, you're not my mother." His eyes are dark as wounds. "All you needed to do was trust me. And you couldn't even fucking get that right."

While I am still reeling, Jordan ushers me into the hallway. "You heard my client," he says formally, and he closes the door behind me.

I stare at it, thinking of Asher's parting sentence.

He may not be his father. But Braden has said the same to me, in nearly identical words.

WHEN COURT RESUMES, neither Jordan nor Asher makes eye contact with me. Before the jury has returned to the courtroom, Jordan approaches the bailiff. "I need to make a statement on the record, but outside the presence of the jury," he says, and the prosecutor raises her eyebrows with interest.

The bailiff gets Judge Byers, who takes her seat. "Mr. McAfee," she says. "You have something you want to note for the record?"

"Yes, Your Honor. My client has decided he would like to testify. I have explained that the State must prove their case in full regardless of whether he testifies or not, and I have advised him it is in his best interests that he *not* testify." He glances over his shoulder at Asher. "Thus it is against the advice of counsel that he is taking the stand."

The judge looks at Asher. "Mr. Fields? Is this correct? Do you wish to testify against your attorney's advice?"

Asher clears his throat. "Yes, ma'am," he says.

"So noted," Judge Byers replies.

Five minutes later, the jury is seated and looking with curiosity at Asher. He is sworn in, and as I watch him place his hand on the Bible I think about how we have never really been a religious family—a random Christmas or Easter service, but that's it. And yet,

I am the cliché, the woman who is praying to a God she hasn't previously acknowledged to protect my son.

"Asher," Jordan says, "you've heard testimony from others about how you met Lily. Is the evidence of how and when you met accurate?"

"Yes."

"Can you describe her?"

A smile steals over Asher's face, like mist, blurring his features. "She could play Bach and Dvořák on the cello, but also the Red Hot Chili Peppers and Metallica. The top item on her bucket list was to go on an archaeological dig with Yo-Yo Ma because she once read that anthropology was his favorite subject in college and she thought it would be nice for him to talk about something other than music for once. When she held a foil in her hand she moved so fast I couldn't even see it." His eyes look over the gallery, but I know it's Lily he's picturing. "She *knew* things—all the lyrics to 'Bohemian Rhapsody,' that McDonald's once made bubble-gum-flavored broccoli for Happy Meals, that the first oranges were actually green, that there's no state with a *q* in its name. We had so much to talk about and she taught me so much. But there were times when we were quiet together—when we just kind of sat, and it was enough to be with each other, because she filled up every space she was in." He draws in a breath. "She's the first girl I ever said *I love you* to."

"Did you disagree sometimes?" Jordan asks.

"Yeah."

"What was your last argument about?"

Asher shifts in his seat. "I wanted to do something special for Lily for Christmas, so I arranged for her father to meet with her," he says. "She hadn't seen him in a really long time. When you're missing a parent in your life, and they actually *want* to connect with you, it's a whole lot better than having an empty space inside you . . . even if that parent isn't perfect." He hesitates. "I understand now that even though that's how I felt about *my* father, Lily's experience was different. But I didn't realize that then."

"How did she react?"

"When she saw I'd invited her father here—without asking her permission—she was pissed off. I tried to explain where I was coming from, but she told me I didn't understand."

"What was your response?"

"I asked her to help me understand. But she . . . wanted nothing to do with me."

"What do you mean?" Jordan asks.

Asher lifts a shoulder. "She stopped communicating with me. She wouldn't see me, even when I begged."

"So," Jordan says, "she didn't confide in you."

"No."

"That was sort of a pattern for her, wasn't it?"

"Objection!" Gina calls.

The judge purses her lips. "Sustained."

Jordan takes a step closer to the witness stand. "What did she first tell you about her father?"

"That he was dead," Asher says.

"Although he was in fact alive . . . and just estranged from her?"

"Yes."

"When you first saw scars on Lily's wrists, where did she say they came from?"

"A car accident," Asher admits.

"Even though they were from a suicide attempt?"

"Yes."

"And Lily never told you she was trans . . . ?" Jordan presses.

"Actually," Asher says, "she did."

Jordan whips toward him, his jaw dropping. The prosecutor looks like she is going to clap her hands together in joy. Time grinds to a stop, as Asher completely and categorically destroys his own defense strategy.

"She told me," Asher says, oblivious to anything but the chance to speak his truth. "And I didn't care."

.   .   .

ASHER COULD NOT have helped Gina Jewett more if he'd drawn a line between her points with a red marker.

She gets up from her table, prowling toward Asher. "Isn't it true that what you were really fighting about the night Lily died wasn't her father . . . but the fact that she told you she was transgender?"

"No," Asher says firmly.

"You didn't like hearing it, and she didn't want to deal with your anger, and that's why she avoided you for five days."

"No," Asher corrects. "She told me a month earlier. After the first time we had sex."

"Right after?"

"No," Asher says. "She was . . . distant right after. I thought she was having second thoughts about . . . doing it. I wanted to talk through it, but she was afraid that whatever she said would break us apart."

"Well, murder's one way to do that," Gina says.

"Objection!"

"Withdrawn," the prosecutor says. "Your first reaction to being told your girlfriend had started her life as a boy was, in fact, negative, wasn't it?"

Asher carefully picks his way through his words. "I needed time to digest it."

"You felt betrayed, didn't you?"

"I felt . . . blindsided," Asher amends.

"You were angry, too, I bet," the prosecutor pushes.

Asher's face reddens. "I punched a wall in at home. I'm not proud of that. But in the end, Lily was . . . Lily. I didn't really care what her chromosomes looked like. She was who I fell in love with." He struggles, trying to explain. "If your favorite band was the Quarrymen and they decided to call themselves something else, you'd still like their music. Even after they became the Beatles." He smiles fleetingly. "I didn't know they changed their name, either, until Lily told me."

"And after that?"

"Then everything was perfect between us."

"Until five days before she died, when you got into a fight so big that Lily wouldn't speak to you again."

"But that was about her dad."

"So you've said, Asher . . . but you've lied before. You lied about being involved in a cheating scandal, but you got suspended from school. You lied to your mother about spending the night at Lily's. You told the police you weren't in Lily's bedroom, but your DNA was found there. You seem to have a pretty shaky relationship with telling the truth, so why should we believe you now?"

His jaw sets. "I'm telling the truth about *this*."

"How would we know?" the prosecutor scoffs. "It seems very convenient, in hindsight, for you to be such a progressive and understanding young man. When in reality, you went over to Lily's house that afternoon because you were still angry—"

"No," Asher says.

"Because you felt like she had deceived you—"

"Objection!" Jordan shouts.

"Sustained."

Asher shakes his head. "That's not—"

"Because you had lost control over the relationship, and you were humiliated and you wanted to teach her a lesson . . ."

I realize Gina Jewett expects rage to break out of him like lightning arcing from a storm cloud.

"But," she jabs, "you lost control over yourself when you got to her house, and *you killed her*."

"You're wrong," Asher says earnestly. His palms are flat on his lap. He doesn't look flustered or cornered. He looks . . . transcendent. "You were not there. *None* of you were. You know nothing about our relationship."

I realize that I am breathless, hanging on Asher's masterful display of self-possession, the same way I used to marvel at Braden's ability to keep everyone from seeing what actually happened behind the drawn curtain of his restraint. Another word for *self-control,* after all, is *discipline.*

"You're right about one thing," the prosecutor muses. "None of us *were* there. Except for Lily, and she's dead." She sits down. "Nothing further."

Jordan is already out of his seat. "A quick redirect, Your Honor?" When the judge nods, he approaches Asher. "After Lily told you she was trans, and you needed some time to absorb that information . . . did you discuss your feelings with her?"

"Yes," Asher says.

"What did you say?"

Jordan is sweating profusely. I realize that he has absolutely no idea what is about to come out of Asher's mouth—a terrible position for any lawyer to be in with a witness.

"I told her it didn't matter," Asher says. "I said I loved *who* she was . . . not *what* she was."

"Thank you," Jordan says, and he sits down. Judge Byers dismisses court. Jordan looks at Asher and says, "Not a word. Not till we get to the car."

INSTEAD OF TAKING Asher alone to the conference room (since I am still persona non grata) Jordan leads a charge to the parking lot, bulldozing past reporters with a muttered *No comment, no comment.* I get into the driver's seat and pull out onto the divided highway for about a mile before Jordan instructs me to stop on the side of the road.

In the rearview mirror, I see Asher's wide, satisfied smile. "That was great, right?" he says, beaming. "I told you."

Jordan twists in the passenger seat. "No, Asher, that was not great. In a single hour, you undermined my entire defense. The prosecution wants the jury to believe that you felt so humiliated when you learned Lily was trans that you killed her. As long as I could get them to think that she never told you, then you had a chance of being acquitted. But you literally just handed the State the information they needed on a silver platter."

"But it's the truth," Asher says, confused.

"The truth has no place in a court of law, goddammit," Jordan snaps. "And since the prosecution's already painted you as an abuser and a liar, how good do you actually think your word is?"

None of us talk the rest of the way home.

THERE ARE A whole host of things that can destroy a bee's home: wax moth larvae, the hive beetle, Varroa mites. Bees can have their trachea infested with mites. There's American foulbrood, nosema, black queen cell virus, sacbrood virus, paralysis viruses, deformed wing virus.

Another threat to honeybees is colony collapse disorder, where entire healthy colonies of bees disappear almost overnight. CCD has been blamed on everything from electromagnetic radiation to pesticides to GMOs to climate change. The only thing scientists agree upon is that stress on the bees from some source is the underlying cause.

When you see colony collapse disorder in a hive, it's eerie. There's honey and capped brood, but otherwise, it's a ghost town. The workers and drones have vanished. The bees are gone.

Except for the queen, who stays behind, and dies alone.

ON FRIDAY, we have the first stroke of luck in the trial: Judge Byers comes down with food poisoning and court is postponed until Monday. We find out when we are halfway to the courthouse in Lancaster, sitting shoulder to shoulder in the truck in uncomfortable silence.

Back home, we retreat to our respective corners. Asher is still refusing to speak to me, even after Selena's attempt at intervention. Jordan huddles over the dining room table, struggling to find something he might have missed in the discovery or witness testimonies that could exonerate Asher, now that his defense strategy has been gutted.

After walking on eggshells for hours, Selena announces that the two of us are going drinking.

I can't remember the last time I was at a bar. Selena drags me to the only one in town—a dive called Le Chez near the railroad tracks with cheap alcohol and sad décor and even sadder clientele.

"I am going to regret this in the morning," Selena says, pushing me my third martini. I don't even like martinis, but Selena says that right now my usual glass of wine isn't going to cut it. She lifts her glass, the alcohol as clear and cold as a winter pond, and clinks it against mine. "Here's to drinking instead of thinking," she says.

"If you drink honey with your booze," I say, my words a little slurred, "you won't get a hangover."

Selena laughs. "Where were you when I was in college?"

I shrug. "Hangovers are caused by ethanol," I tell her. "Honey's got potassium, sodium, fructose—all of which counteract that—and it makes the liver work faster to oxidize alcohol and sober you up." I take a long gulp. "I fucking hate gin."

She takes the glass from me, drains it, and summons the bartender. "My sister needs a vodka martini," she instructs the woman. "What *doesn't* honey do?" she muses.

"Get people acquitted," I mutter, fishing the olive out of the empty glass and eating it. "My son is going to go to jail and he won't even say goodbye to me."

"Technically he'll go to prison," Selena says. "Jail's when it's for less than one year."

I glance at her. "Not helping."

"Right." Selena leans her elbows on the bar. "You never know what a jury's going to do," she assures me. "They could acquit Asher just because he has nice eyes."

"Maybe Jordan will find something," I say. "It's not over till it's over."

Selena doesn't respond, and that's answer enough. She is Jordan's investigator; she knows the evidence better than he does.

I look Selena in the eye. "You know Asher. You've known him his whole life. Do you think he's guilty?"

We both clam up for a moment as the bartender serves me my new drink. "I think you're asking the wrong question," Selena says, when the woman moves away. "Good people do bad things all the time. Even Jeffrey Dahmer had a mother."

"Again. Not helping," I say.

"What I mean is that you're going to support him, whether he's living upstairs at home or in the state penitentiary. Even if he is convicted, Liv, he'll still be your kid."

She is right. I may not be able to brag about his achievements the way I used to when he was a hockey star; I may hear whispers everywhere I go from now on. I may have pictured a future for him that involved college, a job that brought out his artist's eye, a woman he couldn't live without, a house full of children. But just the fact that the arc of Asher's life may turn in a different direction doesn't mean I will stop loving him.

This makes me think of Ava, and I pick up my vodka martini and drain it. I signal the bartender for another.

I know, better than most people, what it means to make a colossal mistake. How you carry it with you; how it alters you at a cellular level. How, if you cannot forgive yourself for your transgression, you snap under the weight of your own flaws.

I also know what it's like to start over.

Asher may not want me around right now, but he is going to need me.

The bartender brings a vodka martini for me, and a gin martini for Selena, although she hasn't ordered one. When Selena starts to object, the bartender shrugs. "This one's on the house," she says.

Selena is the most beautiful woman I've ever met, and I'm used to men and women falling all over themselves to flirt with her, even when Jordan is standing right at her side. I assume that's what's happening, again, par for the course, until the bartender gestures to Selena's bare shoulder, where a dark bruise in the significant shape of a thumbprint stains her skin. "I had a boyfriend who used to hurt me, too," the bartender says, sympathetically. "You should leave him."

Her words shock me. I stare at Selena.

Selena glances down as if she has not even noticed the mark until now. When she sees the horror on my face, though, she says, "Olivia.

Your brother isn't like Braden. He doesn't lay his hands on me . . . unless I expressly invite him to."

I recoil. "Ew," I say, but, as intended, her words divert my thoughts from the path they were on.

She rubs her hand over her bare arm. "Fucking endometriosis. When they did my hysterectomy, they took out my ovaries, too, and put me on estrogen. Ever since then, I bruise if I just bump into something. I don't even notice it anymore." She laughs. "You didn't think Jordan actually would . . . Jesus. I don't think I've ever seen him swat a fly."

"I thought that about Braden," I say quietly. "I thought that about *Asher*, but—"

"Holy fuck." Selena slams down her martini glass. "I just thought of something. Estrogen is part of the hormone cocktail Lily would have taken as a trans woman, right? What if *that's* why she bruised so easily?"

My head snaps up. "You mean it might have had nothing to do with—"

"Abuse. Rage. *Asher*," Selena says. "All of the above."

THIS WAS HOW we wound up, at one in the morning, bursting into Asher's bedroom. We woke him up and asked him why Lily wasn't in school the day she died. Yes, she had been sick, but what were her symptoms? "Fever," Asher said, disoriented, sitting up in his bed. "Headache, I think."

Armed with that information, Selena whirled around and started down the stairs, furiously texting. I was left facing Asher, who took one look at me, and then rolled over and pulled up the covers.

By nine A.M. on Saturday, Selena has connected with a Harvard doctor, a pathologist she used to date before Jordan. He agrees to take a look at Lily's autopsy report. *Lots of people fall down the stairs,* Selena explained. *But not everyone winds up dead. If there's a way to plant a seed of reasonable doubt in the jury that Asher isn't an abuser and that Lily's bruising—and death—had nothing to do with him, then Asher might have a fighting chance at acquittal.*

On Sunday, Jordan gets a text from Selena in Boston: her pathologist will testify in court the next morning regarding his findings—which are different from Dr. McBride's. It is a Hail Mary pass, but it's all we have left. "Why are you frowning?" I ask my brother. "Isn't this good?"

"She called him *her* pathologist."

"Selena never looks at anyone but you."

"I'm not worried about Selena. *He* took her out to dinner to reminisce about old times," Jordan says. "I'm sick of everyone falling in love with *my* wife." But late that night, he sends the doctor's CV to the prosecutor, alerting her of this new expert witness. And he knocks on Asher's door, presumably to tell him about these new developments.

I am not in the room.

Asher hasn't spoken a word to me since Thursday, when he ordered me to leave. We have existed in a silent ballet, him choreographing his movements to elegantly avoid contact with me.

Jordan prepares his questions for the pathologist. Asher hides in his bedroom. I wander the halls like a restless spirit.

It's lonely as hell.

If Asher is convicted, it's something I will have to get used to.

But even if by some miracle he is acquitted, there's no guarantee he'll forgive me for believing the worst.

EARLY MONDAY MORNING, we return to court. Once again, Jordan asks the bailiff to not bring in the jury, so that he can tell the judge he has a new unlisted witness for the defense. After an hour's delay, so that the prosecution has a chance to interview the pathologist and prepare a cross-examination, Jordan calls Dr. Benjamin Oluwye to the stand.

His credentials are impeccable: a Harvard professor who studied at Yale and Stanford Medical School and did his residency at UCLA. He practices as a forensic pathologist in the office of the chief medical examiner in Boston, and is also the director of the autopsy service at Mass General. I wonder if he knows Braden.

"Have you had a chance, Dr. Oluwye, to review the autopsy report of Lily Campanello and the slides from that autopsy performed by Dr. McBride?" Jordan asks.

"I have indeed." His voice is deep, his eyes wise and focused.

Jordan presents him with the autopsy report, which has already been entered into evidence. "At the bottom of the last page of the report, do you see the opinion of Dr. McBride regarding the manner and cause of death of Lily Campanello?"

"Yes."

"Do you share his opinion?"

"No," Dr. Oluwye says. "Not quite."

"Can you elaborate?"

"The autopsy indicates an extensive area of scalp hemorrhage, along the right temporal area extending from the orbital ridge, posteriorly to the parietal area—about ten by four-point-five centimeters. After the removal of the skullcap, the subarachnoid hemorrhage covered roughly forty percent of the right frontoparietal brain, with another focus of two centimeters in the right temporoparietal white matter." He sees the faces of the jury and adds, sheepishly, "As you are looking at me the way my son does when I tell him that Dire Straits was the seminal band of the twentieth century, allow me to break that down. In layman's terms, it means there was a surprising amount of blood in and around the brain. The amount of blood recorded would be consistent with a skull fracture, but the CT and X-rays didn't show one. In the absence of that . . . it means something else is going on."

"Without a fracture," Jordan says, "what *would* you have expected to see in Lily Campanello's autopsy?"

"A contrecoup injury. If she had actually died from the brain bouncing back and forth in the skull, she would likely only have had a tiny bit of bleeding on the opposite side of the brain."

"Doctor, let me get this straight. Lily had more blood in and around her brain than was normal for someone who died because of a contrecoup injury, rather than a skull fracture?"

"That is correct."

"What did that indicate to you?"

"That the deceased had some sort of blood disorder that contributed to her death," Dr. Oluwye says.

"What do you mean by a blood disorder?"

"Anything that causes an abnormality in the way blood moves, clots, or generally behaves," the pathologist explains.

"Like . . . hemophilia?"

"Yes, but that's not what I think led to Lily Campanello's death."

"In your expert opinion . . . what did?"

"Were this my case, I would have signed the autopsy report out this way," Dr. Oluwye says. "The cause of death was one: intracerebral hemorrhage due to blunt force trauma. Two: thrombotic microangiopathy, extensive, consistent with TTP."

Jordan holds up his hands. "Whoa, whoa, whoa. English, please."

"The deceased suffered a blow to the head that led to an excessive brain bleed due to an underlying blood disorder called TTP—thrombotic thrombocytopenic purpura. It's a disorder where platelet clumps form in small blood vessels. As red blood cells pass by these clumps, they get sheared—imagine the hull of a boat scraping up against rocks. The result is that all those passing red blood cells get damaged and deformed and explode."

"The red blood cells *explode*?"

"Yes, and it causes the person to have something called *hemolytic anemia*."

"My mom was anemic," Jordan lies. "She took iron pills. Is this the same kind of thing?"

"No, it looks different from that kind of anemia . . . and it's much more life-threatening. In fact, to scientists, you only see this kind of anemia in two specific underlying conditions: TTP, and DIC—disseminated intravascular coagulation. But DIC almost always has a precipitating cause, like severe infection, cancer, amniotic fluid embolus. My understanding is that the deceased had none of those, which means it would be logical to deduce that she had TTP."

"What happens to a person who has TTP?" Jordan asks.

"When you have platelets clumping together, it means that there are fewer platelets in other parts of the body to help with clotting. As a result, someone with TTP will bruise very easily. He or she often has bleeding under the skin—in fancy pathologist speak, we call that *petechiae*—little clusters of tiny round brownish red dots. Someone with TTP would also have low counts of red blood cells due to the way the cells break down. They also often have kidney, heart, or brain dysfunction."

"How do you get TTP? Is it contagious?"

"No," Dr. Oluwye explains. "You can inherit it genetically, or you can acquire it. There's a gene called ADAMTS13 that helps with clotting. If you don't have ADAMTS13, you get that weird platelet clumping. So, if you inherit a mutated gene, the enzymes that create the protein for clotting aren't made—boom, you get clumpy platelets, and a diagnosis of TTP. But even if you don't inherit that mutated gene, you can still acquire TTP."

"How?"

"Certain diseases—like cancer and HIV—can cause you to acquire TTP. So can surgeries like blood or marrow or stem cell transplants. Sometimes women acquire TTP during pregnancy. Or by taking hormone therapy and estrogen."

"Hormone therapy," Jordan repeats. "Like the kind a transgender girl would be on?"

"Precisely."

"Can someone who has never shown evidence of TTP suddenly . . . show it?"

"Yes. TTP is extremely variable from patient to patient, but five classic symptoms are fever, anemia, thrombocytopenia, and renal and neurological symptoms. The patient might acutely exhibit all of these or just a fraction of them. Even if they've never manifested before."

"Can you cure TTP?" Jordan asks.

"You can, if you diagnose it."

"And if you don't?"

"The patient can die."

Jordan lets this settle. "What evidence did you see in the autopsy and the slides, Doctor, that led you to believe Lily had TTP?"

"I examined slides of the pancreas, liver, and brain to see if there was any indication of thrombotic microangiopathy—that clumping of the platelets. It looks like pink . . . stuff. Almost like paisley. The slides from the autopsy indeed showed classic evidence of the platelet clogging indicative of TTP."

"Is that something a medical examiner might have overlooked?"

"It happens," Dr. Oluwye says, shrugging. "Especially if you're not thinking to look for it. The degree of thrombosis is different from patient to patient, which means that at first glance the microscopic slides of the organs might not have seemed unusual . . . and yet if the medical examiner had looked more closely he'd have seen evidence of TTP."

"Did Lily's body show any of the other calling cards of TTP?"

"From what I understand, she had a fever that kept her home from school that day. She had no evidence of renal failure. I can't speak to neurological abnormality."

"What about those petechiae—the little dots? Wouldn't the medical examiner have noted those?" Jordan asks.

"There were no petechiae found on the deceased's body. However, the cadaver was twenty-four hours old at the time of autopsy and they could very well have faded and gone unnoticed if you didn't know to look for them. Not seeing petechiae in and of itself would not discount having TTP."

"Are there any further tests that could be performed to prove the diagnosis of TTP in Lily Campanello?"

"If the medical examiner had retrieved some blood serum during the autopsy, tests could have been done . . . but that only would have happened if TTP had been suspected prior to death. That isn't possible now, since no serum is available."

"If someone had undiagnosed TTP," Jordan asks, "what would happen if you grasped her arm?"

"She'd bruise easily. Having TTP means your platelets aren't doing what they're supposed to do. For that reason, bruising occurs even when pressure is applied at a low threshold."

"You mean a girl with TTP might wind up bruised, even if she was barely touched?"

"Yes, exactly," the pathologist says.

"You testified that one of the hallmarks of TTP is neurological symptoms," Jordan reiterates. "Could a girl with undiagnosed TTP get dizzy and stumble—even in a familiar place like her own bedroom?"

"Absolutely, the central nervous system symptoms could cause that. In fact, seizures occur in about twenty percent of TTP patients."

"Could this girl with undiagnosed TTP be athletic and graceful one day and feel dizzy the next?"

"Yes, with the onset of symptoms."

"Could a girl with undiagnosed TTP have accidentally fallen down the stairs?"

"Yes."

"And could that fall—particularly on *wooden* stairs—cause blunt force trauma?"

"Yes."

"In the circumstances of this case," Jordan says, stringing the beads together, "if Lily Campanello fell down a flight of uncarpeted steps and struck her head on a stair tread, could the fact that she had undiagnosed TTP have led to a brain hemorrhage that would produce an abnormally large amount of blood for a skull that had not been fractured?"

"Objection, Your Honor," the prosecutor calls. "We are not living in a fantasy world of hypotheticals."

"Judge, Dr. Oluwye has been qualified as an expert witness in pathology and I am asking questions about a possible cause of death in this particular case," Jordan argues.

"You may answer the question, Dr. Oluwye," Judge Byers rules.

The pathologist nods. "Yes, that is exactly what I'd expect to find. In fact, it's really the only explanation for that excessive amount of blood within an unfractured skull. A brain hemorrhage would be more severe in a person with undiagnosed TTP."

"If Lily was unaware of her condition, and not receiving treatment for TTP, could she have become dizzy and fallen down the uncarpeted stairs, hit her head, bled excessively into her brain, and subsequently died?"

"Yes."

"In that scenario, is the boyfriend of the girl with TTP involved in any way?"

"Objection!" the prosecutor says, rising from her chair.

"Sustained."

"Withdrawn," Jordan says, glancing at the jury. "Nothing further."

ON THE CAR ride to court, Jordan had explained the history of the legal concept of reasonable doubt.

It traces back to the United Kingdom, to jurist William Blackstone, who said—in the 1700s—"It is better that ten guilty persons escape than that one innocent suffer." This idea was meant to protect not only the defendant but also the jurors. Since only God could judge a man, it was a mortal sin for a juror to convict the wrong person.

It is, therefore, the prosecution's responsibility to remove reasonable doubt in the mind of the jury. The fun fact, though, Jordan said, is that there's no formal jury instruction that defines reasonable doubt. So if you can produce a different theory—an alternative explanation of a series of events believable enough to lodge in one juror's mind—then they legally should not convict your client.

Should not, he'd said.

Not *will* not.

THE PROSECUTOR IS up and moving toward Dr. Oluwye before Jordan takes his seat. "If Lily had TTP, would it change the cause of death?"

He considers this. "It would still be blunt force trauma to the head, with massive underlying brain hemorrhage caused by that trauma—the only difference would be the additional evidence of the blood disorder exacerbating the hemorrhage."

"Could a girl with undiagnosed TTP still be hit in the head by her boyfriend, or pushed down a flight of stairs by him, and still have the same unfortunate fatal outcome?"

"Objection!" Jordan calls.

"Sustained."

But the pathologist doesn't have to answer for Gina Jewett to have made her point. "Nothing further," she says.

I look at the jury. Some of them are writing on their notepads. Some are looking at Asher with open suspicion.

Jordan stands. "Your Honor," he says. "The defense rests."

AFTER THE JURY is sent out, Jordan and Gina Jewett speak with the judge about jury instructions. Selena, who has been sitting beside me, heads to the restroom. I lean forward until I am only inches away from Asher, who remains facing forward, watching the conversation at the bench, patently ignoring me.

When I sense someone taking the empty seat beside me, I turn. Mike Newcomb is there, his hands balanced on his knees. "How are you holding up?"

I try to smile but fail. "I've been better," I admit.

He nods, then glances toward the counselors at the bench. Judge Byers is on her feet, pacing, shoeless, listening to the lawyers in turn. "First time I ever testified in court," Mike says, "I went down in flames." He shakes his head. "I'd been a cop for maybe three months. My partner pulled over and searched a guy he thought looked suspicious. Guy was clean, and when we got back in the car, he stood in front of our cruiser to take down the license plate. My partner drove forward and hit the guy. In the official report, he said the guy jumped on his car, and that the car was in reverse at the time. I was too new and too scared to contradict him, but in court, I panicked and could barely speak, much less give testimony. You don't know real shame until your own AAG asks if you have a head injury."

"What happened?"

"Partner got fired for *testilying,* as they called it. I got a desk assignment for three months."

"I lost my son's trust," I murmur, "so I guess I win."

He considers this for a second. "I lose shit all the time," he says after a moment. "But you know, it always turns up." He pats the arm of the chair. "You mind? If I sit here?"

"It's a free country," I say, shrugging.

But maybe not for Asher, not for long.

JUDGE BYERS IS still in her stocking feet, pacing behind her chair, as she addresses the jury. "Asher Fields," she says, "has been charged with first-degree murder. A person is guilty of murder in the first degree if he purposely causes the death of another. *Purposely* shall mean that the actor's conscious object is the death of another, and that his act or acts in furtherance of that object were deliberate and premeditated." She looks at the twelve men and women, letting them process that. "A person convicted of murder in the first degree shall be sentenced to life imprisonment and shall not be eligible for parole at any time."

A shudder runs down my spine. I imagine what it will be like to watch Asher growing old behind bars.

I glance across Mike Newcomb's profile to the other side of the gallery, where Ava Campanello sits. As if she can feel the heat of my gaze, she turns and looks directly at me.

"Your verdict needs to be unanimous," the judge says. "You need to listen to everyone else's opinions, but come to your own conclusion."

How ironic. Keep an open mind . . . but shut it, once you've decided.

"We are now going to hear closing arguments from the attorneys, beginning with the defense and ending with the State," the judge says, slipping into her chair again. "Mr. McAfee?"

Jordan rises. "Ladies and gentlemen of the jury," he says, "I'm going to start with the law, and finish with the facts. In every criminal case in this country, the State has the burden of proving every element of the charge, and proving them beyond a reasonable doubt. That means if you have *any reasonable doubt* about Asher's role in this tragedy, you *must* vote not guilty."

If the law is about reasonable doubt, I think, *then—conversely— what do I know* for sure?

"The evidence that you've heard describes a relationship between Asher Fields and Lily Campanello. It began with mutual attraction; it blossomed into mutual respect."

What I know: Once upon a time, this boy fell hard for a girl.

"They went to school together. They went to movies, and out to eat. They shared texts and calls and private moments. They became intimate."

What I know: There is no punishment that could be worse for Asher than the loss of Lily.

"But unlike in many other relationships, this girl told the boy she was transgender. And then what happened? The prosecution would like you to believe that Asher felt betrayed and lashed out angrily. Instead, he showed great maturity. He thought about what she had told him, and came to the conclusion that he loved *who* Lily was, not *what* Lily was. He again showed great maturity by trying to get her to reconcile with her estranged father. The State wants you to connect the dots one way. But is it possible to connect them an entirely different way?"

What I know: You don't remove from your world the one person who fills it.

What I know: Asher can't be guilty.

I feel this certainty flood me, like a light switching on. The prosecution made this a case about Asher's deceit. But there's one thing he has consistently told the truth about: his feelings for Lily.

"You know," Jordan says, "when I was a kid, I was fascinated by optical illusions. I'm sure you have seen them. The vase that, when you blink, looks like two people in conversation; the wavy lines on a page that look like they're moving. There's one where you think you're seeing a profile of a young lady, until someone says, *No, look again*. It's a hag, with a hooked nose, and once you see it, you can't unsee it. Today, I am asking you to blink. I am asking you to see a completely different scenario from the one the prosecutor has directed you to see. Because the evidence you have heard proves there is *also* a scenario in which there wasn't a struggle, but instead a sick girl with an undiagnosed condition called TTP, one whose acute onset led to dizziness that had her staggering around her room, knocking over furniture, and falling tragically to her death. A condition where bruises blossom so easily that even a gentle touch might create what looks like a mark of violence. A condition where a blow to the head during a fall might lead to a brain bleed and instant death. A situation where the defendant was not an abuser, was not arguing, was not lying—only grieving, like he's told us all along." He turns, focusing on Asher. "Blink, and see what I see: a boy who fell in love with a girl."

He sits down beside Asher.

The prosecutor rises and addresses the jury. "Mr. McAfee makes compelling use of words, doesn't he? But then again, so do fiction writers. Strip away his pretty talk about optical illusions and you see the bare facts of this case—and what we have proven beyond a reasonable doubt: in this romantic tale he's trying to sell you about doomed lovers, there was dysfunction throughout. They fought with each other—you've seen the texts. There was abuse—you've seen the bruises. One day, after they had sex, Lily revealed to the defendant that she was trans. They were already in a volatile, combative relationship—and this was the last straw. The defendant, a boy who is easily provoked, realized he had had sex with someone who deceived him. Someone who was born a boy. And that, ladies and gentlemen, pissed him off—enough to tell Lily that *this ends now*."

She turns, gesturing toward Asher. "At the start of this trial, I painted a picture of a defendant who lied, who was abusive, who fought with his girlfriend, and who was found with her dead body. But now we know *why* this particular fight was different. Asher Fields was so furious after finding out his girlfriend was transgender—he felt so *humiliated*—that he was consumed with rage. Ladies and gentlemen, you even saw this happen before your eyes in court, when he felt betrayed by his friend Maya. Imagine that anger being nursed for weeks, ratcheted up. Imagine him going to Lily's house to confront her, to teach her a lesson. But you don't have to imagine the rest, because we've given you proof that Asher Fields murdered Lily—not in a crime of passion, but as a bona fide hate crime."

"Objection!" Jordan yells. "Asher was not charged with a hate crime."

Gina whips around. "None of us knew the victim was trans when this started. Except for your client."

"*Enough*, you two," Judge Byers snaps. "Can't we even get through the closings?" She looks at Jordan. "Sustained." Turning to the prosecutor, she adds, "The attorneys will address the court or the jury, but not the opposing counsel." Finally, the judge looks at the jury. "The jury will disregard that last statement by the prosecutor."

Chagrined, Gina Jewett takes a second to compose herself. "Ladies and gentlemen," she finishes, "the defendant thought he had a relationship, albeit a combustible one, with a girl he knew well. Then he found out that Lily Campanello was born male. He could have just broken up with her. But instead, the defendant's way out of the relationship was to take out his shame, his frustration, his anger *on* Lily. The defense has offered up a list of wild conjectures, hoping that you will be distracted by them enough to ignore reality. After all, isn't it convenient that the only people in the relationship and in the house where Lily was found dead are the victim herself, who can't speak, and the defendant—a proven liar?" She turns cold, assessing eyes on Asher. "Nothing is going to bring Lily Campanello back to life . . . but that doesn't mean this defendant should not be held responsible for her death."

. . .

AFTER DROPPING ME and Asher off at the farmhouse, Jordan and Selena drive to Portsmouth to pick up Sam and bring him back to Adams. We don't know how long the jury will deliberate, and they both want to be present when the verdict comes in.

I know they will return late tonight so that we can go to the courthouse together tomorrow morning, but the house feels cavernous when they are gone. Asher has retreated to his room, still stoic and silent.

I think of something that happened to Asher in second grade. He had been kicked out of school for three days. They had a zero-tolerance policy, and he had decked a boy at recess. He *was bullying* me, Asher had said. *Not the other way around.* I listened to the principal drone on about what was tolerated at this school, and how it was not an auspicious beginning for Asher. When Asher got into my car, I told him we were going out for ice cream. I said that he should always, always stand up for himself, and I would have his back.

The last thing I wanted was for him to turn into someone like me.

In the freezer I find mint chocolate chip ice cream, and I fill a bowl with several scoops and head upstairs.

Asher doesn't respond to my knock, so I open the door anyway. He looks at me holding the bowl. "I'm not hungry," he says, his voice clipped.

"Okay," I reply, and I sit down on the edge of the bed.

"I don't want you in here."

"Well, last time I checked, I still own this house."

He pushes himself up on the bed and yanks his headphones from his ears. "Jesus fucking Christ," he says, "leave me alone."

"No," I say evenly. "I will do almost anything for you. But *that* is the one thing I cannot do."

"Could have fooled me," he says bitterly.

I cleave the ice cream with the spoon. "Do you remember the time you were kicked out of school in second grade?"

His gaze slides to mine. "Yeah."

"Me, too," I say simply.

He grabs the bowl from me and takes a mouthful, which is, I realize, an olive branch. I watch him eat a few bites before he glances up at me again. "I wish you'd remembered a little sooner," he says quietly, still hurt by my testimony. "I guess the pathologist changed your mind?"

I shake my head. It wasn't the pathologist. It was realizing that my doubts had very little to do with Asher, and everything to do with my own experiences.

I think about how, the first night I stayed at Braden's apartment, he already had bought two toothbrushes—one soft and one medium—because he didn't know which one I liked. I believed, at the time, that he was being considerate. Now I know he was being calculating. *No one thinks of you the way I do. No one cares about you as much as me.*

"I used to believe the best of people," I say haltingly.

He studies me, the spoon falling into the bowl. "Why didn't you ever talk to me about what Dad did?"

"Oh, Asher," I say. "Because I was afraid you'd think it was my fault."

"Like he did. You thought I was like him."

"No," I correct. "I *hoped* you weren't."

"Until . . . now." The full force of my testimony, and his, and all the hints dropped by the prosecution swell between us like an airbag that has been deployed to keep us from being hurt even more by each other. Asher runs his finger around the edge of the ice cream bowl. "In second grade?" he says. "When I hit that kid? I did it because the asshole was talking shit about you."

My jaw drops. "What?"

"His mom worked in dispatch at the police department. He heard her say you moved here because you were a punching bag."

The restraining order. I close my eyes, because I don't know how to respond. All this time I tried to hide my past from Asher, and he'd known. All the time I'd tried to shield him, when he was already protecting me.

"When Lily told me she was trans," Asher says quietly, "I didn't know what to say. I was scared, yeah, and freaked out, and I didn't want to betray her by telling anyone else . . . even by telling you. But I wanted to. I thought, *What would Mom say?* And then I figured it out. I went back to Lily, and I told her how sometimes you run into people who knew you when you were married. They always say something in code, you know: *You're like a different person!* And you always just smile and make a joke and say you're who you've always been. I told Lily that when you were with Dad, he wanted you to be someone you weren't. If you'd stayed with him, maybe you would have made yourself into that person . . . but it wouldn't have been you. It would have been who *he* said you were." Asher looks up at me. "And then I told her I loved her. *Her.*"

Tears fill his eyes, and his hands shake. I take the ice cream bowl from him and set it on the nightstand.

"I loved her, Mom," Asher says, crying. "I still do."

I wrap my arms around him, holding him until his chest isn't heaving and his breath evens. Then I pull back, bracing my hands on his shoulders. "Asher," I say, "I believe you."

He knows I am talking about all of it—his pain, his innocence, his truth. And it's not because of a Hail Mary witness testimony or a blood disorder. It's not because Asher isn't like Braden after all.

It's because he is like *me*.

In spite of everything that has happened to me, I still believe in love . . . and so does Asher.

Even more remarkable: that may not be a flaw . . . but a strength.

Asher reaches for the bowl of ice cream and holds it out to me. "Here, Mom," he says. "Help me finish."

LILY ◆ 9

Three months before

There are so many gendered things in this world. Hurricanes. Bicycles. Ice skates. Ships at sea. Even countries—Mother Russia, Uncle Sam? And of course, the planet itself: *Let earth receive her king.*

Sometimes it makes me wonder about all the time we spend tearing out our hair labeling things. And how some of the results of all that work are dubious at best. It was Mark Twain who noticed that, in German, the noun for *fish* is masculine, the one for *fish scales* is feminine, and the word for *fishwife* is neuter.

These are the thoughts that go through my head as we—boys, girls, and even a couple of nonbinary folks—gather here in the Adams High School gym for the first day of the Coös County Honors Orchestra rehearsal. All around me are my fellow musicians, tuning up their instruments, students not just from Adams but from a half dozen other regional high schools. Surely an instrument is neither male nor female—they're just things that make sound—strings and bows, brass and wood, mallets and cymbals and drumskins and little metal triangles.

And yet all you have to do is look around at these musicians to see the way that even sound is gendered.

In the middle of the orchestra is the brass section—tubas, trombones, trumpets, French horn, every last one of them played by boys. It's not all that different in the woodwinds—where the boys play bassoons and clarinets, but all the flutes are played by girls. The strings are even more ridiculous—the deeper the instrument, the more likely it is to be played by a boy. So all the basses? Boys. Most of the cellos? Boys. The violas split half and half. All but one of the violins? Girls.

Then there's the harp, which I guess federal law requires be played by a girl. And the percussion and kettle drums, which are usually played by boys.

How weird is this? Most of us decided to play our instruments in third grade, a bunch of little kids who made our choices without even thinking about them. But even at eight years old, we were already running the gender maze that the world had set for us, without even realizing it.

That's why it's cool when you see someone breaking the expectations a little bit. Like the absolutely huge dude who "mans" the piccolo. And the girl in the back row "womaning" the gongs and kettledrums, twirling her percussion mallets around like a badass.

The oboist is female, too, which is a little bit unusual. She's an Indian girl with a serious face. Mr. Pawlawski, the conductor, taps his baton against his music stand, turns to her, and says, "Maya?"

And Maya gives the A, and the first violin—a guy named Derrick—tunes to it. There's a moment of silence, and then Derrick gives the rest of us his A, and then we all tune up to him.

Mr. Pawlawski is an intense, thin man with a goatee. He looks kind of like a *nice* Count Dracula. He passes out the sheet music for the four pieces we're going to practice this fall—the "Jupiter" movement from Holst's *The Planets;* the Polovtsian Dances by Borodin; a medley of movie music by John Williams; and Prokofiev's *Peter and the Wolf.* The Prokofiev is going to be narrated by the goalie from the hockey team, this huge creature named Dirk Anderson. He's wearing a T-shirt that reads PUCK IT. I met him two days ago, on the first day of school, in my English class. I guess getting the goalie to narrate *Peter and the Wolf* was some kind of coup for Mr. Pawlawski, but just looking at this kid gives me a sinking feeling.

Obviously, no one here has practiced any of this music (except maybe for me, because I played "Jupiter" back in the Pointcrest orchestra two years ago), but Mr. Pawlawski seems to have a lot of faith in his players, because he asks us to give the John Williams piece a go, and just like that he raises his baton, counts it off, and we start in on the theme from Star Wars.

How does it sound? Not good.

What it sounds like, in fact, is the music that would go with that movie if Emperor Palpatine killed everybody in the first thirty seconds. *Good! Good! Let the hate flow through you!*

Mr. Pawlawski taps his music stand with his baton, then raises one hand and holds the bridge of his nose with his fingers. He stands like that for a long time, like his brain is bleeding from the inside, and he's trying to stop it. He sighs, then turns to all of us.

"Again," he says, and the horrible noise begins anew.

It's going to be a long semester.

OF COURSE, I was running the gender maze, too, when I chose the cello in third grade. Even then I was aware of what things boys were supposed to do, and what things were for girls.

My parents had already started having fights about me. Third grade was when my father said that I couldn't wear a dress outside the house. I think his exact words were, *This shit has to stop somewhere.*

I didn't really understand what difference it made what clothes I wore. On the weekends, when I went with Mom to the farmers' market, the cheese lady would tell me how pretty I was. *She's going to break some hearts someday,* she said. I was wearing blue jeans and a T-shirt, but no one thought I was a boy, not unless my father was with me, and he made it very clear that this *young man* was his *son.*

It wasn't about my clothes, so what was it people saw when they laid eyes on me and said, *She's going to break some hearts?* Was it just my hair, which I liked long? Or was it something else, something in my spirit that they sensed?

That fall was when we first chose our instruments for the orchestra. I knew I was going to play cello from the first moment I ever saw one. Like I said, cello is usually an instrument that boys choose, but I wanted it anyway. Was it because of the sweet sound it made, that it's the string instrument that most duplicates the human voice? Or was it the shape, so like the hips and shoulders of a woman?

It's a good thing I found the cello that year, because third grade was when I first felt the world closing in on me. I remember one weekend calling my friend Jimmy Callanan on the phone, asking him if he wanted to come over and play video games. Jimmy just said, *Nah, I don't feel like it. Really?* I said. I mean, I could understand it if he was doing something else, or if he wasn't feeling well, or something. But Jimmy, clearly, wasn't busy. He just didn't want to hang out with me.

After I hung up I sat in the kitchen, trying to understand what had happened. Mom came in, and asked me what was wrong.

I have no friends, I said, and burst into tears.

Oh, Liam, she said, holding me. *I'm sure that's not true.*

But it was. I had stopped getting invited to other boys' birthday parties. On weekends I'd just lie around, playing Zelda, or practicing cello, hour after hour. I got really good with the cello as a result, maybe because I have a good ear. Mostly, though, I was just driven by loneliness. I held that cello in my arms, and let her form the sounds I felt so keenly in my heart but had no other way to express.

Then, one day, my mother came home early from the park. I was in the living room practicing scales. "Liam," sang out Mom. "I have something for you."

I looked up, and there she was, framed in the doorway. In her arms was a puppy, a black Lab. My mouth dropped open.

I ran to my mother and then I held the puppy to my face. He licked me. My nose filled with that great puppy smell.

I was so grateful. My mother had seen how lonely I was, and got this little dog to save me. It was great to have Boris. I loved him.

But it was even better to have my mom.

"There," she said. "*Now* you have a friend."

· · ·

I'M PACKING UP my cello after rehearsal when I hear a voice behind me. "Early one morning," says the voice. "Peter opened the gate and went out into the big fuckin' meadow!"

I turn, and there, grinning from ear to ear, is Dirk Anderson. "How'm I doin'?"

"I don't think that's how it goes," I say.

"Yeah?" says Dirk. "Well, maybe you could teach me." He takes a step closer. "I'm *Dirk*."

"I know," I say. "I'm Lily Campanello. I'm in your English class, with Mr. Jameson."

"Fuckin' *Chopper*, man," says Dirk. "He's gonna bust my balls."

I am not sure how to reply to this.

"Are you good at English?" he asks, and he gives me this look that almost makes me feel sorry for him. Dirk, it would seem, is *not* good at English.

"Good enough, I guess," I say, closing the final latch on my hard case.

"Maybe you can help me out this semester," says Dirk. "You could help me, and I could help you."

He keeps closing the space between us, and I take a step back. Another step and I'm going to be up against the gymnasium wall.

"Hey, Lily," says Dirk. "If I said you had a beautiful body"—he can't believe how clever the thing is he's about to say—"*would you hold it against me?*"

I'm wondering if Dirk has enough of an IQ to realize what an idiot he is, when all at once a guy I've never seen before steps between us. "Dude, what are you doing?" he says. He's beautiful—tall, curly hair, green twinkling eyes. He whispers, "*Play along.*"

"What does it look like I'm doing, Fields? I'm turning on the charm!"

"Too late, Dirk," says the guy, and he slips an arm around my waist. "She's mine." He turns to me, and nods. "You want to go?"

"Okay," I say, and I grab my cello and the two of us head out of the gym arm in arm, leaving Dirk behind.

"You owe me one, Asher!" shouts Dirk.

We pass through the double doors of the gym, and now we're in the hallway, where Asher or Fields lets go of me and says, "Looked like you needed a lifeline there."

"Asher, you're gonna be late for practice. Again," says Maya, the oboist, coming over to join us. "Oh—you're the sick cellist!" She sticks out her hand. "I'm Maya."

"Lily Campanello," I say.

"Lily," Asher repeats, like he's savoring a candy tucked into the side of his cheek.

Maya pokes Asher in the side. "How did *you* meet the new girl before me?"

"I didn't, officially. I rescued her from Dirk."

"Ugh," says Maya. "Can you believe he's going to be in our faces all semester? He's narrating *Peter and the Wolf.*"

"What's his deal?" I ask.

"His deal," says Maya, "is that he's a mouth breather."

"Killer goalie, though," says Asher. He looks at his watch. "Damn. I *am* late."

"See you this weekend?" says Maya.

"Always," says Asher. "It was nice to meet you, Lily," he adds, and then heads down the hall. We watch as Dirk comes through a second set of doors, and he and Asher laugh at something and walk away together, like they are the best of friends.

"So," I say to Maya. "Are you two—?"

It takes Maya a second to realize what I'm hinting at. "Me and Asher?" She blushes from the neck up. "God, no."

We're walking down the hallway now toward the parking lot, where my mother is supposed to be picking me up. "I can always tell when someone's serious about music," she says. "Like you. You're hardcore."

"I've been playing since third grade," I admit.

"Me, too," says Maya. "Maybe we could do some duets sometimes? Unless you're afraid of OD'ing on the nerd factor."

"I don't think it's possible for me to OD on the nerd factor," I say.

"I knew I liked you." Maya laughs. "Do you know the Eugene

Bozza piece for oboe and cello? Why don't you come over to my house this Saturday? We can play, and eat dinner with my moms, and watch a show or something?"

"That sounds great," I say, and I have just enough time to register (1) that she said *Moms* and (2) that it was no big deal. My phone dings, a text from my mother. "My mom's pulling up," I explain.

Maya grabs the phone from me and types her number into my contacts. "I'll text you so we can make plans," she says, and I smile and rush toward the car—well, what passes for rushing what with the cello and my backpack. I'm thinking of what Mom said when she put Boris in my arms. *There.* Now *you have a friend.*

"How was your day?" Mom asks as we drive home, and I tell her about Chopper, and Dirk, and Maya, and everything. I tell her today was wonderful. I tell her I think I'm going to be all right.

The one thing I don't tell her, the thing I keep to myself, is the memory of Asher Fields, and how perfect his arm felt wrapped around my waist. *Too late, Dirk,* he said. *She's mine.*

OLIVIA ● 10

MAY 14–16, 2019

Five months after

Awaiting a verdict. A snapshot: Tuesday.

When I was still married, Braden sometimes operated on patients whose spouses chose not to come to the hospital during their heart surgeries. They gardened or read or worked until the doctor called to say that the operation was finished and the patient was recovering. *Not everyone can handle being at a hospital,* Braden had said to me, but it seemed like a direct violation of marriage vows. Surely the fine print of "in sickness and in health" was the tacit agreement that you would keep vigil.

Now, waiting for the jury to return a verdict, I am starting to reassess my opinion. The problem with waiting is, well, that you have to wait. In the absence of knowledge, the mind is an amazing Tilt-A-Whirl of worst-case scenarios. Pacing a room doesn't make it any bigger; watching a clock doesn't make the time tick by.

Today has lasted six years, by my calculation. This morning we all trekked to the courthouse, even Jordan's son Sam. Jordan says we are required to stay near the courtroom, because the jury could come back with a decision at any moment.

Except, they haven't.

I haven't eaten all day and neither has Asher. I feel jittery and shaky, like I've been mainlining coffee. Asher sits at the table in the conference room with his head pillowed on his arms, eyes closed— but I can tell from the flutter of the pulse at his neck that he's not asleep and not relaxed. Jordan and Selena are reading different sections of *The Boston Globe*. Sam is reading the third book in the Lord of the Rings trilogy.

"Do you like it?" I ask my nephew.

"It's only the best book ever written," Sam says. He quotes: "*Even the smallest person can change the course of the future.*"

"Oh my God," I murmur. "You *are* your father's son."

Sam looks up at me. "You don't like it?"

"Too many orcs," I say.

"Your aunt's lying." Jordan laughs. "She's never even read it."

"That's not true," I tell him. "It's Braden's favorite. He read it to me out loud when we'd drive up to Adams from Boston. He acted out all the characters."

Jordan snorts. "Who would have thought we'd have something in common," he says, and snaps the newspaper back into a shield obscuring his face.

I do not recall much of the book, except for Éowyn, the warrior facing the King of the Ringwraiths, who said no living man could kill him. *But no living man am I,* she said, pulling off her helmet so her hair cascaded to her waist.

Then she hacked him down.

I remember missing much of what Braden read after that, imagining what it would take to see being a woman as a strength, not a weakness.

"What book did *you* pick, Aunt Liv?" Sam asks.

I look at him, puzzled.

"For the car ride home?"

He looks up at me, the innocence in his face blinding. Because in his world, everyone gets a turn to pick. Except, it was *always* Braden's turn. I remember suggesting books by Louise Erdrich and Anne Tyler and Octavia Butler, but we never actually read them on our journeys.

I wonder how long Sam will live in this bubble, until he is older and beaten down by the world. I try to imagine Asher, back when he was Sam's age, but there are scars on him now I cannot see past.

We sit for seven hours in that goddamned room and at about 4:00 P.M. we are finally called into the courtroom by the judge, who's agreed to ask the jury about their status.

When the jury is brought in, the judge turns to the foreperson. "My understanding from the bailiff is that you are not close to reaching a verdict this evening. Is that correct?"

"That's correct."

Judge Byers sighs. "We are going to recess for the night. Do not read anything about the trial, do not turn on the news, or access information on any other media. Do not talk to anyone about the case—not even your spouse."

I tug on the back of Jordan's suit jacket. "What does this mean?" I whisper.

"It means," he says, "that we come back tomorrow and do this all again."

A SNAPSHOT: Wednesday.

Selena has taken Sam back down to Portsmouth, to her mother. It's clear that this trial will not be decided as quickly as she and Jordan had believed.

Jordan and I are at each other's throats. He is breathing too loudly; my chewing of gum annoys him. It is like when we were younger and would try to kick each other's feet under the dinner table.

"I fucking hate the fact that Gina Jewett can sit in her office but we're jammed into this godforsaken conference room," Jordan mutters. The DA's office is in the courthouse building, and presumably it is where she's been awaiting the verdict.

"Why does it matter?" I ask.

"Because she can *do* things," Jordan says. "Make calls. Work. You know."

I fold my arms. "I'm sorry, are we *keeping* you from your busy life? You're retired."

"Correction: I *was* retired," Jordan says.

"Jesus," Asher groans, his hands tunneling through his hair. "Can you two just *stop*?"

We both swivel toward him.

"We have to talk about it," Asher says.

"Talk about what?" I ask.

"What happens when we lose."

"We're not going to lose," Jordan says, a knee-jerk.

"You don't know that," Asher argues. "It can't be good that it's taking this long."

"Is that what you're worried about? Don't be. There was a case in New Haven where a guy was found guilty of murder after six minutes of jury deliberations."

"You're saying it's good that it's taking this long?" I ask.

"I'm saying that there's no way to know."

Asher stands up until he is face-to-face with Jordan. He has a couple of inches on his uncle. "I want you to tell me the truth," he says quietly. "About what's going to happen."

He doesn't have to explain what he means. "If you're found guilty, the penalty will be prison." Jordan hesitates. "For life."

A muscle clenches in Asher's jaw, but he doesn't even blink.

"If that's the verdict, we will appeal," Jordan explains. "But, Asher, I do not think that's going to be the outcome. I have thirty-five years of experience trying cases, including the worst mass murder in New Hampshire history—so you need to trust me when I say that I think your case went well."

By comparison to Peter Houghton, who killed nine classmates and a teacher? I think. *Jesus Christ.*

A SNAPSHOT: Wednesday night.

After another day of unproductive deliberations, we drive home. There's no food in the house. Dinner is canned soup and toast and honey.

Jordan, waiting for Selena to return, dries dishes while I wash. "Were you telling Asher the truth?" I ask.

He nods. "I'm not psychic, Liv. I can't promise him that he'll get acquitted. A jury is twelve total strangers; I have no idea what they're thinking." He carefully wipes down a bowl. "They say that when a jury files into the courtroom, you can tell what they're going to say. If they refuse to make eye contact with the defendant, it's a guilty verdict. If they do look at him, then it's not guilty. But that's basically an old wives' tale."

I take the bowl from his hand and set it into place on a cabinet shelf.

"What I *do* know," Jordan says, "is what they *should* be thinking, based on the evidence . . . and if they're doing their job, then Asher's got a good chance."

"I know. I just . . . I didn't think it was going to take this long," I tell him. "Either way."

Just then Selena bombs into the kitchen. She drops her keys on the counter and brandishes a bottle of Tito's.

"You know what passes the time?" she says. "Shots."

A SNAPSHOT: Thursday, dawn.

I can smell the skunk before I see the evidence—the odor wafting in ripe, rank waves on the spring breeze that blows from the hives toward the house. With my hat and veil and smoker, I head out to check the damage before I have to get ready for court.

Sometimes skunks skulk around the hives at night. They scratch until the bees are coaxed out, swat them till they're injured, and eat them live. Around Lady Gaga's colony I see claw marks at the entrance and scat on the matted grass. Even though it is early and still cool outside, Gaga's bees are agitated and flying, irritably charging my veil, their buzz as high-pitched as a helicopter's whine.

I am weighing the value of opening up the hive to make sure the queen is okay against getting them even more hot and bothered, when I feel a hand on my shoulder.

I whirl, my arms already raised in defense.

"Liv," Mike Newcomb says, shocked. "I'm— It's just me."

My sudden motion has infuriated the bees again. They billow around us both in small, angry clouds. I step away from the hive and Mike follows, until the bees leave us alone.

"I didn't mean to startle you," he says.

"I don't like it when I can't see what's coming."

"Noted," Mike murmurs. "Although to be fair, you were in a lot more danger of being hurt by a bee than by me." He sniffs the air. "Skunk?"

"Yeah. One got in here last night."

"Will you show me?" he asks. "What you do?"

I nod, picking up the smoker, and using it to calm the bees. The few that are still riled up start to settle as I open the cover of Gaga's hive and use my tool to pry one of the frames free. Slowly, I slide it out of the box and watch the bees crawl away so that I can look at the empty cells, the few with larvae curled in them, the rice-grain evidence of eggs. With a flip of my wrists, I scan the opposite side. I set the frame on the ground beside the hive, propped on its side, and unstick the next frame. It's mechanical, methodical. It's like swimming underwater, in a world where it feels like I've been drowning for days.

Three frames in, I find the queen, bustling around. "There you are," I murmur.

"What a beauty," Mike says, but he is not gazing down at the honeycomb. He's looking at me.

Hurriedly, I put the frame back in the hive, and then move the others into formation, picking up the one that was balanced on the ground last. I use my hive tool to set the bee space the insects need to move between frames, and replace the cover. When I pull off my hat, I pretend that my veil is the reason I'm so flushed.

"If this is a work call," I say, "you're here awfully early."

Mike watches me dump the embers from the smoker into a little pit I've dug with the heel of my boot. "Would you believe me if I said I'd come to buy honey?"

"Nobody has a honey emergency at six A.M." I laugh.

"Then I guess I came to see how you're holding up."

I let my breath out in a long stream. "How I'm holding up," I repeat. "Well, I'm overtired, and a skunk tried to get into one of my hives, and I had way too much to drink last night and none of that's enough to take my mind off the fact that jury deliberations are going on their third day."

Keeping his eyes on me the whole time, Mike closes the space between us and kisses me so softly that it might be a breath or a wish. His eyelashes brush my cheek; his hand slides around the back of my neck. He doesn't hold me as much as he anchors me, so that I know that at any time, I could pull away.

But I don't. I lean forward, and I kiss him back.

He tastes of mint and coffee, and I realize that I'm the one struggling to get closer, to bleed into his edges. He waits until I lock my arms around his neck and then he surges toward me, his hands on my spine and my shoulders and tangled in my hair, his lips and tongue consuming me like I am nectar.

Mike nips at me and I gasp, because it's pain but it's not; it's soothed as soon as it stings.

The bees are a soundtrack. The feel of his fingers on my bare skin—my throat, my wrist, my face—is nearly overwhelming. It's been that long since I've been held.

Pressed against me, I can feel how hard he is, how much closer he wants to be. But he is the one to drag his mouth away, to rest his forehead against mine. His voice, when he finds it, is shaking. "How was that for a distraction?" he asks.

I feel capsized, upended, inside out. *I don't like it when I can't see what's coming.*

Maybe this can be an exception.

"It's a start," I say.

A SNAPSHOT: Thursday, 9:00 A.M.

The verdict is in, the bailiff says.

It takes me and Jordan, on either side of Asher, to move him into the courtroom. He is wooden with fear. I take up my position behind him, sitting beside Selena. Asher's face is drained of color, his eyes wide and terrified. "I think I'm going to throw up," he whispers over his shoulder.

If there is a presumption of innocence, why do juries say guilty or not guilty? Why not innocent or not innocent?

Asher's sweating so profusely that the collar of his shirt is soaked.

This is the moment, I think. *This is when I lose my child, or get him back.*

Across the gallery, I see Ava Campanello waiting, her face pinched and drawn.

Judge Byers is pacing again. "Let the record reflect that the defendant and his attorney are present, along with the State represented by its attorney. I have been notified by the bailiff that the jury has sent a message that they have reached a verdict." She nods at the bailiff. "Please bring the jury in."

I think of what Jordan said, and as each member of the jury enters, I scrutinize their faces. Eleven of them sit down in the box, and stare straight ahead.

Fuck.

The twelfth juror looks directly at Asher.

"Madame Foreperson," the judge asks, "has the jury reached a verdict?"

"We have, Your Honor."

Judge Byers turns to Asher. "Mr. Fields," she says. "Please rise."

When Asher stands, dragged upright by Jordan, I grab Selena's hand.

"To the charge of murder in the first degree, how does the jury find?"

The foreperson turns to the judge. "We find the defendant not guilty."

The courtroom explodes, reporters racing outside to file their stories, Jordan folding his arms around a stunned Asher, Selena smothering me with a cry of delight. Dimly I'm aware of the judge banging her gavel, thanking the jury for their service, discharging them. She turns to Asher. "Mr. Fields, the jury has rendered a unanimous verdict of not guilty and thus the charge of murder in the first degree is dismissed. You are free to go." She smacks her gavel. "Court is adjourned."

Jordan jumps over the wooden divider and sweeps me into his arms, lifting me off my feet and swinging me around. He gives Selena a smacking kiss of congratulations. It's almost hard to breathe with the blanket of relief that has settled over us.

There are two people in the courtroom who aren't celebrating.

Without Jordan to lean on, Asher has sunk back into his seat, like his legs have simply given out. He leans forward, his face buried in his hands, sobbing.

About ten feet away, as if she is reflected in a mirror, Ava Campanello is curled in the same snail shell of grief.

JORDAN PREENS FOR the reporters, striking a balance between crowing over his own prowess and humbly remembering that a girl died, albeit not at the hands of Asher. But we do not linger at the courthouse, and after we arrive home, he and Selena pack up their suitcases, intent on getting home to Sam before his school day ends.

I help Jordan load everything into Selena's car. While Selena is saying goodbye to Asher, I stand in front of my big brother. "Well," I say. "Consider your debt clear."

"Debt?"

"You may not have saved me from Braden," I tell him. "But you saved me now."

"I saved Asher," he corrects. "You still get a freebie." He folds me into his embrace, and I tuck my head under his chin and try not to cry.

"What happens now?" I whisper.

"Now you get to be a mom," Jordan says. "He's going to need you."

I nod. "Thanks, Jordan."

"I'd say *anytime,* but let's not do this again, shall we?"

Then Selena hugs me, while Jordan claps Asher on the back.

"Here's the thing," I hear Jordan say. "When you've lost someone, being acquitted doesn't make it hurt any less. So if you want to talk to someone—other than your mother—well, I wouldn't be averse to breakfast at a Chili's, say, once a month."

Asher's lips twitch. "Good to know."

"But you're paying," Jordan says. "Since I took this case pro bono." He grins as Selena ducks into the passenger seat of the car. "Remember, Asher," he says. "You have a lot of people looking out for you."

Asher nods, and Jordan turns to me one last time. "One more word to the wise," he says, under his breath. "Use protection."

"What?"

"My bedroom window looks over toward the hives," Jordan says. "*I'm going to see if a skunk got into the bees,* my ass."

A laugh breaks out of me, but it feels like a butterfly freed from a cocoon. I smack him across the shoulder. "You've officially overstayed your welcome," I joke, but all the same, I stand on the porch and watch him drive away until I cannot see the car anymore.

I HAVEN'T TAKEN a nap since I was in college, but once Jordan and Selena leave I am so exhausted that I fall asleep at the kitchen table, after putting my head down for a moment while sorting through the mail. When I wake up, it's because there is a pounding in my head, or so I think until I sit up, wincing at the sound of hammering.

In the slanting light of late afternoon, it's hard to see what's going on at the edge of the woods near the hives, but I walk briskly along the strawberry fields until I find the source of the noise. The unmistakable rhythmic smack of metal striking wood is coming from inside the tree house.

I know Asher is responsible even before I climb the dangling rope ladder. My head crests through the little trapdoor in the floor of the structure. He is wearing a T-shirt that is damp the length of his spine. As I watch, he wipes his brow on his shoulder, then takes a nail from a row between his pressed lips and hammers it into a board that he's using to close up one of the windows.

"Asher?" I say softly, so that I don't surprise him.

He finishes pounding the nail in, and then turns to me, as if he's expected me all along. "Oh," he says. "Hi."

I look around at the interior: all traces of occupation have been removed. The ship's wheel and the hammock and the wooden box full of old games have been disposed of. The only hint that anyone was ever up here are the initials carved into the rafters, and the afghan, folded carefully.

"Do you need a hand?" I ask, not sure what I am volunteering for.

"I'm almost done."

I watch for a moment as he finishes fastening the board, then I pick up a broom and sweep the dust into piles that I push out the trapdoor. I am careful not to touch the afghan, which feels special, somehow. Sacred.

Asher tucks the hammer into the belt of his jeans and hands me the box of nails. He opens the trapdoor and tosses out a few extra pieces of wood, then motions so I can climb down first. At the base of the rope ladder I wait for him, but he stops on the third rung, curling his arm into the winding twine like a circus performer so that he can anchor himself while he nails the trapdoor shut.

I open my mouth to tell him he's left the afghan behind but then I realize that's exactly what he intended.

When Asher gets down to ground level, he grabs a shovel I had not noticed, and stalks deeper into the woods. I hear the crunch of soil, and then, a few moments later, his footsteps. He holds the shovel in one hand, and in the other, the necks of several bright, wild day-lilies, their roots trailing dirt. He sets them down gently at the base of the tree house, then digs a small hole, and plants a lily in it. As I watch him pat down the ground, I kneel beside him to help—but a low noise from the back of Asher's throat makes me realize this is something *he* has to do.

I step back, and I bear witness.

When Asher is finished, he lets his hand gently trail over the exuberant orange petals, dusting his fingertips with pollen. His eyes are damp, and he's breathing hard, like he's just come off the ice. He swallows, then looks up at the tree house—both an end, now, and a beginning. "Okay," he says, his voice barely more than breath. "Okay."

I loop my arm through his. I lean on him, or maybe he leans on me, as we walk toward the house, leaving his childhood sealed behind.

LILY ⬡ 10

Four months before

We've been in the new house for less than twenty-four hours when I'm reminded that my mom, in spite of being the biggest badass I know, is also really fragile. I'm not the only person under this roof who has a few well-hidden broken places.

We'd done so well together on the long drive east. All the moments when you'd expect us to get on each other's nerves turned out to be fun, even the obstacles and frustrations of the road emerging, in the end, as parts of the adventure.

We stayed at Motel 6s, Holiday Inns, college guesthouses. One night, somewhere in Wyoming, we were both so exhausted that Mom just pulled off the highway and we slept in a field in our sleeping bags, Boris curled up between us. Over our heads was a universe of stars.

I'll never forget that, as long as I live.

When we finally pulled into the driveway of this house last night, Mom turned off the engine and we just sat for a moment listening to the silence, looking at the dark windows. Crickets chirped from a field.

"Well," Mom announced. "We have arrived."

The key was right where the landlords said it would be, hidden under a flowerpot on the front porch. But they'd said that the key was mostly a formality. People in Adams, we were told, didn't go in much for locking doors.

The moving van wasn't supposed to arrive until the morning, so we just spread sleeping bags out on the floor of the living room and pretended we were camping. Mom got the last bottle of chardonnay from the cooler and we drank it out of plastic cups. We opened all the windows and listened to the sounds of New Hampshire at night fill the place, until we finally lay down and closed our eyes. The last thing I thought was *This is my new home. Here's where I can start my life at last.*

We woke up to the sound of the moving van pulling into the driveway. Mom and I got dressed and opened the door. There was the truck, full of everything we'd packed up two weeks before in California. A big guy stood there with a clipboard. He had his name, Hurley, stitched on his uniform. He looked me up and down. *Well, hello, sweetheart,* he said.

Now, late afternoon, we have the rugs down and the chairs and sofas more or less in the places where we expect they'll stay. Mom has opened a big box of framed photos and art and is going through each one gasping with joy, like all these boxes are presents sent to her by someone who knew *exactly* what she always wanted.

Just shy of four o'clock, Mom goes into the kitchen to make herself a cup of chamomile tea. I can hear her rooting through the boxes until, with a cry of triumph, she locates the teapot.

I keep unpacking as I hear the water slowly coming to a boil. I pull an old photo album out of a box; it's an album I don't remember seeing before. I open the cover, and—just like that—my seven-year-old self stares back, wearing a little suit.

I flip the page to discover more photos. Our old house in Seattle. The ranger station in Olympic National Park. Me on the lawn of the Catholic church of our old hometown, holding an Easter basket. There's even the one of me posing with a baseball bat at the Saturday morning T-ball league. I remember that one. It's the picture of me Dad kept in his office at work, the one that was taken the very same morning I'd snuck into the bathroom and put on—and then rubbed off—my mother's lipstick.

"I made you a cup," says Mom, coming into the room. "Do you want—?" But now she sees what I'm looking at.

"What *is* all this?" I ask her, but I know what it is.

"Don't be mad," she says. "I just can't bring myself to throw those photos away." She sits down next to me on the couch. "It's not that I want that life back. It's just—"

And just like that, Mom's eyes fill with tears.

"It's okay," I tell her, and what surprises me is that it *is* okay. There was a time when a photo of me from pretransition would have filled me with shame and anger. Back then, it was as if my womanhood was something that could be taken away from me—by someone saying the wrong thing, by someone using the wrong pronoun, even by an old picture. But now, after this long journey, my womanhood is as solid and true as the earth. If Mom wants to keep her old photos, that's okay.

"Is it?" says Mom. "Because I can throw it all away if you—"

"No," I tell her. "I'm not the only one who went through transition. You did, too."

She wipes her eyes. In the album before us is a picture of me with Puppy Boris. "Sometimes I feel like I don't have any history," she says. "I look in the mirror, and I see this middle-aged woman, and I wonder, who *is* this person? How did I get here?"

I give Mom a squeeze, and it's weird. For a moment it's like I'm the parent, looking out for her. I have a flash of me in the future, in my sixties, taking care of a very, very old version of Mom.

When I was little, on weekends, she let me be as feminine as I wanted. I never wore a dress to school, but I had some cute outfits I was allowed to wear at home. I had a set of hot rollers and some pink tights. I even had a princess costume, with a hanky hem and a pair of translucent wings that strapped over my shoulders.

One day, I swept into the living room with my wings and a wand with a sparkling star. My father, drinking a PBR, looked up and said, "What are you supposed to be?"

I told him the truth: *I'm queen of the fairies!*

My father slapped his hand to his forehead and said, *Jesus fucking Christ.*

I don't know if that's the day that Mom and Dad began fighting about me; my guess is that it started long before that. They tried to hide it, but there were times I was all they talked about, my mother saying, *We have to let him be himself,* and my father saying, *We can't let him get crushed by the world.*

My father kept that photo of me holding the baseball bat in his office, year after year. He never changed it, even after I stopped looking anything like that boy.

By fall of 2011 my parents worked out what my father called *a compromise,* and Mom later told me was her *surrender.* "I thought if I agreed to this one thing," she said, "that I could stay married."

What she agreed to was sending me to a private school, Pacific Day, starting in sixth grade. It was over a hundred years old, had a campus of rolling fields, an old stone library. "They have a fencing team, Liam," my father said, trying to make me feel good about it. "They have an orchestra!" I'd already been playing cello for three years by then.

None of that mattered to me, though, or quite frankly, to him, either. What mattered was that it was an *all-boys school.* We had to wear coats and ties. And call the teachers "sir."

All summer long, I begged my parents, *Don't make me go. Please don't make me go.*

My father: *I'm not saying it won't be hard, Liam. But it's going to be good for you. It's going to teach you how to be a man.*

I so wanted to say the words *That's not what I want to learn.* But I didn't want to disappoint them. Sometimes I thought of the words my father had spoken years before. *You can be anything you want to be, Liam.* And it occurred to me that maybe, if I tried hard enough, I could teach myself how to want to be a boy. That the sense of self I'd had from my earliest memory would somehow disappear, if only I worked harder at it.

By the time of my first morning at Pacific Day, I was determined to be a boy. I thought I could learn it, the way I'd studied the cello: with patience and practice.

But it was clear that at Pacific Day you were already supposed to know how to be a boy. At lunch the first day, I was jumped by a pair of eighth graders. One tied my hands behind my back with a bungee cord, and the other paraded me through the school, shouting, *Hey, you see this faggot!* And everyone laughed, like this was the funniest thing they'd ever seen.

I tried *staying the course,* as my father put it, for a few more weeks, but every day there was another humiliation. I was beaten up a lot. I didn't make any friends. I started doing badly on tests—flailing in class for the first time ever. And worst of all, even worse than the cruelty of the boys, were the teachers. They treated me like I was a joke, as though the way I was in the world was something I had deliberately chosen in order to attract attention. *You'd better get with the program,* said the headmaster, Mr. Parsons.

Mom was working at Olympic National Park that fall, spending four or five days each week on the coast at the ranger station. That meant that Dad and I were alone most nights. We ate takeout in silence, and then I retreated to my room, locked the door, and put on my wings.

Sometimes I wonder if things would have been different if Mom had left Boris at the house while she was out in Olympic. But that fall, Boris went with her to the national park, where he spent hour after hour chasing after the sticks that tourists threw for him into the ocean, and bringing them back.

One day, Mr. Parsons called Dad at work and told him he had to pick me up and take me home. When he arrived at the headmaster's office, Dad found me sitting in a chair. I had the beginnings of a black eye and a contusion on my right cheek from where I'd been dragged against the playground asphalt.

"Mr. O'Meara," said Mr. Parsons. "I'm sorry you've had to be disturbed at work, but I think you'll understand."

Dad took a look at me. "I'm sorry," he said to Mr. Parsons. "I don't know what to say."

"It's not my business, of course," said Mr. Parsons. "But I need to ask if everything is all right at home."

"It's *fine,*" said Dad, his jaw getting tense. "And you're right, it's none of your business."

"I don't mean to pry. It's just that in situations like this, it's often a quiet cry for help."

I just sat there in shame. I *had* called for help, actually, and there had been nothing quiet about it. But no one had come, not until I'd already been hurt. Now, in Mr. Parsons's office, I was learning the truth—that the boys who'd beaten me up weren't the ones who were in trouble.

The night before, when I'd painted my nails salmon pink, it wasn't like I didn't know what was going to happen. But still I was amazed that Mr. Parsons was punishing me—suspending me, in fact, instead of the boys who'd pounded me against the blacktop.

I thought that salmon pink was a pretty conservative color, actually.

My father told me to get my things, and I did. "When can he come back?" he asked Mr. Parsons as we headed out into the hall.

"When he's ready to rejoin the community," said the headmaster. "When he's ready to be a *man*."

We started to drive home. "Well?" my father said. "What do you have to say for yourself?"

I pulled my hair out of its ponytail and shook my head so that it all fell down around my shoulders. "I'm never going back there again," I told him.

"No?" said Dad. "What are you going to do instead, Liam? Tell me that."

I looked my father in the eye. "I'm going to be free."

Dad laughed. "Maybe I should send you to the Porter School, see how you like that. Is that what you want?"

The Porter School was a fancy school on the coast. All girls.

"Could I?" I said, not realizing he was joking. "Could I really?"

"What's the matter with you?"

"Nothing's the matter with me," I said. "Except you."

Dad didn't say anything, but I could tell from the way his jaw was moving he wasn't done.

Finally I said, "You told me I could be anything I wanted."

"What?" said Dad. "When did I say that?"

"At the circus," I said. "Five years ago."

"What circus? I never took you to any circus."

"There was a human cannonball, and a woman who rode on the back of a horse."

"The only circus I've been to," he said, "is the one in our goddamned house."

When we got home, he told me to go into the bathroom and take the polish off. I hated to see it go. The smell of the acetone stung my sinuses. Each swipe of the cotton ball, dripping with nail polish remover, felt like I was erasing a piece of myself.

Finally my nails were blunt and clean, and I stood there, looking in the mirror.

What's wrong with you? I asked myself.

Nothing's the matter with me, said the girl in the mirror. *Except you.*

I can't be you. It's too hard.

Who else are you going to be? said the girl. *Are you really going to spend your whole life pretending to be someone else?*

All my mother's makeup was lying right there on the counter. I dabbed a little concealer on my index finger and smoothed it over the blue bruise beneath my eye. Then I put some foundation on to make the rest of my face look normal. There was a compact, which helped it all set, and a little bronzer to put color back in my cheeks. I traced an eye pencil over my upper lid, and brushed my lashes with mascara. Then I put on one of her lipsticks—a MAC color called Crème in Your Coffee. I brushed out my hair. One of Mom's bras was hanging from a towel rack, and I took off my shirt and put it on, filling each cup with a balled-up sock. Then I pulled on a blouse that was in the hamper, a stretchy scoop-neck print with three-quarter-length sleeves.

I looked in the mirror again. I was beautiful, an unlikely miracle. But I did not see how I was ever going to survive in this world.

You wreck everything, I told that girl. But since I was looking in the mirror, she just said the same thing back to me. *You wreck everything.*

I opened the door and I went down the stairs and into the living room, where Dad was drinking a beer. He looked up. For a second I think he had no idea who I was—was I maybe some nether-universe version of my mother, from when she was a teenager, before he even met her?

Then his jaw dropped. "What the fuck?"

"I told you," I said. "I'm going to be free."

Dad took a moment, as my words sunk in. He slowly crushed the Pabst Blue Ribbon can in his right hand and he threw it on the floor, where it rolled along the hardwood.

Then he smacked me. The blow landed so hard that I was literally knocked off my feet. I flew across that room, and my head cracked against the wall.

A little later, when I came to, I realized that I'd been tied to a kitchen chair with clothesline. I heard a snipping sound. Dad had the scissors out, the same ones we used to cut wrapping paper for birthday presents. "What are you doing—?" I whispered, although I already knew the answer. I heard the snip. I felt my long hair fall onto the floor. He worked his way all around my head. It didn't take long. Dad wiped my face with a damp paper towel. Most of the makeup came off, but not the mascara, of course. It was the waterproof kind.

"I hate you," I said. "*I hate you.*"

"Liam," said Dad. "I'm doing this because I *love* you, Champ. Because I don't want you to get hurt."

He was the one who was hurting me. "Fuck you!" I shouted. "I hate you! Go to hell!"

"Liam, please," said Dad.

"*I. Am. Not. Liam!*"

"No?" said Dad. "Then what's your name?"

I sat there squirming in the chair, trying to get my hands loose, but he'd tied me too tight. I was trapped where I was, until my father decided to let me go.

I wanted to tell him what my name was, but I didn't know it yet.

"Let me fucking go," I said.

"I'll let you go," said Dad. "When you say that your name is Liam."

"Fuck you," I said.

He put his face right in my face. "What . . . is . . . your . . . fucking *name?*"

I spat. The big spitball landed right in his eye, and he reached up with his fingers to clear his vision. Then he set his jaw again, and he grabbed the chair and hurled it so hard I tipped over backward and fell, still tied, onto the kitchen floor.

I watched his shoes through a veil of tears.

Then he said, "I am *not*—a bad person."

There was a jingling of keys, and then the shoes walked out of the room. The front door opened, and closed. The car started up, and then drove off.

I lay where I had fallen. I don't know how much time went by. Hours. Eons. Millennia.

Finally I heard the sound of the front door opening and closing. I shut my eyes tight, preparing for the next round, although what there was left for my father to do to me I couldn't imagine.

Then I heard the sound of dog toenails against the tiles. It was Boris, back from the ocean with my mother.

Liam, said my mother. *Dear God in heaven, Liam, honey.* I heard the snipping of the shears again—the same ones Dad had used to cut off all my hair—and then the clothesline was loose. Mom gathered me into her arms.

"My baby," she said. She said it over and over again. *My poor baby.*

Now here we are, seven years later, in a house in New Hampshire. Boris is old. Mom is going gray. My name is Lily.

BORIS HAS HIS head out the window, his ears flopping in the breeze. There's a fancy opera house downtown, an old river snaking off to the west. Little stores, a church. It's all so cute, like something out of an old movie.

We go around a corner, and there is the high school. It's got a huge gym on one side, and a performing arts center on the other. There's a sign: HOME OF THE FIGHTING PRESIDENTS.

I laugh, thinking about the idea of fighting presidents, but I get a kind of nervous chill, too. Because this is where I'll actually be going to school. My senior year, at last!

Mom looks pensive. "Don't worry," I say. "It's going to be fine."

She blows some air through her cheeks. "I hope so, Lily," she says. "I just hate to think about what will happen, if—you know. Things don't work out."

When Mom and I were driving east, we had endless conversations about what it means to be a woman. Is it about biology, the result of what's between your legs? Or is it more a matter of neurology, or even spirit—something between your ears?

Is it about having ovaries and a uterus? Well, maybe, except that the world is full of women who've had hysterectomies, and they are all still women.

Is it about having breasts and a clitoris? Well, maybe, except that the world contains women who've had mastectomies. Others have had clitoral circumcisions (like the kind I learned Dr. Powers reversed). These women are all still women.

Is it about two X chromosomes that you can't even see? Well, maybe, except that the world contains women who have Y chromosomes and never even know it, women whose genetic makeup contains all kinds of chromosomal variations. These women are all still women.

As we drove east, we kept coming up with a list of all the things people use to define women—but we'd always find an exception or some rare difference that belied the binary definition. Until at one point my mother suggested that being a woman, for some people, might mean *just not being a man.*

Mom said that has been true for her—that being a woman has meant being someone who gets talked over in conversations or ignored; someone who gets judged as a *body* instead of as a sentient soul; someone who, no matter who you are or what you are doing, always has to be on guard, lest someone else decide that you're going to be his victim.

But maybe what was true for Mom won't have to be true for me.

I'm not going to be a victim, ever again. I'm going to live my life with power, and fierceness, and with love.

To be honest about it, I don't actually have a whole theory about who I am or whether I get to live my life as myself. Other women don't have to come up with a reason why they exist. Why is it necessary for me to justify the fact that I'm here upon this earth, to explain and defend the things I have known in my heart since the day I was born?

I think sometimes about all the strange and wonderful things the world contains—the blue potato, the Venus flytrap, the duck-billed platypus.

If there is room under heaven for all of these miraculous things, couldn't there possibly be room for me?

I know that Mom is nervous about this year. *I'm* nervous about this year. But I'm going to be fine. I've been through so much worse.

As I stare at the high school building, I think of all the incarnations of me: who I've been, who I am right now, and—most of all—who it is I might still become.

"Don't worry about me, Mom," I tell her. "I'm a survivor."

OLIVIA ◆ 11

Six months after

You cannot ever really go back to normal. You can approximate the axis of what your life used to be like, but as with an asymptote, all you'll ever really do is get close and never intersect the sweet spot. It is true that the way the legal system works, once you are acquitted you are free to go home, but there's a cognitive dissonance in the realization that the world has spun away without you. Even innocent, you will still be *the boy who was involved in that murder trial.* You are blameless, but stained.

There isn't much point in Asher returning to school for less than a month; instead, we register him to get his GED. We don't go out much, but when we do, people snap surreptitious photos with their phones when they think Asher can't see, or—in some cases—even ask him to take a selfie. He is a curiosity. He has become notorious.

He tries, at first. He shows up at a free skate on a Saturday afternoon where a bunch of other hockey teammates sometimes play pickup. On the ice, he's who he used to be—sure of himself and smooth, every action leading to a consequence he can predict. But he gets hip-checked by another player and they get into a fight and the other kid calls Asher a *chaser.* Asher throws a punch and receives several more and winds up in our kitchen with ice on his black eye, explaining to me that *chaser* is a slur for someone who's attracted to trans people.

Dirk comes over to play video games, but the easy banter between them is missing. He had always managed to invite himself to dinner in the past, so I am surprised to find Asher sitting alone at the table later. "He talked about teachers who wouldn't grade on the curve and who dumped who and who's going to what college next year," Asher murmured. "It's like we're living on two different planets."

Maya doesn't contact him at all.

We fall into a routine, Asher and I. We visit the hives at my pollination contract locations. We add supers where needed, and we monitor how the bees are filling them with honey. Every day, we do the *New York Times* crossword puzzle together. We cook dinner— Asher chopping vegetables like a sous-chef, while I stir-fry and braise and roast. We watch all the Marvel Universe movies, in their correct order.

We are not always in each other's company, but I keep tabs on where he is, because once you almost lose your child you are wary. Asher spends a lot of time sitting among the transplanted daylilies that grow beneath the tree house, but he doesn't pry out the nails and go inside. Sometimes he sketches there. Sometimes he sits with his head bowed, being coronated by the sun. King of solitude; ruler of nothing.

THREE WEEKS AFTER the trial ends, Maya shows up unannounced. She throws herself into Asher's arms. "Oh my God," she says. "I wanted to come earlier but my moms were total assholes about it, like they think Williams will take away my financial aid or something if they find out that we're friends."

Asher looks at her. "You're going to Williams?"

"Oh. You didn't know." Maya sees me standing there, observing all this. "Hi, Ms. McAfee."

I clear my throat. I cannot erase the picture of Maya on the witness stand, of the selfie with Lily's bruises. "Congratulations," I say. "That's quite an achievement."

Her eyes are wide and fathomless as she looks at Asher, as if she is only now realizing that while she was finishing high school, his life was derailed, partly thanks to her role in the trial. "I . . . I wrote my Common App essay about Lily," she admits. "She was all I could think about in December."

"Clearly it paid off," I say under my breath.

"Mom," Asher murmurs. "It's not her fault."

Maya flinches. "I wanted to be there for you, Asher. I've always been there for you. But it was so . . . terrible."

"I miss her, too, Maya," Asher says.

"I hated all the things they said about you in court," she says. "You should never have had to go through that."

Maya bursts into tears, throwing herself into Asher's arms. Over her head, he meets my eye and shrugs. He rubs a circle on her back, and she burrows into him. I turn, heading toward the kitchen to give them privacy.

"You shouldn't even have been arrested," I hear Maya say, weeping. "You weren't supposed to be there." I am just crossing the threshold of the kitchen when she adds, "Lily told you it was over."

The words are dominoes—one trips, and the rest fall. I stop moving, my hand braced in the open door. "Maya," I ask, turning, "what do you mean?"

Maya steps out of Asher's arms, glancing from me to him. "She . . . she texted you."

I think back to the hours Jordan spent huddled over the printouts from Asher's phone and Lily's. Of the motion he filed to exclude evidence, and the judge's ruling. My eyes pin Maya, staking her in place. "Yes," I say. "But Asher never got that text . . . and it wasn't mentioned at the trial."

Maya covers her face with her hands. "It was an accident," she sobs.

A BEST FRIEND just *knows* things. And Maya knew that her best friend was falling apart at the seams.

She also knew her best friend needed her more than he ever had before, even if he didn't realize it yet.

She could see it in the way Asher barely even spoke to her or looked at her. In the way he checked his phone six thousand times a day to see if Lily had finally responded.

Maya had reconciled herself to the fact that the way Asher saw her was not the way she saw Asher. But that wasn't so bad. There were plenty of guys who woke up one day and realized that the girls they pined after weren't as reliable or interesting or worthy as the ones who stood staunchly by their sides. Maya had made an adolescent career out of making sure Asher was happy, even if it meant she wasn't the one who got to be with him. She could be patient. She could befriend the girl he loved.

Until Lily broke his heart.

Maya knew what was best for Asher, and it wasn't Lily.

Lily had been home sick, and was surprised to see Maya at her front door. They'd already texted that day, and Lily said no, she didn't need her homework brought to her. Lily looked like hell as Maya followed her up to her bedroom and sat down on the bed. *What couldn't wait?* Lily asked.

Do you have any idea how Asher feels right now? Do you even give a fuck?

How can you possibly ask me that? Lily said.

There was a ding on Lily's phone, and Maya could read the message over her shoulder. It was from Asher, like the last dozen. *THIS ENDS NOW, I'M COMING OVER.*

Lily looked at Maya, and then down at the phone. *You're right,* she said softly. *Asher and I need to talk.*

It was, Maya realized, the opposite of what was supposed to happen. The details were fuzzy, but she could so clearly see the aftermath she had intended: Lily would dump Asher, instead of stringing him along. He would be heartbroken, and Maya would be there to pick up the pieces.

Lily started to type a reply to Asher.

No, Maya said out loud, and Lily looked up, surprised.

You don't love him the way that he loves you, Maya said, and she was crying, and she didn't even care. *You never will. And let me tell you, Lily. It sucks.*

Lily's mouth dropped open. She looked at Maya, who realized that she'd just revealed her cards.

Maya, Lily said, *I didn't know . . .*

Maya's cheeks were hot. She didn't need Lily's pity. She needed Asher to just open his goddamned eyes and understand that she was here. She had been here all along.

If you really love him, Maya pleaded, *let him go.*

It's because *I love him that I can't,* Lily said. She glanced down at the phone, at the text reply that would reel Asher right back to her. Again.

Without thinking about what she was doing, without thinking *at all,* Maya snatched the phone from Lily's hand and erased her unsent message. *Don't bother, it's over,* she typed instead. But before she could hit send, Lily grabbed for it.

The rest was hard to remember. They were tangled and grasping, both of them, knocking over a lamp and the nightstand. There was glass crunching under her sneakers. Maya clutched the phone to her chest, curling her body around it like an oyster cushioning a pearl, as she backed out of the bedroom. It was Lily who fought for it. If she hadn't, Maya wouldn't have shoved her away. If she hadn't, Lily wouldn't have lost her balance and tumbled down the stairs.

WHEN MAYA FINISHES talking, the truth presses between us like an iron, hissing. Asher is pale, his teeth sunk into his bottom lip.

"I didn't know what to do," Maya tells him. "So I ran. I didn't know you were going to show up." She lifts a shaking hand to her eyes, wiping them. "I never meant to hurt her. I just wanted her to stop hurting *you.*"

A shudder runs the length of my spine. Here is the ultimate irony: Lily Campanello was not killed because someone was threatened by her being trans.

She was killed because someone was threatened by her being a *woman.*

"Maya," I say quietly, "we have to tell the police."

She doesn't even look at me. She reaches for Asher's hand and holds it like a lifeline. "You kept *her* secret," she whispers, broken, hopeful. "Couldn't you keep mine?"

THERE CAN ONLY be one queen in a hive.

When a queen dies, you can either introduce a new one you purchase, or you can wait for the bees to create royalty.

Nurse bees feed royal jelly to all larvae, at first. It's milky and thick, full of vitamins and sugars and amino acids. After a few days, the formula changes to worker jelly, which has lower levels of protein and sugar, or drone formula. But any egg can be repurposed to become a queen, if she is instead fed royal jelly through her entire development. The nutrients trigger different genetic programs, which are already somewhere inside that egg.

This has always been my favorite fact about bees: in their world, destiny is fluid. You might start life as a worker, and end up a queen.

A FEW WEEKS after Asher and I tell Mike Newcomb about Maya's confession, it is time for the first honey harvest. Asher and I are in the barn. He is manning the extractor while I saw through the combs with the hot knife. We've spent the morning collecting dozens of frames heavy with capped honey; now we are sweaty and sticky. The hair that has escaped my braid is glued to my cheek.

Asher opens the extractor and flips the frames so that the centrifugal force can suck the honey from the other side of each comb. I sleek the hot knife along the edge of the plastic tub where I'm collecting the wax cappings, trying to degum it.

"I was thinking," Asher says, "of taking a ride to check out Plymouth State."

Very deliberately, I keep doing what I'm doing. "Oh?" I say mildly. It's the first time since the trial that Asher has expressed an interest in college. In moving on.

"They have a BA in graphic design," he adds. "And a Division Three hockey team."

"Sounds promising," I say evenly.

"But I don't want to leave you here alone."

My eyes fly to his. "Asher," I say, "it is *my* job to worry about *you*, not the other way around."

"I don't think that's a hard-and-fast rule," Asher replies.

I imagine Asher an hour and a half away, reinventing himself. I think of him with friends who do not know he was on trial for a murder, and it strikes me that this will become the thing he hides away. The secret he will have to decide whether or not to tell the next person he loves.

"Can I ask you something?" he says. "Do you think she had it? That blood thing?"

He is talking about TTP, the clotting disorder that Selena's expert pathologist explained at the trial. I know Jordan would say that legally it does not matter whether or not Lily was afflicted; it only matters that the jury thought it was possible. But Asher is not a juror, and I know what it feels like to want to write the ending to a story that you'll never finish living. "I guess we'll never know, for sure. What do *you* think?" I ask gently.

He is quiet for a moment. "I hope she did," Asher says.

A shadow falls across the dusty wood floor, and I look up to see Mike silhouetted by the sun. "Am I interrupting?" he asks.

Asher stills. He's wary, even though Mike has been here a few times since the trial.

"I thought you'd want to know that the prosecutor isn't bringing charges against Maya," Mike says.

Something flickers in Asher's eyes—relief, but also confusion about why she'd been absolved, while he was put through the wringer. Mike turns to me, tilting his head a tiny bit toward the doorway. An invitation.

I put down the hot knife on my worktable. "I'll be right back," I tell Asher, and I leave the barn, pulling the door shut behind me.

We wander a short distance, until we are caught between the whir of the extractor and the hum of bees. "He doesn't like me," Mike says.

"You can't really blame him."

"I can be very persuasive."

I stop walking. "I look forward to that."

It feels strange to flirt. It's like being dropped into a foreign country when you are not fluent in the language. But even then, you can get by on gestures. On nods and shakes of your head. You can build your own language, until one day you dream in it.

Asher is not the only one starting over.

Mike snakes one arm around my hips. With his free hand, he peels my hair away from where it's stuck to my face, and he kisses me.

"Mmm," he says softly. "You taste like candy."

I look down at the streaks of dirt on my shirt and pants, the sticky honey patching my forearms. "I'm a mess."

He shakes his head. "Aren't we all?"

Maybe this is true. Maybe we are nothing more than the confidences we keep, plastered over with a distraction of skin and bone and shadow.

"Does Ava know? About Maya?"

Mike nods.

"She must be crushed that there won't be a trial."

"I don't think so," he says carefully. "I feel like she knows she wouldn't survive another one."

"How come the prosecutor decided not to move forward?"

"It's a funnel," Mike says. "Not every bad thing that happens is a crime. Not every crime can be prosecuted. Not every prosecution results in a conviction. Not every conviction results in jail time or whatever the victim's family may want." He meets my gaze. "Some bad things that happen are just accidents, Liv."

I imagine Asher on a fall day, driving toward his future. I picture Mike standing beside me, as I watch him go.

So are some good things, I think.

EPILOGUE

Ten months after

According to natural selection, bees should not exist. Although workers construct the comb, tend to the queen, and feed the larvae, they're sterile themselves, and don't pass those productive genes to the next generation. Plus, stinging is suicide, and passing on a suicide gene makes no biological sense. And yet, the species has been around for a hundred million years.

Why?

A biologist will say it's because of group selection. Worker bees share seventy-five percent of one another's genes, which is more than they'd share with their own offspring. That means it's in their best interests to take care of their future sisters rather than reproduce.

If you ask me, it's because they're survivors.

In late September, the trees turn vain, wearing their fiery tiaras. I'm getting my hives ready for the brutal winter—storing the cleaned supers for next year, cutting lengths of Styrofoam to screw around the Langstroth boxes, boiling down pounds of sugar into syrup for feeding. One afternoon, as I finish checking on my hives, I hear a car pull into the driveway. I cannot see it from where I am, but I start walking faster.

Mike's supposed to be coming over, with pizza and cider. I turn the corner of the farmhouse, shading my eyes, a smile on my face.

Ava Campanello steps out of her car.

I have not seen her in the months since Asher's trial. We have not crossed paths, although this is not unusual. She works in the White Mountains; I circulate through local orchards and farms and weekend markets. Her car is packed to the gills, and several small pieces of furniture are strapped to the ski rack on the Subaru's roof. A black dog with a gray muzzle leans out the open window, tongue lolling.

I stop a few paces away from her. My heart is beating so hard that I can feel it in my throat.

She draws a line in the dirt between us with the toe of her boot. "I don't know what I'm doing here," she admits.

I wait, because I realize that even though Asher—against all judgment—got to have his say . . . Ava never did.

"I'm on my way out of town," she tells me. "For good."

I nod. I think about Lily's ashes, on the table at the funeral home. I wonder if they are in the car. Where, or if, Ava will scatter them.

She scratches behind the dog's ears. "Boris and I are going to hike the AT for a bit," Ava says. "And after that, I don't know."

"I'm sorry," I blurt out. "I know it's—"

"You *don't* know," Ava interrupts, but her voice has lost its bite. "No one really does. At first, people say that all the time—that they're sorry for your loss. Then a few weeks go by, and only a handful of people check in to make sure you're still functioning. Then you only hear from them on birthdays, holidays, all the things you won't be celebrating. Or they forget, completely."

"I haven't forgotten Lily," I say.

Ava stares at me. "Where's Asher?"

"He's not here." I realize, too late, that I sound defensive. "He's at Plymouth State."

She nods, chewing on a sentence before she opens her mouth. "I'm glad you didn't have to lose your child."

Ava could not have surprised me more if she'd smacked me. I had assumed that the impetus to arrest Asher had come from her, born of a need for closure and answers.

Her eyes shutter. "I lost a son once, but that was okay, because I gained a daughter. But now . . ." She shrugs. "Now I have nothing."

Sadness orbits around Ava, the very atmosphere she breathes. I wish I knew what to say to her, what to do.

"Well," Ava says.

"Wait," I beg. "Just a minute?"

I jog up the steps of the porch, and into the kitchen. On the table is an army of jars, filled with the second harvest of honey. I pick one up and bring it outside to Ava.

Because honey never spoils, it was considered an immortal food, fit for the gods and those who've returned to stardust.

Ava takes the jar and turns it over in her hands. It looks like sunlight trapped inside the glass. A laugh huffs out of her. "I've always hated honey," she says.

But she carries it to her car and turns the ignition. I watch her pull out of the driveway. Her taillights are like eyes, red from crying.

One day, maybe, when Ava has settled in a new home, she will need a sweet substitute for baking, a remedy for a sore throat, some flavor for her tea. She will stand in her pantry, and her hand will close around that jar. Maybe so much time will have passed that she will not remember where it came from. But in all those years, it will never go bad.

It will keep, until she's ready.

RECIPES

BEEKEEPER'S GRANOLA

32 ounces Bob's Red Mill GF
Old Fashioned Rolled Oats

½ cup pumpkin seeds

1 cup sliced almonds

½ cup honey

½ cup canola oil

Preheat oven to 225 degrees. Spray a large baking sheet (21 × 15 inches) with cooking spray. In a large bowl combine the oats, pumpkin seeds, and almonds. Pour the honey and oil over the mixture and toss lightly, making sure the oat mixture is covered. Spread on baking sheet and bake for 90 minutes. Cool on a wire rack.

Granola keeps for several weeks in a sealed container.

CRANACHAN

(Serves 4)

1¼ cups granola, divided

½ cup bourbon, plus
2 teaspoons, divided

3 cups raspberries, plus 8 whole
berries for garnish

1 teaspoon honey, divided

2 cups heavy cream

4 parfait glasses or martini
glasses

Combine ¾ cup granola and ½ cup bourbon and let sit for several hours before assembling dessert. The granola will absorb the alcohol and become soft but not mushy. Meanwhile, chill a mixing bowl.

Lightly crush raspberries with a fork, add ½ teaspoon honey and 1 teaspoon bourbon. Toss to combine. You want a puree texture.

In a chilled bowl, start whipping the heavy cream. When it begins to thicken, add remaining ½ teaspoon honey and remaining 1 teaspoon bourbon. Continue whipping cream until it is slightly firm.

Fold soaked granola into the cream.

To assemble, sprinkle a bit of the reserved granola into each glass. Spoon a layer of the cream mixture over granola and then add a layer of the raspberry mixture. Repeat until you have a few layers, finishing with a layer of the cream. Sprinkle remaining granola and a couple of whole raspberries on top.

QUEEN BEE COCKTAIL

1½ teaspoons honey simple syrup (recipe on p. 435)
Club soda

1½ ounces bourbon
1 teaspoon lime juice
Sliced lime, for garnish

Fill a large glass with ice.

Add honey simple syrup.

Fill glass with club soda.

Add bourbon.

Squeeze in lime juice and garnish with a lime slice.

DO NOT MIX!

BEE'S KNEES COCKTAIL

½ ounce honey simple syrup
(recipe follows)

1 ounce lemon juice (about ½
medium lemon)

2 ounces gin

Lemon peel

Fill a cocktail shaker with ice. Add ingredients (except peel) and shake; strain into a martini glass. Twist the lemon peel and set inside glass.

HONEY SIMPLE SYRUP

In a small saucepan combine ⅓ cup honey and ⅓ cup water. Over low heat stir the mixture until honey starts to dissolve. Let cool and pour into a squeeze bottle or glass container. Will keep for several weeks.

PORK WITH HONEY-LIME MARINADE

(Serves 4)

Juice of two limes

¼ cup honey

¼ cup olive oil

1 garlic clove, grated

1 teaspoon hot sauce (you can
use red pepper flakes for less
heat)

Pork tenderloin, trimmed
(1 pound)

Whisk first five ingredients together. Pour half of marinade into a ziplock bag and add pork tenderloin. Marinate for at least 1 hour. Preheat gas or charcoal grill for indirect grilling.

Brush grate with canola or vegetable oil. Cook pork indirectly 4 to 6 minutes per side until a meat thermometer registers 145 degrees. Remove from grill and brush with remaining marinade. Let meat rest for 10 minutes before slicing.

KALE SALAD WITH HONEY LEMON VINAIGRETTE

1 bunch kale

½ lemon, reserving other half
    for vinaigrette

Pinch of sea salt

Wash and dry kale, tear into small pieces. In a large bowl, squeeze lemon over kale, sprinkle the sea salt over kale, and gently massage the lemon and salt into the kale. This will slightly soften the kale.

VINAIGRETTE

1 tablespoon honey

Juice of ½ lemon

Pinch of ground pepper

¼ cup olive oil

In a small bowl combine honey, juice from remaining lemon, ground pepper, and oil. Whisk gently and pour over kale.

SUGGESTED TOPPINGS

Sliced almonds and sliced pears

Crushed walnuts and sliced
    apples

Goat cheese and pine nuts
    (honey pine nuts recipe
    below can be used)

HONEY PINE NUTS

2 tablespoons honey

½ cup pine nuts (any nut can be
    substituted)

Line a baking sheet with parchment paper and spray with cooking spray. In a small pan stir honey and nuts until honey becomes liquid. Spread mixture on baking sheet and let it set for 30 to 60 minutes. Break into small pieces and use on top of salads or ice cream. Store in an airtight container for up to 2 weeks.

HONEY-GLAZED SPICED DONUTS
(Makes a dozen)

1¾ cups flour

2 teaspoons cinnamon

1 teaspoon nutmeg

½ teaspoon ginger

1 teaspoon baking powder

½ teaspoon baking soda

2 eggs

¾ cup honey

4 tablespoons melted butter

¼ cup oil (vegetable or canola)

1 cup milk (buttermilk can also be used)

1½ teaspoons vanilla

Preheat oven to 400 degrees.

In a medium bowl, whisk together flour, cinnamon, nutmeg, ginger, baking powder, and baking soda. Set aside.

In another bowl, whisk eggs, honey, butter, oil, milk, and vanilla.

Fold dry ingredients into wet and stir until just combined.

Grease a donut pan or cupcake tin and fill halfway with batter. (If you do not have a donut pan, use a cupcake/muffin pan. Create small cylinders of tinfoil, place one in the middle of each cup, and spray each cylinder with cooking oil. If using the cupcake tin with aluminum foil cylinders, transfer batter to a ziplock bag and cut a hole to pipe batter around cylinders.)

Bake for 8 to 10 minutes.

HONEY GLAZE

¼ cup melted butter

1 cup confectioners' sugar

½ teaspoon vanilla

⅓ cup hot water

1 teaspoon honey

Combine all ingredients in a small bowl. Dip warm donuts in glaze.

You can omit the glaze and just drizzle honey on top and, if you like, sprinkle with sea salt.

HONEY VANILLA FROZEN CUSTARD

(Requires an ice cream maker)

5 to 6 egg yolks	1 cup milk
½ cup sugar	2 cups heavy cream
½ cup honey	1½ teaspoons vanilla

In a stainless steel bowl, whisk egg yolks, sugar, and honey until light and fluffy.

In a saucepan, heat milk and cream until it starts to bubble (5 to 7 minutes), stirring occasionally. Temper the egg mixture with a small amount of the milk/cream mixture so that you do not scramble the eggs. Add the remaining milk/cream and whisk to combine. Pour mixture back into the saucepan and return to a low heat, stirring until mixture is thick enough to coat the back of a spoon. Remove from heat and add vanilla. Set a fine-mesh strainer over a clean bowl and pour mixture through the strainer. Chill until completely cool, about 4 hours. Freeze according to your ice cream maker's guidelines. Store in a plastic container.

PAVLOVA

6 egg whites at room temperature (out of the fridge for at least an hour)

1 cup superfine sugar, divided (if you don't have superfine sugar, you can pulse regular sugar in your food processor)

1 teaspoon cornstarch

Squeeze of lemon juice

1 teaspoon vanilla

TOPPINGS

1 cup whipping cream

1 teaspoon vanilla

2 teaspoons sugar

Sliced strawberries

Honey

Preheat oven to 300 degrees.

Line a baking sheet with parchment paper and draw a circle 8 to 9 inches in diameter.

In a medium bowl, whisk together egg whites and ¾ cup of the sugar until light and fluffy (3 to 5 minutes).

In a small bowl, mix together remaining sugar, cornstarch, lemon, and vanilla. Add to egg whites and continue beating until glossy peaks form.

Spread mixture in the circle on the parchment paper. You can also pipe the mixture to create a fancier look.

Place in the oven and reduce heat to 250 degrees. Bake for 75 minutes and then turn off the oven. Remove from oven after 15 minutes.

Let cool.

In a clean mixing bowl, combine whipping cream, vanilla, and sugar. Beat until soft peaks form.

Once pavlova is completely cool, top with whipped cream and strawberries and drizzle with honey.

STRAWBERRY FIELDS

1 cup fresh strawberries, sliced and slightly crushed

1 teaspoon honey

Bread, four slices

Handful of arugula

Mix strawberries and honey in a bowl.

Toast bread. Top each slice with 2 tablespoons of strawberries and sprinkle with arugula.

HONEY LOAF

(Makes 2 loaves)

3½ cups sifted flour

¼ teaspoon salt

1½ teaspoons baking powder

1 teaspoon baking soda

½ teaspoon cinnamon

¼ teaspoon nutmeg

⅛ teaspoon ground cloves

½ teaspoon ginger

4 eggs

¾ cup sugar

4 tablespoons canola oil

2 cups dark honey

½ cup brewed coffee

1½ cups walnuts, chopped

Preheat oven to 325 degrees. In a medium bowl, sift together flour, salt, baking powder, baking soda, and spices. In a large bowl, beat eggs, gradually adding sugar, until light in color and thick. Beat in oil, honey, and coffee. Stir in flour mixture and nuts.

Oil two 9-inch loaf pans and turn batter into them. Bake for 50 minutes or until browned, and when tester comes out clean. Cool on rack before removing from pan.

FROM ASHER'S CALCULUS NOTEBOOK

HOPE CAKES

2 tablespoons butter

8 ounces cream cheese

3 bananas

1 teaspoon vanilla

2 cups white sugar

2 eggs, refrigerated

3 cups flour

½ teaspoon baking powder

½ teaspoon baking soda

½ teaspoon salt

TOPPING

1 tablespoon flour

⅔ cup brown sugar

1 cup butter

½ cup nuts

1. Preheat oven to 350 degrees. Grease a big baking pan with butter.
2. In a large bowl, mix together the butter, cream cheese, bananas, vanilla, and white sugar. Add the eggs.
3. Add the flour, baking powder, baking soda, and salt, mixing all the while. Pour the batter into the pan.
4. To make the topping, in a medium bowl combine flour and brown sugar, then mix in the butter and the nuts.
5. Using a fork, gently lay the topping on the batter.
6. Bake in oven for 40 minutes, or until an impossible thing comes true. Whichever comes first.

AUTHORS' NOTES

JENNIFER FINNEY BOYLAN

On the eighth of May 2017, I woke from a strange dream in which I was writing a novel with Jodi Picoult. There were three characters in the dream: a trans girl who had died; her boyfriend, who had been accused of her murder; and the boy's mother, who was torn between the compelling evidence of her son's guilt and the love she bore for him in her heart. *Wow,* I thought, wiping the sleep from my eyes, *that's pretty specific.*

I got out of bed, went to the kitchen, and made myself a cup of coffee, and then I got back in bed with the newspaper and read the headlines: Emmanuel Macron had won the French presidency; the governor of Texas had signed a bill outlawing sanctuary cities; a nominee for secretary of the Army had withdrawn after comparing transgender people to ISIS militants.

Then I went on Twitter and tweeted out, *I dreamed I was co-authoring a book with Jodi Picoult!*

Moments later, I got a private message back from Jodi. *What was this book about?*

We had never met, Jodi and I, but we'd been on each other's radar for a few years. I'd loved her work since I read *The Pact* back in 2003; for her part, Jodi had read my memoir *She's Not There* and had generously blurbed my 2016 novel, *Long Black Veil*. Quite frankly, I always thought of her as a kind of guardian angel.

As I sat there in bed with my coffee, I told Jodi the plot of the book that we'd written in my dream—although, to be honest, the whole thing was already starting to fade like breath on a mirror.

We hadn't swapped more than two or three messages, though, before Jodi wrote back to me, in all caps, and I quote: "OMG I LOVE THIS LET'S DO IT."

I mention this because it seems not unimportant to me that *Mad Honey* began its life as a dream, and that as a result of that dream Jodi Picoult, whom I had always admired from a readerly distance, became my friend. At that time, she was finishing up *A Spark of Light,* soon to begin work on the novel that became *The Book of Two Ways;* as for me, I was just starting the memoir *Good Boy: My Life in Seven Dogs*. It would take several years before we would be able to actually begin work on *Mad Honey*.

We finally started sketching out the plot in the spring of 2020, at the exact moment that quarantine trapped us in our separate houses. I spent several weeks crawling around on the floor with the two stories—Lily's and Olivia's—and literally cutting them apart with a pair of scissors and taping them into place on a storyboard that, in the end, took up several rooms of my house. We agreed that Jodi would write Olivia's voice to start, and I would write Lily's, but that each of us had to write at least one of the other's chapters, and that as the writing proceeded, each of us would reedit the other's work to make the novel feel like one continuous work, even if told in two voices.

I admit that it gives me great pleasure to imagine readers trying to figure out which one of the Lily chapters is Jodi's, and which one of the Olivia chapters is mine, although to be honest, by the time we were finished editing and reediting, I would frequently read a paragraph and be unable to remember which one of us had written it. Plus, I think there were times when we each deliberately, and diabolically, attempted to imitate each other.

It reminds me of the old Russian proverb *You tell me you're going to Minsk so I'll think you're going to Pinsk, but you really are going to Minsk, so why do you always lie to me?*

Speaking of proverbs, I should also mention that the epigraph to this book from Kierkegaard—the thing about life only being understandable backwards—is actually a simplification of the original text, which says, in part, "that life at any given moment cannot really ever be fully understood; exactly because there is no single moment where time stops completely in order for me to do this: going backwards."

In any case, getting to write this book with Jodi has been one of the greatest gifts of my long career as an author. No one could possibly ever have a more generous co-author than Jodi Picoult. At every moment she treated me with respect and good humor and love. She was fierce, forgiving, and funny. There were days when she had more faith in my ability to find my way through this story than I did.

I admit that as the project neared completion, I was dogged by two melancholy thoughts. One of these was for Ava, Lily's mom, who loses her daughter, the person she loves most in the world, and whom she has done so much to try to save. I am hopeful that she and Boris find some solace on the Appalachian Trail, but I don't know. I think of Paul Simon's line *And sometimes even music cannot substitute for tears.* I briefly tried to talk Jodi into writing a sequel with me, in which we might follow Ava's adventures on the AT, but alas: if that book ever gets written, I suspect I will end up writing it solo. It's not even that I wanted to write Ava's story so much (although that, too) as the simple fact that, as we neared the end of this project, I was not ready to give up working with Jodi Picoult. I'm still not.

It is also worth confessing that we had a brief disagreement over which one of the moms would wind up with Detective Newcomb. I had high hopes that Ava might take off into the wild with Mike, but the day I suggested this, Jodi simply laughed and said, *Bwahaha. He's mine.*

The other lingering sadness I have, of course, is for Lily. I hate the idea that she will never play her cello in the orchestra at Oberlin, that she will never walk down the aisle of a church with her mother at her side, that she will never sit by a fire with Asher as the two of them grow old together.

But the world is full of trans girls and women whose lives have been cut short. During the year that Jodi and I wrote this book, more than 350 transgender people were killed around the world, more than a fifth of them inside their own homes.

November 20 each year is recognized as Transgender Day of Remembrance, a day when we stop to acknowledge the violence that so many trans people suffer, especially trans women of color.

To be trans, of course, doesn't mean only one thing, and as Elizabeth tells Olivia, "If you've met one trans person, you've . . . met one trans person." I have spent many years celebrating the amazing lives of the trans people that I know: airplane pilots and sex workers; fire captains and college professors; astrophysicists and electricians. I regret, in some ways, telling a story of a trans girl who gets killed; there has been no shortage of these stories over the years, and I long for the day when we can instead celebrate November 20 as a day of trans endurance, and courage, and survival, instead of loss. For what it's worth, some of that does now take place on March 31, the Trans Day of Visibility.

Lily, of course, will never get to celebrate that day. But I still hope that her story opens hearts.

After I lost my hearing several years ago, I started trying to learn American Sign Language, and I learned that the symbol for *transgender* in ASL is a hand held over the heart, fingers pointing down as if depicting a flower—*a lily, say*—with its petals closed tight. Then, to make the sign, you move your arm forward, and point the "petals" at the sky, so that they can open. You end by putting your hand back over your heart with the petals now facing upward.

I love this sign because in so many ways it echoes the process we all go through, and not just people like Lily, or me. All of us have something in our hearts like a flower that cannot bloom because it is held in secret. The adventure of life can be to get that thing out of the darkness where it lies and let the sun shine on it.

So it can go back inside your heart facing the right direction.

At the end of that long morning when I dreamed I was writing a book with Jodi Picoult, I signed off of our DM session by reminding Jodi how much I loved her. And also, I said, *I hope tomorrow night I have a dream that I'm co-authoring a book with Stephen King.*

Bahahhaha, she wrote back. And then added, *Don't we all.*

—*Jennifer Finney Boylan*

JODI PICOULT

Those who say nothing good ever happens on Twitter clearly have not had Jenny Boylan—an author I have long admired—post something about co-authoring a novel. What Jenny didn't know at the time was that I had been thinking about writing about transgender rights for a while now. I have had so many readers send me hesitant emails, asking if maybe that was a topic I'd consider in the future—and I had written back, every time, *Yes.* In so many ways my entire career has been about untangling the knots that society tangles itself in as we futilely attempt to separate the *us* from the *them.* It never crossed my mind to think of a trans woman as anything but a woman, or a trans man as anything but a man, but there are cisgender folks out there who do not believe that. Maybe, I thought, I could break down that resistance a little by creating a trans character who was so real and compelling that (as Asher says) they'd love her for *who* she was, not *what* she was.

This was long before I had met Jenny. I thought I'd be writing about trans rights from a theoretical vantage point, because even if I supported trans people, I didn't actually *know* anyone who was trans.

Except . . . I did.

One of my closest friends came out as trans shortly before I started this book. We had known each other for years, but it still took courage for him to have that conversation with me. I know there are people who still do not know this about him or call him by his preferred pronouns.

Here's what changed in our relationship: absolutely nothing.

He still knows how I take my coffee, when to send me a GIF via text to cheer me up, and indulges my addiction to Goobers. The only thing that's different about our friendship is that now, when I look at him, I'm seeing him the way he's always seen himself.

A similar trajectory had happened once before to me, when I was writing *Sing You Home,* about gay rights, and my eldest son came out to me in the middle of it. Suddenly I wasn't writing hypothetically. I was writing as a parent with a vested interest in making the world a safer, more inclusive place for my son. I feel the same way about *Mad Honey.*

I am no stranger to hate mail—and I'm sure I'm gonna get plenty for this book. There is a small corps of people who seem to have made it their mission in life to exclude trans women (in particular) from the greater umbrella of "women." Many of these individuals have suffered abuse at the hands of men. They say men pretend to be trans to get into female spaces and commit acts of violence (this is beyond rare, and it is worth noting that more congressmen have been arrested for misbehavior in public restrooms than have trans women); they say children are being pressured into labeling themselves trans because they don't want to identify as gay (which conflates gender and sexuality); they say trans people often regret transitioning (de-transitioning, in fact, is rare, and the reason for most detransitions is not unhappiness with the target gender, but the cruelty of others, who make life for a newly out trans person intolerable). They most recently have said that support for trans women erases biologically female people (as a biological female, I do not feel personally erased). Do I feel bad that they've suffered their own instances of fear and abuse by men, in a way that might have shaped this philosophy? Absolutely. I chose to have Olivia be an abused wife because I wanted to underscore that violence against women is real and horrific . . . but it is not a reason to dismiss trans rights. In fact, a trans woman is far more likely than a cisgender woman to be hurt or killed by a man. Given how far women—*all* women—have yet to go in terms of equality, it breaks my heart to know that some women spend their time and energy tearing down the rights of other women. As Ava says to Lily, maybe being a woman, for some people, might mean just not being a man.

I also know a lot of very nice cisgender people who are not intentionally cruel to trans folks, but are just plain uninformed. If you're a cis woman, imagine what it would be like if you woke up tomorrow and looked in the mirror and suddenly saw a man's body looking back at you (or vice versa). Imagine how disoriented you'd feel, and how trapped, and how confusing it would be. Imagine having to sneak the moments when you could dress or act to reflect who you truly are; imagine the ridicule at being "outed." Imagine having to justify yourself to people simply because you were born this way. That's a good starting point for understanding.

I know that many cis people have questions, and also are aware that it may not be their place to ask those questions. I hope that Lily's journey can be educational—but more important, I hope it inspires compassion.

I also want to take a moment to talk about co-writing. This book began as a literal dream, and became a metaphorical one. I've only written a novel with one other person before, and I gave birth to her (my daughter, Sammy). I wanted to work with Jenny Boylan because (a) I was already a tremendous fan of her writing, and (b) as a cisgender writer, I was well aware that Lily's story wasn't my story to tell. Even if I did my research, even if I was meticulous . . . trans writers are so underrepresented on bookshelves in general that it wouldn't have felt right or fair for me to write a story about a trans girl by myself. I was honored that Jenny knew my name and had read my books. I wondered, *What if we could combine our voices, and tell both Olivia's and Lily's stories?* The result was a lot of fun . . . and a lot of work.

I realized pretty quickly during the process that we were going to have to treat this as a unified novel, even if it had two narrators, or it would feel like two pigs fighting under a blanket. I admit I didn't realize how much of a control freak I was until we started working together, and I am so grateful that Jenny trusted me when I told her that she *could* tell a story backward (and let me house the master document on *my* computer because I'm possessive that way, LOL). I can't count all the times Jenny made me cry with passages so honest and raw they took my breath away, and made me want to write something equally good. But I am also really pleased at how the end product feels seamless. If ever there was a novel whose scars should be invisible, it's this one.

What would I like you to take away from this novel? Absolutely nothing. I'd like you to *give*—a chance, a thought, a damn. Like gender, *difference* is a construct. We are all flawed, complicated, wounded dreamers; we have more in common with one another than we don't. Sometimes making the world a better place just involves creating space for the people who are already in it.

—Jodi Picoult

ACKNOWLEDGMENTS

The authors would like to thank their guardian angels:

From Jenny
My friend Heidi Doss, of the National Park Service, helped me understand the lives of rangers a little better. The line "I take my paycheck in sunsets" belongs to her. Nick Adams, director of Transgender Representation at GLAAD, provided me with wise counsel as the story took shape, and in particular pointed out how important it is to understand the difference between what is *secret* and what is *private*. My friend Zoe FitzGerald Carter, a distinguished memoirist (and musician), read the book to make sure I got Point Reyes right. The amazing Dr. Marci Bowers—who a few years earlier had served on the GLAAD Board of Directors with me—spent hours with Jodi and me, helping us understand what happens in transgender medicine. And the line "The plumbing works and so does the electricity" belongs to my friend Kate Bornstein, author of, among other works, *Hello Cruel World: 101 Alternatives to Suicide for Teens, Freaks, and Other Outlaws.*

From Jodi
There's nothing like writing a book during a pandemic. If not for Zoom, the research for this book would have been impossible. I'm indebted to my legal gurus: Jen Sargent and Jen Sternick and *especially* Christine Turner (who likely didn't know what she was getting

into when she said yes). Thanks to John Grassel, my detective on call, who worried about Asher as much as I did. I'm also grateful to the doctors and pathologists who helped me understand estrogen and bruising, and TTP: Dr. David Toub, Dr. Joel Umlas, and Dr. Betty Martin.

Thanks to Katie Desmond, for all the honey recipes.

There was one bit of research I could not do from behind a computer—and that was beekeeping. Luckily, you can learn bee-keeping from six feet of social distance, while wearing a mask under-neath your netting. I am grateful to Laura Johnson, Alden Gray, and Lorenz Rutz for allowing me to tag along during an entire season of work, and for teaching me so very much.

Thanks, too, to my beta readers: Brigid Kemmerer (who was there chapter by chapter, thank God), Jane Picoult, Reba Gordon, Elyssa Samsel, Kate Anderson, and Melanie Borinstein.

We would both like to thank our agents, Kris Dahl and Laura Gross, for taking a dream and making it come true. The entire team at Bal-lantine has our gratitude for being enthusiastic about a co-written novel and for making it shine in so many different ways: Gina Cen-trello, Kara Welsh, Kim Hovey, Deb Aroff, Rachel Kind, Denise Cronin, Scott Shannon, Matthew Schwartz, Theresa Zoro, Paolo Pepe, Sydney Schiffman, Erin Kane, Kathleen Quinlan, Corina Diez, and Jordan Pace. Emily Isayeff and Susan Corcoran get special kudos because they looked at Jodi's gross finger when her bee sting got infected and because they are likely more enthusiastic about this book than anyone else on the planet. Our remarkable editor, Jennifer Hershey, is currently being nominated for sainthood. If you think wrestling a book into shape is hard, try doing it with two different authors—and yet Jen manages to be brilliant and graceful *always*.

Finally, we'd like to thank our significant others: Tim van Leer and Deirdre Finney Boylan, for love that will last as long as honey.

—*Jodi Picoult & Jennifer Finney Boylan*

JODI PICOULT is the author of twenty-eight novels, with forty million copies sold worldwide. Her last thirteen books, including her most recent, *Wish You Were Here,* have debuted at #1 on the *New York Times* bestseller list. Five of her novels have been made into movies, and *Wish You Were Here* is currently in development at Netflix. A musical adaptation of *Between the Lines* (co-written with her daughter, Samantha van Leer) recently debuted Off-Broadway. She is the recipient of multiple awards, including the New England Bookseller Award for Fiction, the Alex Award from the YA Library Services Association, and the New Hampshire Literary Award for Outstanding Literary Merit. Picoult is also the co-librettist for the original musicals *Breathe* and *The Book Thief,* which debuted in the UK this fall. She lives in New Hampshire with her husband.

jodipicoult.com
Facebook.com/jodipicoult
Twitter: @jodipicoult
Instagram: @jodipicoult

PROFESSOR JENNIFER FINNEY BOYLAN is the bestselling author of eighteen books, fourteen under her own name and four others under a pseudonym. In addition, she is the inaugural Anna Quindlen Writer-in-Residence at Barnard College of Columbia University and a 2022–2023 Fellow at the Radcliffe Institute for Advanced Study at Harvard University. A nationally known advocate for human rights, she serves on the board of trustees of PEN America. For many years she was the national co-chair for GLAAD as well as a contributing opinion writer for *The New York Times.* Her memoir *She's Not There: A Life in Two Genders* was the first bestselling work by a transgender American. She lives in New York City and Belgrade Lakes, Maine, with her wife, Deirdre. They have a son, Sean, and a daughter, Zai.

jenniferboylan.net
Facebook.com/JenniferFinneyBoylan
Twitter: @JennyBoylan
Instagram: @jenniferfinneyboylan